Good Grief

Good Grief

— A NOVEL —

LOLLY WINSTON

WARNER BOOKS

New York   Boston

This book is a work of fiction. Names, characters, places, and incidents are the product of the author's imagination or are used fictitiously. Any resemblance to actual events, locales, or persons, living or dead, is coincidental.

Warner Books
Time Warner Book Group
1271 Avenue of the Americas, New York, NY 10020
Visit our Web site at www.twbookmark.com.

Printed in the United States of America
First Printing: April 2004
10 9 8 7 6 5 4 3 2 1

Library of Congress Cataloging-in-Publication Data
Winston, Lolly.
   Good grief / Lolly Winston.
      p. cm.
   ISBN 0-446-53304-1
   1. Grief—Fiction. 2. Widows—Fiction. 3. Young women—Fiction. I. Title.
   PS3623.I667G66 2004
   813'.6—dc22   2003015207

For Anders

And in memory of
Marvin Winston, Mary Anne Winston,
and Sam Winston

Contents

Part One

DENIAL

How can I be a widow? Widows wear horn-rimmed glasses and cardigan sweaters that smell like mothballs and have crepe-paper skin and names like Gladys or Midge and meet with their other widow friends once a week to play pinochle. I'm only thirty-six. I just got used to the idea of being married, only test-drove the words *my husband* for three years: *My husband and I, my husband and I . . .* after all that time being single!

As we go around the room introducing ourselves at the grief group, my heart drums in my chest. No wonder people fear public speaking more than death or heights or spiders.

I rehearse a few lines in my head:

My name is Sophie and I live in San Jose and my husband died.

No. *My name is Sophie and my husband* passed away *of Hodgkin's disease, which is a type of cancer young adults get.* Oh, but they probably already know that. This group seems up on its diseases.

A silver-haired man whose wife also died of cancer says that now when he gets up in the morning he doesn't have to poach his wife's egg or run her bath, and he doesn't see the point in getting out of bed. He weeps without making a sound, tears quivering in his eyes, then escaping down his unshaven cheeks. He looks at the floor and kneads his sweater in his hands, which are pink and spotted like luncheon meat.

We sit in a circle of folding chairs in a conference room at the hospital, everyone sipping coffee out of Styrofoam cups and hugging their coats in their laps. Fluorescent lights buzz overhead. They are bright and cruel, exposing the group's despair: the puffy faces, circles under the eyes like bruised fruit, dampened spirits that no longer want to sing along with the radio. There should be a rule for grief groups: forty-watt bulbs only.

The social worker who leads the group balances a clipboard on her knees and takes notes. She has one tooth that is grayer than the others, like an off-color piano key. Is it dead, hollow? I want to leap up and tap it with my fingernail. Surely she's got dental insurance. Why doesn't she fix that tooth?

My name is Sophie and I've joined the grief group because . . . well, because I sort of did a crazy thing. I drove my Honda through our garage door. I was coming home from work one night and—even though my husband has been dead for three months—I honestly thought I would run inside and tell him to turn on the radio because they were playing an old recording of Flip Wilson, whom he just loves. *Loved.* Ethan had been trying to find a copy of this skit for years, and now here it was on the radio. If I hurried, we could tape it. Then I had the sudden realization that my husband was *gone,* dead, and the next thing I knew the car was lurching through the door. The wood creaked and crunched as I worked the car into reverse and backed through the splintery hole; then Flip Wilson got to the punch line, "And maybe we have a banana for your monkey!" and the audience roared. My shrink, Dr. Rupert, pointed out later that I could have hurt myself or someone else and insisted I join this group.

The Indian woman sitting next to me lost her twin sister, who was hit and killed by a drunk driver. Her long black braids hang like elegant tassels down the back of her pumpkin-colored sari. She says she and her sister shared a room until they left home, and after that they talked to each other every day on the telephone. Now she dreams that the phone is ringing in the middle of the night. But when she awakens the house is silent; she picks up the phone and no one is there and she can't fall back to sleep and she's exhausted during the day. She hears phones ringing everywhere, in the car, at work, at the store. Now, she shudders and cups her ears with her slender brown fingers. I want to get her number and call her so that when she picks up someone will be on the other end.

Suddenly everyone in the circle is looking at me expectantly, and I wish I'd had a little more time to prepare for the meeting before racing here from work. I can feel my uncooperative curly brown hair puffing in crazy directions, as if it wants to leave the room. On some days it forms silky ringlets, on others Roseanne Roseanna-danna frizz.

"My name is Sophie Stanton and my husband died of cancer three months ago . . . ," I stammer, tucking my fingers into the curls. My voice sounds loud and warbly in the too bright room. I try to talk and hold in my stomach at the same time, because my slacks are unbuttoned under my sweater to accommodate a waist-line swollen from overmedicating with frozen waffles; I think I feel the zipper creeping down my former size six belly. That seems like enough for now, anyway. "Thank you," I add, not wanting to seem unfriendly.

"Thank you, Sophie," the social worker says. Her voice is as high and sweet as a Mouseketeer's.

Maybe later I'll tell the group how I dream about Ethan every night. That he's still alive in the eastern standard time zone and if I fly to New York, I can see him for another three hours. That I'm mixing chocolate and strawberry Ensure into a muddy potion that will restore his hemoglobin. When I wake at three or four in the morning, my nightgown is soaked and stuck to my back and the walls pulse around me. But by the time I get to Dr. Rupert's office, I've sunk into a zombie calm. It's sort of like when you bring your car into the shop and it stops making that troublesome noise.

Dr. Rupert says to keep busy. For the past three months I've been rushing from work to various activities: a book club, a pottery class, volunteer outings for the Audubon Society. We rescued a flock of sandpipers on the beach. Something toxic had leaked from a boat into the water, and the birds reared and stumbled and flapped their wings as we scooped them into crates. I rented a Rototiller and turned over the hard, dry earth at the very back of our yard and planted sunflowers and cosmos that shot straight through the September heat toward the sky. Everyone said how well I was doing, how brave I was.

Then I drove my car through the garage door.

"Screw the birds!" I yelled at Dr. Rupert in my session that afternoon. "Screw the books, screw the sunflowers!" He scribbled on his little pad, then told me about this group.

There are fifteen of us in the circle. My eyes scan the sets of feet, counting: two, four, six, eight, ten. Two, four, six, eight, ten. Two, four, six, eight, ten. Thirty feet. Fifteen people. Hush Puppies and Reeboks and penny loafers.

The group meets at the hospital where Ethan died. I haven't been back since his death. But I remember everything about this place. How Ethan lay in bed, gray and speckly as a trout. The smells of rubbing alcohol and canned peas and souring flower arrangements. The patients, wrapped like mummies, being wheeled on gurneys through the halls. The monotone pages over the PA, the operator saying things like "Code five hundred" and "Dr. So-and-So to surgery" as calmly as if she were reporting a spill in aisle six.

Great idea! Let's go back to the *hospital* once a week. You remember the hospital.

Now everyone is looking at me again, and the social worker is saying something.

"Pardon?"

"What did your husband do, Sophie?"

I push my glasses up on my nose (a little problem with oversleeping prevents me from wearing my contact lenses these days) and peer out at the circle of forlorn faces. "He was a software engineer."

"I see." She adds that to her yellow pad.

How odd to reduce a person to a job title. While he didn't like sweets, he did eat sugared cereals, I want to tell her. His feet were goofy. A couple of those toes looked like peanuts, really. And what a slob. You would *not* want to ride in his car, because it smelled like sour milk and you'd be ankle-deep in take-out wrappers and dirty coffee mugs. He loved Jerry Lewis movies. One movie made him laugh so hard that beer shot out of his nose. I fight to suppress a giggle as I think of this. Or maybe it's a scream. A dangerous tickle lurks in the back of my throat, and I check to see how close the door is, in case I need to escape.

"And how did you two meet?"

Unfortunately I am clear on the other side of the room from the door, stranded in this circle of feet. A pair of laid-back Birkenstocks scoffs at my uptight career pumps. I clear my throat.

"While I was visiting college friends here for Thanksgiving." I think of how Ethan sat beside me at dinner, moving someone else's plate to another spot while the person was in the kitchen and wedging himself in beside me. *Geez,* I thought. *Strangely overconfident software geek.*

"How nice. Did you date from afar at first, then?"

"Yes, we had a long-distance relationship for a year, then I moved here and we lived together for a year and then we married."

"Very good."

I feel as if I could have said we were embezzlers and the social worker would have thought that was nice.

A few of the other women are widows, too, but they're older than me. One has white hair and glasses with lenses as big as coasters that magnify her eyes, making them look like pale blue stones underwater.

There's a man whose wife was killed in a car accident on Highway 1, and his ten-year-old daughter is having her first sleep-over party this weekend. She told him this morning that she hated him because he didn't know what Mad Libs are, and she wanted Mad Libs at her party, and why did her mother have to die and not him since he's so stupid? The man's voice speeds up and his Styrofoam cup cracks as he squeezes it. A dribble of coffee leaks onto his khakis. He tells us about the dozen girls coming to sleep in his family room this Saturday night and how he wants to surprise his daughter with an ice-cream cake; he's pretty sure that's what she wants, but his wife didn't leave any notes about the party and he's afraid to ask his daughter because he doesn't want to upset her any more.

"I think she likes mint chocolate chip," he says, looking down, his pink double chin folding over the stiff collar of his white work-shirt, which looks impossibly tight.

I want to squeeze his plump hand and tell him it's going to be all right. I know, because I was thirteen when my mother died in a car accident on her way to work, and my father and I were left to fend for ourselves.

That was my first experience with death, and I wished then that I'd gotten a dress rehearsal with a distant, elderly relative. A great-aunt Dolores whose whiskery kisses I dreaded. The only death experience before my mother was my hamster, George, who somehow got confused and ate all of the cedar chips in his cage. I came home from school to find him lying still as a stuffed animal, his water bottle dripping on his head. But there was a new hamster by that weekend who performed all of the old hamster's tricks: running in his wheel and fidgeting with his apple slice and popping his head through a toilet paper roll.

"The death of a loved one isn't really something you ever get *over,*" the group leader explains, leaning forward in her chair. She wears a fluffy white angora sweater with a cowl neck reaching to her chin, so it looks as though her head is resting on a cloud. "Instead, one morning you wake up and it's not the *first* thing you think of."

While I know she's right, I can't imagine that this morning will ever come to my house.

By now, everyone in the group is sniffling and honking, and a box of Kleenex is making the rounds. As the gold foil box comes my way, I pull out several tissues and hold the wad in my hand like a bouquet. But I'm the only one in the circle who isn't crying. You don't cry at a scary movie, do you? Dr. Rupert thinks the group will help me move from denial to anger to bargaining to depression to acceptance to hope to lingerie to housewares to gift wrap. But it seems the elevator is stuck. For the past three months I've been lodged in the staring-out-the-window-and-burning-toast stage of grief.

Now my cuticles demand my attention. *Pick at us,* they insist. *Yank away. Don't mind the blood. Keep going.* At last, a use for Kleenex. As I blot at the blood, the counselor glances my way and says you have to find ways to release your anger.

"Keep a box of garage-sale dishes you don't care about," she suggests. "And break them when you're upset." She says you can lay down a blanket and throw the dishes at the garage, then roll the whole thing up when you're done. She's enthusiastic about how easy this is, as if she's relaying a remarkably simple recipe. It's hard to imagine her stepping on an ant, let alone breaking a service for twelve.

Would it be all right if I threw dishes at my former mother-in-law? I want to ask the counselor. Marion, Ethan's mother, calls every other *day* now to insist that she come over and help me pack up Ethan's stuff for Goodwill. I dread the thought of her snoopy paws all over his Frank Zappa CDs and Lakers T-shirts. She'd probably want to chuck his frayed flannel shirts, which I've started sleeping in because they're as soft as moss and smell like Ethan. *Marion's* house is as neat as a museum. The only trace of the past is one family photo on the baby grand piano. It was taken the day of Ethan's college graduation, and he stands between Marion and Charlie, his father, who died a few months later of a heart attack. Ethan's smiling and the tassel on his graduation cap is airborne, as if it might propel him through the future. Marion looks up at him, bursting with awe.

Marion's always needling me to get ahold of myself. "You have to get back on the horse, dear!" she'll chirp. "Chin up, chin up!" Get-your-act-together euphemisms that say, *Look, I'm a widow, too, and now I've lost my only son, but you don't see me driving through my garage door or inhaling pralines and cream out of the carton for breakfast.* I would like to bean Marion with a gravy boat.

Now, even the men are weeping. I'll bet the counselor feels she's making real progress here. I'll bet tears are to a grief counselor what straight teeth are to an orthodontist.

Still, dry eyes for me. Maybe I need the remedial grief group. Maybe there's a book, *The Idiot's Guide to Grief.* Or *Denial for Dummies.*

Maybe this is going to be like ice-skating backward, which I never got the hang of. Or like Girl Scouts, which I got kicked out of for having a poor attitude. I didn't have any badges and wasn't enthusiastic about making my coffee-can camp stove and wouldn't wear that Patty Hearst beret while selling cookies. (It was hot and made your ears itch!) The troop leader, Mrs. Swensen, called my mother to say that I should find an after-school activity I was more enthusiastic about. She didn't know that I had been *working* on the cooking badge. I'd written a little report on paprika—although it was mostly copied out of the encyclopedia—and learned to make pie crust, rolling out the dough until it was as thin and transparent as baby's skin. "Too thin, sweetie," my mom commented, pointing at the huge disk of dough glued to the countertop. Anyway, I was relieved to be free of Girl Scouts, preferring to lie on my bed and listen to Casey Kasem's countdown, chewing banana Now and

Laters and reviewing the repeats in the daisy wallpaper pattern to soothe my nerves. Flower, flower, stem. Flower, flower, stem.

Now, it doesn't look as if I'm ever going to get the grief badge.

I look out the window at the brittle, leafless trees, their branches like bones in the sky.

And that's all the time we have today.

"The warmth of the body causes the patch to adhere," I explain to the *Herald* health care reporter who's interviewing me by telephone for an article he's writing. As public relations manager at Gorgatech, I'm supposed to improve the image of a scrotal patch product that's prescribed to men whose testosterone production is off-kilter on account of illness. A scrotal patch! Why can't I work on the headache product? The problem is, the patch doesn't always stick. Just imagine some poor guy in a sales meeting looking down and suddenly discovering a thing like a big square Band-Aid clinging to his sock.

"For some patients the patch may not adhere completely," I admit. "In which case it should be warmed gently with a hair dryer before application."

The reporter snorts. He points out that another company markets a gel. The disdain in his voice suggests he'd rather talk to a used-car salesman than a PR flack.

"True, but the patch provides a steadier dose," I explain. I look over the padded beige walls of my cubicle at the pockmarked ceiling tiles. Someone's piping sleepy gas into the office. I want to curl up on the floor with my head on my purse and just *sleep.*

My boss, Lara, a size two Armani jackhammer, says I have to get two positive media stories on the patch—one local and one national—by the end of November. That leaves about five weeks for me to redeem myself. Lara's quick to point out that there haven't been any media stories on our company or products since she hired me. She says that if I don't nail the two stories, she'll slam my hands in her desk drawer, severing several fingers, and I'll never be able to type again. Then she'll fire me, and the mortgage company will auction off my house. She didn't say this with words. She said it with her eyes, with the quick cock of her head, her lips pursing into a little red knot. If this guy writes a positive story, I'll be halfway through my quota.

"Most patients aren't bothered by the minor inconvenience of using the dryer," I tell the reporter, reading from my tip sheet, "because of the benefits of the product." I imagine my mailbox at home stuffed with property tax statements and soaring electric bills. The problem is, I like to keep lots of lights on at night so it seems as though people are home. "On *low* heat, though," I tell him. "Never high."

The clacking of the reporter's keyboard and his intermittent chuckles make me nervous. He wants to know if I really think guys travel with blow dryers, if they *own* blow dryers.

"We provide complimentary dryers upon request." At least I think we do. I probably shouldn't stray from the tip sheet.

The reporter says he has to go so he can meet his deadline. As I listen to a long silence and then the dial tone, I think of how my other English major friends have more noble jobs: one's a travel writer in Paris, another teaches creative writing to women prisoners.

Finally I hang up the phone and get back to work on the press release I'm composing about the patch. It's nearly lunchtime and I've made little progress. There's a pea-size hole in my panty hose just under the hem of my skirt, and I've taped it to my leg so it doesn't head south.

I think of the white-haired lady in the grief group whose husband drove her everywhere. I picture them in a Chevy Impala driving forty-five on the freeway, two cottony heads peering over the dashboard. I wonder if it is worse to be widowed later in life, when you and your spouse are as attached as roots to a tree.

The cursor on my computer screen blinks: *mort-gage, mort-gage, mort-gage.*

When I first moved to Silicon Valley to be with Ethan, I found a job I liked editing university publications. I had my own office, with ivy growing along the windows, and went home every night by six. But at parties, other women in their thirties compared BMW models and how many direct-reports they had at work, and I decided I needed a higher-paying job with stock options. What kind of loser worked at a place without stock options?

I got this job during Ethan's remission, after he'd finished his radiation therapy and it seemed that he would be all right. This gave me a brief surge of confidence, during which I drove down the freeway at eighty miles an hour with the moon roof open, the wind in my hair, old songs like "I Will Survive" and "A Girl in Trouble (Is a Temporary Thing)" blasting on the stereo.

Then the cancer came back, this time as a tumor in Ethan's chest. It was the home wrecker that stole my husband. I almost wished it *had* been another woman—a slutty thing in a miniskirt whose tires I could have slashed.

I hardly took any time off after Ethan died—just the three allowed bereavement days and the two sick days I'd accrued. Co-workers stopped by my cube and asked, "How are you doing?" I wanted to tell them not to worry; my husband was only out of town, maybe at a trade show. He'd be back.

Ethan's presence in our house was palpable, his loafers and sneakers lined up in the closet and his *Smithsonian* and *Wired* maga-zines still arriving every month. But all too soon floury dust coated Ethan's shoes, and his toothbrush grew dry and hard in the cup on the sink, and his pile of unread magazines toppled over. People stopped saying, "How are you doing?" and Lara started assigning the black diamond projects again. This damn patch.

Lara whistles into my cube now. "Don't *bother* with a press re-lease," she says, looking over my shoulder at my keyboard, hands on little StairMaster hips, blond hair pulled into a high, tight pony-tail. "Just get a story. Call *The Wall Street Journal.*"

I cower at the keyboard, thinking of the leak underneath my house. A few weeks ago a plumber in coveralls crawled through a trapdoor in the front hall closet and reported that it would cost $2,000 to repair the leak and install a sump pump. Money I don't have right now. "You folks need a pump," he said.

"It's just me," I told him.

If you reach behind the coats and lift the slab of wood, you can see the black puddle, which smells like iron. My car would like a piece of my paycheck now, too. It's been making a grinding noise and pulling to the right, as though it would rather drive through the trees.

"Okay? *Okay?*" says Lara. Although she's only five-three, she somehow manages to tower over people.

"Okay." I flip slowly through the Rolodex on my desk. Later, when I can breathe, I'll tell her about the *Herald* story. She huffs a sigh of exasperation and leaves me in a pit of Willy Loman cold-call despair.

On my way home from work that night, I get in an accident: I'm broadsided by the holidays. It happens when I stroll into Safeway and see the rows of tables by the door stacked high with Hal-loween candy: Milky Way, Kit Kat, Butterfinger. Halloween, Thanksgiving, Christmas. *Stop, turn, run!* I try to shove my cart toward produce, but it won't go. One stubborn wheel tugs like an undertow toward the candy. I kick the cart and focus on my shop-ping list: eggs, milk, ice cream.

I make it safely to produce, but there the pumpkins lurk. *Look!* they shout. *The holidays are coming!* I spot the bunches of brown corn you can hang on your door and the tiny gourds—the bumpy acne ones and the clown-striped green-and-yellow ones. I lean into the cart for support. How can a place called Safeway seem so dangerous?

Last Halloween Ethan and I took Simone, the daughter of my college girlfriend, Ruth, trick-or-treating. Ethan dressed up as Yellow Man, his own made-up superhero. He wore a yellow T-shirt, yellow rubber gloves, and a yellow rain poncho for a cape. He made Simone laugh so hard, she choked on a Gummi Bear.

I remember the yellow yarn dust mop bobby-pinned to his head. I remember his hair—the sweet, almost eggy smell of Flex shampoo. Beautiful hair! Thick, straight, shiny, and brown. The hair I always dreamed of having instead of my wiry curls. Sometimes a Dennis the Menace piece stuck straight up on top of Ethan's head, which is probably why he got carded. He was thrown together in a boyish way—baseball caps and too-big sweatshirts, Converse sneakers with no socks, dirt on his knees from crawling around in the backyard looking for his Frisbee. Why did I ever sign that paper to have him cremated? That's what he wanted. To have his ashes spread at Half Moon Bay, where we went for our honeymoon. It made sense at the time. But now there isn't even a grave to visit. How can I be a widow when there's no grave?

"Miss?" A clerk clutching a bunch of basil stands beside me. "Are you okay?"

"Yes." He said miss and not ma'am. Sweet. There are streaks of cranberry red spots on his cheeks, and his nose shines. I try to think of something to say, a vegetable to inquire after. Instead I blurt: "My husband died." Maybe this is the first time I've said this. I'm not sure. I think it is. Suddenly I'm crying, that little-kid gulping kind of crying, where you can't catch your breath. The morning after Ethan died, I resented the mourners collecting in my living room. How could they fall into the role and accept Ethan's death so readily? While they wept and carried on, I cleaned the house. Scrubbed the shower grout with a toothbrush and Clorox. Now I'm one of the howling mourners. But they've wrapped it up already, moved on.

The clerk touches my elbow and leads me through the big swinging double doors by the coolers with the chicken. He says, "Careful," as we walk up a narrow flight of stairs. There's a leaf of lettuce on one stair. We shuffle into a break room and he seats me at a long brown Formica table. He's probably only in high school or junior college. He sets a cup of tea and a box of tissues on the table.

"You take your time," he says.

I'm suddenly embarrassed and want something to do to look busy. I grab one of the tissues and begin cleaning my glasses.

Okay, so Ethan *isn't* coming back. The sympathy cards reverted to phone bills months ago. Even telemarketers have stopped asking for him.

Oh! The tissues have lotion for sore noses, and the lenses of my glasses now look as though they've been dunked in salad dressing. The room is blurry. The boy is gone. The holidays are coming. Can I stay in this break room until after New Year's?

At home the phone rings as I'm peeling off my coat. I let the machine pick up.

"Hello? Sophie? . . . Dear? Are you there?" It's my mother-in-law, Marion, who's not really comfortable around answering machines, VCRs, and other newfangled devices. She clears her throat.

"Well, I'm calling for two reasons. One, there's a sale at Talbot's, and I'd like to take you to buy a few new things. I thought that might cheer you up." Marion always seems to wish I'd shop at Talbot's, that I'd dress more like a country club wife than a frumpy neo-hippie—frayed jeans and clogs and my husband's too big sweaters. Once in a while Marion wears jeans, "dungarees," she calls them, but she irons stiff creases in the legs that stand up like little tents. "The other thing is, dear, I'd like to make a date to come over this Sunday and pack up Ethan's things for the Goodwill. Remember, we talked about that? I really feel it's time, and it'll be a breeze if we work on it together. . . ."

A breeze?

A tornado.

There are no groceries to unload, since I abandoned my cart at Safeway. I head straight for the bedroom and crawl under our king-size quilt, choosing to sleep in my clothes to ward off the icy corners of the bed.

I dream that I run into Ethan in downtown San Jose by the convention center when I'm on my way to the library. His hair glistens like a mink coat and I want to touch it. He's with a policeman. They explain that Ethan's been in a car accident and the officer is trying to help him find his way home. I look down and see the edge of Ethan's hospital gown hanging out from under his parka, the little blue snowflakes on the fabric fluttering in the breeze. I want to tell him that he wasn't in a car accident. He had cancer and now he's dead. But I'm afraid I'll hurt his feelings, like telling someone they could lose a few pounds or their clothes don't match.

When I make it to work the next morning, the *Herald* is spread across my desk. I'm supposed to read the paper every morning *before* getting to work, so I'll know if the company has been in the news. I'm also supposed to scan the national press and be up on current health care issues so I can pitch stories relating to our products. Spins, pitches, angles. I always mean to do this. But mustering the courage to leave the house every morning leaves me too enervated to lift the pages of *Time* or *Newsweek*.

I read the health care reporter's lead for the patch story.

Gentlemen, start your hair dryers.

I can't read the next line, because there's a Post-it note stuck over it with a note from Lara: *See me.*

The bum fluorescent bulb over my cube ticks and buzzes like a cicada.

I head straight for Lara's office without taking off my coat. Lara and I are opposites, and in our case opposites deflect. She's only two years older than me—thirty-eight—but she's already a vice president. She's as polished as a lady news anchor, and her whole *being* seems dry-cleaned. She meets her personal trainer at the gym every morning at five, arrives at work by seven-thirty, eats lunch at her desk—peeling the bread off her turkey sandwich to avoid the evils of carbohydrates—and leaves at seven-thirty in the evening. I get up at five in the morning, too, but only to pee, my sole workout being a shuffle to the john. The next time I wake it's ten minutes before I'm supposed to be at work, never mind the forty-minute, second-gear commute and the fact that my hair is in one long snarl like the Cowardly Lion's in *The Wizard of Oz*.

As I stand in the doorway to Lara's office, she's on the phone.

"Un-huh, un-huh, un-huh," she says impatiently, punching her PalmPilot, sipping coffee out of a giant mug, and checking her e-mail. She motions me in. I hover at the threshold. *Simon says: Go into your boss's office!* I take a big step in. She yanks off her headset and tosses it on her desk. Her expression is in the fully upright and locked position.

For the first time, I almost *wish* I'd get fired. I would probably be eligible for some kind of severance or unemployment. I could get roommates to help pay the mortgage. We could do the Jumble together and cook pot luck suppers. I can live off a couple weeks' salary for a little while. I actually *like* chicken pot pies. . . .

"Sit," says Lara.

I sit. Good dog? Bad dog.

"We'll get a correction printed." She smiles, containing her irritation. Her teeth are so white, they're almost transparent; I think she used her bleaching trays a few too many nights.

"Right," I tell her, as though I've planned this all along. I realize I'm still wearing my coat.

"Did you take this reporter to lunch?"

Lara has a real thing for taking reporters to lunch. She thinks you can control the media with smoked turkey and fusilli salad. I shake my head. Bottom line: The patch doesn't stick.

"I'd like to be able to tell Ed by noon that a correction will be printed tomorrow morning."

Ed's the CEO. *Turn down your teeth,* I want to tell Lara. *I can't hear you.* Instead, I nod. "I'll get on it." First, get me out of this oxygen-depleted room.

Of course, this doesn't count as one of my two media placements due by the end of November, since it didn't even mention the downsides of the competing product. But when I get back to my cubicle, I realize there aren't any *errors* in the story. It's all about tone. It's a tone piece. Tone, voice. This reporter has found his voice! It is the voice of an asshole.

The phone rings. I pick it up.

"Hello?" a man says.

I know he'll ask a question I can't answer. I'm supposed to be able to remember scads of facts for this job: each product name, its generic name, its indication, whether it has a trademark or service mark, how long it's been on the market, whether it's part of a joint marketing and distribution agreement. Then there are the common side effects, adverse reactions. But since Ethan died I can barely retain a seven-digit phone number. I slide one finger over the button on the phone, hanging up. The man will think we got disconnected. When the phone rings again, I let it drop into voice mail.

I open a new file on my computer and start typing what to say to the *Herald* reporter about the patch story. This is a trick I employ when I have to make a nerve-racking media call: Type my story pitch or sound bite in all caps, then follow the script.

MUST PATCH THIS ALL UP. HA, HA, HA!

I remember when I first joined the company how I felt I was finally making it in Silicon Valley. I stood in the coffee line chatting with the women from marketing, all of us wearing cute but sensible chunky black pumps, my day planner bulging, my checkbook balance growing, my self-esteem swelling. But now I feel like an impostor in a cubicle—like the artificial crabmeat of public relations managers. Then there's the fact that I have to say "scrotum" to people all the time. Is this really the color of my parachute?

If Ethan were alive, I'd call him and we'd meet for lunch. We often did this when one of us was having trouble at work. We had a knack for solving each other's job quandaries, maybe because our ignorance of each other's fields made us objective. Sometimes he'd pick me up after work and I'd be so flustered by this new job, I was ready to quit and start a yard service. By the time we got home, though, Ethan had me laughing and contemplating a solution.

Of course, I can't call my husband. (But why not! What good is all this technology if you can't call a deceased loved one? Who cares if you can buy movie tickets and bid for antiques on-line if you can't dial up your dead husband?)

The cursor on my computer screen pulses impatiently, and the red voice mail light on my phone flashes. My stomach growls and my head throbs. But I can't call my husband. Because, here's the thing: I am a widow.

OREOS

Ethan's former boss invites me to a party at his house. It's nice of him and his wife to include me. What do I do to thank them? Drink too much Cabernet and swipe Xanax from their medicine chest.

The problem is, it's a family-friendly party, and everyone seems to have a baby. Babies with sweet doughy arms and tiny toes like erasers. Ethan and I tried for two years to have a baby, up until his prognosis was terminal.

Month after month, I peed on the drugstore pregnancy test sticks while Ethan pretended to be busy in the next room. I closed my eyes, listening to the clanky whir of the bathroom fan, trying to will the second pink line into the result window. But it was always empty. No one home. Like the vague Magic 8 Ball message: *Try again later.*

I felt duped by my body. What's going on in there? Who's in charge here! Ethan held my hands in his, rubbed my neck a little too hard, and said not to worry. There was always next month. Then he'd come up with a fun, kidless activity: a late-night dinner at a French restaurant or an R-rated movie or a pitcher of beer and game of pool.

I studied fertility books until their diagrams haunted me. The vines on our quilt turned into fallopian tubes and the inverted U shape of a papaya half in the refrigerator looked like a uterus, its slick black seeds a crazy wealth of eggs. Our sex life, dictated now by the coy, shadowy purple line on the ovulation test sticks, suddenly seemed like work.

We went to a fertility specialist, who concluded after several tests that I was ovulating but possibly had an "egg quality issue." Suddenly I felt about as feminine as a log. I imagined my ovaries shrinking like those little Japanese roasted peas, my eggs reduced for quick sale. Neon orange stickers shrieking *Half off!*

Now, thirty minutes into the party, I feel a slow leak of crazy juice seeping into my brain. My palms sweat and my throat squeezes shut. It's hard to talk or swallow.

I work a splintery wedge of spanakopita down my throat as a marketing communications director tells a funny story about her Emma's play date that morning.

"Chocolate pudding. In her *ear!*"

The other mothers hoot and toss back their heads. I laugh, too. But the thing is, Marion's coming over in the morning to corral Ethan's earthly possessions for the Great Goodwill Giveaway, and suddenly I can't breathe.

I lurch into the powder room, lock the door, and stand at the sink, peering into a china saucer of pumpkin-shaped soaps. Their cinnamon smell burns in my nose. I could call Marion and tell her I'm sick, but she'd drive over anyway and let herself in with her key. Stamp her little brown loafers on the front mat, roll up the sleeves of her pressed white blouse, and get to work packaging up Ethan. I'd like to get that key back from her, but I'm not sure how I'd ask, so I burrow into the medicine chest, finding baking soda toothpaste and unopened toothbrushes, then the Xanax. I have my own prescription at home—from Dr. Rupert—but I've taken it only once so far, preferring to rely on frozen waffles instead of pills. This *is* the guest bath and clearly the toothbrushes are for guests, so maybe the Xanax is, too. Probably not, but my throat is so tight and the air in the room is so thin.

"What's your number?" the hostess asks as I emerge from the bathroom.

Why? Does she need to give it to her lawyer so he can call and sue me for stealing her drugs? I stutter out my home phone number.

"No, silly," she says, caressing my arm and leading me back into the crowd. "Your raffle ticket number." I remember that when I arrived at the party, her daughter handed me a curly pink ticket, dropping its twin half in a paper bag.

"Oh." I dig into the pocket of my slacks, pull out the ticket, and hand it to her.

"Read the number again," she tells her daughter, a pretty girl with long strawberry blond hair.

The girl reads the number, and her mother hugs me and says, "It's *you*, Sophie. We have a winner!" She smells good and I would like for her to keep hugging me, but she pulls away, raises my arm over my head, and spins me toward the crowd. Everyone claps and I feel my face heat up. It turns out the party prize is a week's worth of free home-delivered meals from Waiters on Wheels. If anyone sees the irony in the fact that it's "dinner for two," they don't let on.

At home, even though my brain is a dim wad of Xanax and red wine, I can't sleep. I miss having Ethan to gossip with about the party. It was kind of a mean game, but sometimes we'd play Who am I?, imitating the guests.

I sit up in bed with a family pack of Oreo cookies, twisting them open and licking the cream filling until my tongue feels raw. The walls around me creak and sigh, as if the empty house can't settle down and get comfortable. I stack the cookie shells on the clock radio, then get to work on the pile, chewing and swallowing without pleasure until I can't really taste the chocolate anymore—until the cookies begin to seem more utilitarian than sweet, more like glue or caulking that welds things back together.

I dig two, four, six more cookies from the family pack, noting that in a *normal* family, each person would eat maybe four. I chew and chew until my gums burn and my head tingles from the sugar. Sandy crumbs spray the sheets, and chocolate collects in the corners of my mouth like potting soil.

It's morning and I'm dreaming that I'm getting up and then I'm down again and then I'm trying to lift my head and arms but they are as heavy as logs and then I'm underwater and then I am not underwater, I'm just perspiring under this quilt, which is like a lead blanket. Finally I'm awake. My mouth is filled with moss. No, that is my tongue caked with cookie sludge. A crack of sunlight shoots through the blinds and slices into my head. The morning is uninvited and overly cheerful, like a Jehovah's Witness ringing the doorbell. I shield my face with my arm. *Sorry, nobody home!*

I roll over and an Oreo crunches beneath me. The TV's on and cartoon characters chatter. Damn. Marion's due at ten-thirty.

I get up, shower, dress, fix coffee for Marion, and defrost blueberry muffins I find in the freezer. I arrange the muffins in a circle on a paper plate, wondering if Marion's going to make me give away *all* of Ethan's belongings. Even his books? In my nervousness, I eat all the muffins. Blueberry. Soft, sweet, cakey, crumbly, gone.

I lie down in a patch of sunlight on the sofa in the living room, bracing myself for Marion's burst of efficient energy. I always suspected that she didn't approve of me but was nice in order to be supportive of Ethan, the way a parent would try to accept a child's pierced nose or decision to join the Peace Corps. Still woozy from last night, I drift back into a syrupy sleep.

"Dear?"

I awaken to Marion hovering over me and furrowing her brow, her arms embracing an empty cardboard box, her pretty white hair curling around her freshly powdered face. She always smells flowery and clean, like the first floor of a department store.

"I used my key," she says brightly.

I remember Ethan telling me that his mother was "remarkably together" after his father's death, tending to all of the necessary details and procedures, soldiering on with an eerie resolve.

Now I follow Marion as she heads for Ethan's office, drags his suitcase out of his closet, and parks it by the coat closet in the front hall.

"I might need that," I tell her, pointing to the suitcase that I bought for Ethan last Christmas. We made a jaunt that spring to Napa and shared the bag. I vowed never to share a suitcase with Ethan again, though, because he didn't have a system for separating his dirty laundry (muddy socks on top of clean underwear!). But we never traveled after that.

"You *have* a suitcase, don't you, dear?" Marion asks, looking up at me impatiently. "You don't need two."

I stand with my arms at my sides and watch as she fills the bag with Ethan's coats. Oh! The suede jacket with the lamb's-wool lining that we dubbed the Marlboro Man coat. She tucks the arms inside the suitcase carefully, as though she's making hospital corners. You don't need a coat when you're dead. It's that simple.

I reach into the closet, pull Ethan's ski sweater off a hanger, and curl it against my belly, massaging a pinch of the wool between my fingers. The familiar scratchy fabric is as soothing as a hot bath. I didn't know how to ski when Ethan and I first started dating. He patiently rode the T-bar up the bunny slope with me for hours until I could make a parallel turn and graduate to the chairlift. "Take your time!" he called up the hill as I doubled over my skis, rear in the air, eight-year-olds whizzing past me.

Now, Marion takes the sweater from me and folds it into the suitcase. When she reaches for Ethan's down parka, a spider lurches out of the sleeve. Marion smacks it with her bare hand, making me jump, then brushes the creature onto the floor and gives it one swift stomp.

"They bite, you know," she says, returning to the coats with dour concentration. She is a first-rate widow. Not a woman who needs a man around to kill her insects.

We lug the boxes into the garage, creating stack after stack, and pretty soon I have to move my car into the driveway to make more room. The concrete is cold and gritty on my bare feet, and Marion says why don't I put on some shoes. Then she tells me that the Goodwill truck is coming Monday morning between eight and noon. Can I be home then? *Yes, yes,* I nod, and smack invisible dust from my hands. I survey the boxes, locating the one with Ethan's ski sweater.

After we finish packing Ethan's belongings, Marion takes me to a salad bar restaurant for lunch. I drizzle nonfat ranch dressing onto nonfat honey corn muffins, spoon nonfat sour cream into a steaming baked potato, munch Chinese chicken salad, and sip diet soda. I've always enjoyed food, especially lobster, blueberry pancakes with real maple syrup, and beer, but I've never felt so *compelled* to eat. In the year before Ethan died, food actually seemed like a nuisance—having to worry about what to make for dinner or where to find take-out lunch close to work. But now eating's like crawling under the covers, food a tunnel to burrow into. The green salad is cool and soothing—the kidney beans as soft as felt.

Marion eyes my salad, which is loaded with raisins and croutons and chopped eggs. "Looks like you haven't lost your *appetite,*" she says, her tone of voice somewhere between talking and singing. "I lost fifteen pounds after Charlie died. Couldn't bring myself to eat alone."

Marion's right. All of the grief books say that widows *lose* weight. There's nothing in any of the chapters about wanting to devour a minimart.

I dab my mouth with my napkin and fold my hands in my lap. "It feels good to eat and sleep," I try to explain.

Marion nods and butters a ladylike corner of corn muffin. She has never lost control, of course, never ransacked the host's medicine chest at a party or inhaled a box of Thin Mints. She probably thinks I'm not a very good widow. I wish I could be. I want to be a classy widow—a Jackie Kennedy kind of widow. Slim and composed, elegant and graceful. White gloves and a string of pearls. But I seem to be more the Jack Daniel's kind of widow—wailing in the supermarket and mowing through the salad bar, hair all crazy like an unmade bed.

Lately, life requires so much self-discipline. While most people have a to-do list, I have a don't-do list. Don't eat Oreos until your gums bleed. Don't sleep in your clothes. Don't grab the produce boy's teenage wrists and sob.

Marion excuses herself and heads for the fruit. I get to work on the potato and then the gluey soup. But I'm interrupted by a chubby toddler who stumbles up to the table and rudely points a waxed-bean finger at me. He blurts something incomprehensible, foamy spittle bubbling up around his pacifier.

It sounds like "How come *you* don't have a baby?"

On Monday morning I stay home from work to wait for the Goodwill truck. I figure I've got a few hours to rummage through the boxes and retrieve Ethan's ski sweater and those wool socks that I like to wear to bed and the Marlboro Man coat. But the doorbell rings just after eight and two guys are standing there, ready for business. There's a tall, lanky man with a mustache that's got a bit of scrambled egg or something in it, and a squat guy who looks as if he could move pianos. The skinny one has a clipboard.

"Stanton?"

Nope, I want to tell him.

"Yes, hi, come in."

We stand in the entryway while the guy studies his clipboard.

"Boxes?" he finally says.

My palms are damp. "Furniture, actually." I lead them to the living room and point to the burgundy tapestry sofa that Ethan and I bought on sale at Macy's along with a matching armchair. The pieces are fairly new and don't feel like part of the house yet; they're guests rather than family members. Still, the furniture was expensive, and we coveted and saved up for it.

"Take the armchair and the end tables, too," I tell the man, waving at the whole ensemble. "And the lamps." I unplug the lamps and wind up the cords.

The skinny guy raises his eyebrows as if to say, *Crazy, fickle lady.*

The stocky guy pulls the cushions off the sofa, and the skinny one jogs back to the truck and returns with sheets of plastic for wrapping everything. As they grunt and shove the sofa through the front door, Ethan's money clip falls out from a crack, clanging to the floor. I gave it to him on our first anniversary, and we hadn't been able to find it for the past year.

"There that thing is." I shove the clip into the pocket of my jeans.

The mustache guy points to the coffee table and raises his eyebrows. I nod and he passes it through the door to his partner. Then he hands over the clipboard for me to sign and they're off, their truck rumbling down the street.

I stand on the front porch and look at our neighborhood, quiet, since everyone is off at work or school, then turn back inside. The sound of the front door closing echoes through the empty living room, making the house sound hollow. I close my eyes, dip my hand into my pocket, and run my fingers over the engraving on the money clip—*SS loves ES*—the bumpy writing like Braille.

That night Waiters on Wheels shows up with my first free dinner. The waiter is dressed in black pants, a stiff white dress shirt with too-long sleeves, and a slick black vest. A red bow tie hangs askew at his neck.

"Evening," he says, bumping past me into the hall, a red insulated bag tipping him to one side. "Living room, dining room, or kitchen?" he asks, mopping his brow with his free hand.

"Kitchen, I guess." I stand in front of the living room door, hoping he won't notice the lack of furniture.

He quickly unpacks the dinner and sets two places at the kitchen table, the oily-looking vest making swishing noises as he works. There's even a little vase with a red carnation and candles in plastic holders.

"It's just me," I tell him.

He looks around the room helplessly. "Should I put the other dinner in the fridge?"

"No, leave it," I tell him. "But I don't need the extra setting." I wonder what it's like to have a job delivering fancy restaurant dinners to the Valley's high-tech workers, many of whom have gourmet kitchens—six-burner Vulcans, Corian counters, and gleaming stainless appliances—but rarely cook.

The waiter's neck is red and bumpy along the collar of his shirt. I consider asking him to sit down and eat the other dinner with me, take a break, but I worry this will come off as a romantic advance. Besides, I'm sure he's got more food to deliver.

"I won the dinners," I try to explain in case he thinks I'm crazy for ordering two meals when I'm only one person. "At a party."

He smiles weakly and I tip him. Then he's gone.

Instead of sitting, I stand at the table and eat, the earnestness of the red carnation breaking my heart. It's trying too hard. The foil-wrapped butter patties glitter like gold coins. I unwrap one and place it on my tongue. Eating plain butter! But a "Why bother" mantra prevents me even from buttering a roll. Besides, the yellow tabs are soothingly smooth and sweet and salty. I eat another, then another, and then the rolls, followed by the risotto, then the second serving of risotto—Ethan's risotto—finally sitting down.

The truth is, I often ate alone when I was married, when Ethan worked late. Sometimes he'd get so sucked into writing software code that he'd forget to call or show up in time for dinner. I bought him a watch that was water-resistant up to 330 feet and told time in five different time zones. I set the alarm for six-thirty P.M. and insisted he call home even if he was at the bottom of the ocean or in Paris.

The first night after I gave him the watch he called at six-thirty sharp, then at seven, eight, and again at nine. At ten he strolled through the door, laptop tucked under one arm. As I jammed wilted asparagus down the disposal, he tried to hug and kiss me, but I was not talking to him. I slammed pots and pans into the dishwasher and lusted after my next husband, an attentive podiatrist who'd always arrive in time for dinner, because no one really needs their feet tended to after five.

Ethan hovered behind me, his belly warm against the small of my back. Lifting my hair, he kissed the nape of my neck and cheeks, nibbled at my ears.

"Quit it," I grumbled, swatting him away. But he moved in closer. As I felt the thump of his pulse in his neck and breathed in the cottony smell of his shirt, I was soothed by his significant otherness.

He said he was sorry and suggested we both work from home the next day.

"Maybe," I mumbled, still refusing to turn from the sink.

"I can't guarantee you won't get sexually harassed in the workplace," he teased, pulling my arms against my sides so I couldn't fuss with the dishes anymore.

I tried to suppress a giggle, forcing a cough instead. Ethan's arms were strong and certain as he steered me down the hall to our room, his mouth warm, salty, and familiar.

Now, as I swallow more gummy risotto, I imagine that Ethan and I dined together every evening at a table like this. But a post–Thanksgiving dinner sort of cramp starts to rise up in my throat, and I have to push the food away.

. . .

The next time I see Dr. Rupert, I explain that I'm always tired yet never sleep well and that I can't stop double-checking things. Before I can go to sleep at night, I have to circle through the house and check the locks on the doors two, three, four times. Whenever I leave a restaurant or coffee shop, I have to go back and touch the table and look under the chairs in case I've forgotten something. When I'm taking aspirin for a headache, I have to spit the pills back into my palm and double-check, making sure they're not buttons or pebbles.

"Obsessive-compulsive behavior," he explains calmly. "It's part of working through the loss. It should subside."

But I feel too exhausted to work through the loss. I'd rather *outsource* working through the loss. That's what you do in Silicon Valley: hire help. A nanny to look after the kids, a nutritionist to plan the meals, a gardener to tend the wisteria, a trainer to monitor your workouts. I need a grief underling. *This is Helga, and she'll be working through the loss for me. Helga, before you leave today, please touch all of the doorknobs and locks and eat all of the Oreos in the house. I'm going to sleep now.*

Dr. Rupert laughs nervously when I share this idea, sliding a little pad from his desk drawer. "Grief-caused depression," he explains, writing a prescription for an antidepressant. "These will help. But they may take up to six weeks to really kick in."

On Halloween, angels and ghosts and pirates flock to my doorstep. A tiny pumpkin hoists her leg over the threshold and clings to my calf like a koala bear.

"No, Jenny," the baby's mom says, and laughs. "We don't live here."

This is a busy year for trick-or-treaters. It's only seven and I'm already running low on candy, since I never made it back to

Safeway to load up. Every time I passed the store my throat tightened, and I decided to make do with the limited selection at the drugstore by my house.

I wish Ethan were here now, because he always dressed up on Halloween and made the kids laugh. During a lull, a Butterfinger burst of energy inspires me to dig my witch costume out of the basement: pointy black hat, black cape, rubber nose, and green makeup. I add a little water to the makeup to get it working again and blacken one of my front teeth with an eyebrow pencil.

Next time the doorbell rings, I throw open the door and let out a cackling laugh. A tiny cat and ladybug shriek and hide behind their mothers' legs. The ladybug sobs and tears off her antennae.

"Oh, I'm sorry!" I pass out handfuls of Baby Ruth bars to show I'm not one of those just-pick-one ladies. The mothers chuckle and say not to worry. But one of the mothers doesn't want the Baby Ruth.

"Little ones can choke on nuts," she says primly. She's wearing khakis, white ankle socks, and loafers. I feel as if I offered the kids Drano.

After the group is gone, I crack open a beer and sit on the living room floor, leaning against the wall where the sofa used to be, unwrapping and eating Baby Ruth bars. My witch's hat hangs over my eyes. I knew it had to be too good to be true: this fleeting feeling that the holidays could be fun.

As I'm working my way through a peanut-butter cup, the phone rings and I climb up to answer it.

"I'm a *ticky* tahk," a small voice squeaks.

"Pardon?"

"I'm a *ticky* tahk!"

Then there's a grown-up voice. "She's a kitty cat," says Ruth, my college friend. Ruth lives in Ashland, Oregon, now, and she's called me at least once a week since Ethan died. "Sorry, she's got candy in her mouth," she adds, laughing. "We lost her tail."

"I'm a *ticky* tahk!" Simone squeals in the background. Then she says, "Uncle?"

"No, *Auntie*," Ruth says, and sighs. "How are you *doing*?"

"Fine. Good!" Then I confess that I'm flubbing up at work and driving over curbs and mailing letters without stamps and I'm afraid to go to the store.

"Get out of there, Soph. Come and stay with us. *Live* with us. Honestly, I could use the help." Ruth's ex-husband is a flake who rarely visits Simone.

"I'd have to sell the house."

"So?"

So. I'm already one living room ensemble closer to leaving Silicon Valley. A step toward escaping my mortgage and that deadline at work. Part of me wants to say, *Screw this place.* Another part of me still wants to make it here for Ethan. Yet another part of me wants to get back to work on the Oreos.

While Ethan was sick, all I thought about was whether he was comfortable—whether he wanted a malted or a pain shot or a cool cloth for his forehead. As soon as the memorial service ended, though, it was time to think about the future. Suddenly what to do with the rest of my life and what shirt to wear became equally daunting decisions. Gradually I was able to think ahead a little bit: Maybe in a few minutes I'll get dressed. Maybe in a few hours I'll get dressed. Maybe *tomorrow* I'll get dressed. But nothing like moving to a new state.

"I don't know," I tell Ruth.

"You'll love it up here."

"Thanks, it sounds great. I'll think about it."

After we hang up, I open the front door and peer out at the street, flashlights bobbing in the night. The air is cool and moist against my face, and overhead Venus glitters and blinks as though it's breathing.

— *3* —

"You would not *believe* how the smells of cinnamon and vanilla draw in a buyer," says Melanie the realtor, pivoting on one pump and surveying my living room. "Hmm, you don't have any furniture in here, and *that's* a problem." I got her name from a SALE PENDING sign in a neighbor's yard on a day when selling the house and moving into a condo with no memories and a smaller mortgage seemed the only logical thing to do. But now I'm not so sure. Melanie's making me a long list of chores before the place can go on the market: replace drapes, buy houseplants and throw pillows, rent living room furniture. She's already sold four houses on our block and she drives a champagne-colored Lexus, but she looks young, maybe only thirty.

"Buy scented candles or bake a pie or something," she says, waving a hand in front of her face and wrinkling her nose. "This place smells . . . *musty.*" Cancer. Maybe three months later my house still smells like cancer.

Ethan and I never discussed selling the house. During his last visit to the hospital he rattled off reminders for taking care of it: repair the sagging fence, hire a chimney sweep before lighting a fire this winter, schedule the tree pruner. I sat on the edge of his bed, even though the nurse said not to, and listed the chores on a yellow pad, pretending to be concerned about them. We had worked hard to buy our house, so I didn't want to tell him that after he was gone I didn't care if I lived at the YWCA.

I had imagined there would be *Love Story* speeches by Ethan's deathbed, like in the movies, but mostly we just held hands and talked about the house and whether he wanted Chap Stick or a sip of milk, and I realized that this is what happens when someone's dying. It's not like a soap opera, where the patient clutches your arm and rasps, "My whole life I have loved you the most," or, "I have always wanted to tell you that you have a sister living in Albany." Your loved one is more apt to remind you to feed the cat when you get home.

Melanie says we have to stage everything, whip the place into shape. Her diamond earrings shimmer against her downy pink earlobes. She frowns at my empty living room, indents in the carpet marking where the furniture once was.

"I'll bake," I promise.

The first week of November brings gusts of wind that send lawn chairs tumbling across the patio, dead leaves swirling, and garbage can lids clanging against the side of the house. The autumn sky is a bright gray that hurts to look at. I imagine the earth tilting on its axis away from the sun and feel dizzy and weak and wonder when the pills will start working. Of course, the fact that I sometimes forget to take them probably doesn't help. Also, I've started playing grief group hooky, dreading the bitter coffee, bright lights, and public speaking at the meetings.

Medical bills and insurance statements continue to arrive in the mail, the "Explanation of Benefits" as nonsensical to me as Ethan's death. I try to read the "Description" column, but everything's abbreviated: "morphin inj 10 M, Elctrd EKG 3, Ans breath cir, SPNG 4x4 TRI10." Finally I give up and just pay the patient responsibility portion, my checkbook balance waning, the vague medical terminology bringing back images of Ethan's hospital days. The cool, damp sheets and ammonia smell of his bed. Dry, thin flamingo legs.

Melanie's sign on the front lawn says FOR SALE. The ad in the paper says *Perfect for a growing family!* It rains and rains, and the puddle under the floor in the coat closet creeps higher, a few skeletal leaves floating at the top.

I attend a day-long meeting with a committee writing the label for a new drug. The wording on the label is important, because that's what you have to work with in the promotional materials that follow. The FDA is touchy, though, and won't allow any promotional-sounding language. Each word has to be debated. *Reduces* versus *prevents. May cause* versus *has been known to cause.*

As I'm trying to find my place on the handouts, the tag in my sweater jabs the back of my neck. I raise my hand to adjust it.

"Sophie. Question?" the vice president of marketing asks impatiently. His legs are crossed, and one slick loafer shines under the bright lights. Everyone in the group turns to look at me. Obviously I haven't been paying attention. Worrying about the leak under my coat closet!

The VP drums his fingers on the table.

I want to explain that I wasn't raising my hand, but suddenly I'm overcome with stage fright. *Meeting* fright. Trying to take a deep, cleansing breath, I discover that thin-air feeling again, my lungs shallow and woolen. Stars shimmer up the wall. My only thought is: *I need a sump pump.*

Lara leans toward me, her eyebrows raised so high that they look as though they're trying to crawl under her hair. Clearly they didn't cover nut jobs like me in her MBA program.

One guy—a product manager who wears an earring in his tongue when he's not at work—laughs, but everyone else is quiet. I excuse myself and then I'm out of there. Down the hall, down the stairs, papers flying behind me. *May cause? Has been known to cause?*

As I run past the receptionist in the front atrium, forgetting my coat, I tell her I have a dentist's appointment.

She points a red fingernail at the sheet on the counter and calls after me, "Sign out!"

The next day I set out to shop for the houseplants, pillows, and curtains Melanie wants for "staging" the house, even though the thought of going to the store fills me with what I know is an irrational sense of doom. I haven't been to a *real* store since I fled Safeway before Halloween, limiting my shopping since then to the less overwhelming inventory at the 7-Eleven—squishy wheat bread and bologna and only one kind of eggs to choose from.

It's not even Thanksgiving, but there are already poinsettias and Christmas decorations for sale at the nursery. A big spruce towers above me, choked with garland and winking white lights. I must write a memo to the Minister of Happier Days requesting that the holidays be canceled this year. As I browse for paper whites and amaryllis, *Nutcracker* Muzak rushes to a crescendo, all those violin strings screeching at me. I give up on the flowers and race to get out of the store, knocking over a display of potted African violets on my way. I stumble to my hands and knees, gathering up clumps of soil.

"I *told* Renaldo we shouldn't put those there," a voice behind me says. A slender man in a green apron stands with his hands on his hips. "Don't worry," he adds. "I've got it." But it is better down here on the floor with the brown-speckled tiles and thin layer of dirt. Not overly festive like the rest of the store.

I can't get up because the air's too thin and my head's too light. But I need to get out of the nursery *now*. The floor is cool and chalky against my palms as I crawl toward the exit.

"Ma'am?" the salesman calls out.

Surely this is worse than crying by the acorn squash at Safeway. If I hurry, I'll be out of here in no time. I scuttle faster, passing a dirty noodle of a rubber band, my coat hiking up around my waist.

"Ma'am?" The salesman's voice is farther away now. Grow lights buzz around me.

"Sophie? Dear?"

Marion! I crouch lower and peer up at her. Of course. She lives right near the nursery. She clutches a wicker reindeer lawn ornament by the neck. He has a big plastic cherry nose. It looks as though she's choking him.

"Did you lose a contact lens?" she asks.

"Yes." I begin to get up.

"But you've got your glasses on."

"Right. Gosh." I am on my knees, at eye level with the hem of Marion's loden jacket. She reaches a small hand down for me. The fingers are pink and gnarled with arthritis, and there are no rings, just fingernails rounded into white crescent moons.

"What did you do with your wedding ring?" I ask her. "Where do you keep it?"

ANGER

Thanksgiving is on its way now, like a storm pumping across the weather map. I'd like to hide under the covers for the four-day weekend, but I'm determined to keep busy and get in the spirit. I decide to take off the Wednesday before the holiday and bake pies. Lure those buyers in with the smells of cinnamon and vanilla.

While I'm nowhere near placing two media stories by the end of the month, I call Lara and tell her that I'm making progress working from home. Then I flip through cookbooks and bookmark recipes, comforted by the ingredients as I read them aloud: flour, eggs, butter. Cinnamon, cloves, nutmeg. I decide to bake a pecan pie with the top almost burned, the way Ethan likes it, and a sour cream apple and a pumpkin cheesecake with gingersnap crust. And a pumpkin pie. You have to have one plain pumpkin.

When I finish the pies maybe I can deliver them to a homeless shelter. One Thanksgiving, Mother and I bought store pies and took them to the veterans hospital. A man with scissors-sharp stubble on his chin wept and grabbed my arm and hollered, "Marjorie!" I knew then that the holidays spelled trouble.

The year Ethan and I were engaged, we volunteered as Meals on Wheels drivers, delivering dinners in Styrofoam cartons in East Palo Alto. I baked pies at Thanksgiving and we brought slices to everyone on our route. One woman, Mrs. Tucker, didn't want to let us in. She peered warily through the crack in her door with one glazed eye. "I'm not celebrating this year," she grumbled. Her two tiny nostrils flared at the smell of the dinner.

Ethan pulled off his baseball cap, smiled, and said that it was okay not to celebrate the holidays. "But you gotta eat, right?" he asked. "So why not let us in and we'll sit with you?" His voice was a low, smooth ballad, and pretty soon Mrs. Tucker's face loosened and she opened the door.

We sat at her kitchen table as she ate turkey and cornbread stuffing, and Ethan poured her a glass of milk.

"Madam," he said as he spread the napkin across the lap of her quilted robe, and she giggled. In the car on the way to the next house, Ethan said thank God we had each other to grow old with.

Now, as I unpack cans of pumpkin and condensed milk that I ordered from an upscale shop that delivers, the phone rings.

"I'm buying you a plane ticket to come home," my father insists. He has called me once a week since I left home and has always offered to buy me plane tickets for the holidays, even when I was married. I picture him across the country, sitting at his kitchen table in his retiree uniform—blue chamois shirt and khakis speckled with paint.

"Oh, no, Dad. I told you, I can't take time off from work." I cut open a sack of flour and pour it into the canister.

"It's a long weekend. You could leave tonight and be home on Sunday."

After years of living alone, Dad recently remarried and seems happy at last. He and his new wife, Jill, do everything together. He washes and she dries. They split restaurant entrées and share a suitcase when they travel. I don't want to bring grief back into his house. I'm afraid it will linger after I leave, like cigar smoke clinging to the drapes.

"I have to work this weekend," I tell him. A lie. While some people are going into the office Thanksgiving weekend, Lara hasn't asked me to. She probably figures I'll do more damage than good. "I still have so much to learn." The truth.

"Working through the holiday doesn't sound fun."

"Fun?" My expectations are much lower than fun. "Maybe for Christmas," I tell him.

After we hang up, I get to work on the pies, creaming butter and sugar, sifting flour, scalding milk, chopping nuts. My feet ache as the hours drone by. Pretty soon pies are spread everywhere, cooling on the kitchen counters and table, even on the washer and dryer. As I'm eating a slab of apple crumb over the sink, the phone rings and I hope it'll be Dad again. Maybe this time I'll give in. It's only a long weekend, after all; I can't pollute his whole life in one weekend. But it's a telemarketer who wants to know if I'll switch long-distance phone companies. In my married days, I would have hung up quickly. *The nerve!* But now I ask questions. Maybe I *will* switch. Is it cheaper on the weekends? I want to know more. But I have to say good-bye and hang up, because the doorbell's ringing and I hear a key turning in the lock.

"Hel-l-o-o-o!" Melanie the Realtor calls out. I hear a baby squawk and a woman trying to comfort him. Melanie peeks around the corner into the kitchen. Her cheery expression suddenly rolls up like a window shade.

There's a snowfall of flour across the floor and a tower of dirty dishes in the kitchen sink. My arms and hands are caked with bits of pie dough, and I'm not officially dressed yet. I'm wearing Ethan's clothes: baggy jeans that are more forgiving of my new Oreo waistline and a T-shirt with no bra.

"Sorry to interrupt," the wife says, the mommy. She cradles a chunky toddler around her hips and is clearly pregnant with her second. The husband wears a T-shirt with a company logo, and his hair is tousled.

"We can come another time," he offers.

"No, please, have a look," I insist, wiping my hands on my jeans, hoping they're taking in the cinnamon and clove aroma.

Where's your husband? the toddler seems to say with his relentless stare. *Where's your baby? How come you didn't fix the fence out
back? How come you're selling the house? Are you sure your husband
would want you to sell your house?*

I offer the baby a plastic measuring cup to play with. He shrieks
with glee and chomps on it.

"It's an adorable kitchen," Melanie coos, splaying a hand across
her chest, talking to the couple as though I'm not there. "Just *look*
at this breakfast nook."

Ethan and I made love once in the breakfast nook, before we
bought a table. It was during a heat wave before we installed air-
conditioning and it was too hot to sleep and we found that the only
way to keep cool was to lie naked on the kitchen floor with ice
cubes on our foreheads. We got to laughing and tickling each other,
and one thing led to another.

The oven buzzer goes off and the baby starts to cry.

"There's a room upstairs that would make a *wonderful* nursery,"
Melanie says, herding the couple out of the kitchen.

"Really? Which one?" I ask her. But she is already heading up the
stairs.

"Have a look and I'll be right there," she tells them. Then she
turns back toward me. "What about the new living room furniture?" she hisses through the banister.

"I got a reindeer," I whisper. I did. I bought one of the reindeer
lawn ornaments that Marion found at the nursery and jammed it
into the ground next to the FOR SALE sign. Surely it adds cheer.
Melanie looks quizzically at my hair, which I've pulled into a ponytail with one of Ethan's stretchy black dress socks.

"Look," she says coolly, "I can sell this house in no time." She
snaps her fingers. "But you have *got* to be a motivated seller. Please,
get some furniture and *do* something about that leak."

I want to explain that I won't have money for furniture or

repairs until *after* I sell the house. But she darts up the stairs two at a time, commenting on my grass cloth wallpaper.

"That is *so* easy to tear down," she tells the couple.

On Thanksgiving I join Marion for dinner at Ethan's aunt's house, bringing two of my pies.

As Marion drives, she peers over the backseat intermittently to make sure her yam puff casserole is anchored. She wears a camel's-hair coat and brown felt hat with a stiff black feather perched in the brim. She is more formal than my mother was and a better house-wife and cook.

Mother was more interested in reading Russian novels than in keeping house. She'd spend hours in the basement laundry room, ironing and listening to art history books on tape. Everything in our house was neatly pressed—even nightgowns and draperies— but caterpillar dust collected on the blinds, and our kitchen floor was always sticky with something. She was a dreadful cook. Her Minute Rice burned and stuck to the pan, and her green beans were always slightly frozen, squeaking between your teeth. My father and I struggled to pretend we enjoyed her murky stews of canned tomatoes and stringy meat. Marion is just the opposite, and now she makes me miss my imperfect mother.

The hugs at Ethan's cousins' house are tighter and longer than usual. I haven't seen these relatives since Ethan died. "How *are* you?" they want to know.

As the afternoon progresses—from football to relish trays to salads to the main course—I begin to have a floating sensation, as though I'm one of the floats in the parade, billowing unsteadily down the street headfirst, a maniacal grin stretched across my face. The women fawn over my pies. *Homemade crust!* Their cheer rings in my ears.

"Sophie, you sit here," Mrs. Waxman says, pointing to a seat in the middle of the table. "Girl, boy, girl, boy." I'm seated between two of Ethan's cousins: a political science professor and a TV news cameraman whose bristly sweater rubs against my arm as he pulls out my chair. Men. My age. I'd forgotten how good-looking Ethan's cousins are. Their tenor voices reverberate as they talk and laugh, and the hair on their wrists peeks out from under their cuffs as they pass potatoes and peas. They are attentive, piling turkey on my plate and telling funny Ethan stories. *Remember the time, remember the time.*

I move the turkey around on my plate and try to laugh at the stories: ha, ha! But my laughter comes out: herp, herp. The turkey is dry and sharp. I gulp water and cough, then excuse myself to go to the bathroom. Instead, I hurry past the bath to the end of the hall and duck in the laundry room, closing the door. At least in here I can't smell the cinnamon and sage. At least in here it could be any day of the year.

Ethan couldn't really eat last Thanksgiving—he was weak and slept most of the time—but the orderly brought him a tray of food anyway. I loved the cafeteria trays for their optimism. *Look here,* they said. *You can't die. Because we've got turkey, yams, milk, and cranberry Jell-O!* I picked up the carton of milk and shook it, and Ethan's eyes widened suddenly. *Maybe he's going to make the* Love Story *speech now,* I thought. *Words of courage to carry me through.*

"Why," he gurgled, "are you *shaking* my milk?"

I squeezed open the carton and white bubbles foamed out the top. Ethan blinked at them. I stuck the straw in. *I don't know why I'm shaking the milk,* I thought. *I'm shaking the milk because I want everything to be just a little better here. I want to improve on this hospital carton of milk the way you'd fluff up a pillow.*

I shrugged, handed it to him, kissed his forehead.

Now, I bend over the concrete sink in the laundry room and splash water on my face as if trying to put out a fire.

There's a knock at the door.

"Sophie?" Marion whispers loudly.

"Yes?" There's no towel, so I quickly dry my face on a shirt of Mr. Waxman's that hangs on a water pipe. It smells perfumey, like detergent.

"Oh, now," Marion says when she opens the door. She gives me a brisk military hug, then pulls a hairbrush from her purse to fix my hair.

"You can't really *brush* my hair," I try to explain, picking at the curls with my fingers. Then I just stand with my hands at my sides and let her use the brush. It feels good against my scalp and her body gives off warmth.

"It's all right," Marion says. "You're among family." She hands me a lipstick called Coral Reef. It's too bright and orange, but I dab some on anyway.

"Now let's see about those lovely pies of yours."

Clearly, Marion and I are never going to talk about Ethan, about how we miss him.

Marion drops me at home late Thanksgiving afternoon. I sit alone at the kitchen table and pick systematically at the crumb topping on one of the remaining sour cream apple pies. My reflection stares back at me from the French doors. *Do something,* it says. *Read a book. Work on your media pitch letter. Bundle up and go for a walk. Call someone. Call Ruth.*

I don't want to bother Ruth. A single working mother doesn't need her kooky college roommate pestering her. Our friends Sonia and Alfie invited me over for dessert, encouraged me to sleep over, stay the whole weekend. But I called and canceled last night. I've become an expert canceler in the past few weeks, telling friends at the last minute that I can't make it after all, feigning a sore throat or oncoming migraine. I hate to impose my glumness on them. Besides, everything about them reminds me of Ethan.

The pies seem pointless now, spread across the kitchen. Melanie said bake *a* pie, not *nine* pies. The idea of spending the weekend alone with them makes me nervous. I don't want to eat them, yet I don't have the heart to throw them away. I get up from the table and carry the pies one by one out into the driveway and load them into the trunk of my car, so I won't have to look at them anymore.

Last year I didn't bake because Ethan and I spent Thanksgiving in the hospital. The Thanksgiving before that we went to our friends Sonia and Alfie's house, but not until late in the day, because Ethan insisted on working. I close the trunk and head back inside. That was our last *real* Thanksgiving. Screw him for working on Thanksgiving. I slam the front door behind me. The pictures on the walls shake and rattle. "Screw Ethan!" I holler into the empty house, at the hall table and the TV, at all the inanimate objects that have become my aloof roommates. "Screw Thanksgiving! It's all about women doing all the work and men doing as they please. Watching football. Working. Getting cancer!"

In the kitchen I reach into the cupboard for cereal and a bowl. Unable to swallow my turkey at dinner, I'm hungry now. My hands tremble and I fumble and drop the bowl on the floor, sending it spinning like a dreidel. As I scoop it up I remember the exercise the grief counselor suggested—smashing dishes. She also said you could knead bread or yell in the shower.

The bowl is cold and hard in the palm of my hand. How do you break a dish on purpose? Do you fling it sideways like a Frisbee or hurl it overhead like a softball? Maybe you could stomp on a cup the way you'd crush a tin can.

I don't have any unwanted china—only my grandmother's Limoges. My everyday dishes are the white retro-looking set with the black-and-yellow stripes that Ethan and I picked out before the wedding. There we were, a typical couple registering for kitchen accessories in preparation for our Special Day. The world was our oyster. Then red tide seeped into our oyster. Now the cheerful yellow trim annoys me.

I look at the tower of dishes in the kitchen sink; it seems it would be easier to smash them than to wash them.

I remember feeling overwhelmed by the choices of dishes at Macy's and wanting to ask my mother's opinion, wishing she were there to meddle in our decisions. Now I want her here, to fix me soup and tell me not to worry about my stupid boss and to help me arrange the photos of Ethan for the album that Dr. Rupert said I should make.

I last saw Mother on a snowy morning when I was thirteen and she sped off for work in her Chevette, even though ribbon-candy sheets of ice covered the roads and radio DJs said motorists should stay home. The museum wasn't even *open* that day, but Mother was eager to prepare for an upcoming exhibit. She loved her job as docent. I think she liked being among the paintings as much as she liked being home with us. How I resented that job.

When the policeman came to the door to tell us about the accident, my father's reaction was remarkably calm. He said nothing, just nodded, smiled faintly, and pushed the door shut as the officer described the icy conditions and sharp curve in the road. I remember the officer's badge shining under the porch light and how his inky eyebrows shot up as the door swung closed in his face.

"Wrong house, I guess," my father told me cheerfully.

After Ethan and I were married, I made him buy a big car with double air bags. Fortunately he was a cautious driver. Still, as he looked both ways and stuck to the speed limit, malignant cells crept into his lymph nodes.

There's no milk for cereal. But who cares? Because now the bowl is flying out of my hand. To lose a mother *and* a husband! The bowl bursts against the wall, shards like pointy teeth shooting across the floor.

A heavy cape of nausea hangs over me, and my knees feel

wrong. Cap'n Crunch smiles maniacally, his blue hat like a ship on his head. *Outside, silly,* he says. *You're supposed to break the dishes outside!*

I open the cupboard and peer in at the plates. They are inviting, smooth and white and neatly stacked. I recall how carefully I packed them when Ethan and I moved into our new house, sliding each saucer into a padded liner as if it were a treasure from King Tut's tomb.

Now I understand why rock stars wreck hotel rooms—to shatter the relentless stillness of a room. My arms are prickly and my hands feel as swollen as baseball mitts. I've got to get hold of more dishes.

I drag the wheelbarrow clanging from the garage into the kitchen and load it with the dirty dishes from the sink, then plates, bowls, mugs, saucers, and cups from the cupboards. The wheelbarrow wobbles under the weight as I heave it through the French doors and shove it across the grass, dishes clacking and rattling.

As I fling dinner plates against the back of the garage, they pop and shatter. Pieces of china fly back at me. Teacups split into crescent shapes like shells. Little Pyrex custard bowls explode. I wish that I were the one who got cancer, since I can't even do my stupid job. My legs give out and then I am on my knees, chucking saucers with both hands, my pulse a crazy metronome ticking in my head. Charcoal dusk envelops the yard. The wind picks up, the branches on the bushes beside the garage swatting like arms. As the French doors to the house blow shut, the blinds crash against the glass.

I know I should stop breaking my dishes, just as you know you should stop eating cashews or potato chips. But who needs twelve special bowls for pasta? My right shoulder burns as they sail through the air.

My neighbor Mrs. Selman pushes open her sliding glass door and calls out, "Sophie? Are you there?" I see her silhouette through the bamboo hedge lining the fence between our yards, standing on tiptoes and trying to look over. I dive into the grass and crawl on my belly into the bamboo, the ground soggy and cold beneath my knees. A branch scrapes my cheek and my glasses fog up, turning the world white.

"Hello?" Mrs. Selman says. She gives up and slides her door shut. I wait for the click of the lock, then scramble out of the bushes.

Broken dishes are spread across the lawn like remnants from an archaeological dig. It begins to rain. Maybe I should be kneading bread or yelling in the shower. Kneading bread in the shower? The air is moist and cold and my hands are raw and my nose is running. I dab at it with the sleeve of my coat and peer in the wheelbarrow, which is empty.

Just as I'm wondering whether I've got paper plates, a policeman rounds the back corner of the house, the automatic porch light clicking on.

"Ma'am?" he says, blinking and peering into the yard.

My hands shoot up over my head. "Yes?"

"Do you live here?"

I hear my voice bark an enthusiastic, "Yes!"

He looks at the broken dishes. "Everything all right?"

"Sure. It's just that I'm sick of these dishes. And believe it or not, the doctor advised me to break them. She's not a *real* doctor, she's an MSW." Stupid. Babbling.

"Do you mind if I see some identification?" The policeman's face is round and chubby. He's probably younger than me.

"Yes, of course. *Please,* come in." My voice slides into jovial unctuousness. We step through the French doors into the kitchen, the officer taking care to wipe his feet.

In the front hall, I show him my driver's license, with my address and photo, tiny face surrounded by hurricane hair. He looks at me, looks at the picture, looks at me.

"Okay, thank you." He hands back the license. "Your neighbor called and said she thought someone was breaking and entering over here."

"Just breaking." I laugh.

He tries to laugh. "Right," he says. Then he says good night and ambles down the front walk to his cruiser, the radio scratching out a message that I can't hear.

"You can break the rules now," Dr. Rupert said during our last session, encouraging me to do something entirely different for Thanksgiving. "The big rule was broken: Your loved one died." But I'm pretty sure he meant fly to Hawaii or eat roast beef instead of turkey. I don't think he meant break all of my dishes, and I don't think I should leave the house anymore.

DEPRESSION

5

Since Ethan died our bed has grown from the size of a California king to the size of an aircraft carrier. It seems to take up the whole room now, the vast white bedspread screaming: *empty, empty, empty.* I decide it will be easier to sleep alone if I lie on Ethan's side. That leaves my side open, but I'm here, so it's not as though anyone's missing, right?

I try the middle.

The sheets remain cold and indifferent.

I give up and drag the covers to the living room, inflate our camping air mattress, and push it against the wall where the couch used to be. Without furniture, the living room rug is as expansive as a lawn and there are little things that fell underneath the sofa: a dime, a Frito, a Scrabble tile with the letter O.

Oh. Friday night. Two more days of this dreaded four-day holiday weekend. I remove the key to the house from the realtor's lockbox, so Melanie can't get in for her drive-by showings, which are like scary surprise parties. I should take my medication and wash my hair and rescue the pies from my trunk and find a place that rents living room furniture. Instead, I curl up on the air mattress with a blanket, stick my legs in the sleeves of Ethan's down parka for extra warmth, and turn on the TV.

It would be better if my mother were here. When I was home sick from school, she'd fix a tray with soup and crackers, a Pyrex cup of Junket custard, ginger ale, and two tiny orange aspirin tablets. We'd curl up on my bed and watch *Perry Mason*. I remember the swell of her breasts against my back and how the tickly down on her cheeks was as supple as tennis ball fuzz.

The blanket is as soft as an animal, and I pull it over my head and knead the nubby fabric between my fingers. I would like to touch someone. It seems the last time someone touched me was a few weeks ago when I went to the dentist and he had to wrap his arms around my head to check my fillings. He patted my chin and cheeks and asked me to say *ahh*. I liked the comforting curve of the chair and the sweet, soapy smell of his hands and my eyes teared up and he asked if he hit a nerve and I nodded yes.

On a TV program called *Cops*, a shirtless man strung out on something called sherm stick beats down an old girlfriend's door to reclaim a box spring. There's a channel that's showing a weekend marathon of *Cops* episodes, and now I see the attraction of the show: It makes your own life seem pretty together.

Mother would insist that I turn off the TV, shower, get dressed, eat a piece of fruit, and call to rejoin the grief group.

I will call Ruth and then the hospital to find out when the next group meets. I *would* call, if I could get to the phone. But my limbs are weak and heavy and won't go. My brain says, *Get up,* and my body says, *Screw you, I'm watching* Cops.

If Ethan were here with his annoying habit of clicking through the stations, I wouldn't be stuck on *Cops*.

A police officer on the TV talks over the backseat of his patrol car to the camera. He says, "Some folks don't know how to stay out of trouble."

Instead of showering, I build a fire. The reindeer lawn ornament makes excellent firewood. You don't even need a saw. You can just break him apart like Ramen noodles and toss him into the flames. I forget to take off his nose, though, and it pops and oozes, melting like a candied apple.

The phone rings and the answering machine picks up. I hear Melanie leaving a message, asking if I've had a change of heart about selling the house. Even though it's nighttime, she's still working. Her voice is tinny on her cellular phone. It sounds as though she's calling from another world: the land of the capable.

Over the weekend, my sleeping schedule moves around the clock because I can't sleep at night and I can't stay awake during the day, and pretty soon I seem to be missing daylight altogether.

One morning (*what morning?*) a garbage truck (*Tuesday morning!*) screeches and roars down the street, and then I am awake, floating on the air mattress through the middle of the living room. The good news is that the four-day Thanksgiving weekend is finally over. The bad news is that I forgot to take out the garbage and I'm at least a day late for work. I hear my neighbor's car door slam as he pulls out of the driveway.

The grief is up already. It is an early riser, waiting with its gummy arms wrapped around my neck, its hot, sour breath in my ear. Now it follows me down the hall to the bathroom, tapping my shoulder the whole way. *Try to pick up your toothbrush*, it says.

I clutch the edge of the sink and stare at the drain. A spooky *Voyage to the Bottom of the Sea* monster that's all dark circles and chapped lips peers out from the bathroom mirror.

I'm sure that the toothbrush is as heavy as a hammer. My hand won't go, won't pick it up.

My skin itches, probably because I haven't showered all weekend. Sticky dribbles of ice cream are caked to my pajama top. Instead of showering and dressing for work, I carry the tube of toothpaste back to the air mattress. I rub a little across my teeth as a guy on *Cops* in a Firebird screeches away from the police, speeding the wrong way down an exit ramp. They shoot out his tires, but he keeps driving on the rims, sparks spraying everywhere, oncoming cars spinning out and crashing into the guardrail, and then I am asleep again.

When I awaken again there's a square of sunshine on the carpet and I hear the mailman's feet shuffling on the porch. I resist the urge to throw open the door and embrace him. *A J. Crew catalog. You shouldn't have!*

Instead, I creep to the kitchen and root for carbohydrates. I stack a plate with toasted frozen waffles and pull a carton of Cherry Garcia from the freezer. I know I should be eating fruits and vegetables, but they don't carry produce at 7-Eleven.

Tomorrow will be different. Tomorrow I'll start a high-protein, low-fat diet and sign up for yoga, as Dr. Rupert suggested, and start walking thirty minutes a day. Order that light box. I will overcome my fear of the produce section. Speaking of tomorrow, I scan the kitchen calendar, trying to find today. Here it is: Tuesday, November 27. Ethan's birthday. You are here. I swallow a bland, dry lump of waffle.

The night Ethan died I wasn't even *with him*. I went home around eleven to get clean clothes and a book of Thurber essays that were the last thing that made him laugh. Even though he hadn't spoken for two days, and he lay so still that you couldn't tell if he was breathing unless you stared straight at the little snowflakes on his hospital gown and made sure they were rising and falling, I read to him. Because they say hearing's the last thing to go, even when you're on morphine. So like an idiot I went home for a shower and the book. Marion stayed at the hospital with her cup of Sanka and her knitting, the steady *click-click-click* of the needles filling the room. I was packing jeans and a sweatshirt into a paper bag when she called.

"We lost him," she said.

We'll find him, then, I thought.

Christmas is coming, the calendar says now. *What are your plans for Christmas?* It is a bossy gardening calendar that wants me to start a mulch pile and stock my pantry with pretty jars for impromptu floral arrangements. I do not have a pantry. I rip the thing off the wall and stuff it into the overflowing garbage. A tuna fish can clatters across the floor.

I *see* myself bending over to pick up the can. I *see* myself taking out the garbage and rinsing off the lid, which has smudges of food all over it. I *see* myself loading the stack of dirty dishes in the sink into the dishwasher and showering and ironing something to wear to work. But I don't do these things. Instead, I call our department secretary and tell her I've got the flu. She reminds me to get a flu shot; it might not be too late. It could be, but she's not sure. I tell her that I will put that on my to-do list.

Taking a shower is a good thing. I know this, but I can't seem to turn on the water. I'm staring at the insanely busy scallop-shell pattern on the shower curtain when the phone rings. The answering machine picks up and Marion's voice echoes through the house. She says that she tried my office and cell phone, and she wants to know where I am and whether I'd like to drive over to Half Moon Bay, where Ethan's ashes were scattered, and maybe have lunch. She sounds a little frantic. I trudge through the kitchen and pick up.

"Sure," I say. Somehow this plan seems easier than taking a shower. I'm surprised that Marion sounds relieved. I've always assumed that she calls and takes me places to be polite. But maybe she needs me. Although she has her volunteer work and bridge club and luncheons, she lives alone, too. Maybe she needs me to be her basket case. Just as sometimes you need a person to be strong for you, maybe sometimes you need a person to be weak for you. Maybe I am to Marion what *Cops* is to me. Kooky screwups who help you tell yourself: *Hell, I could be worse.*

I pull on overalls over my pajamas and tie a kerchief around my snarled hair. As I'm getting a coat out of the closet, I notice spotted brown mildew creeping up the wall near the leak under the house. It smells funny—damp and sour. Maybe the house is filling up with invisible spores. Spores that drain the energy I would otherwise have for renting living room furniture. Maybe the whole place is going to rot and crumble and sink into the swampy earth with a giant sucking noise, taking me with it. They might find me thousands of years from now in my pajamas, like those bog people whose leathery brown bodies they discovered curled up under miles of earthy peat, their woolen cloaks still clinging to their limbs.

Marion doesn't mention my pajama top. Normally she would

ask if I wanted to go back inside and put on a blouse or turtle-neck. Her posture is always perfect—straight spine, chin leading her through a room—but today her composure seems manic. I notice she's got her coat buttoned crooked.

Ethan was an only child, and he said his mother always planned lavish theme parties for his birthday when he was little—dinosaurs or cowboys and Indians, with hours of games and bulging goodie bags. Even when he was grown she still baked his favorite, banana cake, every year for his birthday.

We head up I-280 and over the hill on Highway 92.

"Is this the right way?" Marion asks, suddenly panicked. There's really only one way to get over the mountain to Half Moon Bay, so I'm not sure why she's asking. Certainly she wouldn't forget this route. I nod and her grip loosens on the steering wheel.

"Beautiful," she says vacantly, pointing to the wisps of fog strewn through the eucalyptus trees, which smell sharp and clean.

We stop at a greenhouse, where I choose six yellow roses to throw out to sea for Ethan. It takes me a while to decide how many: A dozen seems like overkill, hard to throw into the surf, yet one or two seems too sparse, like when only a few people show up at a party.

"Good afternoon, ladies," says a white-haired man behind the counter, bowing ceremoniously at the flowers. "Will that be all?"

"I'll get those," Marion says, waving a $20 bill at him.

"You look *just* like your mother," the man tells me. I glance up from a package of crocus bulbs and realize he means Marion. She looks shyly at the floor, her lips turning up slightly at the corners.

I say, "Thank you."

We pass fields striped with rows of brussels sprouts as we head toward the sea, which is gray and chalky on the horizon.

Ethan loved the ocean—scuba-diving and boogie boarding. After we were married, we had time for only a short honeymoon because he had just joined a start-up company and could take only five days off. We drank champagne on the beach and stayed in bed until two in the afternoon. But then engineers from his company started calling on his cell phone and he'd talk them through fixing bugs in the software code.

"Enough," I told him after we missed the sunset and our dinner reservation one night. I snatched his phone and tossed it into the bushes outside our room.

"This is for *us*," he said, running out to get the phone. It was always for us. He said I needed to realize that and focus more on the future.

Now, here I am in the future with a handful of yellow roses.

At the beach, angry waves pound the sand. I take off my sneakers and socks and roll up my pants, but I can't make it out to where the water is even a little bit deep. A thorn on one of the roses pricks my finger.

Marion stands facing the sea with her hands on her hips, as if commanding it to settle down. The wind blows her white hair straight back, and I see her pink scalp underneath. Her eyes tear from the cold.

The weather was almost this blustery on the day of Ethan's memorial service, even though it was summer. Marion, Dad, Jill, Ruth, and our friends Sonia and Alfie and I gathered on the shore to sprinkle the ashes. The wind whipped everyone's hair into their faces, and sand stung our eyes, and the ocean churned impatiently, tugging at our ankles as if to say *You, too; I want you, too*. Technically we were supposed to get a permit to disperse the ashes, but no one had done this. Marion looked around furtively and struggled to open the stubborn lid on the urn. She finally pried it off and tossed out the ashes, which tumbled straight down into the foam around everyone's feet. She glared disdainfully at the urn. Clearly, this wasn't what she'd had in mind. She must have imagined a crisp but windless day, the sky a big blue bowl overhead, the ocean twinkling, the ashes flying in a graceful arc toward Hawaii.

Now, I fling the roses as hard as I can. They're airborne for a second, spread out like a fan. Then they bob and rock in the white foam just a few feet away. The waves push them to shore, drag them back, push them in again.

A German shepherd splashes through the surf, barking at the flowers. "Shoo!" I yell at the dog, who clutches one rose between his teeth. "Scram!" There's no owner in sight, no one else on the beach. The salt water stings my calves. My feet are numb.

I'm startled when Marion comes up from behind me, takes my hand, and squeezes it. I squeeze back. While her fingers are cold and dry, her palm is warm and cushiony. She says we should have remembered our gloves. Then her hand is gone. We turn away from the ocean, the roses, and the barking dog and climb up the hill toward the parking lot. The sand is so deep that it's like one of those dreams where you're trying to run but you can't.

Marion and I are the only ones at a restaurant that overlooks the beach. We order crab and a bottle of wine for lunch. I work at the claws and dredge a slice of sourdough bread in melted butter and drink some of the Chardonnay. Marion finishes her wine and pours another glass but doesn't touch the crab.

"Too much work," she says. "Too much." She looks at my pajama top suspiciously but doesn't seem to have the energy to comment.

"Maybe you'd like something else?" I ask her. The waiters, who outnumber us, stand by the coffee machines and glance over at our table.

"No, thanks." Marion smiles and tucks her napkin beside her plate. "Actually, know what I'd like?"

I shake my head.

"A cigarette."

"A *cigarette*?" I can't imagine Marion smoking. "We could get you some."

"Oh, my gosh, no." She waves her small hand over her plate.

Across the water I think I see the ghostly sail of a boat on the horizon. Or maybe it's just a whitecap or a cloud. Soon it's gone, swallowed up by the ocean.

I know, I *know* as I drive up 280 to work the next morning, that I should not be wearing my bathrobe. But I can't stay home from work another day, and I simply couldn't get dressed this morning. All of my clothes were either too small or mismatched or dirty. But mostly they were too small—the skirts unforgiving of my new apple pie middle. I tore blouses and dresses off hangers and laid them across the bed, trying to put together an ensemble, but nothing worked. I couldn't get dressed and I couldn't *not* go to work, so I climbed in the car in my bathrobe and started driving.

Now, it's already nine-fifteen. Who do I think I am, taking so many days off? This is Silicon Valley, for God's sake. Is the NASDAQ going to shut down because my husband died? There's business-to-business e-commerce valuation to shore up and leverage!

I crank up the heat and take another slug of coffee from my travel mug. My bowels rumble.

My head itches because I haven't washed my hair in how many days? Who knows. The thing is, account executives from our New York public relations agency flew out last night and they're meeting with Lara and me today to hammer out a strategy for East Coast story placements—*The New York Times, The Wall Street Journal.* Lara always says "hammer out." She called last night to make sure I'd be there. I promised I'd be in by nine-thirty.

Mastodon Suburbans and Land Cruisers chug past me. Maybe I feel fragile because my car is too small. Maybe I should be driving a van, a school bus, a tank. On *World's Scariest Police Chases,* a guy stole a tank and plowed through a neighborhood, crushing cars and boats and bicycles. I can relate to having this kind of bad day. I wince when I realize what's clunking from side to side in the trunk: my pies.

I'm supposed to give a presentation after lunch to Lara and the PR women on patch strategies. But I don't have a single idea yet. *We're the client. Why doesn't the agency come up with a strategy?* Their job is to implement the strategy under my direction, says Lara.

I listen to the traffic report, hoping for a multiple-car crash to halt my commute, but there isn't any.

In the elevator, the CFO smiles at my slippers in an absentminded sort of way. Maybe he would like a slice of apple crumb. We both concentrate on the red square numbers overhead, which wink knowingly as we shoot toward the fifth floor. Two, three, four, *here we are!*

I fetch *The Wall Street Journal* from the little table in the hall.

"Oh!" the admin two cubes over says when she sees me. *"Oh."*

As I steam toward my cubicle, suddenly the floor seems all uphill. *I think I can, I think I can!* More and more employees are finding it hard to juggle work with family, an article in the *Journal* says. I envy *that* dilemma.

My in-box is piled high. Doesn't anyone at this company know we're becoming a paperless society? I pick up the whole thing and dump it into the garbage. I move my ficus tree to where the in-box was. It looks pretty there, its wrinkly leaves outlined in white. I decide the other plants around my desk would look nice on the floor. I arrange them in a row that closes up the opening of my cube. The potted palm, ivy, Christmas cactus, and African violet create a much needed fourth wall.

My presentation is in less than two hours. I turn on my machine, open PowerPoint, and get started on the slides, but I can't decide whether to make the text centered, flush left, or flush right, let alone what to say. I pull my lunch out of my desk: a bag of old hot dog buns and a few restaurant packets of honey. I drizzle the honey on the buns and start eating. Not so bad, really.

There's a rustling in the plants and a knock on the edge of my cube. I love how people try to knock on your cube, as though you've got privacy.

Someone says, "Sophie?"

I'll huff and I'll puff and I'll blow your house down!

Lara slides through the plants. She is small and lithe and can wedge herself into narrow spaces, like a bat.

"Um," she says. "What happened?"

"Erm." The buns and honey stick to the roof of my mouth. "My hug-band thied."

Lara crouches on her haunches beside my chair. She bites into her plump lower lip and draws in a long breath through her teeth. Finally, she clears her throat and speaks. But I don't have *any* idea what she's saying. I try to listen, but suddenly my brain can't string words together.

"Media streep froop," she whispers.

"Wha?" I swallow a dry lump of hot dog bun.

I don't think this is a sentence. Not in a hammer-this-out kind of way. No way.

"Way," Lara insists. "Flood mires grow blood brambles."

Supposedly, hearing is the *last* thing to go, but in my case it seems to be the *first* thing to go. I knock the side of my head, trying to get the water out.

Is everyone speaking a new language starting today? I've always dreaded changes in the rules like this. Daylight saving time. The threat of a conversion to the metric system.

"Flood mires grow blood brambles, hon," Lara coos again, bending in closer. I've heard her on the phone calling her friends "hon." It is a term of endearment for her. A derm of entearment for hoo.

"Hoo!" I hear myself exclaim.

I dig into the bowl of Starburst candies on my desk and begin unwrapping and eating them, first orange, then red, then yellow, then pink, then orange again. The orange ones are the best. The air is warm and Lara is fuzzy and then she's gone.

I swallow the candies and pat my hair, a tangled nest on my head. I try to tuck the clumps behind my ears.

In a little while an HR guy is in my cube, a bearded man who wears a lavender dress shirt and black jeans. His eyes are brown— two mud puddles staring calmly out of his face. He touches me, a hand on my shoulder that gives off warmth, even through the thickness of my robe.

Oh, my voice echoes in my head.

"Sophie, why don't we go downstairs to my office?" he says, slowly pushing a box of Kleenex across the desk toward me.

"That sounds good to me," I hear myself stammer. I slide down in my chair and burrow my feet under my desk to hide my bunny slippers. I don't want him to see how casually I'm dressed when it's not even Friday. At least I don't think it is. I believe it's Thursday or perhaps Wednesday. Maybe *that's* why he's in my cube. There is a company dress code, after all. Jeans are one thing. But slippers? I've had them for years, since before Mother died, and the ears are frayed from getting stepped on.

"Okay, then," he says. I look at his hand on my arm. The fingers are big and square and pink.

"That sounds good to me," I repeat. Then I can't stop saying "That sounds good to me." I dig my hands into the sleeves of my robe. I want to move on and say something else, but everything's stuck. "That sounds good to me," I tell him.

"Ready?"

I nod. But I can't get up. I need to rest a minute first. Some would argue that wearing your robe and slippers is enough of a rest, but I need something more. I lay my head on my desk, and the faux leather blotter is cool against my cheek. The branches of the ficus tree bend toward me, the small, pointed leaves stroking my hair.

6

Seventeen, eighteen, nineteen, twenty. There are lots of white lines in the road on the way to Dr. Rupert's office, and I can't help counting them.

Dad's come to stay with me, and he's been driving me to my appointment twice a week, just like when I was a teenager and he drove me to the library and community pool after Mother died. His wife, Jill, sent me a care package of apricot bubble bath and lotion, gourmet chocolate peanut-butter cups, and movie star magazines.

Dad had only one girlfriend between Mom and Jill, an accountant from his office named Beverly who bore down on him like a tropical storm about a year after Mother died. Everything about Beverly was big and loud—big bones, big bosom, big white teeth that always had a dab of orangey lipstick on them. She stayed over once when I was at a friend's sleepover party. I came home early the next morning and found her in our kitchen wearing chiffon baby-doll pajamas and frying bacon. She offered me a cigarette even though I was only fifteen. There were so many things wrong with her that instead of being angry I was actually drawn to her, the way you might be drawn to an exotic bird or lizard if one wandered into your yard.

After he and Beverly broke up, Dad quit dating and took up bee-keeping. He wrote away to the U.S. Department of Agriculture for information and set up two colonies. One of his queens died right away, and I worried that even a seemingly therapeutic hobby might break his heart. But he prevailed by cheerfully merging the two colonies with the one queen. Every morning he trudged out to the backyard to check on them, looking like an astronaut in his stiff white coveralls. As he lifted the lids off the white pine boxes the bees swirled up to meet him, dripping off of his black mesh bee veil. The precision and steadiness and underlying threat of danger involved in beekeeping seemed to calm him. Soon we had buckets of thick blond honey, and he and I worked at the kitchen table decorating jars with labels and bows to hand out at Christmas. Whenever the word *apiculturist* showed up on one of his crossword puzzles, he'd say it aloud proudly, his title—beekeeper—and he seemed grateful to be something other than just a widower.

Now, I feel bad that Jill's alone in Vermont while Dad's stuck out here chauffeuring me around. But it's a good thing he's driving because Dr. Rupert switched me to a new antidepressant that makes my head feel light, as though my scalp might float away. I feel more like a gas than a solid, and driving doesn't seem possible with all these lines in the road.

According to Dr. Rupert, I had a depressive breakdown brought on by grief. "It can happen after such a large life loss," he explained, as though showing up at the office in your bathrobe is perfectly understandable. I don't like having to take the pills twice a day. I don't mind relying on eyeglasses or vitamins or mousse, but relying on pills confirms that I'm feeble.

"You look nice today," Dad says, clicking on the signal to change lanes and dipping his head to peer over the top of his glasses at me.

"Thank you." He's probably referring to the fact that I actually *got* dressed—shed my pajamas, showered, and wriggled into jeans and Ethan's boxy old ski sweater. The rest of my wardrobe seems to belong to someone else: a happily married thin woman who's too busy to spend her evenings baking and eating rolls of refrigerator biscuits. I smooth a hand over the yellow, red, and navy stripes on Ethan's sweater.

"It's the new black," I tell Dad.

"Oh," Dad says.

"That's a *joke*, Dad."

"Oh!" He laughs a little too hard, then tugs the handkerchief from his back pocket and dabs perspiration from his forehead. He perspires when he's worried, even when it's cold out. I feel bad for causing him anxiety. Mother was the calm one in the family, the one who soothed our nerves.

Dad wears his retiree uniform of khaki pants with a navy chamois shirt. He sticks to blue because he's color-blind and if he strays into reds, greens, and browns, he ends up clashing and looking like a kid who dressed himself. A stub of pencil sticks out from behind his ear for doing *The New York Times* crossword puzzle in the waiting room while Dr. Rupert stares at me and I stare at the Oriental carpet. What does he scribble on that pad, anyway? *Wacko, hopeless, weird sweater.* Or maybe it's just his list for what to do on the weekend: *weed, prune, mulch.*

"Almost there," Dad says as we exit the freeway.

Gorgatech has given me a three-month leave of absence without pay. LOA. They said I probably wouldn't be PR manager when I returned, but there will still be a place for me at the company. I wonder if that place is in the cafeteria or parking garage. The HR manager presented a long document that I tried to read before signing, but the papers shook in my hands and the tiny type crawled across the page. I still have a job, technically, a business card to hand out at parties, but no paycheck. LOA. LoserOutofA job.

The state of my house has thrown Dad into a panic. Dirty dishes and laundry and unopened mail and overflowing garbage. Moldy pies in the trunk of my car and newspapers littering the driveway, their dry, yellowing pages curling into newspaper jerky.

"Soph, honey, why don't you bring the paper in in the morning?" he asks, worrying that the pile signals burglars that no one's home. I try to explain that the end of the driveway has become impossibly far away, but then he wonders why I don't just call and cancel the paper. Frankly, that hadn't occurred to me. Despite the fact that I've been dying to talk to someone, the phone confounds me with all its crazy buttons.

Dad wants to know what happened to my dishes. Are they in those boxes in the garage?

"Yes," I fib. "I didn't want to look at them anymore."

He nods understandingly. But the boxes, and the fact that I have to park in the driveway, make him chew nervously on his lower lip, which has become red and raw since he arrived.

"I'll rent you a storage locker," he offers, flipping through the Yellow Pages.

"No!" I snatch the phone book away.

Dad still owns many of Mother's things—her art history books, cashmere sweaters, letters from friends, old hats in festive striped boxes. But they are tucked away on shelves or in drawers—woven through his house unnoticeably. While this makes more sense to me than a towering shrine of boxes in the garage, I'm not sure how to merge Ethan's things back with mine.

I see Dr. Rupert on Tuesday and Thursday; it's not clear why I need to get up Monday, Wednesday, and Friday. Dad's in my room every morning by eight, though, opening the curtains and windows and coaxing me out of my flannel shell.

"We've got a lot to do today," he says, clapping his hands like a camp counselor. "How 'bout you put just one foot on the floor?"

I slide a foot out and explore the chilly wood floor with my big toe, the covers tugging me back into the warm center of the mattress. *Don't listen to the father,* they insist. *Just sleep.*

Finally I stumble out of bed and into the shower while Dad

tidies my room. He's a neatnik who can't stand the sight of an unmade bed or clothes on a chair. By the time I emerge from the bathroom, the covers and pillows are as smooth and plump as a Macy's display ad, making it hard for me to crawl back in. The next thing I know, he's herding me outside to rake leaves or sweep the driveway, the air and light clearing my head.

Dad fixes my favorite grade-school dishes—Cream of Wheat for breakfast, Fluffernutter sandwiches for lunch, and creamed tuna on toast for dinner. He frets over the creamed tuna, which he hasn't made for years, hovering over the stove and stirring the white sauce, the *Joy of Cooking* laid out on the counter with recipe steps outlined in highlighter pen.

"Please, *thicken,*" he begs the sauce, frantically scratching the bottom of the pan with the wire whisk as though he might dig through the burner into the oven.

I'm grateful. All this for bathrobe-can't-hold-down-a-job me. I stand beside him at the stove, watching the white liquid finally congeal. Suddenly I worry about when Dad's going to die. I hope I die first. I'm not afraid of dying. I'm afraid of everyone *else* dying and leaving me behind. I wonder if I need more than a leave of absence from work—maybe a leave of absence from the planet. Dr. Rupert says I'm doing well and just need to give everything more time. There are no miracle cures; there's only time.

Dad and I shop for folding lawn chairs and TV trays to refurnish the living room and a set of dishes that serves four. I'm relieved when we don't buy the bigger eight-serving set, which seems painfully optimistic.

We eat dinner in front of the TV, and I take a quarter of a tablet more of the antidepressants every other night. You have to go on the pills gradually, like shifting gears to merge onto the freeway. After supper we have pralines and cream ice cream and play cassino. Dad's large block letters spell out BERNIE and SOPHIE on the back of an envelope, with our scores underneath.

He's going to leave soon, a little voice nags as I watch Dad shuffle the cards. *He can't stay here and take care of you forever. You're an adult!*

But Dad stays for three weeks, and then Jill joins us for Christmas. I want so badly for her to like me, like *us,* stay with Dad, keep him happy, that I set the alarm and get up on my own at seven-thirty every morning and stumble out to the kitchen to fix them coffee and toast.

Jill, whom I'd met only once before, at their simple backyard wedding just before Ethan died, seems perfect for Dad. Sweet, smart, and funny. Even though they're still newly married, she encourages me to come and live with her and Dad in Vermont for the winter. She brings pages from the classifieds with jobs circled—one for manager of fund-raising at the local public radio station. I'm flattered that she thinks I'm this capable. I suppose I could stay with them for a few months, as I did in college, when I'd go home to sleep off *Anna Karenina* and the categorical imperative and all those cafeteria carbohydrates. I imagine snuggling into Dad's down coat and heaving the snow blower down the driveway. Tapping syrup from the maple trees in the yard. But I don't want to barge in on them.

Dad and Jill come up with so many holiday activities, it's impossible for me to sleep in the afternoons. We string cranberries and popcorn, bake Christmas cookies, go to matinees, and drive around town to see the colored lights. When it's time to decorate the tree, I'm a little irritated by how agreeable they are. I miss having Ethan to argue with about the decor. He was from the garland-and-colored-lights school, while I favored the more understated tinsel and plain white lights. After much grumbling we would compromise, layering everything on until our tree looked like Las Vegas.

Now, Dad's cheer and optimism about the holidays still seems unfamiliar to me. After Mother died, he and I grew to dread Christmas. That first winter he sank into a foggy depression. We were supposed to go to New York City for Christmas and stay at the Plaza, like Eloise, but he said he was sick and we couldn't go. He sat in his chair in the living room all day for a week, a shadowy layer of beard creeping across his face. It didn't seem as though we would have Christmas that year. No tree or stockings or turkey. I called my aunt Athena—my mother's sister in Wisconsin—and she flew out and helped Dad find a psychiatrist and took me to pick out a tree and shop for all the groceries we needed. She layered a ham with canned pineapple rings, put it in the oven, then flew home to be with her own family. Somehow during Aunt Athena's visit Dad snuck out of the house and bought me a new ten-speed bike.

On New Year's Eve, Dad, Jill, and I celebrate with lobster and champagne. Dad looks relieved and victorious to have gotten me through the holidays, as though he hiked the entire Appalachian Trail. I'm not sure what to choose as a New Year's resolution. Don't crawl on the floor at the store anymore? I read an article in a women's magazine that suggested choosing one easy, fun thing, so you can feel good about yourself. I decide my resolution is to wear more lipstick.

The morning that Dad and Jill go home, I bravely smear on a rock-star serving of Saucy Salsa lipstick and drive them to the airport, firmly planting my hands at ten o'clock and two o'clock. This is the first time I've driven in a month, and I manage not to count the lines in the road.

I follow Dad and Jill to the security checkpoint, where a guard tells me I can't go any farther without a boarding pass. We hug quickly, not wanting to hold up the line. Dad says he'll call as soon as they get home. I watch the backs of their silvery heads bob along with the crowd of passengers. The guard asks me to step back, please, step *back,* and I realize I'm lurching into the line. *Let me through!* I want to holler. I move away and sit in a row of green plastic chairs scattered with newspapers. Once through the metal detector, Dad turns, smiles, and waves. I jump up to wave back. Then he vanishes.

In the airport parking lot, I have no idea where I left the car. I stand swaying like a boat bumping a dock. The whole garage looks unfamiliar; the whole dadless planet looks strange.

I find my parking ticket in my purse and turn it over in my hands, noticing Dad's big square handwriting on the back: *Level Two, Row G.* Thank you.

As soon as I see the EXIT sign in the garage, I lift my foot off the gas and the car slows. There's no way I'm going back to that empty house. What if I can't get up in the morning or rake the leaves or break out of the Oreo food group again? What if I'm terrified of the shower curtain and can't wash my hair? I should have gone with Dad and Jill. Flying to Vermont to stay with them or moving up to Oregon to live with Ruth seems easier than going back to sleep alone in my house. Ruth worked up a good sales pitch for Ashland when she called on Christmas Day.

"There are lots of cute actors and there's river rafting and plenty of jobs up here," she said. "Not fancy jobs, but, you know, low-stress jobs." She added this apologetically, not wanting to insult my career capabilities.

I told her I'm afraid of men and rivers and jobs, but she urged me to come ahead anyway. "Hang out. Hunker down," she said.

A car pulls up behind me. Stepping on the gas, I veer up a ramp toward more parking. My tires screech. An oncoming car swerves to avoid me, the driver glaring and making a "What the hell?" gesture.

Level three. Maybe Ruth's right. What's the point of staying in

Silicon Valley? It doesn't make sense for a jobless English major to live in a place with the highest cost of living in the country. I could help Ruth with Simone, cook them dinner every night. Home-made macaroni and cheese.

Level four. While I don't want to impose on Ruth, I know I would urge her to come and stay with me if our roles were reversed.

Level five: the roof. Sun blasts through the windshield. I flip down my visor. Plenty of parking up here. I pull up to the wall facing the airport, turn off the engine, and watch the planes take off.

It's exhilarating being at the airport, surrounded by the possibility of traveling anywhere. At the same time, it doesn't feel right being a thirty-six-year-old woman with no place to be on a Wednesday morning. No job or children or husband. I could pack up and rattle off across the country, no one knowing for days where I am or whether I'm safe.

Another plane rumbles overhead, its bright silver belly tipping and turning over the bay. Actually, I *do* have someplace to go: the mall. Not a very glamorous destination. No passport required. But I need to shop for curtains, decorative throw pillows, and house-plants, so I can stage and sell my house, then leave Silicon Valley.

"I could live here," I told Ethan the last time we visited Ruth in Ashland. We sat by the Rogue River on a hot August afternoon, reading Shakespeare aloud and eating cheese and apples with wine.

"No jobs," Ethan said.

"No *high-tech* jobs," I said.

I imagine giving my new throw pillows decisive karate chops, creating *House Beautiful* creases Melanie would approve of.

I turn the key over in the ignition and reach for my parking ticket.

ESCROW

7

One bright February morning Melanie shows up with a buyer for my house who looks as though he walked out of a men's underwear ad. Broad shoulders, square chin, shelf of sandy blond hair.

"Steve Cunningham," his deep voice rumbles as he steps through the front door. His handshake is warm and firm, and suddenly I'm glad that I fussed over contact lenses, mousse, and Juicy Tubes lip gloss. "Love the place," he says.

"Thanks." I feel myself blush and wonder how it's possible to be both lonely and terrified of social encounters at the same time.

Steve has made an offer on the house that matches the asking price, and Melanie says we'll soon be on our way to escrow. Steve just wants to have another look. He rattles on about how he loves the neighborhood and the proximity to the freeway. I agree, smiling and nervously spinning my wedding ring around my finger with my thumb. He says this will be an easy commute to Whatevertech, where he's VP of sales.

After Steve takes measurements in the living room for his wide-screen TV, Melanie tells me to show him the garden. She nudges the two of us into the backyard. I point out the hydrangea, roses, wisteria, lantana, and salvias, all of which are dormant now. The "mow, blow, and go" guys have been by, but I haven't done any yardwork for months.

"It looks like the Addams Family lives here now," I tell Steve, bending over to pull up a weed, "but I promise it'll all come back in the spring."

Steve smiles, looks at my hair. For some reason it hangs in silky ringlets today. For the first time in months I feel attractive. Even *female*. For so long I've felt like an androgynous lump. Grief on a stick.

"Now that I've found a place, I can get back to skiing on the weekends," Steve says. "You ski?"

"Not lately. Used to." Used to before Ethan turned into a work slug and we had to go to a marriage counselor just to get him to come home on Saturday for a few hours, let alone go skiing.

"I could take you sometime," Steve offers.

"Ha!" This response comes out involuntarily, like a sneeze. I peer through the kitchen window for Melanie, wishing she'd show up to nag me about some decor blunder. I look at Steve, who's studying the spindly peach tree. Maybe I should wear a placard around my neck that says: WIDOW, KEEP BACK. I tell Steve that the tree will look better after it's been sprayed in the spring.

"You shouldn't be so apologetic," Steve says, laughing. "It's a beautiful yard." After feigning interest in the calla lilies, he asks if I'd like to go to dinner some night to celebrate the sale. "That is, if you have a free spot on your calendar," he adds.

"Uh . . ." I don't want to tell him that I'm all free spots. Shrink visits and free spots. My PalmPilot retired with my pumps and panty hose, cell phone battery not even charged. Dinner sounds good. Someone to eat with. Since Dad and Jill left, I've grown to dread the dinner hour again, choosing to slurp a bowl of cereal over the kitchen sink rather than sitting down alone. Still, I should explain that I'm not really available, that my mental health is hanging like a loose tooth.

"Sorry. That was too forward," Steve says.

"Sure," I tell him. What's the harm, since I'm moving away? I realize that I've been staring intently at the azaleas, as though trying to will their fuchsia buds to bloom. "Sounds great," I add, looking up at Steve. Green eyes. Pressed shirt. Dinner date. Where the *hell* is Melanie?

She steps through the French doors onto the deck and winks at me. Then she points out the view behind us of the Santa Cruz foothills. As Steve turns to look, she mouths the word *divorced*. Melanie's always selling something.

Heading back into the house, I fret over the fact that I've agreed to go to dinner with a guy I've met only once. Isn't lunch more appropriate, especially since we haven't even gone into escrow yet? What if he's the bogeyman? Am I being paranoid? I don't remember how to be single.

Dear Ethan: Not only did I sell our house, I'm going out with the guy who's buying it.

This is not a *date*, I tell myself, tell Ethan, driving to meet Steve at a French bistro in Mountain View. For most people, a big step in life would be a promotion or a new baby or a bigger house or corrective eye surgery. For me, it's eating dinner with a man other than my husband.

Steve has a just-showered allure that's intoxicating: a citrusy clean smell and glowing skin, blond hair damp around the edges. I'm a little dizzy as I scan the menu. The choices, which don't include Cap'n Crunch or Eggos, are overwhelming. Steve conspiratorially consults the waiter over a bottle of wine. It's probably fancy and expensive. Everything in the restaurant makes me nervous: the crisp white tablecloth and single red rose in a vase, the direct eye contact with Steve. The possibility of running into friends who might wink and nudge each other when they find me splitting escargots with a male underwear model. *Relax!* I can hear Dr. Rupert and the grief books on my shelf at home chide.

Already, I dread the awkwardness of the bill and who's going to pay. Then there's the potential kiss good night. What was I thinking, agreeing to this? I'd rather just be friends with Steve. Maybe we could rent movies and order pizza and he could tell me about his dates with other girls. I could be the sisterly buddy.

As the waiter pours a Cabernet, Steve explains to me how wine doesn't really breathe in the bottle. It should be poured into glasses first and allowed to rest, then swirled a bit to provide aeration. Many people don't realize that the narrow neck of a bottle doesn't allow enough oxygen for the wine to "breathe." Steve makes air quotes when he says "breathe." He's a talker who covers Silicon Valley topics with ease: wine, technology, cars.

His face is boyish, his blond hair falling over his green eyes. How come he doesn't already have a girlfriend? Maybe it's the weird way he doesn't really look at you when he talks but stares at your forehead, sort of talking *at* you. You don't feel as though you're having a conversation, more as though you're listening to a book on tape, the title *Steve the Sales Guy Goes on a Dinner Date.*

He's had a rough week, he confesses, digging into his salad and finally asking the dreaded question: "Where do you work?"

"I'm sort of unemployed."

"Did you cash out and retire, or are you between gigs?"

"Between gigs, I guess. I kind of lost my job." I wish I could add something interesting, like I love to windsurf or I'm planning a backpacking trip through Thailand.

"Oh, I'm so sorry," Steve says sweetly, leaning across the table toward me. "I had no idea."

Of course not, I think, since you haven't asked me about myself. But I find that oddly comforting. Companionship without having to be the center of attention is a relief. If someone took my hands in his, looked straight into my eyes, and asked personal, getting-to-know-you questions, I'd run.

"We need marketing people," he offers.

I shake my head. "I'm taking a break." This seems like the best way to sum up my twice weekly shrink visits and my struggle with the produce section. "I'm going to move up to Oregon."

Steve looks disappointed. "To do what?"

Good question. I shrug, embarrassed by my lack of a plan. Everyone in Silicon Valley has a plan.

"Well, this is great," he says, cutting into his steak. "I usually eat alone on the run." He explains that he's recently divorced, which is why he needs a new place to live.

"I'm sorry about your divorce," I tell him, pretending that nosy Melanie didn't already tell me. "Kids?"

He shakes his head, pauses, chews. Despite all his enthusiasm, there's something sad about him, shadows under his eyes and a line of worry indented in his handsome forehead.

Over glasses of port and a shared chocolate soufflé, we exchange wistful memories of marriage and confess to each other that we're both lousy date material at the moment. We just want our spouses back. Steve's sweet, treating me with a sibling reverence a fraternity guy might have for his "little sister."

"Here's to a great house," he says, raising his glass.

I thank him. Our glasses clink. Now I can check a huge item off my to-do list: sell house. Who knows, maybe checking off this big task will make littler tasks easier, such as buying produce and packing for Ashland.

"What sold you on the place, anyway?" I ask. "The tapestry pillows? Melanie said those were *essential*."

Steve looks up at the ceiling, thoughtful. "The place just has a *vibe*." He looks at me. "A happy vibe."

"Seriously? I look at that house and all I see is cancer."

"Did your husband die there, at home? I mean, it doesn't matter—"

"No." I shake my head. "Hospital."

"Well, I'll bet you guys were really happy in that house."

Before we struggled to get pregnant, and before Ethan's diagnosis, we were happy there. I've almost forgotten that.

"You're right," I tell Steve, grateful for his company, grateful for the sleepy, full feeling after a good meal. "We were."

ASHES

— *8* —

The day after I sign the closing papers to sell my house to Steve Cunningham, I'm sorting through my dresser drawers and packing for the move up to Oregon when I come across the empty urn that held Ethan's ashes. I'd hid it under my jeans while Marion was in the garage during the Big Pack-Up, afraid she'd confiscate it.

"Urn" seems too glamorous a word for the container. It's plastic and square and the color of eggplant. More like a box for recipe cards or miscellaneous screws. Why did I settle for this Kmart urn? Probably because after someone dies it's hard enough to decide what socks to wear, let alone choose a receptacle for their remains.

I barely recall making the arrangements after Ethan's death. I do remember the salesman at the funeral home, how one of his hands was small and withered. Polio, maybe. I wanted to reach out and cover the hand with mine. I also remember how alarmingly heavy the urn was. I expected the ashes to be light, ethereal, but when I picked up the urn it felt as heavy as a half gallon of milk. I let out a yelp and dropped it on the table, and the salesman asked if I wanted to sit down.

I could barely talk during the weeks after the memorial service. "Herg," I'd stutter when people asked how I was doing. They would touch the small of my back or gently cup a hand under my elbow. They would not say, "Honey, 'herg' is not a word." Instead, they'd smile and speak softly, as though I were going to be all right, as though I weren't wearing one navy and one black loafer. As though I weren't driving down the street with my purse on the roof of the car or leaving the oven on preheat all night.

Now, it's hard to imagine that this urn is all that's left of Ethan. I wish there were a grave to visit. A place to plant flowers. Sure, I can go to the beach at Half Moon Bay where we scattered his ashes. But the ocean always seems so irritated and preoccupied, as though it has better things to do than comfort a widow.

I shake the urn; it clinks and I shudder. What's in there? A shard of *bone*? The lid is stubborn and won't come off. Finally I wedge it open and peer inside to find Ethan's wedding ring at the bottom. A simple gold band. I slide the ring over my middle finger, but it's too big; so I slide it over my forefinger, where it's still too big. I remember the safe feeling of being the smaller one. The ring fits on my thumb, but it looks silly there. I pull it off and place it in my jewelry box beside my mother's sorority pins and her docent nametag from the museum and a folded piece of yellow lined paper. I unfold the paper and find that it's a note from Ethan: *Gone to Home Depot. Be right back.* Dizzy, I lose hold of the paper. It drops and floats like a leaf over my pearls.

I squeeze my eyes shut, open them. After carefully refolding the note, I tuck it under the amethyst bracelet that my father gave my mother in junior high when they won a dance contest. Then I close the jewelry box, patting the top.

Picking up the urn, I sniff the inside. Nothing. No odor. No smudges or flakes.

I carry the urn downstairs to the kitchen and set it on the counter while I mix up a batch of martinis. The martini shaker is cool in my hand. Ethan loved martinis on the weekends. When he got sick he couldn't drink anymore, but he still nibbled olives out of the jar.

I decide to have one last drink with him.

I twist the lid off the martini shaker, pour gin into the urn, and swirl it around. Now the urn smells like something, like a party.

Closing my eyes, I inhale the cocktail party smell and imagine fresh vacuum marks on the carpet and ice tinkling into glasses. Jazz piano music rumbling on the stereo. I hear the doorbell ring and see our friends standing on the front porch, their faces flushed, expectant.

I drink my martini from the urn, its square edge sharp against my lips. Everything in the room begins to soften, and moving up to Oregon doesn't seem so scary.

After a few more sips I carry the urn out to the backyard, swirling the martini as I go. I swirl and swirl until there's a vortex of swirling martini, then I spin my whole body in circles, my arms outstretched, the martini flying out of the urn in an arc across the lawn. I am some kind of crazy gin sprinkler. I hear myself laughing as the sky spirals overhead: clouds, then trees, then roof, then clouds trees roof, and then just grass as I tumble down, the earth cold and squishy beneath my hands and knees. I topple into a fetal position, clutching the urn to my stomach. The lawn smells sweet, like summer. Our house towers above me.

I remember that when I got home from Ethan's memorial service I couldn't believe the house was still *there*. How could the clocks tick? How could the air-conditioning run? How could there be mail in the box? The relentless soldiering on of the world hurt my feelings.

As I roll onto my stomach, grass tickles my neck. Maybe Ethan would have preferred a beer to a martini. "Grab me a beer?" he used to holler from the living room. I spot a chunk of broken china in the grass—pointed, like an arrowhead—and remember smashing all of my dishes. It's a relief now, not to have to pack them. I kneel, the mud beneath the lawn seeping through my jeans. Then I crawl up onto the deck and scramble back into the kitchen.

Behind a snowy box of chopped spinach in the freezer, I find an old package of cigarettes. This is where people who don't really smoke but might need a smoke once a year to remind them why they don't smoke keep their cigarettes. I tap one out, light it on the burner, pour another martini into the urn, then head for the yard again. The lawn furniture is stored in the shed for the winter, so I sit on the deck, the wood splintery beneath my jeans.

The cigarette doesn't taste good. It burns the back of my throat. But its forbiddenness is somehow right. I remember that Marion longed for a smoke on Ethan's birthday. The other day, when I called to tell her that I was moving to Ashland, she was oddly complacent.

"That's nice, dear," she said. "Who's Ashland?"

"It's a town," I told her. "In Oregon. Where the Shakespeare festival is? Ethan and I visited there a few times."

"That's nice," she repeated. I almost yearned for some of her bossy advice: *Now, Sophie, you must purge all of those ratty paperback novels before you move.* . . .

The deck creaks as I shift my weight. I'm glad I'm not going to have to worry about renovating it, as Ethan recommended. He wanted me to tear out and replace the wood with flagstone and add lights. For what? For whom?

I hope Steve Cunningham will be happy in our house. Maybe he'll remarry and fill the rooms with new memories—kids charging through the halls on Thanksgiving with black olives stuck on their fingers.

I stub out the cigarette. Rinse the gritty feeling off my teeth with the last bit of martini. When I move up to Oregon, I'll start taking better care of myself. Jog. Try soy milk.

Back in the house, I wipe the urn dry with a paper towel, then work the lid back on. I turn off the lights in the kitchen but leave the radio on low. I like hearing the distant murmur of voices.

In the bedroom, I pack the urn and my jewelry box into my suitcase with my clothes and toilet articles. I've sold most of my furniture to Steve and hired the neighbor boy to help me load my boxes into a rented U-Haul, which I'll drive up to Ashland. Dad offered to fly out and drive up with me, but I don't want to make him travel again, so I insisted I'd be fine. Still, I have terrible U-Haul anxiety. Dad says not to worry, those things aren't so hard to maneuver. (I certainly won't parallel-park on the way!)

I wrestle open a dresser drawer that bulges with socks and panty hose. I close the drawer. Tomorrow. I'll pack my socks and shoes and dresses and books tomorrow. Start again on starting over tomorrow. Finish packing and move up to Oregon and find a new job and maybe a little Victorian house to rent and plant some flowers out front. Daisies and delphiniums. Something sturdy and easy at first.

Part Two

Lust

9

Ruth was the most beautiful one among our group of college friends. The tall, willowy dance student with perfect posture and delicate hands, long fingers storming through moody Chopin preludes on the piano. She was so focused and independent that she seemed aloof, which drove guys crazy with longing. Jocks, nerds, professors—every variety of guy was in love with her. In awe of her perfect cheekbones, high grades, and killer volleyball serve that always sent the other team ducking and stumbling. She could have any guy she wanted. So I don't understand why she has this loser boyfriend in Ashland: Tony. He reminds me of a ferret—thin and slithery, with a pointed nose and two protruding front teeth. I swear I've seen him on *Cops.*

I figured it would be just Ruth, me, and her daughter, Simone, in Ashland, both Ruth and me single, the way it was when we were roommates the first year out of school and we'd stay up late painting each other's hair with henna (hers "honey," mine "mahogany"). But now this Tony sleeps over at her house every night.

Ruth, Simone, Tony, and I eat breakfast together every morning. Simone spoons cereal into her mouth, looking at Tony, looking at her mother, Cheerios falling in her lap and on the floor. She's only four, but you can see the thought bubble over her blond little head: *Who is this guy? Where's my father?* Ruth's dentist husband, Mark, took off with his hygienist shortly after Simone was born.

For the most part Tony ignores Simone, whom he begrudgingly calls the Munchkin.

"Where are you from, Tony?" I ask as we sit down to the buckwheat pancakes I've fixed.

"Albuquerque."

Ha! They are always filming *Cops* in Albuquerque. I'm about to ask what brought him to Ashland when Ruth shoots me a look that says, *That's enough, Barbara Walters.* She pushes away from the table, leaving her pancakes unfinished.

"Gotta run," she says. She manages the admissions office at the university in town and she's always there by eight, dressed in her sensible wool kilt and sweater and clogs, her long blond hair pulled into a pretty French braid. She kisses Simone, then Tony gives her a long, wet kiss. I look away, feeling embarrassed, peripheral.

While I clear the dishes and clean up the kitchen, Simone plays in the living room and Tony watches TV. Whatever his job is, it doesn't start until after noon. I've volunteered to watch Simone, whose baby-sitter is sick with bronchitis. As I rinse the plates, I try to think of something to fix for supper. I want to contribute by cooking, but it's a bit of a challenge since Ruth is a healthful vegetarian and I've been on the Godiva plan. In the next room Simone plays with her jack-in-the-box—an annoying toy that plays "Pop Goes the Weasel" until you'd like to pop the thing with a hammer.

"The *end!*" Tony snaps. I hear him grab the gadget out of Simone's little hands and hurl it into her toy box. She shrieks and cries. I poke my head out of the kitchen in time to catch Tony standing over her.

"Crybaby," he hisses. He steps away from her when he sees me. I bolt over and gather Simone into my arms. She digs her little red Keds into my thighs, wraps her sticky fingers around my neck, and buries her head in my shoulder.

.   .   .

"Do you think Simone minds that Tony sleeps over every night?"
I ask Ruth later that night as we sit down to dinner. Tony's still at
work; he usually doesn't show up until after Simone's in bed.

"We have a consistent schedule," Ruth says crisply, taking a
mouthful of tofu casserole and chewing vigorously.

"Sorry to be nosy." I pour her more wine and pile salad onto her
plate. "But is he really your type?"

Ruth stops chewing and narrows her eyes. "I guess I don't *have*
a type."

I shrug. "It's just that he's not very nice to Simone."

Ruth puts down her fork and folds her arms across her chest.
"Yeah, he's far from perfect." She pushes her plate away.

"I'm not saying you need someone who's perfect. But you and
Simone need someone who's good for you."

"Good for me? Mark was supposedly *good* for me."

Mark was Ruth's first real boyfriend. In college, he won her over
essentially by wearing her down—filling her dorm room with
roses, singing to her from under her window. A month after graduation they were married. Now, Ruth seems worn down by everything, raw and brittle. It's mind-boggling why Mark took off with
his hygienist, Missy, who's the opposite of Ruth—a silly laugh that
bubbles over without cause and a childish collection of stuffed
animals in the back window of her car.

"I don't need you critiquing my love life," Ruth says.

"It's just that I'm *sure* you're the most eligible woman in Ashland, and—"

"Right. With a four-year-old!" Ruth clears her plate. I'm a little
hurt as she shoves her casserole down the disposal.

She's hardly aged since school—beautiful smooth skin, two rosy
knobs for cheeks, thick blond hair the color of corn. We nick-
named her Dove for that perfect skin. Tony or no Tony, I want to
start the evening over. When you live far away from your best

friend, all you remember are the General Foods International Coffee ad moments. You forget that you ever had the capacity to fight.

"You're a snob," Ruth continues. "Just because Tony didn't go to college—"

"It's not about him going to college. It's about you and Simone having someone you deserve."

"It doesn't matter what I deserve. MIT graduates aren't strolling the streets of Ashland, Soph." She faces the sink with her back toward me, scrubbing her plate. "I would rather be with Tony than be alone. I know you find that despicable, but it's the truth." She sighs, sets the plate in the drainer, and drops her hands at her sides.

"I'm not saying you have to date Einstein. But what about Simone? He yelled at her." My hands tremble as I clear my plate. I haven't been this forceful in a long time. "Tell me you disagree with me. Tell me that Tony's good for you and Simone."

In the next room, a group of syrupy children on a *Barney* video sing a song about Mother Goose, and Simone giggles.

Ruth turns toward me and brushes tears from her cheeks.

"Yeah. He doesn't seem crazy about kids." She pours her wine down the drain.

"That's all I'm saying."

"All right. Point *taken*."

I sleep in the guest room at the back of Ruth's old Victorian until I can find a rental of my own. The room is spinsterish, perfect for a widow, with its prim lace curtains and yellowing doilies on the dresser, the faint smells of mothballs and stale rose sachets. The arthritic wood floor that creaks under my bare feet. It's as unsexy a dwelling as you could possibly find. Which is good: Nothing about the place reminds me of Ethan. It's hard to miss the absence of his weight in the single bed that droops like a hammock. And I can't really imagine him showering in the old claw-foot tub in the adjoining bathroom.

Still, I dream about Ethan every night. He's always sick in the dreams, and it seems as though I'm not dreaming about my husband, I'm dreaming about cancer. While Ethan was dying I hid my fear, worrying that it would only make him feel worse. You constantly try to be optimistic when someone's sick, to look on the bright side, even if the bright side is only their ability to swallow a spoonful of applesauce or walk to the bathroom. After they're gone, you're left with endless fodder for nightmares.

In one dream Ethan's driving us across the country.

"You don't want to live in Oregon," he says. "It rains all the time."

There's something wet, warm, and sticky on the seat. I look down and see that it's blood, as slick and dark as motor oil.

Some nights I can hear Ruth and Tony on the other side of the bedroom wall: low voices, giggles, the steady bump of the headboard. Intimacy. Then there's the swell of TV show music and laughter. The top ten reasons why you should get a job and find your own place.

I stash my boxes in a storage facility out on I-5, figuring I won't need them until I find my own apartment or house. But after a week at Ruth's I begin to miss Ethan's belongings. I buy an X-Acto knife and drive out to the locker and cut through the layers of cardboard and packing tape back into his world—closing my eyes and inhaling the smells of his musty old textbooks and leather belts and shoes.

Sitting on the cold cement floor, I flip through Ethan's high school yearbooks, running my fingers over the spidery ballpoint inscriptions from his classmates. One of the smartest kids in his class, he obviously helped a lot of pretty girls with their homework. *Dear Ethan,* wrote a girl with feathery blond hair and lots of mascara, *thanks for helping me with my trig!* Someone named Emily wearing a puka shell choker scribbled, *Hey, Ethan, thanks for show-ing me how to work the Bunsen burner.* I have the urge to look these women up and see if they remember my husband. I'm afraid the fickle world will forget him entirely.

I rescue Ethan's flannel shirts, sweatpants, and baseball caps, packing them into grocery bags to carry back to Ruth's house. Finally, I find his ski sweater. As I pull it on over my head, the tightly knit wool is like armor against the damp Oregon air.

"I have sweaters you can borrow," Ruth says, eyeing Ethan's boxy sweater skeptically when I get back to her house. I haven't had it cleaned since he died, and there's a long teardrop-shaped tea stain in the middle of the yellow stripe.

"I like this one," I tell her.

It's an easy walk from Ruth's house to downtown Ashland, and the town is much prettier than the strip mall landscape of Silicon Val-ley. The Siskiyou Mountains scoop around East Main Street, shrouded with capes of cottony clouds and sprinkled with sugary snow. Colored flags for the Oregon Shakespeare Festival top the lampposts lining the street.

I discover Kit Whittaker, a realtor who handles rentals in town, in an upstairs office across from the Chamber of Commerce. Kit's friendly and handsome—olive skin, green eyes flecked with gold, and thick, curly brown hair. But I find filling out his rental applica-tion form daunting. I don't have enough of a life to answer the questions. No employer or set annual income. For references I put down my father, which seems childish. Then there's the worst part: *Person to contact in case of emergency.* I pause, then fill in Ruth's name. Next to *Relationship,* I write *friend,* hating the absence in my life of the word *husband.*

I look up at Kit, who sits behind his big oak desk, peering thoughtfully through wire-rimmed glasses at paperwork. There's a picture on his desk of a pretty woman with long black braids standing beside two little girls.

"Twins?" I ask him. He smiles and nods, and I have the urge to write *his* name down on the form in case of emergency. I imagine him stooping over the gurney in the emergency room, green eyes glittering, and whispering, *Don't worry. Everything's going to be all right.*

Kit picks me up at Ruth's house the next morning, bringing me a cup of coffee with milk and sugar and a fresh pile of rental listings. The real estate market is slow in Ashland in the winter, so he has time to point out landmarks and actor hangouts and fill me in on town gossip—the rivalry between bed-and-breakfasts and the story of a terrible flood that ruined much of East Main Street one winter. The coffee is hot and sweet, and Kit's car door is heavy and a little difficult to close. I feel safe inside as he snaps the locks shut.

After two days of touring rentals with Kit, I've got a crush on his whole life. His corduroys and cable-knit sweaters, his appreciation for wood floors and French doors, his conscientiousness for always calling his wife when he's running late, his two little girls, even his car: the sweet cowboy smell of new leather seats.

I imagine that Kit becomes a widower, his wife and girls suddenly gone somehow. Poor Kit! Then I'm bringing dinner to his house—maybe Bolognese sauce—and then, don't ask how, we wind up making love on his kitchen floor. I imagine Pergo cold and hard against my back. No, this is plain crazy! I would never have an affair! Besides, Kit's married. I'm married. *Was* married. Still *love* Ethan. It's just that Kit has this calm, thoughtful expression and broad shoulders punctuated by a narrow waist. A waist you could curl your arms around while skinny-dipping in the ocean. That's all I want. Not to have an affair. To go skinny-dipping in the ocean, just once, with my realtor. Loneliness. This must be loneliness talking. As much as I hated my job, suddenly I wish I were trapped back in the office, the fluorescent lights and bad coffee sucking the vitality out of me. Now that I'm regaining my energy, I'm not sure I like how it makes me feel: alive again, with all the weaknesses of the living. Realtor lust! Surely this isn't a stage of grief.

It's not just Kit. Suddenly I'm noticing guys everywhere. Even Tony's denim-clad rear is something to consider, despite his weaselly face. For months, men have been genderless blurs, nondistinct shapes orbiting around me, occasionally moving close enough to give off heat or the soft brush of a cotton sleeve.

I feel guilty because I don't miss just my husband. I miss *men*.

The truth is, I developed little crushes on other men while Ethan was alive. The attentive guy at the nursery who knew the names of all the salvias (unlike Ethan, who couldn't tell a plastic palm from a blooming rosebush). The cracks of the nursery guy's palms were caked with soil. Once, as he loaded gallon containers of lantana into my trunk, I imagined helping him wash his hands. That night I *dreamed* about the hands—that his fingers swept up under my shirt, calluses tickling my belly. Then there was nuzzling and necking, and I awoke next to Ethan, gasping for air.

"Are you okay?" Ethan asked tenderly.

"I'm *fine!*" I shouted, clutching the duvet under my chin and telling myself: *You did not just have a lusty dream about that twenty-something nursery guy. You're* married.

Kit must think I'm a little off, because now when he picks me up in the morning I don't want to look at him. Shyness envelops me, and small talk sticks in the back of my throat.

"Not changing your mind about Ashland, are you?" Kit asks as I stare pensively through the rain-splattered windshield.

"Oh, *no*," I assure him. But the truth is, I want to go home. I feel the way I did as a kid at camp, with a pit of homesickness in my gut that no amount of s'mores or bug juice could fill.

10

Dr. Rupert gave me the name of a shrink in Medford, the next town over, but the new doctor doesn't take my insurance, which I've extended through COBRA. I call around and find that none of the psychiatrists or psychologists in Ashland seem to take insurance. It turns out that COBRA is an ill-tempered snake who wants to cover only 50 percent of "allowable" charges for out-of-network doctors, which is much less than what the doctors actually charge.

I meet with the Medford doctor once and he agrees to refill my prescription for antidepressants as long as I see him every three months and attend a weekly grief group in Ashland, which is free.

The group meets Tuesday evenings at the Ashland Community Center, a log cabin across from Lithia Park that looks as though Daniel Boone should live there. The first meeting is on Valentine's Day, and I feel grateful to have a date, even if it's with a room full of strangers.

Inside, a fire burns in the fireplace and there's the familiar circle of folding aluminum chairs and bitter coffee served in Styrofoam cups, clumps of stubborn nondairy creamer floating on top, and little heart-shaped sugar cookies with pink icing.

The leader's name is Sandy, and he's good-looking in a sandy sort of way—tousled blond hair, as though he just got out of bed, golden skin, two apricots for cheeks, a sandy goatee. A silver wedding band flashes between his tanned fingers. He asks us to take our seats. He's tired, he explains, because he was up late last night with his daughter, Emma, who has a cold. Perfect name for a daughter, Emma.

"Hello, everyone, let's get started," Emma's dad says.

We go around the room introducing ourselves. Since I'm sitting next to Sandy, we start with me. I tell the circle of faces that my husband died of cancer seven months ago. I used to feel faint whenever I told someone that Ethan died—as though I were floating above the earth, watching a movie of two people talking about his death. But now I'm able to state the fact as though someone merely asked what kind of car I drive. I'm surprised at how Ethan's death is no longer a cruel impossibility, but rather an inherent part of my life, like my address or middle name (Enid, horrible, after an aunt). Sophie Enid Stanton: widow. Starting over.

"Tell us something you miss about Ethan," Sandy says.

This seems too big a question to answer. Besides, wouldn't we make it easier on ourselves if we tried to recall something we *didn't* miss about our loved ones? If we tried to remember the time they locked the keys in the trunk or forgot our birthdays? But that's the problem with dead people. They're perfect. They never argue or chew with their mouths open.

Actually, it bothered me the way Ethan chewed. He ate quickly with big bites, his cheeks bulging as he stared vacantly into space, his mind spinning around some piece of software code.

Sandy clears his throat, leans forward in his chair, waiting.

"His hair," I tell the group softly. "Going to sleep with him at night." I feel myself blushing, hoping they don't think I mean just the sex part. "Someone to put down in case of emergency."

People smile and nod encouragingly, and we move on to the man sitting next to me, Al, a piano instructor who's been a widower for nearly a year. "It's just not the same," he says, shaking his head and tugging at his black beard. He looks at the coffee urn on the table at the back of the room. "Are there doughnuts?" he asks.

Then there's an older man whose wife recently died of Alzheimer's. She didn't recognize him anymore, and when he visited her at the rest home she yelled at him to get the covered bridge out of her room.

After we finish introducing ourselves, Sandy wants us to write letters to our loved ones. He passes out yellow pads and Bic pens. More hard work! I concentrate on shredding my cuticles.

The empty pad stares up at me coolly.

Dear Ethan, I begin. I look around the room. Everyone's bent over, scratching away with their pens. Where are we going to mail these letters—to the North Pole?

I moved up to Ashland and I'm staying with Ruth until I can find my own place and we sort of had a fight. It's beautiful here, but it's lonely. I thought I could leave the loneliness in San Jose, but it followed me up here like a stalker. Do you think I'm doing the right thing?

I should probably tell Ethan that I sold our house. Oh, screw it. He can't read this. I tear the sheet off the yellow pad, crumple it, and start over.

Dear Sandy. Can I sleep with you? How come none of the grief books talk about how widows get crushes on everyone? Anyone who's even remotely kind or good-looking? You become like the bird in that children's book that loses its mother and starts thinking everything is its mother, even a steam shovel. Are you my mother? it keeps asking. Are you my husband?

I look up, watching everyone writing. Sandy clears his throat again and shuffles some papers. Finally he asks if anyone would like to read their letter aloud. People squirm, glance at the door.

"We're doing some hard work today," Sandy says, looking around the room, smoothing his goatee. "I understand if you don't want to read your letters. Would anyone like to?"

He turns toward me, eyes big and brown. My heart speeds up. I fold my letter and stuff it into my jacket pocket, then look at the floor. My anxiety-rattled brain expresses a sudden desire to run a hand over the golden hairs on Sandy's arms. A desire to have sex with him in a sleeping bag under the stars. He's not even my type! I don't go for earthy goatee guys. Still, sitting this close to Sandy, I can't help but notice that he smells earthy in a good way, like potatoes. It would be a down sleeping bag and we would be naked and I'd have my flat stomach back. We'd be on another planet where there's a lot more to console a person than an empty legal pad.

A woman whose husband fell through the ice and drowned on an ice-fishing trip reads softly to the venetian blinds. Her letter is all about how her husband never should have gone fishing in the first place. It wasn't cold enough for the ice to be solid and they already had a freezer full of fish at home and it was dumb to drink and fish and be so careless when he had two kids and a whole family who cared about him.

"And hello!" she says, her quavering voice getting louder. "They *have* fish at Safeway. We didn't need any more fucking fish out of that cesspool of a river!" She looks up at us and says, "That's as far as I got."

Sandy says thank you and it's okay to be angry and keep going, don't be afraid to keep going.

After the meeting, Gloria, an older woman in a black wool cape whose daughter died of leukemia, crosses the room toward me.

"You remind me of my daughter," she says, giving me a hug. "She had curly hair, too." I feel her knobby vertebrae under layers of cape and sweater. She smells spicy, like cinnamon and cloves, like apple pie, and I don't want to let go of her.

Gloria takes a step back, looks at me, then touches my curls. "You take care," she says. "See you next week."

Then the piano teacher is at my side. "Is it Sophie?" he says.

"Yes."

He extends a hand. "Al." The hand is damp, a little slippery.

"Hi, Al."

"Would you like to have dinner with me tonight?" He wears a

Mr. Rogers cardigan sweater, and his wiry black hair is combed over in a swirl from the nape of his neck, like a shadow across his head. He's probably at least ten years older than me. "You mentioned not liking to eat dinner alone," he explains sheepishly, "and I'm trying to get out of myself by reaching out to others."

"Um . . ." I am searching for an answer. Looks aren't everything, after all, and it is Valentine's Day, and maybe it's a good thing to have a friendly dinner with a man I can't possibly lust after. Besides, Al's a musician and he's probably talented and sweet and interesting. Lonely, like me.

"Sure," I say, trying to smile. Al reminds me of my geometry teacher, Mr. Rowinson, who wore similar brown polyester pants but was kind and patient and let you retake quizzes to bring up your grade.

After the meeting, Al and I walk to the warehouse-type brewery in town that serves gourmet pizzas and beer. I order a wheat beer and vegetable pizza for dinner; Al orders pasta and wine. As we're sipping our drinks, he leans over the table and tries to take my hand. My arm jerks back instinctively and Al gets only two fingers. He squeezes them and gives me a mournful look.

"I know it's hard," he says.

"For you, too," I tell him, unlooping my fingers and folding my hands in my lap.

Here's what happens in the movies: A single woman moves to a small town in the country to start over, and a rugged Sam Shepard kind of guy—lean and muscular, a cleft chin, and a thirty-three-inch waist in faded Levi's—finds her. He's got an old Ford pickup with a friendly black Lab in the back and a big, soft bed with a brass headboard and miles of flannel quilt you could hide under all day.

Here's what happens in real life: A single woman moves to a small town in the country to start over, and Professor Tweedly—his breath smelling faintly like the cat box, his hands as oily and plump as sausages—finds her. Despite his feeble comb-over, she figures maybe he'll offer a bit of benign companionship, a bit of dreamy Mozart that will take her mind off things.

But no! After dinner I agree to walk the four blocks over to Al's house for coffee and he seats himself at the piano in his living room and begins playing a Barry Manilow song.

"'I write the songs that make the young girls cry . . . ,'" Al swoons, closing his eyes and swaying. Suddenly I can imagine why Ruth lowered her standards for Tony. If this is the alternative! The wheat beer makes my head throb. I curse myself for agreeing to this evening. My weak spot: desperate for a dinner mate.

"Al?" I say, raising my voice over the second chorus. "Al, I have a migraine." I clutch my temples.

He stops playing, quickly pulls the cover down over the keys, and rushes to my side on the sofa.

"Let me give you a massage." He reaches for my shoulders.

"No." I squirm away. "I need to get going."

"Of course, let me drive you."

It's pouring now, and I'm exhausted and don't have an umbrella.

"All right." I grab my coat. As Al tries to help me into it, I duck my head, fighting back tears. *Ethan, I need a ride!* Wherever my husband is, however dark that place might be, I want to go there, right now.

Al's car is parked in the street in front of his house. We get in and he starts the engine, then he puts his hands in his lap instead of on the steering wheel.

"I was hoping . . . ," he says, looking down. But then he stops speaking and lunges across the seat, trying to kiss me. His beard is coarse and scratchy, like Easter basket grass. I turn my head, and his lips, warm and sticky, brush my cheek. Then his arms are around me and his grasp is firm. I spot a tennis racket in the backseat and reach over and grab it, smacking the window as I try to hit him with a cramped backhand swat.

"Quit it!" The racket bounces against the back of his head with a *twong!*

"Yeow!"

I hold the tennis racket in the air between us, watching him through the squares in the netting. He slides back against the door.

"Okay. Sorry! It's just that you're so beautiful. And I'm so lonely."

"Well, get a *hold* of yourself."

Just then a woman in a yellow slicker rounds the corner by Al's house. When she sees us in the car, she speeds up, swinging her arms and huffing, her scarf flying in the wind behind her.

"Al!" she screeches.

Al sinks to the floor of the car, the upper half of his body folded over the seat.

"Shit! My wife!"

"Your wife? Your *dead* wife?"

"She's not exactly dead," Al moans. Then he grabs a piece of newspaper—the "Local and State" section—and pulls it over his head.

"Dead or alive, she already *saw* you."

"Al!" The woman charges toward the car and raps on the window with her umbrella. "Where's the check, Al? We're on instant oatmeal, Al. And I don't mean for breakfast. I mean your daughter, who you can't be *bothered* to call on her birthday, is eating instant oatmeal for dinner!" She gives the window another smack with the umbrella.

"And who's this? Suzie Coed? One of your piano students? Did you take her out for a nice roast beef dinner while your daughter ate instant oatmeal?" She looks at me. "Honey," she says, poking the umbrella toward my face, "this man couldn't even get a job playing the piano at Bob's Bar."

"You're a deadbeat dad?" I ask Al.

"It's a long story," Al says.

"You posed as a widower to get a dinner date?"

"I am filled with pain and loss," he says, pulling the paper farther down over his head, trying to get smaller on the floor of the car.

I open the passenger door and get out.

"I'm not his student," I tell the woman. "I met him at a grief group. He said he was a widower—that his wife was dead."

"Yeah, well, he's killing me all right." She leans into the car and beats at the newspaper with the umbrella. "You worthless man. You worthless bad comb-over bastard!"

I realize I'm still clenching the tennis racket. I use it to give the newspaper over Al's head a good swat, then hand it to his ex-wife.

"Liar!" the woman shrieks, whacking the paper with the racket and then tossing it into the backseat.

"Liar!" I agree.

"Ow. Yeowch!" Al hollers.

"See you in court, Al," the woman says. She slams the car door and the engine stalls, then quits. The woman and I look at each other for a moment. She seems to decide that I am no threat. Then we head off down the street in opposite directions.

Al. As in *no alimony.*

Droplets of rain dot the rhododendron bushes like glass beads. As the wind blows, water from the trees stings my scalp. It is a different kind of rain in Oregon, sharp, cold drops that seem to find a way of getting *inside* your body, of seeping through your clothes into your blood and bones and making everything ache.

BARGAINING

11

Isn't there some way out of this? I wake up thinking in the middle of the night, desperate to negotiate a deal. *Isn't there some way around having to start this new life without my husband?*

Maybe there's been a mistake. A clerical error. Maybe the angel of death is a bumbling bureaucrat who took the wrong Ethan. "Oh, *your* Ethan," the sweet volunteer in the daffodil-colored uniform behind the front desk at the hospital lobby would say if I called the hospital to check. "He didn't die. He went *home.*" Then I'd climb into the Honda, drive back down to San Jose, and find Ethan in our kitchen waiting for me.

"I've been at the hardware store," he'd say, shrugging and holding out a tiny brown bag of drill bits.

That's it: My husband went to the hardware store for seven months. You know how men are!

I wish life were like one of those cheesy movies where ghosts come back to visit their loved ones. Hover around and knock stuff over. Breathe a tickle of warm air on your neck while you're flossing your teeth or opening the mail.

Maybe if we had gone to the doctor a month earlier, when Ethan's glands first started to mysteriously swell and ache, he'd be here in Ashland with me now. We'd be starting over together. He could work for the festival managing their Web site and make it home every night in time for dinner.

But Ethan's not here and Ruth has to go to work early and Simone needs her Cheerios. So I get up every morning and try to make a contribution. If not to the world, or my life, at least to Ruth's household.

Ruth's stalwart work ethic inspires me to at least do my grief group homework: exercise twenty minutes a day. Even if I'd rather eat a roll of cookie dough than walk around the block, Sandy promises that exercise will make us feel a little better. Back in San Jose I would have chucked this advice, but now I'm wistful for my waistline, for my former energy level. I treat myself to a new pair of sneakers, cushiony white socks, and a snug sports bra that feels as if it's giving me a supportive you-can-do-it hug.

Every morning after breakfast I set out with Simone in her Baby Jogger, hoping to shed the fifteen gummy pounds I've packed on since Ethan died. I run across the bridge from Ruth's house into town, pushing her past the bookstore, and into the park. Simone seems as heavy as a sack of cement. At first my chest tightens and my thighs cramp. Then the moist Oregon air pushes the fear of rejoining the world out of my lungs and my body tingles with possibility. Pretty soon I'll find a house. Then a job. My feet pound the earth with determination. "Pretty soon," I tell Simone.

"Pretty soon," she chants.

I collapse on a bench by the duck pond, exhausted. Mothers pour down the paths toward the water, pushing babies in strollers, plastic wheels clacking along the pavement. As I pull Simone out of her jogger, the smell of her baby-shampooed ringlets shoots straight to my heart. If I don't have a job, then I should have a baby. If you can rent a house and a car and a storage locker—rent a new life—why can't you rent a baby? It's odd not having anyplace to report to or anyone to care for at eight-thirty in the morning. These mothers in the park obviously have routines: walk, nap, lunch. Warm onesies from the dryer to fold in the afternoons.

I hand Simone a bag of cracked corn and the ducks swarm

around her, orange beaks lurching toward her little fingers. On the other side of the park, beyond the community center where my grief group meets, a pretty row of houses lines the street. I wonder if any of them are for rent. But they're too big for a single person living alone. Rental houses should come with families, the way wallets come with photos of families. I think of Kit's rental applications with the many boxes to check for available features: *Furnished? Washer and dryer? Garage? Wall-to-wall carpet? Husband? Child? Twins?*

I've always hated an empty house. When I was eight, I would beg my mother, who was already forty by then, to have another baby, to fill the kitchen table with siblings.

"Honey, I can't have any more children," she said, smoothing over my hair, trying to tuck it behind my ears.

"Why not?"

"Some women have a harder time than others. That's why I'm lucky to have you."

I was suspicious about the difference between *can't* and *won't* and would wait only a few days before asking her again.

When Ethan and I struggled to get pregnant, I wished I hadn't nagged Mother about having a baby, that I'd been more sympathetic.

At least if I had a baby now, I'd have a part of Ethan with me: his peanut toes or inability to carry a tune. At parties I could trade play date anecdotes by the Havarti with the other moms.

In college, Ruth sort of rented a kid. She joined Big Brothers/ Big Sisters and brought a tiny freckled girl to our dorm every weekend. We taught her how to play checkers, do needlepoint, and dribble a basketball. Maybe I could get a little sister, a girl like Simone, who needs help fastening butterfly barrettes in her hair. I remember Ruth and her little sister sitting cross-legged on the dorm room floor, singing along to *The Sound of Music*'s sound track.

Simone pokes the toe of her sneaker into a puddle rimmed with duck glop. I scoop her up and wrestle her back into the jogger. As I run out of the park, I imagine my own rented bungalow, a sunny kitchen with an old refrigerator decorated with construction paper collages and finger paintings by my own "little sister," the smudgy shapes of tiny hands.

When I return to Ruth's house, I call Big Brothers/Big Sisters. The woman who answers schedules me for an intake meeting. She says they'll ask me lots of questions about myself and why I want to join the program, then do a background check. I try to mask my disappointment. Of course they can't drop off a kid at my house tomorrow morning.

"Mama?" I hear Simone say as I hang up the phone.

"She's at work," I say, trying to pump enthusiasm into this fact. But when I round the corner into the kitchen, I'm surprised to find Ruth sitting at the table in her robe. Her forehead rests in her hands, a curtain of blond hair covering her face. Having recently returned from Planet Bathrobe, I don't like the sight of her trapped in pink terry cloth as lunchtime approaches.

"Taking the day off?" I try not to sound judgmental. The coffee has turned as dark as molasses in the pot. Simone sits on the living room floor, speaking soothingly to a stuffed tiger, assuring it of something.

"Taking a mental health day," Ruth says, looking past me and out the window. Her eyes are red around the rims. She stares straight ahead without blinking. I kick off my sneakers and sit next to her at the table.

"Hey." I wrap an arm around her shoulder. "You're not thinking about a career as a bathrobe model, are you?"

"I asked Tony not to come over anymore."

"Broke up?"

She nods.

"I'm sorry." I try to conceal my relief.

"You were right about him."

"Well, I didn't want to be right. I wanted to be proven wrong. He just—"

Ruth holds up her hand to stop me, then passes me a note written in Tony's fourth-grader handwriting on a flattened paper bag.

Baby, the note says. *Your the greatest. Call me when you change your mind. Love, Tony.*

"The pathetic thing is," Ruth says, "I want to call him. No. I don't want to call him. I want to *sleep* with him. I think. Fork!" She pounds her fist on the table. She has a medley of faux F-words so she never swears in front of Simone. "Frittata," she adds. Then she lowers her voice. "I feel sick. I'm going back to bed." She spreads her hands across the table but doesn't get up. "I think I'll take the rest of the week off."

"Oh, no." I fetch her a glass of water. "We can go out for a three-martini lunch or you can sleep all day. But tomorrow you have to go back to work."

She looks at the glass of water on the table.

"I'll dress you if I have to, but you only get *one* bathrobe day." I say this as firmly as I can, finding it odd that I'm the one trying to convince *her* not to crumble.

"You're right," Ruth mutters. But she doesn't move. Her gaze wanders to a smudge of butter on the kitchen table. She frowns, as though she'd like to wipe it up but can't muster the energy. I know this feeling. Smudges moving in on you while you're trapped in an inertia as sticky as flypaper.

"I know you'll miss Tony," I tell her. "But being alone is better than being with him, trust me." How do I know? I'm so lonely that I'll go to dinner with No Alimony Al.

Ruth rubs the butter smudge, then licks her finger.

"This used to be the other way around," I remind her. "You'd encourage *me* to ditch the loser guys. You're the *originator* of the good-riddance list."

Ruth shakes her head and the corners of her mouth turn up a little. She dabs under her eyes with a napkin, blots at her cheeks.

The good-riddance list was a list of annoying qualities about a guy that you were supposed to make after a breakup. Whenever you missed the guy, Ruth said you had to consult the list.

I dated this golden-haired law student in college named Tad Pennington, who looked like Robert Redford in *The Way We Were* but turned out to be a liar and a cheat who had another girlfriend he didn't tell me about. I was devastated when we broke up, but Ruth made me write a good-riddance list and carry it in my wallet.

"Tad threw his gum out the car window," I tell her now. "And he was rude to waitresses. See? I still remember."

Ruth blows her nose and laughs. "Tad the Cad. He was cute." She frowns again and tightens her robe across her chest, two fists of terry cloth in her hands.

"I was always a little envious of your perfect marriage," she says softly. "I wish I weren't so pissed off and could cherish boxes of my lost husband's stuff and wear his dirty ski sweater."

I'm taken aback by this confession. How could you be envious of a dead husband?

"The sweater's not *dirty*," I stammer.

Ruth looks at me, raising her eyebrows.

When she found out about Mark and Missy, she didn't make a good-riddance list. Instead, she cut all the buttons off Mark's shirts and coats, threw his clothes onto the lawn, and changed the locks. This was a side of her I'd never seen, a side that seemed healthy compared to her unflinching composure over the years. Later, she mailed the buttons to him with the divorce papers.

"My marriage wasn't perfect," I insist, our knees bumping under the table as I lean toward her. "We couldn't have a baby, for one thing, and Ethan was a workaholic. Even cancer couldn't get him to make our time together a priority over work." While this is true, I think part of the reason Ethan went back to work right after he went into remission was to get back in cancer's face. A steely resolve not to submit to the disease.

"But he didn't leave you with a baby for a bimbo in Mickey Mouse scrubs."

"Oh Ruth." I stand up and rub her shoulders. "Mark must have lost his *mind*."

Maybe the only upside of your husband dying is that he didn't leave you for someone else. At least you can't take cancer personally.

I look over at Simone, who is concentrating on keeping her small hand inside the lines of a picture in a coloring book. She makes the sky brown and a house blue and a tree yellow. I refill her sippy cup with watered-down juice, then head to Ruth's room and fetch her clothes and a hairbrush. When I place the jeans, sweater, and underwear on the table, Ruth closes her eyes, as though they're too much to contemplate right now.

I tug off her ponytail holder and brush her silky hair, amazed at how easily the brush sails through it. Ruth's shoulders drop and she tips back her head. I turn over the paper bag with Tony's note and write, *Tony's Good-Riddance List,* on the other side. Then I hand her the pen.

Terrible with children, she writes. *Greasy hair.* She pauses to read what she's written, sets down the pen, looks at her clothes. Then she scoops them into her arms and heads for the bathroom. I'm relieved when I hear the shower running.

— *12* —

Kit and I pull up to a Queen Anne house painted a hopeful powder blue with white gingerbread trim and a picket fence surrounding the yard. A lattice arbor loops over the gate to the front walk, which is lined with box hedges.

"This place is for *rent*?" I ask Kit. Ivy drapes out of an old milk can set beside a wooden porch swing.

"It's a B and B, but one of the owners got sick. They're renting the place for a year until their son can move to town and take over the business." He says the place is called Colonel Cranson's, after the original owner—a retired Civil War colonel who used to manage the railroad station back when the train ran through Ashland.

"It looks like the Happily-Ever-After Institute."

"We can commit you on the first of the month."

"Do I have to like scones?"

The inside of the house smells like an attic—like mothballs and cedar and musty fabrics. Sunshine spills through the warbly glass in the windows onto the long oriental runner in the front hall. I admire the doors' glossy porcelain knobs. We creak past the living room, which is crowded with antiques that remind me of old ladies. Wingback chairs with tea party posture. Pedestal tables with demure padded feet. A grandfather clock at the end of the long hall lets out a loud gong. I jump and grab Kit's arm, then quickly let go, embarrassed.

The bright kitchen still smells of yeast and coffee. I run my fingers over the grain of the oak table, which is surrounded by chairs with embroidered seats.

"Sold!" I tell Kit.

Dear Ethan: Don't worry about me. I live in a Pepperidge Farm ad now.

"There might be mice." Kit swipes cobwebs from a windowsill. "And rumor has it there's a ghost." He pushes open the back door, which leads to a porch alongside the house. We step outside. "This is where the guests eat breakfast." Directly across the street there's a gas station equipped with a car wash. Machinery whirrs and water gushes. A car chugs through the giant spinning black and blue brushes, the driver blinking into the sunlight as he emerges. "It's a little noisy," Kit admits. He's sort of the anti-realtor—without bluster or hype.

I shrug. "My car will always be clean."

We sit in wicker rockers on the porch and review the rental agreement. Kit lowers his voice and leans toward me. "The ghost's name is Alice." He laughs. "She's the Cransons' daughter, who died of pneumonia. The owners claim she rustles around in the kitchen in the middle of the night and once she left the milk out on the counter."

I can relate to Alice. Restless and hungry in the middle of the night, milk carton absentmindedness.

"No problem. I'll take it." I'm used to living with ghosts.

Soon after I sign the lease for Colonel Cranson's, Big Brothers/Big Sisters calls to say that my background check has been cleared and that I've been matched with a thirteen-year-old eighth-grader named Crystal Lowman. During the intake meeting, I told the counselor that I didn't care what age the child was. She said this might make for a faster match. But secretly I hoped for a littler girl, like Simone, with whom I could finger-paint and build Legos. "It's a henhouse!" Simone shrieked with glee the time we built a simple red Lego building. Will a teenage girl be this easy to please?

Now the counselor explains that Crystal lives alone with her mother and has trouble at school. "She's bright enough but spends a lot of afternoons in detention," the woman says. "Her mother doesn't seem to participate in her life much. But I'm sure you'll make a great role model."

Role model! Sure, let me show you how to lose your job and your house and gain fifteen pounds in no time.

Crystal, her mother, and I meet for the first time at the agency with a counselor. Crystal looks young for thirteen, with a thin, boyish figure. Her face is pretty, though, with high rosy cheekbones like Ruth's and a small pointed nose that's chapped on the end. Her skin is flawless and translucent, with an almost bluish tinge, like skim milk. Her short hair is so blond that it's nearly white. Roxanne, Crystal's mother, is a larger version of her daughter—thin and sinewy, with long legs. She looks younger than me, more like a sister than a mother.

When we discuss what day of the week to get together, Crystal's indifference makes my stomach drop. "Whatever," she says with dramatic exhaustion when I suggest Sundays at two. It's as though she thinks our get-togethers will be about as fun as detention. She barely looks at me during our meeting. Instead she systematically examines her split ends, her eyes crossing as she tugs pieces of her short hair in front of her nose. As for her mother, she's either had too much caffeine or there's someplace else she has to be. Her Reebok-clad foot circles the air frenetically, and she keeps checking her watch. She and Crystal exude an impatience that makes me wonder why they came to the agency in the first place.

A few days later, I attend an orientation meeting for "Bigs." The counselors recommend that we take our "Littles" on outdoor adventures, such as hiking or ice-skating. They warn against letting our Littles persuade us to always take them shopping, to the video arcade, or out for junk food.

"It's not about you being their sugar daddy," a counselor explains. "It's about forming a friendship and being a mentor."

Wrong house? I wonder, standing on Crystal's front porch the afternoon of our first date. I double-check the address on the paper in my purse. No, this is right. I've been stood up. By a thirteen-year-old! This isn't supposed to be like dating.

Wedged between the aluminum storm door and front door of her house, I ring the bell a second and then a third time. Nothing. I knock, but no sounds come from inside the house, which is painted the weirdest color: a pale powdery pink that makes it look like a giant after-dinner mint.

There are probably a hundred other things a teenager would rather do than hang out with a thirty-six-year-old on a Sunday afternoon. I peer into Crystal's empty living room. Everything is tidy and sparse—a TV with little flags of tinfoil attached to the antennae, a sofa with square red pillows nestled neatly at each end.

Finally I give up and jot a note on the back of a checkbook deposit slip for Crystal: *I stopped by, but you weren't in,* I write, wanting to sound casual. *Call you later. Sophie.* I tuck the note in the mailbox so that one corner's sticking out. As I head back down the porch steps, I don't feel like a very big Big.

Stepping onto the front walk, I notice a white starfishlike clump in the grass. I jump when I realize it's a hand, palm open, fingers spread wide. The long sleeve of a navy blue sweatshirt snakes into the rhododendron. I crouch and peer into the bushes, where I see Crystal sprawled on her back, arms and legs spread open as if she's making a snow angel.

"Crystal?"

"Yeah?" A white wisp of breath curls up from her mouth.

"Hi."

She rolls her head to look at me. "I was waiting for you," she says. Her smoky blue eyes are outlined in heavy black liner, and her lips shimmer with pink gloss.

"Usually people wait in the house or on the porch." I laugh nervously, realizing this isn't particularly funny.

"No shit! My mom told me to wait outside."

"In the bushes?" My thighs ache from my morning jog. I sit cross-legged on the cold, hard sidewalk.

"She's a bitch."

"I see. Well, what would you like to do today?"

Crystal turns onto her side and hoists herself up onto her elbow, resting her head in her palm. A crescent of short blond hair falls across her forehead. "Do you have a cigarette?"

"Sure, I have a cigarette and some crack. Would you like some? *No,* I don't have a cigarette. I don't smoke. And if I did, I wouldn't give you one, silly."

Crystal rolls her eyes and collapses back onto the ground, squinting through the bushes. Already I feel as though I'm not fun or cool. I want to be cool. I wish Ethan were here. He wouldn't be shy or nervous. For a computer nerd, he was cool.

Crystal reminds me of those girls in junior high who were sexy and moody and gravelly-voiced early on, while the rest of us still piled stuffed animals on our beds. I remember cowering in the last stall in the girls' room as they smoked and talked about the boys they planned on cornering behind the gym after school. Crystal doesn't look as voluptuous as those girls, though; she's too skinny and childlike.

She rolls over suddenly, crawls out of the bushes, and stands up, the hood of her big sweatshirt falling onto her shoulders. Her jeans are slung low around her narrow waist, with flared bell-bottoms tattered and caked with mud. She smacks dirt from her hands. "*Dude,*" she says. "Let's go to the movies."

. . .

"Nice wheels," Crystal says of my Honda as we head toward Medford to the multiplex.

"Thanks. It's practically the only thing I *own* right now. Except for cardboard boxes of stuff."

She rests the waffle soles of her clunky platform sneakers on the dashboard and jams two sticks of gum into her mouth. "How come?"

"Just moved here."

"You mean you, like, live in this hick hole on *purpose?*"

"Yes. And I wouldn't exactly call Shakespeare a hick."

"You work at the festival?"

"No."

Silence. Gum snapping. "Seen the plays?"

"I hope to see all of them."

Crystal turns up the heat. "My class went last year?" She poses most of her statements as questions. "Sucked hard core."

I try not to seem alarmed by Crystal's language.

"If you like plays, you'll like this movie." She juts a chunk of newspaper in my face to show me an R-rated movie circled in pen. I've read reviews and I know there's lots of sex and swearing involved.

"Oh." I push the paper away so I can see the road. "Well, that's rated R. How about we compromise and pick a PG-13 movie?"

"How is that a compromise, chiquita? My mom doesn't care if I see an R-rated movie. You want to call her?" Crystal cracks her knuckles, pulls a cell phone out of her jacket pocket, and flashes it at me. "I'm not allowed to call anyone but my mom on this. It's like the Mom Police hotline. She's at work. We can ask her."

"Okay," I agree warily. Already I'm faltering! I should be able to put the kibosh on this movie without having to bother Crystal's mother.

Crystal presses one button on her phone and it automatically dials a number. She shoves it across the seat toward me and the next thing I know there's a voice on the other end.

"Roxanne Lowman," a woman says briskly. I explain that Crystal wants to see an R-rated show.

"It's a coming-of-age story," Roxanne says, annoyed. "It's better to be open with teenagers than to try to hide everything. Teenagers *have* sex, you know."

"I, uh . . ." They do? *Crystal* does? I look at her across the seat, her arms and legs as thin and delicate as willow tree branches.

"Okay," I tell her mother, trying to sound confident.

"See?" Crystal says, vindicated as she snaps the phone shut. "All my mom cares about is that my grades don't fall below a C average and that I don't go to jail. She's, like, all about attaining a respectable level of mediocrity."

This seems a sadly grown-up interpretation for a thirteen-year-old.

In the theater, Crystal takes a long sip from her barrel-size Coke, then tugs at the straw with her teeth, making it squeak loudly.

"*Hush,*" scolds one of two college-age boys in front of us.

"Okay, douche bag," Crystal says, lightly kicking the back of the boy's seat with her chunky sneaker. I doubt she'll ever want to play checkers or sing along to *The Sound of Music.*

He snaps around and glares at me, and I shrug.

"Sorry," I whisper.

Crystal giggles.

"Watch the language," I tell her.

She huffs a sigh and crosses and recrosses her arms and legs. She's in constant fidgeting motion, as though her bones are trying to get out of her body. I wonder if what she really wants is someone to set boundaries for her. Maybe I just need to work up a tough-love shtick. I'd rather call Big Brothers/Big Sisters and ask for a younger, easier-to-manage kid. A little girl with pigtails who would want to color or bake. But I know I should give Crystal more of a chance. No one said this would be easy.

The movie starts and there's tons of swearing and sex. Crystal finally stops fidgeting, her mouth hanging open, her pointed chin still. I swear next Sunday will be different: Jiffy Pop and a game of Risk by the fire.

"Married?" Crystal asks, pointing at my wedding ring. She digs into the whipped cream and nuts cascading over the giant banana split I bought her after the movie. So far I've established myself as a pushover, letting her mow through all the popcorn, soda, and ice cream she wants. But it looks as though she could use a few extra pounds.

"Widowed." I take a bite of pralines and cream.

"What happened?"

"Cancer."

"How come you still wear the ring?" Crystal doesn't swerve tactfully around the questions everybody really wants to ask.

"It's not like I'm divorced."

"But you're not married and you're, like, *never* going to get a boyfriend if you wear that thing." She raises her eyebrows and nods at the ring.

My ice cream is bland and waxy. Suddenly I would rather not be sitting at Baskin-Robbins with Crystal. I've run away from Silicon Valley to Ruth's house, and I've run away from Ruth's house to the movies with Crystal, and now I want to run away from Crystal to the rest room and lock myself in a stall for six months, surviving on Lifesavers and purse lint.

"That's not the point," I tell her. "Anyway. Your house is an unusual color."

"Yeah, my mom likes pink. Hello! What a freak show!" Her eyes brighten. "Hey, you can buy me beer."

"I'm not buying you beer. And we're not seeing any more R-rated movies, either."

"What*ever.*" There's fudge sauce on her chin, and I resist the impulse to lick my thumb and rub it off. I push my ice cream aside and watch her eat, noticing for the first time that there are pea-size red rings across the tops of her hands. Some have rusty scabs, while others shine like red licorice. Crystal catches my gaze and tugs the sleeves of her too big sweatshirt over her hands, bunching the fabric in her fists.

After digging around in her black backpack, she pulls out a compact of blush. She rubs her forefinger into the pink cream and dabs it across her cheeks. It's too bright and uneven, making her look a little like a clown.

"Let me help you." Laughing, I get up to sit next to her. (As if I'm the makeup pro!) She doesn't move over to make room, and I have to balance on the edge of the booth, inhaling her cigarette and baby powder smells. As I rub my fingers in circles over her cheeks to even out the color, she tips her chin up and closes her eyes.

"Your skin looks pretty without makeup," I tell her, studying the thick globs of eyeliner stuck in her lashes. "You should skip it."

"I already look like I'm about ten years old." She wrinkles her nose. "I need all the help I can get."

I rub what's left of the blush onto a napkin.

She checks her reflection in the blush's dusty mirror, clicks her mouth in disgust, then snaps the compact shut. "I'm the smallest girl in my class." She wraps her arms around her chest. "You know, *here.*" I sneak a closer look at the mottled red rings on the tops of her hands.

"What are these?" I brush my fingers over the welts, which are surprisingly smooth.

"Nothing." She shoves her hands in her lap.

"Are you sure?" Her chest whistles faintly as she breathes. I remember that the Big Brothers counselor told me that Crystal has asthma and that I should remind her to carry her inhaler on our outings. "What happened?"

"I burned myself." She licks her mouth and looks sideways at me, edging away.

"How?"

"With a cigarette."

"On purpose?"

"*No*, you think?"

Crystal's sarcasm is irritating and heartbreaking at the same time. "You should use an ashtray next time."

"Hah, hah."

"I'm not kidding."

"What*ever.*"

She clutches her backpack to her chest. I change the subject, pointing to the silver band just below the knuckle on her thumb. "That's pretty."

"It's my father's wedding band." She sits up straighter. "My mother, like, threw it in the *garbage,* but I found it."

"Where does he live?"

She licks the back of her spoon and shrugs.

"Does he ever visit or call?"

"He called from a place in Arizona once and left a message? But when I dialed the number that he left, the lady who answered could, like, *barely* speak English and she didn't know who my father was. I think my stupid mother wrote his number down wrong. He probably thinks I never called back and that's why he never called again. He probably thinks I don't *want* to talk to him."

At least the possibility of a wrong number means it could all be an accident.

"He looks like Mel Gibson," Crystal adds, pushing aside her empty goblet and burping.

"Wow."

"Yeah. I don't blame him for leaving my mother. She's such a bitch. I can't believe I have to live with her. It's like being held *hostage*."

I can't imagine having this much disdain for my mother. When I was Crystal's age, my mother was dead and I missed her so much that sometimes it hurt to breathe. In junior high there was a TV ad for salad dressing in which a mother in a red-and-white-checked apron showed her daughter how to fix salad. "You must never cut the lettuce, but always gently tear it," the mother explained kindly but firmly to the daughter as they broke up chunks of iceberg and tossed them into a wooden salad bowl. I assumed all mothers, except maybe Joan Crawford, were like this, and I wanted my mother to come back and insist that I be gentle with lettuce and wear a sweater and use sunblock.

"Hey, how come you don't live someplace cool, like L.A.?" Crystal asks.

"I don't feel up to L.A."

"Why?"

"It's expensive and I don't know anyone there."

"I'll bet it's killer."

"You've never been?"

She shakes her head.

"Well, maybe we can go one day. Maybe we could see the taping of a show."

"*Dude!* Maybe we'd see rock stars."

Crystal bounces in her seat, and I realize I probably shouldn't make promises I may not be able to keep.

Waitressing

13

"Whatever," Crystal says when I call to ask her if she'd like to visit my new house for a barbecue on Sunday.

I picture her on her sofa, cradling the phone between her chin and shoulder so she can use both hands to examine her split ends. She has a way of sitting so that she's nearly horizontal, slouched down with her head tipped against the back of a chair or sofa, long skinny legs stretched out in front of her.

"Okay, Miss Enthusiastic."

"Well, it's like, *March*."

"The barbecue still works, and you'll like my new place. It's got tons of rooms and a ghost."

"What*ever*."

I hang up wondering how many more weeks I can handle this level of disdain. Or is it just indifference? Crystal doesn't seem to have any more disdain for me than she does for the rest of the world. I'll try not to take it personally for now.

"Whatever" is her answer to most questions. She has two ways of saying it. She either exhales a weary "Whatever," as though the thought of doing anything other than preening her split ends is too enervating, or she indignantly snaps, "What*ever*," as though the question is a personal attack. I'd like to adopt this approach.

Sophie, your husband died.

"What*ever*."

And you're fired.

"As if I even *liked* that job."

And you're depleting your savings with no means of income in sight.

"That is *so* not a problem. I could, like, *totally* get a new job."

And that, of course, is what I must do.

As I crack open the classifieds the next morning, my stomach burns and there's a raw, bitter taste in the back of my throat. Job hunting means job *interview*.

The newspaper feels dry and chalky, and ink smudges my fingertips. Fortunately, there are no "real" jobs in Ashland in the winter. No listings under Marketing or Public Relations. Waitressing lingers between Underwriting and Welding. I never waitressed in college. While I shelved books in the library, other women in my dorm *cocktailed*—donning nylon heart-shaped black aprons with pockets that bulged with dollar bills and artfully balancing glasses overflowing with beer on tiny trays. But this isn't what I tell Bill, the food and beverage manager at Le Petit Bistro on East Main Street.

"You've waitressed before?" he asks, scanning my application.

"Right! In college." I didn't plan on lying. I planned on admitting that I didn't have any waitressing experience but that I'm confident I can do the job. I seem to have left that confidence in the car, however, and now I'm fibbing my way into the restaurant industry.

We sit in a booth at the back of the bistro, which emits a dark pinkish glow—lit only by little Tiffany-style lamps on the tables. Bill wears a stiff white dress shirt and a tie dotted with martini glasses. I think he's the dressiest person I've seen in Ashland.

"What's your long-term goal?" he asks, leaning across the red-checkered tablecloth. "I imagine it's not waitressing?"

The dining room smells like burned butter and pine cleaner. I'm not sure what to tell Bill. To make it through a year in Ashland? To wake up in the morning twelve months from now and not want to dive back under the covers and hide? Maybe one morning a year from now there will be a bit of news on the clock radio that I'd like to share with Ethan—who won the World Series or who's running for president. But this won't make me cry. Instead, I'll think of my husband and smile, flicking away grief the way you'd brush off a fly or piece of lint. Then I'll climb into the shower and iron a crisp white shirt like Bill's to wear to work here at Le Petit Bistro.

Bill leans closer and blinks.

"Not to spill anything," I tell him, and laugh. I pinch the creases in my khakis, which I ironed over and over this morning.

Bill laughs a dry laugh and cocks his head. "What would you say your strengths are?"

Strengths? Certainly not leading department meetings or wearing panty hose. Hopefully memorizing specials. Strengths. I can peel an apple in one long spiral.

I'm still not saying anything when Bill moves on to the next question: "Weaknesses?"

Real butter. Kodak ads featuring husbands or mothers.

Bill skips to the next question. "How do you work under pressure?"

Crumble, weep, wear my bathrobe to work. "Pretty good," I tell him. I mean, how hard can waitressing be?

Here's how hard waitressing can be: Try balancing a tray loaded with entrées on your shoulder without stooping like Groucho Marx. Try opening a stubborn bottle of Merlot without snapping the cork in two and pouring cork crumbs into diners' glasses as they squint and frown. Try remembering who ordered the escargots and who ordered the onion soup and who wanted their dressing *on the side, please, I said on the side!*

A week into the job, I'm struggling to navigate a scalding plate of shrimp scampi around an older, bargelike woman who's flailing her arms as she tells a Shakespeare festival actor and his date a story about trying to hail a cab in New York City.

The actor is handsome, with a square chin and deep dimples. He smiles at me and suddenly I'm self-conscious in my uniform of black pants, white dress shirt, and black vest. I probably look as though I should be playing the piano at Nordstrom. His actress girlfriend or wife who sits next to him is all Isadora Duncan scarves and eyeliner. She crosses her slender, shapely arms and raises a tweezed brow at me.

"Here we go!" I announce, trying to slide the big woman's entrée under her gesticulating arms and onto the table in front of her. The scalding plate burns through my towel and into my fingertips. Suddenly her baseball bat of an arm swings through the air to make a point, sending her plate careening out of my hand and shrimp scampi splashing across her back. Hot oily sauce hits a wedge of flesh above her collar, and shrimps tumble down her gray wool suit. She pops out of the booth and does a dance, because now one or two shrimp seem to be *inside* her blouse.

The actor's eyes widen, but he doesn't say anything. I realize that he's the one playing Hamlet this year. I remember him from a dress rehearsal I sneaked into—how my pulse pounded when he cried, "O God, God / How weary, stale, flat and unprofitable / Seem to me all the uses of this world!"

The woman in the suit swats madly at her back with her napkin. Meanwhile, the two entrées that I've left on the tray stand aren't centered and the whole thing flops over, dumping the other dinners on the floor. The classical piano CD pounds to a crescendo. The actress girlfriend suppresses a giggle. I try to help the flailing woman, who is peeling off her jacket and throwing it on the floor. Her face is red and her eyes bulge. The actor is trying to help her, too, standing with a glass of water as if he's not sure whether to pour it on her. He tells me not to worry, it wasn't my fault; it certainly wasn't my fault.

Bill rounds the corner by the coffee machine, his martini tie flapping as he hustles over, panting, "What the . . . ?"

On Sunday I drag the barbecue out of the garage and set it up on the lawn by the side porch. Cooking makes me feel disoriented; some of my kitchen stuff is still in storage and I can't find tongs or salt and pepper shakers. I imagine my belongings dividing into smaller and smaller subsets, like cells dividing, until all I've got is a pair of socks and a few old *National Geographics*.

While I loathed the quiet cavernousness of my house in California after Ethan was gone, I miss living in my own place now. In the mornings before work, I wander through Colonel Cranson's bedrooms, running my hands over the bumpy chenille bedspreads, fingering the soft fringe on the yellowing lampshades, and sniffing the odorless china bowls of potpourri, tiny dried roses, and cedar chips coated with dust. Everything in the house is pretty, but few things are mine. I'm a visitor, temporary.

Crystal gets to work building a fire in the barbecue that worries me: newspaper rolled into tight logs, followed by a heap of dry sticks and leaves, then a mound of charcoal. Although it's a balmy spring day, the sun making the roofs steam, she wears her usual heavy uniform of low-rider bell-bottom jeans and a giant hooded sweatshirt.

"Let *me*," she says, swiping the lighter fluid from my hand. She pumps the can several times, a long silver stream arcing over the charcoal.

"Okay, enough!" Sometimes it seems her goal in life is to make people nervous.

She slides a pack of matches out of her back pocket, and with one hand and one swift movement—like a magic trick—she flips them open, lights a match, and tosses it onto the grill. The newspaper and branches snap and crackle. Then the fire explodes with a *whoosh*, orange flames shooting above Crystal's shoulders and licking the wisteria branches on the trellis overhead. I leap back, swatting at her.

"Give me that." I grab the lighter fluid. "Gosh!"

She lets go of the can but doesn't look at me. She's entranced by the flames cascading over the edge of the grill.

I sit on the edge of the porch, setting the lighter fluid behind me, and wipe my forehead with the back of my sleeve. The fire methodically pops and chews through sticks and newspaper. I hope the neighbors aren't home to see the black smoke curling over the fence. They're friends with the owners of Colonel Cranson's and I want them to think I'm a good tenant.

I've set the little wrought-iron table on the porch with plates, napkins, silverware, goblets of iced tea, and three kinds of toppings for our baked potatoes. It looks silly now—not something a thirteen-year-old would enjoy.

Crystal rips open a bag of marshmallows, jams one on the end of a stick, and shoves it into the flames. It instantly ignites and droops, falling into the fire. She stomps her foot in the grass. While grocery shopping for the steaks and marshmallows, I pictured us making s'mores, just as in Girl Scouts. I'd earn the Big Sister Badge, while Crystal earned the Learning to Behave Badge. But now Crystal grabs the plate of steaks from the table and tosses the meat onto the grill.

"Not yet!" I jump up from the porch.

The steaks sizzle and hiss. Crystal snatches the lighter fluid and pumps more into the flames. A tube of black smoke spirals toward the sky. She lunges toward the fire, as though she'd like to climb into it. I grab her arm.

"Crystal!" My mouth is dry and tastes metallic, like smoke and lighter fluid. Crystal doesn't seem to hear me. Her bicep is sinewy and strong, and I can't loosen the lighter fluid from her grip. I reach my arms around her, trying to grab the can, thinking: *I am in over my head here.*

"Quit it!" Crystal shrieks, reeling around. My arm is hooked inside of hers, and she sends us both stumbling into the barbecue, tipping it over with a crashing clang like cymbals. Flaming paper and coals tumble into a pile of raked leaves. I end up on top of Crystal, staring into her face. Her cheeks are flushed magenta and her forehead is beaded with sweat. I crawl over her and get up.

A stick in the leaves whistles, then spikes into a sharp flame. I stomp it out. The leaves smolder and smoke, then an obstinate arm of fire snakes through them. I can't find the hose anywhere. Finally, I see it lying in a tangle at the end of the porch. The stubborn faucet is sharp in my hand. I twist it on and drag the hose toward the leaves. A lazy stream of water dribbles onto the low flames, dousing them. Then the wind picks up again, sending smoldering leaves under the porch.

Crystal leaps back as though the water is more dangerous than the flames around her.

"Help me!" I shout at her. My nose stings and my eyes water. She snatches our glasses from the table and tosses iced tea at the fire.

"Don't worry," she grumbles, lighting a cigarette. "It's pretty much out."

Crouching on my hands and knees, I try to peer under the porch. It's too dark to see anything. Perspiration drenches my face and neck. I glance up at the house, which looks old and fragile, and decide it would be best to have the fire department check everything. I head inside to make the call, leaving the hose running under the porch.

When I return to the yard, Crystal is leaning against the garage, smoking.

"What were you thinking?" I pluck the singed steaks out of the grass and toss them on a plate.

"I was bored." She gets to work examining her split ends, the lit cigarette dangling between two fingers.

"You were *bored*? So you thought you'd light the yard on fire?"

She makes a clicking noise with her tongue and rolls her eyes.

"It's time for you to go home," I tell her quietly. "That's all the action I can handle in an afternoon."

"Can we go to McDonald's?"

"No. You need to go *home*." I sink my teeth into my lower lip so I won't say anything more.

"But I'm hungry," Crystal whines.

"Now, damn it!" I point toward the street. I'm supposed to be a mentor, to lead by example. But aren't there any guidelines for the little sisters?

"Okay." Crystal's voice lowers and she sniffles. Maybe she *wants* me to yell at her. Ruth says kids want you to be firm, to set boundaries. Crystal flicks her cigarette in the grass and stomps on it.

"Take that with you." I point at the cigarette butt. She picks it up and cups it in her hand, wrapping her arms around her chest, folding herself inward. Her platform sneakers clomp loudly as she crosses the porch. The screen door creaks as she opens it. She pauses, turns toward me.

"Later, dude."

I don't say anything.

After I hear the front door of the house click shut, I collapse, sitting on the edge of the porch. I tip my head back and look up at the sky. It's bluish white and looks thin, like fabric that's been stretched too tight. In the distance I hear the wail of a siren and the impatient blare of a fire engine horn. I subdue a howl that lingers like a flame in the back of my throat.

That night, I dream that Crystal's been burned badly in a fire. She lies still and flat in a hospital bed, her gown dotted with the familiar blue snowflakes, her pointed face as black and leathery as burned meat. Her hair is matted to her head, stinking like singed carpet. Her blue eyes twinkle like marbles and peer up at me, imploring, pleading, but I'm not sure what she wants. Morphine? Ice cream?

"Honey, can you hear me?" I say, and I'm not sure why I'm calling her honey. This is what a mother calls a daughter. Crystal raises a stiff arm toward me, her hands mottled with red rings, rust-colored foam bubbling up around the wounds. I feel guilty, because I don't want to touch her. Hopefully she'll fall asleep so I can leave. I back away from the bed, trying to think of a reason to get out.

"I'll be right back," I gurgle. "I forgot something." I turn toward the door and Ethan's there, in a wheelchair, sunken eyes, chattering teeth, a Foley bag bulging with too-yellow urine. I want to hug him, but I don't want to touch him.

I turn back toward Crystal. Her brown monkey hand reaches for me. Her eyes are sharp, wanting to know why I'm leaving. I can't leave anyway, because my feet won't go. They are heavy and numb and welded to the floor.

When I awaken, I'm already sitting up. Something presses on my chest, and my pulse pounds in my temples. My arms are asleep, prickly and heavy as logs. I shake and pinch them. A sour burned taste sticks in the back of my throat, and I'm sure a whorl of smoke hovers by the ceiling; when I snap on the light and fumble for my glasses, it vanishes. Every surface of the room is papered with swirling calico wallpaper, even the ceiling and the light switch plates. When I close my eyes I still see the dizzying sprays of cornflowers.

I try to calm myself by slowly inhaling and exhaling, but my lungs fill only partway. Something woolen clogs them. I imagine my lungs shrinking until they are as small as kidney beans, only two teaspoons of air for my whole body.

"I'm having a heart attack!" I shout into the room. My voice sounds thin and strange. The wood floors glisten sternly. A walnut from the tree in the yard blasts the roof. I stumble out of bed, pull on jeans and a sweatshirt, grab my purse, keys, and coat, and lunge out of the house into the moist night.

At the emergency room I can't sit down. Driving fifty miles per hour down the quiet streets of Ashland, I failed to realize that I was driving myself right back into my nightmare: the hospital. Suddenly I picture Ethan sick and curled in bed, the covers a white snarl around his shrunken waist.

I pace in front of a woman whose husband fell and hit his head on a wood stove. Her eyes dart back and forth from the big black clock on the wall to the clerk sitting behind a sliding glass window.

When I was a teenager, I baby-sat for a very literal-minded boy who thought that Colonel Sanders actually worked at every Kentucky Fried Chicken and Jesus actually lived in every church. This is how I think of Ethan—that he's somewhere in every hospital now. That's where I last saw him, where I left him. I imagine he might roll by on a gurney, thin white arms reaching toward me.

A doctor wearing pale green scrubs hustles down a nearby corridor. I remember loathing that green—the color of illness and surgery. The color of death. I *had* to come to the hospital tonight, though; I don't want to die of a heart attack at home alone, where no one would find me for days. I picture the polite but finicky bowtie man who sits at the same table in my section every Thursday night at Le Petit Bistro and orders the Caesar salad and coq au vin with no garnish because he can't stand parsley. He might pipe up eventually and ask, "Where's my usual waitress?" Then Bill might show up at Colonel Cranson's and find me sprawled in some sad corner of the house.

The clerk behind the admissions desk yawns and stretches. Things are moving too slowly here. Adrenaline is sharp and bright in my blood, and I want to run to my car and drive back to San Jose, the Honda slicing down I-5, my heart a rocket in my chest. I should call Ruth. I should call Dad. I should call some Person in Case of Emergency.

"Sophie Stanton?" a voice calls through the emergency room door.

I sit alone on a gurney behind a curtain gulping air until a tired-looking doctor in a white coat appears. He presses two cushiony fingertips to my wrist, studying the floor thoughtfully as he takes my pulse. Then he tips up my chin and peers into my eyes with a sharp white light. His hair is silvery gray and cut short. It looks soft, like a dandelion. I have the urge to cup it with the palm of my hand.

"I'm thinking this is merely your garden-variety panic attack," he says a little apologetically, resting a warm palm on my shoulder. "Been under stress lately?" He straddles a black stool and wheels it up to the edge of the examining table.

I explain that my husband died, I just moved here, and I'm trying to learn to wait tables without throwing boiling shrimp on people. I stop talking, embarrassed that I'm taking his time away from patients who are truly sick or injured.

The doctor smiles. He pulls a prescription pad out of the pocket of his white jacket.

"These will help you sleep." He scribbles out a prescription. I explain that I'm already on antidepressants, but he says these tranquilizers are okay to take occasionally, too.

I clutch the slip of paper a little too hard, and it crumples.

"You can take them during the day, but not if you're going to drive."

"Thank you."

"I'm also going to have you checked out by a cardiologist." He writes a doctor's name and number on another sheet. "Just remember, though," he says, patting my arm, "the death of a loved one, moving, and changing jobs are among the most stressful events in life."

Ha. Three down. I've scored a hat trick. I want to go home with this dandelion doctor, become his adopted teenage daughter, and lie on his sofa all day, drinking coffee milkshakes and reading movie star magazines.

The cardiologist wants to run a few tests, which worries me. That's how it all started with Ethan. *Probably nothing. (Reassuring slap on the back.) Let's just order a few tests to be sure.*

For twenty-four hours I wear a monitor strapped to my chest that records my pulse as I scramble eggs and dash from the house to the car, chased by the neighbor's belligerent German shepherd.

Back at the hospital, I have an echocardiogram, lying under a nubby cotton blanket in a dark room while a technician moves a wand across my chest, ultrasound peeking at my insides. At the foot of the bed I watch my heart, a squishy frog of a thing on a black-and-white TV screen. It looks lonely in its murky surroundings.

Cheer up, I want to tell it. *You look good.*

My heartbeat creeps along the bottom of the screen. *What if in the end, you're all alone?* it seems to say. *The shrinks, doctors, grief groups. None of them can help.*

"This is some kind of machine," I tell the technician.

"Un-hunh. I know it," she says.

I ask her about her degree, how long it took her to learn to run the contraption. Maybe this is a job for me. I'd like to spend my days in this warm, quiet room, keeping tabs on people's hearts.

The technician smiles and tells me I better hold still.

The cardiologist calls a few days later to report that my tests are fine. He suggests that I drink plenty of fluids and get enough sleep and exercise. He adds that I can take the tranquilizers as needed.

Negative test results! This is the relief I craved when Ethan first got sick. That's when I wanted the doctor to peer over his reading glasses and say calmly, *It's nothing. You can go home now.* Instead, he nervously straightened the manila folders on his desk, checked his watch, cleared his throat, and began discussing options.

14

What if I have a panic attack at *work*? I ponder this possibility the next morning as I'm pressing my blouse and vest. I lean into the iron too hard and the vest starts to melt like caramel.

What if suddenly I get that wool sock sensation in my lungs and can't breathe or speak to the customers, can't ask them if they'd like a baked potato or rice? What if I'm in the middle of taking an order and my throat closes up and I cough and choke and have to hide in the bathroom or drive back to the emergency room?

I yank the iron's plug from the wall and bolt into the kitchen. After digging the bottle of tranquilizers from my purse, I crank off the childproof top and tap two tablets into my palm. They're the comforting pale peach color of baby aspirin. I swallow them, then slip on my vest and sit at the kitchen table. Nothing. I lace up my sensible black rubber-soled work shoes and try eating a piece of toast. But my throat won't open. The doctor at the hospital said that I shouldn't take the tranquilizers every day, but rather keep them in case of emergency, like a fire extinguisher. This morning the blaze seems insatiable. As I delve into the bottle for a few more of the tablets, I think of the helicopters that fly over forest fires dumping buckets of flame retardant from the sky.

I swallow another pill with a few sips of juice, then another. Finally my throat loosens. I wedge the clip-on bow tie under my collar and head off on my walk to Le Petit Bistro, the trees outside seeming more affectionate than usual.

I arrive at work to discover that the restaurant is underwater now. Everything is dreamy and blue. The other waiters swim and float by me, words bubbling out of their mouths toward the surface of the room. As I approach my first table of customers, a three-top, I feel rubbery, boneless, and decide it would be best if I sat down. I slide into the booth beside a man in a lovely gray jacket. I wonder if it's flannel or wool and explore its mossy surface with my fingertips. Very nice.

"Let me tell you about the thpethals," I begin. While I don't know these people, I do love them. I ask the woman sitting across from me where she got her fabulous pink-and-red silk scarf. I adore how older folks dress up for the theater. She fingers the scarf and looks at her husband.

The man next to me removes my hand from his sleeve and sets it in my lap, where it looks strange and far away. Bad hand! The couple sitting across from me leans over the table in unison, swimming my way, their mouths parted, lips forming fishy Os.

"Do you work here?" the man asks.

"Serpently," I tell him. "I do." But my head doesn't want to stay up anymore. I lay my cheek on the tablecloth, which is stiff with starch.

"Sophie, get *up.*" That would be the voice of Bill, the food and beverage manager. He leads me to a chair in the back of the restaurant and sits me down by the coat rack. "Have you been drinking?" Instead of waiting for an answer, he rushes back to the table and apologizes to the customers. I hear him say "recently pickled." Or maybe it's "recently widowed." Bill calls a cab to take me home. I clutch the coat rack for support, hoist myself up, and drag it like an IV pole across the crowded room.

"Good Gob," I hear Bill mumble as the door of the restaurant thumps me in the rear on my way out.

I sleep for thirteen hours, and when I awaken, Ethan is whispering in my ear. He wants to know why I didn't pick him up at the airport. "I had to catch a cab, silly," he murmurs, caressing my arm. He's been in New York, meeting with stock analysts. His company's going public, the market's soaring, and I can quit my waitressing job now. We're going to fly to Paris for a week and sit at sidewalk cafés, sipping strong coffee out of china cups as white as bones, the sun warming our backs, Ethan's hair glowing golden. His fingers tickle my arm and I giggle.

The doorbell rings and I open my eyes, enveloped by the expanse of white ceiling above me. I'm still in my clothes. My sleeves are rolled up and the lace curtain by the bed brushes my arm. I'm usually relieved to awaken from a dream about Ethan, because he's always sick in my dreams. There's at least one cancer detail—a mottled IV bruise or the row of brown prescription bottles lining the kitchen windowsill, each with its troubling side effect. But this was a cancer-free dream. The pain of Ethan being there and then not being there shoots to the pit of my stomach, and I grab a handful of the bristly lace curtain, desperate for something to hang on to.

The doorbell rings again. I let go of the curtain and get up to see who's at the door.

Ruth stands on the porch, her cheeks flushed, shooting a look of concern at my mailbox.

"This mailbox is no good." She's glamorous even in frump mode—shapely calves outlined in leggings, a bulky sweatshirt, and square-toed hiking boots that make her look as though she walked out of an L. L. Bean catalog. Her face is freshly scrubbed and her hair is pulled back in a high ponytail, shining in the sunlight. "People can steal your identity."

My head feels heavy, and the mail seems like too much to deal with right now. "They can have my identity," I tell Ruth. "My vanishing waistline and minuscule checkbook balance and lousy waitressing skills." The fact that I've probably lost my job.

"Aren't we optimistic!" Ruth scoops the mail out of the box, steps inside, and sets it on the table in the hall. "How come you can be cheerleader for me but not for yourself?" She tugs off her hiking boots.

"Sorry. Horning in on your job as chief pessimist."

"Ha!" She gives me a quick hug, then scans my outfit. "On your way to work? Or are you going to perform a magic show?"

I yank off the bow tie. "Ha, ha. On my way home. Sort of." I don't want to tell Ruth about my mishap. I finally got a job and now I'm screwing it up.

Her eyes dart past me into the living room. "Well, I need a cocktail."

In the kitchen, Ruth opens the refrigerator and discovers there's nothing inside but a bag of oranges and a carton of nonfat sour cream.

"I decided the best way to lose weight is to stop buying food." I duck my head under the tap and drink water from the faucet, closing my eyes, the liquid a cool silver creek against the back of my throat.

"Your inner critic is delusional. You've got a very cute figure." Ruth roots through the empty cupboards, rings on the checked shelf paper where bottles and jars once sat.

"Yeah, well, I can't zip my jeans."

"Reality check: The world won't end if you go up a size."

"Reality check: I've already gone up two sizes. I've sprouted third and fourth buttocks." I pirouette to show Ruth my rear.

"Don't be ridiculous." She climbs onto a chair, cracks open the cupboard high above the refrigerator, and finds a bottle of Mount Gay rum.

"Bingo," she says.

"There's a store down the street," I tell her.

Ruth's remarkably resourceful, though. She earned *every* badge in Girl Scouts, even the esoteric Textile and Fibers Badge and the Weather Watch Badge. She slices and juices the oranges, crushes ice in the blender, pours in the rum, then adds confectioner's sugar she finds caked in the bottom of a box.

As we sink into the sofa in the living room, dust swirls out of the flowered damask fabric.

"Cheers," Ruth says, clinking my glass.

"Cheers." I take a shallow sip and the rum warms my chest going down. But my tongue is mossy from the tranquilizers, and my brain feels about as useful as a clump of masking tape. The last thing I need is a drink. I set down my glass, and Ruth and I prop our feet side by side on the coffee table.

"He wants to come back," Ruth says.

"Tony?"

"Mark. He wants to come home."

"Home? What happened to Missy?"

"He claims he never loved her. That she was his midlife crisis, which is over." A rim of orange foam lines Ruth's upper lip. "He misses Simone and wants to come home."

"Are you going to let him?"

She takes another neat sip of her drink, wipes her mouth. "He *is* Simone's father."

While I always liked Mark, I want Ruth to meet someone new, someone wonderful—maybe a professor at the university, or even the university president—and live happily ever after, filling her house with babies and feeding them fresh-squeezed orange juice with confectioner's sugar.

"He'll still be Simone's father," I remind her, "even if he doesn't move back in."

Ruth lays a hand over mine. Her long fingers are cool and

smooth against my skin. She's wearing her wedding ring, which I haven't seen since I've been in Oregon.

"You put your ring back on?"

She nods, takes her hand back. "You never took yours *off.*"

I shrug and circle my ring around on my finger. After Ethan and I were married, I had my engagement ring and wedding band melded into one interlocking piece. The soft gold tugs at my swollen flesh, and the small, bright diamond is sharp under my thumb. "I guess the diamond would look pretty in a brooch or something," I say.

"I guess mine would look pretty hocked and in a bank account." Ruth yanks off her ring and tosses it clanking onto the table. "Fah! Fruit salad!" she curses. "What was I thinking?"

"That maybe you and Mark could get back together and become a family again. That everything might work out somehow. We're trying to be optimistic, remember?"

Ruth closes her eyes. After a minute, she nods at my ring. "How long do you think you'll wear yours?"

"Good question." I should probably have taken it off by now. Moved it to some less married locale, such as a simple gold chain around my neck. I tug the ring over my knuckle and set it on the coffee table next to Ruth's.

I recall the panic that used to pass over me whenever I slipped off the ring in the bathroom, how any open drain looked gaping and greedy. Now, an itchy indentation circles my ring finger, which feels much lighter than the others, as though it might fly away. I sit on my hand, squashing it. The pressure is a relief.

"It's okay if you want to wear it," Ruth says. She's always easier on others than she is on herself. If she was widowed, she would have had that ring off two weeks after the funeral, her naked willowy fingers steadily writing out mortgage checks and a poignant obituary for the alumni magazine. She'd use the same self-discipline she used for studying in college, marching off to the library while the rest of us procrastinated over foosball and beer. That's why I can't understand why she's caving in to Tony and Mark.

I tell myself I don't need to wear my ring anymore. Ethan will still be woven around my fingers like a glove. Leaning to one side, I press my weight onto my hand, which is numb and tingly.

I consider our rings sitting on the table. They look pretty and hopeful, like girls waiting to be asked to dance.

When I arrive at work later that afternoon, Bill wants to see me in his office. I follow him past the bar, where the other waiters fold napkins in silence. Usually they joke and gossip, but today they frown at the napkins. Maybe they know something I don't; maybe I'm going to get fired. Fired for the second time in six months. I breathe in the smell of burning butter and the dizzying fumes of the brass polish that the bartender's rubbing into the railing along the bar. I follow Bill down the hall to his office. His scalp shows pink and shiny through the hair on the back of his head. He closes his door.

"Have a seat," he says, pointing to the chair in front of his desk. I was called to the principal's office once in high school, when I wrote a paper for Danny Glutcher, a track star who lightened his hair with lemon juice and had a knack for getting people to do things for him. The paper was on *The Scarlet Letter*, and it was a little too passionate to be a boy's essay—a little too sympathetic toward Hester.

The dark brown wood paneling in Bill's office closes in on us. A paperweight in the shape of a head of lettuce anchors a sea of pink forms on his desk.

"I'm sorry to have to do this," he tells the lettuce. "But you can't work in the dining room anymore."

"I see." A part of me says, *Tell him you can work in the dining room. Tell him you will learn to uncork wine properly and not let plates of food tip over.* But another part of me doesn't want to worry about the dining room anymore.

"But I can offer you another job, in the kitchen."

"Washing dishes?"

Bill chuckles, rubs his eyes. "No, no." I know he has a baby at home, and I don't think he's been getting much sleep. He'll probably get more rest once Lucille Ball isn't bumbling through his dining room.

"As salad girl."

"Salad girl?" From corporate manager to salad girl! What will I tell Dad? What would I tell Ethan? I wish I could tell him that I got promoted to director at Gorgatech and fixed the leak under the house and installed the flagstone patio in the backyard. "Isn't salad girl kind of a politically incorrect job title?" I ask Bill, not being critical, merely thinking aloud. I imagine myself as a food group superhero, with radish head, eggplant body, and carrot arms and legs, celery leaves for hands. Salad girl is a job you're supposed to have in high school.

"Well, food prep assistant level three, technically," Bill says.

I imagine that level two is dishwasher and level one is amoeba. The funny thing about rock bottom is there's stuff underneath it. You think, *This is it: I'm at the bottom now. It's all uphill from here!* Then you discover the escalator goes down one more floor to another level of bargain-basement junk.

"I'll need you to come in at two and do prep for a few hours," Bill adds. "Then stay until about ten making salads and assembling dessert orders and cleaning up. You won't make as much—no tips—but it's very low-key."

I want to tell Bill that I was capable at one point in my life. I was hired out of seventy-five candidates for my PR manager job. Before that, when I was a publications manager, I edited two award-winning four-color newsletters, wrote speeches for the university president, and managed a small staff. I spoke in front of large groups and drove a stick shift in rush hour.

"Meanwhile," Bill says, rubbing his eyes, then his forehead, then his temples, as if he's trying to rub something out of his head, "if you find something else—you know, a better job in town, I'll understand. You might find something at the Chamber of Commerce, for example. Or maybe the Shakespeare festival has an opening?" He says this hopefully, as if he's worried I might goof up as salad girl, too—maybe drizzle chocolate sauce on the romaine.

"Thanks. This will be great in the meantime." At least I'll be earning something. A little cash for COBRA and Colonel Cranson.

Bill spins around in his chair, grabs a pile of clothes off the credenza behind his desk, and hands them to me: a pair of black-and-white-checkered pants, starched white chef's jacket, apron, and a paper toque. This seems like an excessive getup for making salads, especially since there are only two on the menu: a house salad with hearts of palm and roma tomatoes and creamy dressing with little peach-colored shrimp on top, and a Caesar.

"This looks serious." I take the uniform.

"Chef Alan is very serious about his kitchen," Bill says, rolling his eyes.

"Well, thanks again." I hug the bundle of clothes and carry them to the rest room, where I wedge myself into the stall and change. I emerge looking something like the man on the cover of the Cream of Wheat box. Only the chef's hat doesn't really want to stay on top of my curly hair. It sort of floats on my head, as though a flying saucer flew down and landed there.

MENTORING

15

"How *come*?" Crystal whines when I call to tell her I can't get together at our usual time on Sunday.

"Because I need a break."

"From me?"

"From you."

"But you're my big sister. The rules say you're supposed to hang out with me every Sunday."

"I'm sure the rules also say you're not supposed to set your big sister's yard on fire."

"*You're* the one who wanted to barbecue."

I suppress the compulsion to slam down the phone. "We're not going to argue about this."

I stretch the rotary phone's long curly cord across the kitchen and sit at the table, reviewing the festival play schedule. Instead of being terrorized by Crystal on Sunday, I'm going to see *Blithe Spirit*, by Noël Coward, a comedy my mother took me to in New York when I was in grade school. I remember riding the train with her, visiting FAO Schwarz, and sipping tea at the Plaza, nibbling triangles of cinnamon toast on china plates rimmed with pink roses.

"What about *next* Sunday?" Crystal asks. I hear her suck on a cigarette and wonder if her mother knows she smokes.

"We'll see." I'm surprised Crystal's pushing to get together. So far she's seemed annoyed by our outings.

"Uh!" she snorts indignantly. "Are you, like, *ditching* me?"

"No." Or am I? I'm not sure yet. "But you need to think about being nicer."

"What am I supposed to *do* on Sunday?" she asks. "I don't want to, like, spend the day alone."

"Call your friends."

There's a silence and Crystal drags on her cigarette; it occurs to me that maybe she doesn't have any friends at school, that she's a loner.

"Whatever. Okay!" I'm ready to hang up, but Crystal wants to keep talking. "This girl at school, Tiffanie, has the same shirt as me? She says I have to take mine *back*."

Maybe there are girls in Crystal's junior high who are meaner than she is. Something tells me the other kids don't appreciate Crystal's wry sense of humor or pretty features or chutzpah. They probably just see her as a spooky girl who lives in a strange pink house.

"Listen," I tell her. "Here's what I want you to do on Sunday. Start a journal. Get a notebook and write about that girl. Write about anything you want for half an hour." Maybe Dr. Rupert's tricks will help Crystal, too.

"What are you, like, my teacher now?"

"No, I'm just making a suggestion."

"Are you going to read it?"

"Nope. It's for you. To help you feel better."

"I don't feel bad."

"Okay. Well, just try it."

"What*ever*."

"I gotta go now, okay?"

"Okay." But she stalls and keeps talking, and I let her rattle on a bit. Maybe she's being manipulative, but now I feel guilty for breaking our date. I know about those long weekends when you're an only child. In grade school, I'd often talk Leslie Bennington—an aloof blonde who stood next to me in choir—into sleeping over. She had an arsenal of siblings and didn't really need me but liked to stay over because my mother served unlimited heaps of Tater Tots and let us stay up to watch *Laverne & Shirley*. When it was time for Leslie to go home, I'd hide a piece of her clothing to stall her departure, hoping she'd stick around to play one more game of Trouble or practice a duet on the piano.

"And so like—" Crystal is about to launch into another diatribe about the two bully girls in her class, Amber and Tiffanie, but I tell her that I have things to do and firmly say good-bye.

Ruth can't make the play, and I'm not crazy about going to the theater alone, but I'd rather go alone than miss the show. This is my least favorite thing about being thirty-six and single—when your only choice is to hit movies and restaurants alone or stay home with your Lean Cuisine and remote control. You tell yourself you should *appreciate* this "me time." You take a bubble bath, just as the magazines tell you to, then curl up with one of the books you've been meaning to read, reminding yourself: *This is relaxing!* But you can't concentrate. Your brain skitters around like a squirrel in the road, wondering: *Will I ever find someone? Will I ever get to watch a daughter or son walk down the aisle? Will I even have a* date *this New Year's Eve?*

On Sunday, I decide to have lunch at the deli on East Main Street before the matinee.

It's hard to know where to look when you're eating alone in a restaurant. Do you focus on your salad or glance eye level at the empty space above the chair across the table? I choose the latter, trying to muster a cheerful look that says, *I don't mind this.*

I spot Sandy, my grief group counselor, and his wife, sitting side by side in a booth across the room. They're cuddling and laughing. I think of how Sandy said there are two kinds of loneliness: intimate, when you're cut off from physical contact, and social, when you're cut off from people. He said most widows suffer from both. His wife's black hair is cut short, revealing small, pretty ears. Her belly swells against the edge of the table, pregnant with another baby. Sandy laughs and she wrinkles her nose. I feel shy and don't want to say hello. I duck my head, turn, and stare through the rain-flecked window at the street, my turkey sandwich tasting bland and stringy. Still, I finish the whole thing and all of the French fries, chewing and swallowing without pleasure, filling in the fifty minutes before the play. Then I order a piece of peach pie to go and eat it in the car, listening to the rain drum the roof.

Anyone else would be thrilled with my seat at the theater: tenth row center. But I've always been a little claustrophobic, and I don't like being wedged in the middle of the audience. If Ethan and I were trapped in a full elevator, I'd press his hand for comfort, concentrating on the warm, padded flesh and network of little bones. I count the theater seats to the exits and find that I'm equally far from both doors—a narrow passageway of feet and purses between my seat and the aisles.

I squeeze my pocketbook, locating the bottle of tranquilizers through the leather. Should I swallow one dry pill in the middle of the theater? I'd rather not rely on the medication. Besides, I don't want to end up chewing through half the bottle and collapsing into someone's lap, like at Le Petit Bistro. I concentrate on breathing instead, counting and twisting my playbill into a tube. My turtleneck feels tight against my neck. A scratchy tickle flutters in the back of my throat. It's probably only a cough. But what if it's a scream?

In elementary school, one of the mothers screamed during a piano recital in the middle of Eva Cross's performance of a Chopin prelude. The woman stood up, her camel's-hair coat forming an A shape around her, screeched like a pterodactyl, then clutched her perfectly curled black hair. We all watched as her husband put his arm around his wife and led her out of the auditorium. The funny thing is, Eva kept playing, and her dour A-Minor Prelude became a sound track for the outburst.

Finally the theater lights dim, cloaking the audience in darkness. A hushed wave of throats clearing and cough drop wrappers rustling crosses the theater. Yellow stage lights slowly dawn. Then the play explodes into heat, light, and laughter, making the audience's faces glow golden. The uneasy tickle in my throat vanishes.

I remember the time Mother and I saw this play in New York and we snuggled together in the dark theater, laughing and eating linty butterscotch LifeSavers from her purse. If Crystal were better behaved, I could have brought her to the play. Then again, if she were better behaved, she probably wouldn't need a big sister.

A good-looking man in a velvet smoking jacket glides onstage. The husband, Charles. *The shrimp scampi actor from the restaurant.* I slide down in my seat. He's movie-star handsome—a cleft chin and high forehead swept with a boyish fop of brown hair. The audience adores his caustic comebacks and witty repartee.

Dry martinis, fringed lamps, grand piano, constant fun. I want to climb inside the play and live there. Wake up every morning in a drawing room comedy, with the jolly *b-r-r-ing!* of the doorbell and telephone—visitors always stopping by, laughter always bellowing through the house.

The audience howls around me. I'm no longer at the theater alone; we all seem to have one set of laughing lungs and clapping hands, one joyous pulse.

I wish I hadn't dropped that theater class in college. But it was so silly: *Everybody be a tree! Everybody be a color! Be green!* Still, when Charles leaves I want to follow him through the door of the set and into the bowels of the dark, warm theater and out to the cast party, where I'm sure the actors will laugh and sing until dawn.

— 16 —

I'm leaning against my workstation at Le Petit Bistro—a long stainless steel counter with a sink at one end that's as big as a car trunk—deveining a mound of shrimp and daydreaming about the handsome scampi actor in *Blithe Spirit*, when a sticky hand creeps up the back of my neck. Chef Alan. I flinch, banging my shin against the shelf under the counter. I smell his oniony breath, see the tips of his black clogs behind me, flecked with butter and brown gravy.

"*Relax.*" He chuckles, twisting and pulling the hair on the back of my neck as he massages. "You're so tense."

My shin burns and Chef's little white towel tickles my shoulder. He always clutches it to hide where his right ring and pinky fingers are lopped off just above the knuckles. The dishwasher says Chef used to work at a big restaurant in New York City and one busy night he sliced off two fingers while hurrying to cut more prime rib. Supposedly Chef screamed and sobbed and smashed dishes, then served a plate of meat with blood on it—*his* blood—and got fired. Now, his rubbery nubs prod my shoulders.

"Cool it," I grumble, twisting away from him. "There are *laws*, you know."

Chef stiffens, shifts into bitch mode. He dunks a giant pair of tongs into the sink, plucking out a piece of lettuce that I've got soaking in ice water. "No good!" he barks, waving the lettuce in the air like a flag. There's a black spot on the leaf.

Maybe the only way I'll ever achieve career serenity is to become my own boss. I pull a stringy brown strand from the fleshy center of a shrimp.

"Smaller batches ensure better quality." Chef flings the offending lettuce into the trash. "Maybe they didn't *care* about quality where you used to work."

Chef doesn't know that this is my first restaurant job. He seems to think I've always worked at a restaurant. I cross my arms, which are chronically sticky from digging into the big vats of vanilla ice cream for à la mode scoops.

"This is not Pizza Hut," he adds. "This is not Red Lobster. This restaurant is a *destination*." His skin is as oily and pockmarked as the broiled cheese on the onion soup.

"Okay, Alan." I leave the shrimp and begin sorting through the lettuce, the cold water in the sink making my hands ache.

"*Chef* Alan," he says, snapping his towel in the air.

"Okay, Chef." I consider how this job will look on my résumé. I'll probably have to leave it off. A hole in my life requiring explanation.

One day the baker at Le Petit Bistro, who works mornings preparing the desserts, walks out on Chef after an argument. I arrive at work in time to find her storming down the back steps of the restaurant, the layer of a chocolate cake sailing through the air after her like a Frisbee. It lands in the parking lot near my feet.

"I don't need this bullshit," she says, throwing her apron toward the back door and climbing into her car.

"I know," I tell her, picking up the cake.

Inside, Chef hands me a black binder of recipes. "You'll need to come in two hours earlier to prepare these. I'll give you a raise." He stomps into his office and slams the door, leaving me in peace.

I like the solitude in the kitchen. No specials to memorize or stubborn bottles of wine to open. No meetings or media calls. Within a week I learn to bake all of the desserts in the binder:

chocolate rum cake, raspberry crème brûlée, carrot cake, cheese-cake, marionberry pie.

Puttering with an old set of frosting bags with curious tubes and nozzles, I take my time icing and decorating the cakes. Chef says why bother, since the customers see them only a slice at a time. I wish I worked at a real bakery, where people would appreciate customized cakes. There's something satisfying about perfecting iced pink roses. I'd rather glaze a crème brûlée than coach a company CEO for a TV interview—worrying about how to fix his wandering comb-over without offending him.

After mastering the desserts, I invent a grapefruit avocado salad with curry-citrus dressing. Chef pronounces it "tangy and complex" and adds it to the menu. Next I improvise with the cheese-cake recipe, creating a savory version with blue cheese and Brie. My first attempt is too runny, the second too crumbly. By the third try I come up with a smooth pie that tastes wonderful with a glass of Cabernet. Upon sampling it, Chef closes his eyes, smacks his lips, and then adds it to the menu as well.

After work I usually take a long hot bath, then crawl into bed with cookbooks piled around me. Their weight is almost as heavy as a lover's limbs. As I flip through the batter-splotched pages, I imagine completing each step of the recipes until I begin to feel sleepy.

The restaurant is closed on Mondays, when the theater's dark. Tuesdays are slow, typically just a meek crowd ordering French onion soup. These are my two days off, my weekend. At home, the hours drone by, marked by the gong of the grandfather clock and the relentless clanking of the radiators, which are always having noisy tantrums. I'd like to round them up and send them to an anger management class. I clean and shop and weed and launder and walk and read and nap, and by four in the afternoon, I'm ready to iron washcloths or tear down walls.

I try to work on my laptop computer, but the thing keeps crashing, as though boycotting Colonel Cranson's. I want to e-mail Dad, write a letter to Marion, and search online for a Gore-Tex raincoat.

In fact, I could use an entire Gore-Tex wardrobe to ward off this beastly Oregon rain. I'd order Gore-Tex underwear if my damn machine would just cooperate. As it freezes for the third time, I cry and pound my fists on the dining room table. I want Ethan here to fix the thing. He had a way of showing electronic devices who's boss. I give the computer a little shake, as though it's a pinball machine, probably damaging its innards. I snap the lid shut and yank the plug from the wall. Worthless piece of junk! I curse myself for depending upon my husband for all things technological. But there were tasks Ethan relied on me for, albeit simple stuff. Refolding road maps. Carving a turkey. "You," he'd say, rocking back and forth nervously and pointing at the roasting pan. And I always fixed his swim goggles. It was easy, but I didn't want to show him how. I liked having this one trick that my highly capable engineer husband depended upon me for.

Some afternoons I practice my crossovers at the ice-skating rink in the park in town, circling on the jagged ice, teenagers shrieking and whipping past me. I drag Ruth to see every play at the festival, the characters' woes helping to diminish my own. Henry V may fit into all of his pants, but he's got to worry about conquering France, plus those three creepy guys who are plotting to kill him.

During my Crystal moratorium, she shows up at my house one Monday afternoon. I answer the door to find her slouching on the front porch, her bulging backpack pitching her to one side.

"Wanna hang out?" she asks. The air is moist and musky. Behind her, the street shines with rain.

"We're taking a break, remember?" I fold my arms across my chest. This is me, enforcing boundaries.

She nods and glances eagerly past me into the house. Her damp hair sticks out in crazy spikes and her cheeks are flushed.

"Did you *walk* here?" It's about two miles between my house and hers. She nods again. "No umbrella?" She shakes her head, clutching the sleeves of her jean jacket in her raw, chapped hands.

"I brought stuff. I thought I could, like, crash here." She takes a resolute step forward, but I lean against the doorjamb, blocking the doorway. I want to let her in, but on my terms, which I need to establish before she crosses the threshold.

"What about school tomorrow?"

"Spring break." Her eyes scan the porch. "I need help with my pre-algebra. My teacher's gonna, like, flunk me if I don't finish this take-home test." Her backpack is so swollen that the zipper has burst and she's fastened it with safety pins.

I wish Ethan were here to help Crystal with her test. He had a knack for tutoring, asking questions and leading you to the right conclusion, making you feel as though you figured everything out on your own. I picture him spreading Crystal's books across the big wooden kitchen table and saying, "All right, what have we here!" and somehow managing to make a take-home pre-algebra test fun.

"I don't know how to do algebra," I tell her.

"*Dude!* But you're, like, a grown-up."

"I know. Theoretically." I've decided I don't mind being called dude; if you can't be called miss anymore, why not dude? It's better than ma'am.

Crystal slides off her backpack and collapses cross-legged on the porch. The trees shudder in the wind, water spilling from their leaves. I don't have the heart to send her home. First of all, I don't think she'd go home. Even if she did, there's probably no one there.

"Come on, you're getting wet." I extend my hand and she grabs it, her skin cold and rough against mine. She's remarkably light as I tug her through the door.

"Can we order a pizza?" she asks, peeling off her jean jacket and tugging off her clunky boots. They look several sizes too big.

"You walked in those?"

"They're my dad's." She lines them up by the front door. As someone who wears her dead husband's ratty ski sweater, who am I to judge?

We eat in silence at the kitchen table, pizza staining our paper plates bright orange with grease. I scoop salad onto my plate and reach for Crystal's.

"I don't want that," she snaps, swatting at the lettuce and tomatoes with her fork.

"You mean 'No, thank you'?"

"Whatever. You sound like my mother."

"Well, thankfully I'm not."

Crystal plucks the pepperoni off her pizza and piles it like a stack of coins on the edge of her plate, then polishes off her crust in big bites, lips glistening with grease.

The radiators in the house have only two settings—scorching or off—and the kitchen feels as hot as Death Valley today. Crystal chews and stares into space, absentmindedly pushing up her sweater sleeve. The inside of her forearm is striped with red marks. At first I think she's drawn all over herself with a red pen. No. The marks are *cuts*. I stop chewing. She quickly tugs down her sleeve, clenching the cuff in her fist.

"Don't like pepperoni?" I swallow and lean toward her.

"I'm a *vegetarian*," she says disdainfully. "Probably I'm going to be a vet."

"A veggie vet?"

She nods. "I saw a nature show on a guy who saves horses? Sometimes he can't fix them and he has to, like, give them a shot so they die." She fans herself with her dirty paper plate.

"Why don't you take off your sweater?"

"No." She finishes her soda in two big gulps. I notice that the cuffs of her sleeves are caked with something reddish brown. Blood? Food or dirt, I hope.

"Crystal, will you show me your arm? It worries me."

"Okay." But she doesn't move.

I reach across the table and wrap a hand around her wrist. With my other hand, I push up her sleeve, then turn over her arm. The soft white underside is slashed with crisscrosses of cuts, raised like argyle. Her skin feels hot and jagged. Crystal sucks in her breath, blinks.

"What happened here?" I feel my pulse race but try not to seem alarmed. Some of the wounds are fresh, congealed blood at their edges.

Crystal jerks her arm away and yanks down her sleeve. Her shoulders curl into a hunch.

I move my plate aside and fight to maintain the same even calm I kept when Ethan's skin was as gray as oatmeal and he was too weak to climb the stairs. You don't want a sick person to see in your expression or hear in your voice how frightened you are for them.

Crystal bites her lower lip.

"Did you do that on purpose? Like the burns?"

She rolls her eyes. *"Duh."*

"I see."

"Can I smoke?"

"Okay. On the porch." Earlier, I decided I wouldn't let her smoke during our outings, but now smoking seems like coloring with crayons compared to the cuts. I follow her outside, helplessly grabbing a plate of lemon-frosted sugar cookies on the way. We sit in the big wicker chairs, watching cars chug through the wash across the street.

Crystal tugs up her pant leg, slides a box of Marlboros out of her sock, and lights one. What else is she hiding under that cloak of black clothing?

"Doesn't it hurt?" I ask her.

"Yeah. But it, like, makes it feel better, too." She exhales a huge puff of smoke.

"What it?" The wind slams a door shut in the house and I jump.

"You know."

I nod, but I don't know. I can't understand being this kind of broken. I want to know, though. "Better? You mean like putting

your fist through a wall better?" I can imagine doing this. I know
that horrible, helpless feeling of wanting to bang your head against
the wall until all the moths and spiders fly out. But cutting yourself?

"I started out digging my nails into my skin?" Crystal tries to
explain. "But cutting works better." She takes another long drag on
her cigarette. "A serrated knife hurts more."

"And that's a good thing?"

She shrugs and puffs out little smoke rings that break into question marks and parentheses.

"I see." I dig into the cookies, sugar and flour soothing my
nerves. "Does your mom know?"

"Yeah."

"What's she say?"

"She yells. What am I doing to myself, what am I doing to her.
She called me a freak. *Hello!* She's the freak." Crystal gets up and
stubs out her cigarette in the wet grass.

"Please don't leave that there," I tell her.

She shoves the cigarette butt in her pocket and slumps back in
her chair.

"What about your dad? Does he know?"

"I guess not. Since I haven't, like, *seen* him for ten years." Her
lower lip trembles and she jams a cookie in her mouth.

"Right."

"I bought him a card for St. Patrick's Day?" she says thickly, her
mouth full. "I send him one every holiday. Even on Passover, and
we're not Jewish." She swallows. "Even on Secretary's Day. 'Dear
Dad, Thank you for being such a great secretary. Your coffee's the
best!'" She slides down in her chair and gets to work chewing her
nails. "None of the cards have come back. So I think he got them
or they're, like, holding them for him. He might be in Alaska on a
fishing boat." She kicks the porch with her bare foot, thinking. "It
would be cool to live on a boat."

It's stopped raining and the sky brightens overhead. We sit listening to the high-pitched whir of the brushes and the rumbling *whoosh* of the dryers at the car wash.

"Does anyone else know?" I finally ask. "About the cutting?"

"I go to a shrink on Tuesdays after school."

"Does he help?"

"It's a lady." She shrugs, raises her eyebrows. I can relate to this reaction. How exactly do you know if you're getting better? "You're not grossed out?" she asks.

I shake my head.

"My mom says it's disgusting."

"There's nothing about you that's disgusting. Besides, I've seen it all: tubes, bandages." I recall the incision in Ethan's back, which oozed and scabbed over, how I cleaned it gently with Q-tips, chattering while I worked, trying to distract him from the pain.

"I'm sorry about Edgar," Crystal says softly. I think this is the first nice thing she's said to me.

"Ethan."

"Ethan." She says his name again slowly, her tongue resting for a moment on her front teeth. "E-than." She looks at me and wrinkles her nose. "Was he, like, your boyfriend for a long time?"

I cave in and let Crystal sleep over. She calls her mother's cell phone twice before reaching her. Roxanne doesn't seem to mind *where* Crystal spends the night. Isn't this beyond the definition of a latchkey kid?

I set Crystal up in the guest bedroom beside mine. She sits cross-legged on the bed, jams her Walkman headphones over her ears, and cranks up the volume. Tinny music tinkles around her head. I've noticed from her CD collection that she favors dead musicians—Jim Morrison, Jimi Hendrix, Janis Joplin, Kurt Cobain—as though death's the ultimate cool sulky thing to do. She pulls her math book from her backpack. The spine makes a cracking noise as she opens it.

"You're going to study now? With music?"

"Dude, I'm going to *ace* this test." She is serious, manic.

I shrug and head off to bed.

As I crawl under the covers, I wonder if there are cuts anywhere else on Crystal's body. I've never seen her bare legs. Colonel Cranson stares down sternly from the sepia portrait on the wall, his handlebar mustache drooping into a permanent frown. Mrs. Cranson's black dress is buttoned to her chin, and her slick black hair is pulled into a tight braid. The sheets are chilly as I tug them over my shoulders. I still hate sleeping alone, hate the absence of heat and weight and someone to discuss the day with. I pull *The Joy of Cooking* from my night table, lay it open across my lap, and turn to meringues. I imagine the Cransons spooning in this big brass bed. Maybe the colonel wore a nightshirt and cap, like the man in "'Twas the Night Before Christmas." I inhale the crisp smell of the bleached pillowcase, imagining Mrs. Cranson's long white eyelet nightgown. Then the bed is a cloud and I'm floating and the colonel is leaning over to whisper that the house's smoke alarm is shrieking.

Fire, Crystal, slippers, run, my sleepy brain tells my feet.

As I lurch out of bed, the cookbook smacks the floor. I bound across the hall and shove open Crystal's door. She's perched on the edge of her still-made bed, peering into a metal trash can. Thin gray smoke spirals toward the ceiling. An orange flame curls over the top of the can, then dips back inside.

"Crystal!"

"Take *x* and *y* and shove them up your ass," Crystal grumbles, tearing a page from her math book and stuffing it into the fire.

"Crystal!"

She stands and stares into the trash basket, her arms straight and stiff at her sides. "What?"

"Fire, that's what!"

"It's *in* the can." She scratches through the fabric of her sweater at the scabs on her arms.

"My God!" I scramble down to the kitchen for the fire extinguisher and sprint back up the stairs two at a time, repeating the words I once learned during an office safety drill: *Pull, aim, squeeze, sweep. Pull, aim, squeeze, sweep.*

As I grab the fire extinguisher's cold chrome handle, yellow foam shoots across the room, hitting the trash can and caking in globs on the bedspread. The fire dies. I cough, waving my hand in front of my face. Stinky yellow talc coats the Oriental carpet, which is strewn with Crystal's broken pencils and torn papers. I should have just thrown water in the can.

"Ruined." It's the only word I can muster and I think I mean this relationship, too.

Crystal sits on the edge of the bed, one foot maniacally tapping the floor.

"I don't even know if I can fix this beautiful carpet now." I hear my voice quaver. "It's old and fragile." Like me.

"I got stuck on a problem." Crystal flops onto her back and talks to the ceiling. "Besides, *you're* the one who wrecked the place with the fire extinguisher."

I snatch a towel from the bathroom and swab the carpet, tapping and then pounding the foam. "You got stuck on a problem so you're going to start another fire?" I hear my voice getting louder and faster, like a train approaching, and can't stop it. "Burn down this beautiful house that's in the *Historical Register* and I can barely afford to rent?" I'm shouting now. My head pounds, and the tacky fire extinguisher powder makes my fingers itch.

"My mom says there was no Colonel Cranson."

I stop blotting the carpet and stare at the baseboards, fighting the urge to throw something, to break a lamp.

"Get your things together," I finally tell Crystal. "I'm going to call your mother and have her pick you up."

"No! Don't call her." Crystal sits up and frantically rubs the insides of her arms. "She's sleeping at her boyfriend's."

I spread the towel over the stained carpet, crawl into the armchair beside the bed, and lean my head against the wall for support. "I'm confused," I tell her. "Do you want to spend time together?"

She nods, squeezing the insides of her arms and rocking.

"Well, we can't do that if you have no respect for me or my house."

"Okay. Sorry," she mumbles.

I move to the edge of the bed and peer into her face, looking for a sign of anything I can reason with. Her pale blue eyes are smoky, vacant. She nods and rocks, nods and rocks, working her jaw back and forth, her teeth sawing into her lower lip.

I sink toward the soft center of the bed. "Don't bite like that." I grab her chin. "Here, have a drink." I pass her a can of root beer she left on the night table. "Algebra's hard. A *lot* of students struggle with it. Did you know that?"

She shakes her head, holding the soda between us. Her lips are swollen and cracked, and the color has drained from her cheeks.

"I barely passed," I tell her. "Then guess what? You get geometry. It's worse, like someone's forcing you to learn to play the tuba. But that doesn't mean you get to start fires."

I feel bad that Crystal has no one to help her with her homework. It took me lots of help from my dad just to get a C in algebra. On Sunday mornings he fixed us pancakes and sausages, then helped me study at the dining room table.

"If Lucy baked three more than twice as many cookies as Sally, and Julio ate a fourth of them, how many would be left?" he'd coax gently. My brain seized up like a tangled bicycle chain. Instead of answers I produced tears. I'd hunch over the sour-smelling pages of the book as the sunny morning passed outside the window, the smooth, empty street begging me to roller-skate.

"I think you need a tutor," I tell Crystal now. "I can't help you, because I stink at algebra. But I'll help you find someone."

"I don't care if I flunk! I fucking *hate* school." Her face tightens into a red grimace, like a baby's. She sobs.

I loop my arm around her shoulder, my elbow sore from where I smacked it while taking a corner too fast with the fire extinguisher. She recoils from my touch.

"I hate fucking Amber and Tiffanie. As if I *want* to be invited to their stupid parties. They don't even know who Janis Joplin *is*. They are such losers!"

She starts to rock again, hugging herself and shivering. I want to tell her to watch the language. Instead I try to hug her. Despite the fact that she's skinny, it's hard to get my arms around her. She's sharp and angular—all elbows and shoulder blades. I pull her closer. I'm embarrassed by my effort and give up. But as soon as I let go of her, Crystal's arms tighten around me.

"Here's a secret," I say, rocking with her but slowing her down. "Ninety percent of the world hated junior high." Her short hair is bristly against my cheek.

"Not my *mom*."

"Okay, not your mom." My realtor, Kit, told me that Crystal's mother was quite popular in junior high school. "Oh, Roxanne Lowman's daughter," he said, blushing and tipping his head when I told him about Crystal. Turns out she was two grades ahead of him and all the boys had crushes on her. They called her Foxie Roxie. I got the sense that this was her apex, though, and it's been downhill for her since.

"If you want to know what hell's like," I tell Crystal, "you're in it: junior high. You're not crazy." I remember bumbling through school without a mother, doing my best to avoid the scary gum-snapping girls who trolled the halls in packs. Fighting every morning to wrestle my curly hair into Farrah Fawcett feathers like theirs.

Crying in quiet hiccups now, Crystal untangles herself from my grasp and leans back into the pillows, listening attentively, as though I'm telling her a bedtime story.

"I know school's hard, and your dad left you, and you don't get along with your mom. I'm sorry, and I do want to help. I'm on your side." I nod at the carpet and the disaster of a room. "But you have to go easier on me."

Crystal rubs her eyes until they squeak under her fingers. "Okay."

I take her hands and hold them in mine, examining her bitten fingernails, which are raw and rubbery, like erasers. "You have to realize that life isn't easy for other people, either, Crystal. That's the part you're missing, and that's the part that's hard about growing up. It seems like a conspiracy—like life's only hard for you, but it's not the case."

"But those bitches have *dads,* at least."

"I know they do. It's not fair."

Crystal slides under the quilt with her clothes on.

"You can stay tonight. But this is your last chance. *No more fires.*"

She nods.

I reach under the covers and help her tug her sweater off over her head, static electricity snapping at my arms. Her little white T-shirt exposes her mottled arms.

"Where are your pajamas?"

"I don't have any."

"Well, what's in there besides matches?" I point at her bulging backpack.

"Stuff."

Clutching her wrists, I examine the cuts, some of which are snagged with black sweater fuzz. From the bathroom I grab a bottle of hydrogen peroxide and box of cotton balls. As I swab Crystal's skin, pink foam bubbles up from the rust-colored incisions.

"This doesn't look so bad," I tell her, averting my face toward the wall. Crystal's shoulders relax.

I fold her arms under the covers, then get up to leave the room, stopping in the doorway. "I bet your arms will heal nicely in a few months and you can wear short-sleeved shirts this summer," I say, switching off the light. "You know, if you don't cut them again."

The streetlight casts a stripe of yellow across the floor.

"I don't care," she says.

"I know. But—"

"Leave the door open?"

In the morning I wake to the cloying smell of burning butter and rush downstairs to see if Crystal's started another fire. She's curled on the sofa, showered and dressed, watching a nature show on TV. Her brown corduroy hip huggers expose a creamy stripe of flat belly, silver studs outlining the pockets. Instead of her bulky black sweater, she wears a little pink tank top that shows off two knobby bones on the tops of her shoulders and the crisscrosses of cuts along the insides of her thin arms.

"Hi," I say.

"Shh!" She points to a plate with a bowl over it on the coffee table.

Lifting the bowl, I discover two soggy pieces of French toast. I sit on a pillow on the floor and dig in. The slices are lukewarm and a little underdone in the middle. "Yum," I tell her, but she's concentrating on her program.

On TV, a tiny brown mole digs a hole in the sand and hides. I like nature shows for their slow, matter-of-fact approach. "In the desert," the narrator says quietly, as though narrating a golf tournament, "a hole . . . is a *very* good thing."

You can't argue with that.

17

Breathe, I remind myself, looking up from the library book on cutters. The fluorescent lights buzz noisily overhead and the library air is dry and dusty, parching my throat. I close my eyes for a minute, then continue reading.

Cutting the skin with a knife, razor blade, or other sharp object. Sometimes the skin is scraped with a coarse edge, such as that of a bottle cap, or burned. This is a symptom of severe underlying depression, anger, or anxiety.

I draw a deep breath through my nose and spread my palms across the cold, greasy-feeling table, bracing myself.

When the body is injured, it releases endorphins, natural painkillers that have a numbing effect. In this way, cutting may literally be a form of self-medication.

The book goes on to say that cutting is often misunderstood as a suicide attempt or dismissed as being a fad, such as body piercing, but that it's actually a coping mechanism.

It can also be said that cutting replaces overwhelming emotional pain with more comprehensible physical pain. . . . Cutters feel compelled to injure themselves, and the activity is typically performed in a trance-like state.

I look up and around the room. A man draped in a giant green rain poncho snoozes in a nearby chair. A sign made out of a wedge of brown cardboard is propped against his backpack, large print reading: ATTENTION IM HUNGRY.

I run my fingers under my sleeves and over the warm, smooth skin on my arms, which feels remarkably thin. And I thought smashing dishes was desperate. As I picture the delicate underside of Crystal's forearms sliced up like lattice pie crust, I shudder. While I can imagine the urge to cut yourself—an urge like wanting to smack yourself in the forehead, only ten times stronger—I can't imagine the ability to actually go through with it. In an odd way, I admire Crystal for being able to cut herself—for being able to endure this much pain. I shudder again, snap the book shut, and gather a small stack of volumes to check out.

I hear the clacking of a keyboard in the background as I explain over the phone to the counselor at Big Brothers/Big Sisters everything that's happened with Crystal so far—the fires, the cigarette burns on her hands, the cuts on her arms.

"What are you typing?" I ask her.

"I have to file a report," she says, sighing.

"Okay. But Crystal's not going to get in trouble, is she? She can't help it. And I know she's already seeing a psychologist."

"Right. But we have to file a report on any activity that may be harmful to the little sister, big sister, or others."

"I see."

"The social workers will review the report and contact Crystal's mother and the school." The woman takes a gulp of something. "Don't worry," she adds. "You're doing the right thing." She stops typing for a minute and says apologetically, "I know this is more than you bargained for. Please be honest and tell me if you think it's too much for you to handle. We would certainly understand—"

"No, it's okay," I assure her. "I figured from the beginning that this might be difficult." But that's not really true. I pictured games of Candyland and Disney movies. I never imagined self-mutilation and fires. Still, I can't return Crystal as though she's an appliance that broke before the warranty expired.

.   .   .

At work, I'm determined to master fondant—a stubborn mixture of sugar, water, and cream of tartar that you heat and cool, then knead into a doughlike icing that forms a lovely satiny outer blanket for a cake. That is, if things go well. My fondant is more like cement than satin, gluing itself to the counter and under my fingernails. I'm working in a little more confectioner's sugar one afternoon when suddenly the Shakespeare festival actor who played Charles in *Blithe Spirit* shoots through the swinging doors of the kitchen. I jump, dropping the measuring cup on the floor. The sugar explodes into a little white cloud.

"Sorry!" Charles says, and smiles. Two deep dimples and a flash of bright teeth. I scoop up the measuring cup and toss a towel over the mess. It's the quiet part of the afternoon before the waiters and waitresses arrive. Chef's in his office. I'm not sure how Charles found his way into the kitchen.

"How's the scampi today?" He's wearing jeans, a black leather jacket, and a black turtleneck that frames his square, cleft chin.

Heat surges up my neck and into my face. The last thing I need right now is a handsome actor. I've always had a knack for getting crushes on performers. It started when I was ten and wanted to marry Elton John, obsessively sewing sequins that spelled E-L-T-O-N onto a T-shirt when I was supposed to be studying for French quizzes.

"Honey, you can't get married, you're only ten," my mother said gently. "Besides, I think Mr. John is gay." What did this mean? I asked her. That he would marry a man, she explained. Still, I didn't see how this would prevent him from loving me.

"Drew Ellis," Charles says, extending a hand. His narrow face is slightly wrinkled with laugh lines, and his blue-gray eyes are like slate. I squint, searching for flaws to prevent me from falling for him—a chipped tooth, bad grammar, dirt under his fingernails.

"Um, hi. Sophie Stanton." My thumb circles my naked ring finger, which is chalky with powdered sugar. I wipe my hands on my apron and reach for his hand. His palm is warm, electric. A bit of sticky fondant smudges his thumb. He smiles, looks around, licks it off.

"You work in the kitchen, too?"

He's probably here to see if I'll pay the dry-cleaning bill for the scampi screwup.

"Uh," I tell him, "I'm the salad girl now." I hear my voice speed up and feel my smile stiffen. Although I was married for three years, suddenly I don't know how to talk to a man. My mind is as blank as a sheen of lemon fondant. I spread my arms, showing off my workstation—the gleaming stainless steel counter and giant mixer on the floor, the case of butter lettuce waiting to be rinsed.

"I hope that's not my fault." Drew has an actor's perfect diction, with crisp consonants and slightly British pronunciation.

"No, I'd say it's pretty much my fault. I accidentally sat on a customer's lap." I smack my forehead. *Goofy! Don't tell* that *story*.

Drew laughs, throwing back his head. He's one of those hearty laughers who makes you feel clever. I giggle, remembering how nice he was when I spilled the scampi.

"They don't want to offer lap dances here," I add. "Family restaurant and all. Would you like a piece of cake?" Before he can answer, I slice a wedge of chocolate rum cake and hand him a fork.

"How long have you lived in Ashland?" Drew asks, digging into the cake. He's got Ruth's dance-student perfect posture.

Suddenly I can't open my mouth. I'm certain there's spinach between my teeth. I haven't eaten spinach all day or all week, as far as I recall, but I swear I feel a greenish black piece wedged there now. I want to dash to the bathroom to check.

"Almost two months," I finally say, casually covering my mouth with one hand. I realize that I've been counting my time in Ashland as a finite, temporary period that will eventually end. Then I'll go home and my husband will be alive again and my life will return to normal. But my Gorgatech leave of absence ended a month ago. (When I called to tell Lara I wouldn't be returning to work, she sent a dozen white roses and a bon voyage card signed by everyone at the office wishing me good luck. *Good riddance!* they probably thought.)

"I'm sorry I spilled food on your guest," I tell Drew, leaning over to escape eye contact by wiping globs of pie dough off the big mixer.

"My mom."

"Oh, gosh! I'm sorry. How's she doing?"

"Fine. Preparing for the lawsuit."

I swallow hard, wondering what happened to the Isadora Duncan date he brought to the restaurant that night.

"I'm joking," Drew says.

"You were great as Charles," I tell him, wiping the counters now. *Stupid. Gushing!*

"You saw the play?" His eyes brighten. He polishes off the cake and sets the plate in the bottom of the big stainless sink. "Delicious."

I busy myself folding a pile of kitchen towels.

"Listen . . ." He bows his head toward his white Nikes. "I thought maybe you'd like to go to dinner sometime."

I fold the last towel until it's too small to fold anymore.

Drew glances across the kitchen at the giant boxes of canned apricots and olives. "But maybe you're sick of food. Maybe something else? Bowling?"

"You mean a date?"

"I've wanted to ask you out since the night you were our waitress."

"Right. You were with . . ." I pause, remembering the Isadora Duncan girl's tiny nose and elegant neck—how her lustrous strawberry blond hair cascaded over her shoulders. "Your girlfriend?"

"Friend," Drew says.

Friend. What*ever*! I already hate this woman. Hate her loud theatrical cackle and silk scarves with their pretentious fringe. What a glamour-puss.

"Oh." I reach into the refrigerator for a new clump of chilled pie dough, even though I'm finished making pies for the day. I want to climb in and hide behind the butter.

"I hope I'm not being presumptuous and you don't have a significant other."

"Nope," I tell the bottles of milk. "I'm significant otherless."

"Great." Drew catches himself. "I mean for me. How about Monday, around seven? That's my day off." He adds this fact apologetically, I guess because Monday is a B-list date night, unlike Saturday.

I close the refrigerator door. "Sure."

"Great. It's a date."

A watery wave of nausea rises in my throat, the word *date* like a food I got sick on. I had to fend off my last *date* with a tennis racket.

"Monday," I repeat, rolling out an unnecessary ball of dough.

"Shoot, I've got a rehearsal." Drew peels back his sleeve to look at his watch. "May I call you?"

After ripping the corner off a sack of flour, I jot down my number and hand it to him, then return to the dough.

"Great," he says. "Great to meet you. Again."

Good, he's leaving. By the time he calls, maybe I'll be a new person with self-confidence and cute comebacks. Straight hair, a better job, a smaller waistline.

Drew disappears through the swinging doors. I collapse onto a cardboard box filled with giant cans of tomato juice. Then Drew stumbles back through the doors as a woman crashes past him, lunging toward me.

"Sophie *Stanton*?" she barks accusingly. Crystal's mother, Roxanne. Rage in a blue angora sweater.

Drew pauses, a questioning look crossing his face.

"Yes?" I take a step backward.

Roxanne's tight-fitting sweater outlines a small waist and large breasts. Oddly enough, I'm optimistic for Crystal—hoping she'll inherit this figure soon and become as popular as her mother was in high school. "Where you from, anyway, hunh?" she asks in a low, gravelly voice.

"Be with you in a minute," I say cautiously. I peer past Roxanne and wave at Drew, hoping he'll leave.

"You one of those *East Coast* girls who's moved to Oregon to help straighten out the white trash?" Roxanne has ramrod posture instead of Crystal's unconfident hunch. Her white-blond hair spills past her hips.

Drew's face sinks into a concerned frown.

I wave at him. "See you soon!" This comes out like a command, and he disappears through the kitchen doors. I wonder if he'll ever really call or if the fondant moment was our first and last date.

"Daddy send you to college and now you're the authority on raising a kid?" Roxanne flips her hair behind her shoulders, Cher style, snapping her head from side to side.

Listen, Old Yeller: I earned a partial scholarship to college and took out student loans and worked at the library to pay for my books. Of course, all this is beside the point. "Can we please just—"

She cuts me off, rising on her toes. "You need to butt outta my life, Big Sister Suzie." Her full, heart-shaped lips shimmer with pink lip gloss. It's the same color Crystal smears clumsily across her thin mouth. I wonder if maybe, despite claiming that she hates her mother, Crystal yearns to be like her. "'Cause you have *no* idea what it's like to raise a bratty teenager."

"I'm sure I don't," I tell her. "Can you please call me after work and we'll discuss this?"

"You think I don't know she sets fires?" Her eyes are slightly sunken, with dark circles, the only thing about her that isn't pretty. "You think I don't know she hacks up her arms? I know. The shrink knows. And now, thanks to your little *report*, the school knows. You think that makes junior high better for Crystal? Hunh? When everybody *knows* she's a freak?"

"Crystal's not a freak." I can't believe this woman has so much disdain for her own daughter.

"She *cuts* herself."

"I know, but you shouldn't write her off as a freak."

"Who the fuck are you to tell me what I should do?"

"I'm not telling you what to do. I'm just saying maybe we should have a little more faith in her."

"*We?* This isn't about we. This is about me and my daughter."

I clench my hands into fists to stop them from shaking. "Well, your daughter almost burned down my house. Did you think I couldn't say anything about this?"

"Just mind your own business, that's all."

"How do you expect me to spend time with Crystal *and* mind my own business?"

Chef Alan charges out of his office, his toque tipping to one side on his head.

"What's the deal here?" he demands.

"We're just having a discussion," I tell him.

Chef's eyes shoot straight to the U shape of blond hair that sweeps across Roxanne's small rear, and suddenly the air is let out of him. He straightens his back, broadens his chest, and bows ceremoniously in her direction.

"Well, *hello,*" he says.

Crystal's mother reels around toward Alan, ready to tear into him. She stops when she sees him and tilts her head to one side, like a lion trying to decide whether an antelope is worth the hassle.

"I don't believe we've met," Chef murmurs, sashaying toward her.

Roxanne curls her upper lip, irritated. But Chef begins layering on the compliments and slowly she melts, like an ice sculpture losing its edge and definition.

"Are you an actress with the festival?" he asks. "You *are* stunning." Roxanne looks up at him through lashes thick with black mascara. Her tongue sweeps across her small, even teeth. She seems to be calculating the benefits of Chef's attention.

I step back, clearing the path between them. Alan glides over, takes Roxanne by the elbow, and leads her toward his office.

"May I interest you in some fresh cracked crab and a glass of Chardonnay?"

She shoots me a glare over her shoulder, as if to say, *I'll catch up with you later.*

"I just love the veal Oscar here," she coos to Chef. It seems easy for her to forget about Crystal for the moment.

"Allow me to give you a tour," Chef says. They disappear around the corner into the pantry area, Chef telling Roxanne how he has his olive oils shipped in from Italy, that olive oils are like fine wines, really, and many people don't realize that.

DATING

18

Status quo: I'm thirty-six years old, and my husband died nine months ago, and I'm locked in the bathroom getting ready for my first date in nearly six years. I stand over the bathroom sink watching with horror as my last disposable contact lens slithers down the drain. Boys don't make passes at girls who wear glasses! And my scratched tortoiseshell frames are about as stylish as saddle shoes. Choosing vanity over depth perception, I forget the glasses for now and move on to my hair. It's the dull, unglamorous texture of yarn today. It doesn't want to go on a date. It says, *Let's stay home and eat rhubarb pie!*

I believe every woman with curly hair has a graveyard of products under her bathroom sink that she resorts to in emergencies such as this. Canisters of mousse, gel, and pomade—each promising to be the miracle cure. The pathetic part is I *moved* my mousse collection from California to Oregon. Towed it up in the U-Haul. And now I'm on my hands and knees, burrowing through the bottles. I choose one: Frizz Eaze—the z's on the can mirroring my own kinks. I rub the goo between my palms and pat my head. Now my hair has a shellacklike sheen. It's frizzy, sticky, and crunchy all at once. I give up, tug it into a ponytail, and slide on my glasses for an overview. Great. The librarian look. *Allow me to recommend this volume on the Dark Ages.*

I remember holing up in the bathroom getting ready for the prom in high school while Dad cowered out in the hall, wanting to help. "Sweetie, is there anything I can do?" he called through the door.

"No!" I shouted over the roar of the hair dryer as I worked at straightening my curls—a forty-five-minute chore that left my scalp scorched and my arm muscles aching.

I am thirty-six years old and my husband died nine months ago and here I am getting ready for a date to go bowling with a too-handsome actor who must have some sort of dark, psycho-killer secret because everyone *knows* all the nice, smart, normal men are married. Only the trolls are left.

In the past hour I've changed from corduroys to jeans to a skirt. How could I have managed to lose my husband, my job, my house, *and* my ass all in one year?

Oddly enough, I didn't fret over my first date with Ethan. We went to see the Lakers, who'd come to town to play the Warriors, and I wore jeans and a flannel shirt. As mustard dribbled down my front, I distinctly recall not worrying about what some goofy engineer thought about me or my hair. Maybe because I didn't fear then that I might be alone for the rest of my life.

Now I know Ethan would want me to start dating. *Go for it,* he'd say. *Don't sit home alone.* I feel a pang of jealousy imagining him remarrying if I were the one who died. Who would it be? That woman engineer at his office who was smart and funny and had the teeniest feet? I *hate* her.

I rub blush into my cheeks, trying to work up a healthy glow.

I didn't tell Ruth about my date because you never want to tell Ruth when you're doing something inappropriate, and I'm not sure this is appropriate. Yet. She'd never *say* anything, she'd just bristle, her dance-student posture straightening a notch.

The only thing worse than being widowed is being widowed and single. Well, how could you *not* be widowed and single? The thing is, though, there's this grace period right after your husband dies when you're sort of widowed and still married. When it's okay to burrow under the flannel sheets with a family pack of Oreos. When you're not expected to take off your wedding ring and go on a date with a man whose slate-blue-gray eyes give you goose bumps. But eventually you *are* supposed to get on with things and start bowling with actors.

How will I know if I really even *like* Drew Ellis? I'm so eager for intimacy, I would date a tree.

Drew called the night he visited me in the kitchen at Le Petit Bistro to make sure I was all right after "that crazy woman started yelling." I explained what had happened with Crystal and he immediately took my side, saying that I should call and report Crystal's mom, too. Oh, well, I told him. What was the sense in that? We talked for almost an hour, and I learned that he's from New York and put himself through Juilliard waiting tables at Brew Burger in the garment district and sometimes people left pennies in the ketchup as their tip. He said he hated waiting tables and could understand how the kitchen would be a much better place to work. Suddenly I didn't feel so embarrassed by my job. I learned that he's been with the festival for five years and he turned forty-one last month and his parents are retired schoolteachers. I cursed myself for imagining flying east with Drew to meet his parents for Thanksgiving. I'd apologize for the scampi incident, and we'd all gather around the piano to sing show tunes in their living room.

I explained that my husband died of cancer and I recently moved here from California after quitting my job. I left out the part about wearing my bathrobe to work.

Now, my heart leaps at the sound of the doorbell. Punctual! Another annoyingly charming characteristic. I jam the bottles of hair goo under the sink, throw the cupboard door shut, and lurch out of the bathroom.

In the front hall I pull off my glasses and set them on the table, take a deep breath, and consider not answering the door. Later I could claim that I got the day wrong. I wonder if Drew can hear me from the porch. Suddenly I imagine my mother saying: *Oh, sweetie, you're being* silly. After one final smooth and pat, I clutch the brass door handle with determination.

Crystal stands on my front porch, hopping from foot to foot.

"I gotta pee," she says.

I wish I hadn't opened the door. "You should call first." I put my glasses back on.

"Our phone's broken."

"Broken?"

"Well, like, shut off. My mom didn't pay the bill. The power's out, too." She shoots past me into the bathroom.

I recall how tidy Crystal's pink house was, with potted geraniums lining the steps up the porch and neat rows of pillows along the sofa, making me think that Crystal's mother must be very organized. Apparently not.

"Okay, you can use the bathroom, but then you have to go. I have a—" The word *date* sticks in my throat.

"We have no heat at night?" Crystal says through the door. "I've been freezing my ass off."

"Do you know when they're going to turn everything back on?" I feel bad for trying to get rid of her.

"This happens all the time." She flushes and opens the door. "My mom sends in the check? But she doesn't sign it on purpose or she dates it wrong. First they think it's a mistake and then she gets more time to pay. But they're, like, totally *on* to her now, so they shut everything off. Then she goes to stay at her jackass boyfriend's house and he pays the bill and they turn it back on."

"I see." While I can't think of a single redeeming quality in Crystal's mother right now, it doesn't seem helpful to disparage her. "Well, you know it's hard being a single mother. Working and making ends meet."

"What*ever*," Crystal says. She adds in a prim, grown-up tone, "I think it's her organizational skills and her priorities."

I look at my watch. Seven minutes until Drew's due to arrive.

"Okay, well, I have an appointment and when he gets here you have to go, okay?"

"*He*? You mean a *date*! Really? With who? Do you have a boyfriend? Do you think Edgar would mind? I mean Ethan?" She points and cocks her head, considering my skirt. "Is that what you're going to wear?"

I freeze, wishing I'd stuck with the jeans. Too late to change now. I brush my teeth for the second time in the last hour. Crystal stands behind me at the sink. She always stands a little too close, her knobby knees bumping me, her baby powder and cigarette smells lingering. I spit and gargle and we look into the mirror together.

"Um . . ." she says, biting down on her lip. "Is your hair, like, on *purpose*?"

I look at her in the mirror, look at my hair, look at the floor.

"I mean, it's not, like, a perm, right?" she adds optimistically, reaching out to finger a renegade curl.

Seven-thirty. Drew's officially half an hour late. Crystal drones on about how Amber and Tiffanie, the two girls at school she could supposedly care less about, got their belly buttons pierced.

"They totally didn't tell their moms, and they are in *big* trouble," she says, crossing her thin arms over her chest.

I glare at the phone, then pick up the receiver. The dial tone hums.

Seven thirty-five. The only thing worse than being a widow and being single is being a widow and being single and being stood up.

"I think I've been stood up," I tell Crystal.

"Oh, no. He's coming." She hands me her tube of pink lip gloss and I layer a little on top of my Rose Potpourri lipstick.

"You want me to fix you some supper?" I ask her.

She nods and we move to the kitchen, where I make her a grilled cheese sandwich. I've resigned myself to the fact that she's my date for the night and we're going to discuss Amber and Tiffanie, not Hamlet.

"Thank you," she says as I set the plate in front of her.

Wow. *Manners.* "You're welcome."

She hops up from the table and roots through the refrigerator for the ketchup. I'm relieved that she makes herself at home at my place now, alleviating some of the pressure to entertain her.

Since I'm obviously not going anywhere this evening, I kick off my shoes and unbutton my skirt, which digs into my waist despite the fact that I've eaten nothing but scrambled egg whites and canned peaches for two days.

"So does your mom let you stay home alone with no electricity while she's at her boyfriend's?" I ask, trying not to sound judgmental.

She bites into her sandwich and a string of cheese hangs down her chin. "Sometimes. Or I stay at this kid's house down the street, Melvin. He's a grade behind me and he's a geek, but his parents are totally nice, and they have awesome food like Pringles and Pop-Tarts." She pauses, in a reverie. "The *frosted* ones."

The lipstick tastes soapy. Using a napkin, I rub it all off.

"Hey, can I stay here tonight instead of at Melvin's?"

"Sure." What difference does it make? Drew's not coming.

Crystal perks up, talking faster. "I know what we can do. You can help me sew quilts for the animal shelter."

"Sew?" I ask skeptically.

"Yeah, there's this volunteer program? Where you cut up old quilts and sew the edges over and make littler ones for the animals 'cause they have to sleep alone in cages on newspaper and they, like, get cold." She looks around the kitchen. "Where's your sewing machine?"

How do I break it to Crystal that I can't sew? Can't do algebra, can't sew. What kind of mentor am I? Home economics was mandatory for girls when I was in junior high. We baked Rice Krispies bars and learned how many calories were in ten medium-size potato chips and sewed wraparound skirts while the boys made clay ashtrays in shop down the hall. I sewed through the front and back of my skirt while trying to get the pocket on, the sewing machine gobbling up the paisley fabric until Miss Crawley had to unplug it from the wall. Thankfully, my dad let me stay home the day of the fashion show when we were supposed to model our garments.

I clear my throat. "Ruth has a sewing machine," I tell her. "She knows how to sew. We could go over there."

Crystal makes a clicking noise with her tongue and rolls her eyes. "What*ever*. Never mind." She doesn't care for Ruth or anyone who takes my attention away from her.

She reaches under her pant leg and pulls a pack of Marlboros out of her sock. Her nose is red and raw, and her breath whistles in her chest.

"Sweetie, your asthma sounds terrible. I don't think you should smoke."

"Hey, you called me sweetie!"

I'm embarrassed by my corny term of endearment. "Sorry."

"That's okay. You can call me that. My dad? He called me muffin." She slides the cigarettes back into her sock. "I'm pretty sure he did."

Two hours after Drew was supposed to show up, Crystal's arranging a game of Risk for us to play when the phone rings. I jump but then let it ring several more times, not wanting to seem interested or desperate or even *home*.

"Hello," I say casually.

"Sophie?" Drew's voice sounds thick, as though he's been drinking. Great! A boozer.

"Hi. Is this Drew?" I try to sound as though I forgot we even had a date.

"I'm so *sorry*," he slurs.

"No problem." I obsessed over *mascara*, asshole. Fifteen minutes in the aisle at the drugstore debating between clump-free or luxury lash.

Crystal hovers beside me, cracking her knuckles and mouthing, *Is it him?* I swat her away.

"I'm at the hothpital," Drew moans. "I got hit."

"Hit? By who?" I'm thinking bar brawl. DUI, maybe.

"A truck. I was crossing the street. That's all I saw. The grill of a *very big* pickup truck." He giggles. "Sorry," he says apologetically. "They gave me a pain pill." He pauses, then perks up. "Hey, you want to come down here? I'll buy you some peanut-butter crackers from the vending machines."

The Ashland emergency room. My old stomping ground.

"I could use a lift home," Drew continues. "I'm not supposed to drive, and besides, I don't have my car."

Dating *and* the hospital. Two phobias for the price of one. "Uh . . . sure." I hope my hesitation doesn't make me sound stingy about giving him a ride. I'd like to ask if they'll wheel him out to the end of the parking lot so I can fetch him there. Explain that I've depleted my lifetime supply of hospital bravery. But I don't want Drew calling that red-haired actress friend for a ride. She'd probably have him home and sprawled across her sofa with his pants off in no time. "Sure," I repeat.

"Great," says Drew.

"Can't I come?" Crystal whines as I drive her to her friend Melvin's, where she's supposed to spend the night.

"Nope, sorry."

"But you said we could sew!"

"We will, just not tonight."

"I'm really good at bowling."

"We're not *going* bowling. My friend's been hurt."

Crystal kicks the dashboard with her bare foot.

I glare at her. She bows her head and frowns, hugging her grungy backpack to her chest.

"Think about something fun you'd like to do this weekend," I tell her.

"I could watch your stuff while you're in the hospital, and then we could all—"

The glass hospital doors jolt open automatically, revealing the cavernous hallway into the ER.

"Move!" a man shouts as he bumps past me toward the front desk, clutching a bloody towel to the side of his head. I scramble in after him. The doors slice shut behind me.

At the front desk I tell an admitting clerk that I'm there to pick up Drew. "I'm Drew Ellis's . . ." *Person to contact in case of emergency?* "Ride," I tell her, not wanting to elevate my status.

She leads me down the hall to Drew, who sits behind a tan curtain on a gurney, examining a pair of crutches. His face brightens when he sees me. Even his *wrinkles* are handsome—intelligent lines across his forehead, crinkly crow's-feet when he smiles. Ethan's face always lit up when I walked into a room. I was grateful for being loved this unconditionally—loved for just showing up! But he knew all of my flaws and foibles.

"No breaks," Drew says proudly. His right arm is held close to his body in a sling, his fingers poking stiffly out of an Ace bandage. He wiggles them. "Only a few stitches." He points to his knee, lumpy with bandages under his jeans, which are torn and streaked with blood.

I must blanch; he quickly insists that he's fine, only a little banged up.

As I listen to Drew's story of getting hit—a pickup truck packed with teenagers turning right on red without stopping—my pulse takes off and my head swims. I'm distracted by the red sharps container on the wall behind him. It overflows with a tangled plastic catheter dotted with tiny beads of bright red blood. Beyond that, a row of empty gurneys lines the wall, their black cushions gleaming under the bright lights. I wonder what happened to the people lying on them, whether they got to go home.

Drew says he stopped at the store to buy me daffodils and was headed back to his car when *wham!*. I picture him sprawled in the gutter. Then my train of thought is interrupted by an awful smell: rubbing alcohol. The stark odor of illness. The smell of the prep pads I rubbed over Ethan's hip before giving him his pain shots.

There must be a place to sit down here. I take a step toward Drew's gurney, but there's no chair. I consider the floor, spotting a brownish quarter-size stain on the linoleum that could be blood. Then the whole room turns inside out.

"Miss Stanton?" A blurry nurse hovers over me.

I'm a Mrs., I want to tell her. No, I'm not.

"I'm not," I stutter.

"You're not Sophie Stanton?"

"I am."

"Okay, honey. What day is it?"

"It's, um . . ." It's my day off. The day the theater's dark. My first-date day. "Monday," I stutter.

"You fainted. You're fine. You didn't hit your head."

"What *did* I hit?" Fainted! How mortifying.

"You fell forward, onto the gurney."

Which gurney? *Drew's* gurney? It's been a long time since I've dated, but I'm pretty sure you're not supposed to do a face plant on your suitor's gurney on the first date.

"Are you all right?" Drew asks, hobbling over to me.

He's got his jacket on, one sleeve dangling at his side, and he's clutching some paperwork.

"I'm fine," I tell him.

Drew and I head across the hospital parking lot toward my car. Although I promised the nurse that I was all right, I'm still light-headed. Drew fumbles with the crutches, leaning into me acci-dentally. I cup his elbow in my hand. He leans closer for support, readjusts. His body gives off warmth. My knees wobble.

I try to suppress the dawning realization that this is a stellar first-date story. *Your father and I had our first date at the hospital!* No. Stop that. How can there be a nuclear family in my future without Ethan?

"Oh, *ow*," Drew moans as he hops along the uneven asphalt.

"Look at us." I laugh and touch my fingers to the side of my head, as if to be sure it's still there. "I'm sorry I fainted," I add. "Since my husband died I don't do well at hospitals."

The word *husband* hangs in the air before us.

"Oh. *Oh*." Drew stops, touches my shoulder. "God, I shouldn't have asked you to come down here."

"It's okay."

A car swerves into the driveway of the hospital, the driver gun-ning the engine up to the ER. Drew rears back and we both almost tumble over. We right ourselves, laughing.

"Let's rest," Drew says, making a U-turn toward a nearby bench.

We sit side by side on the bench in silence. I feel as though we're two kids who don't know each other yet, waiting for the bus on the first day of school.

19

Drew Ellis is a laugher. He throws his head back and pounds the table with his fist until his face reddens and tears fill his eyes and you can't help but feel that you're the funniest person on earth when you're telling him a story.

Over dinner on our second date (which is really our first date, since our hospital get-together ended after a short ride home), I recount my corporate demise at Gorgatech. When I get to the "Gentlemen, start your hair dryers" part, I'm afraid I'm going to have to perform the Heimlich on Drew.

"What a *terrible* job!" he gasps, drying his eyes.

I never thought of it as a terrible job. I thought of myself as a terrible employee. For the first time, I see the humor in my public relations career.

"Yeah!" I agree, laughing. *Laughing* for the first time about Lara and the patch. *For immediate release: This job sucks!*

We eat at a restaurant downtown that features oddly vertical entrées, ingredients stacked high and topped with feathery sprigs of rosemary, making them look like ladies' hats.

Drew Ellis is a listener. He leans forward and makes direct eye contact, tilting his head as if to bring one ear closer. I hate to make comparisons to my husband, but I can't help it. Ethan never listened this carefully. He was always distracted—a part of his brain working over chinks in software code. Sometimes several sentences into a conversation Ethan would yelp, "What? *What?*"—a tip that he obviously hadn't been listening. This made me feel boring and sometimes, as I told a story, my voice would lower until I decided that what I had to say was dumb. "Oh, never *mind*," I'd grumble.

"I'm listening!" he'd insist.

Drew Ellis is decisive. He glances at the menu for only a moment before choosing the filet. And he seems to have made up his mind right away that he likes me. Or is he this way with all of his dates? Fawning and laughing and complimenting. Either way, I'm not sure I'm up to this undivided attention, this pressure to break out of the sweatpants comfort zone and be clever all the time.

Drew Ellis has lots of friends. We sit at a table overlooking the street, and when festival actors passing by the window spot him, they burst in to say hello, lavishing us with hellos and handshakes.

Drew Ellis is generous. He leaves our waitress a big tip and waves people ahead of him in traffic as we pull away from the restaurant in his rattly old BMW.

Drew Ellis is tidy. His car is immaculate on the inside, nothing but a fountain pen and a small box of Kleenex on the seat and a notebook for recording gas mileage. It's not like riding in Ethan's car, where you'd be ankle-deep in a heap of take-out trash and used coffee mugs.

Drew Ellis smells sweet, like clothes that just came out of the dryer. As we say good night on my front porch, he gives me a once-on-the-mouth, respectful, I-know-you-recently-lost-your-husband-and-more-than-anything-you-just-need-companionship kiss. Despite its simplicity, it is the most complicated kiss of my life. My first post-Ethan, widow kiss. But it is also a relief, like peeing after a long car ride. Drew whispers, "Good night," and heads down the front walk. I stand paralyzed on the porch, a warm boozy feeling pooling in my knees. I hate him for being such a terrible good-riddance list candidate.

. . .

Drew Ellis keeps calling my house.

"Hi, just wondering how you're doing," he says, his impeccable actor diction echoing through my answering machine. "Thought maybe you'd like to take a drive out to Jackson this weekend."

I can't call Drew Ellis back. If I call him I might go out with him again and if I go out with him again I might fall in love with him and if I fall in love with him he might dump me or die.

"'Feelings, nothing more than feelings . . . ,'" he croons into the machine the next evening, hamming it up and then laughing at his own joke. "Listen," he adds, his voice lowering with seriousness, "I completely understand if you'd rather not go out again. Just give me a call to let me know you're okay."

Instead of calling Drew Ellis, I fill out a registration form for night classes in the culinary arts program at the local university. Because I don't think I'm going to master this fondant thing on my own. Besides, I don't need an actor boyfriend; I need a vocation, a new career. When I get to the dreaded question that stains every starting-your-life-over-again form—*Person to contact in case of emergency*—I write: *George Clooney*. I seal the application, stick it in the mailbox on the porch, then start a double batch of vanilla cake batter so I can practice frosting.

Soon the whole house smells like a bakery. For hours I work on perfecting fondant, until the edges of the cakes are crisp and even and the sheen on top is as smooth as glass. When I run out of cake layers I ice a shoebox, then an old Styrofoam kickboard I find in the garage. Squeezing pink, blue, and yellow icing through the tubes over the fondant, I try roses, balloons, and cursive writing. I wish imaginary people happy birthday—*Quentin* and *Zachary*—so I can master more challenging letter combinations.

Despite the sweet, buttery smell of the cakes, I have no desire to sample them. It seems the more I work with food, the less I feel like eating it. Maybe it's simply that finding enjoyable work is as satisfying as curling up with a box of Mallomars.

Exhausted, with fondant cemented under my fingernails, I fall asleep in my clothes on the sofa. I dream that Chef Alan takes all the entrées off the menu at Le Petit Bistro, replacing them with desserts. As he crosses out the veal Oscar and shrimp scampi, I notice that his tangle of a beard is made of spun sugar.

Drew Ellis shows up at Le Petit Bistro to invite me to his house for dinner.

"Sorry I haven't called," I tell him, hoping for once that Chef Alan will charge out of his office and interrupt. "I've been busy."

Drew nods with interest. "What have you been up to?"

"Um . . ." *Decorating shoeboxes with frosting?* "Signing up for cooking school. . . ." My voice trails off. I'm not sure if I'm ready to tell anyone about my new career ambitions. It's like telling people you're quitting smoking or going on a diet. You feel silly later if things don't work out.

"Great." He points to the strawberry rhubarb pies cooling on wire racks, ruby filling bubbling through golden brown lattice crust. "You've obviously got a natural talent."

Sometimes I'm wary of Drew's knack for saying just the right thing. Before I know it, I'm agreeing to have dinner at his house on Monday night when we're both off from work.

"Great," he says. "It's a date."

There's that word again.

Drew Ellis can't cook. There's nothing in his refrigerator but a bag of potatoes that have grown eyes and tentacles, and the smell is so sour that I wonder what decaying matter he threw away just before my arrival. This isn't in keeping with his tidy car!

He's set the coffee table in front of the fireplace in the living room with a bottle of Chardonnay, wineglasses, paper plates (one of which looks used), candles, and a little bouquet of double delight roses from his garden. He hands me a take-out menu from a Chinese restaurant and insists that I make all the choices.

Drew Ellis keeps books in his dishwasher. Books! After we finish our kung pao and mu shu, I clear the coffee table and open the dishwasher to load the forks and knives. There, where the plates go, are plays by Tennessee Williams and George Bernard Shaw, lined up in alphabetical order, spines facing up.

"Oh, my bookshelves are all so full!" Drew says, waving at the books. "I hand-wash." He adds that he rarely eats at home, buying most of his meals at the diner off of I-5, where they serve "great" biscuits and gravy. I'm disappointed by this overall disregard for food.

Despite his stinky refrigerator, Drew Ellis is a neat freak. As he fixes us coffee, I notice that all of the handles on the mugs in his cupboard point in the same direction. On our way back to the living room, he's compelled to straighten my shoes by the door. When I start the crossword puzzle in pen, he gasps and fetches a jar of freshly sharpened pencils.

Don't ask *why* I'm doing the crossword puzzle on a date. Suddenly I feel the need to keep occupied. The room's too primed for romance. Logs crackling in the fire, jazz piano moaning on the stereo. I swear I can hear the wine breathing in our glasses. While I wouldn't mind a little post–kung pao ravishing before the fire, I'm certainly not brave enough to facilitate it. As Drew adds a log, I sneak a peek at him from behind the newspaper. He's handsome, but not *impossibly* handsome, as I'd first thought. Slightly beakish nose, brown hair thinning a bit at the crown of his head. His forehead is a little too high, his eyes set a little too deep. Only a little, but still. He looks up. I return to the puzzle, the pencil point snapping and flying across the room.

Drew Ellis suffers from stage fright. Stage fright! Mr. Hand-some-self-confident-voice-projected-across-the-room-like-a-javelin. As we split a Toblerone bar for dessert, he tells me about his job as an actor, describing intense preperformance jitters.

"I'm fine once I get *on* stage," he explains, "it's the hour leading up to the show."

"What happens?" I've given up on the crossword. We sit cross-legged in front of the fire, our knees barely touching, an electric current running between them. I try to seem unfazed by Drew's closeness.

"Shaking, sweaty hands, racing pulse. All the symptoms of a heart attack, basically. A thirty-second, three-pound-weight-loss trip to the bathroom. You get the picture."

I'm about to tell Drew just how *much* I get the picture when I recall the magazine article I read last night: "Dating Dos and Don'ts." *Don't share your insecurities!* I even used a highlighter pen on the article, studying up on how to be single again the way you'd prep for a final.

"What are you afraid of?" I ask him.

"That I'll forget my lines."

"Have you ever?"

"No." He sits up straighter, eyes widening. "But it's more than that. That I'll lose my job. That I'll be a washed-up actor doing the dinner theater circuit in the Catskills, singing 'Copacabana' to a roomful of geriatrics."

"Wow. That's a very specific fear."

"My shrink helped me put it into words."

"*You* go to a shrink?"

"I'm *from* New York."

"Drew, I've read your reviews. There's no way you'll ever lose your job."

"Once I was in a musical in Manhattan that opened and closed the same night. By noon the next day I was filling out an application at Brew Burger."

"Right. And how many years ago was that?"

He laughs. "Twenty."

"That's all I'm saying."

He kisses me. Cool, sweet mango lips, warm tongue. Not my husband.

He pulls away and we both stare into the fire.

Finally I ask to use the bathroom.

Drew trails behind me. He says he wants to explain his bathroom floor. He started remodeling months ago but couldn't decide on tiles. Brushed limestone or plain linoleum?

As I step onto the splintery plywood subfloor, exposed nails cutting through my socks. Drew pulls back the shower curtain to show me a case of tiles in the tub that he doesn't like but hasn't gotten around to exchanging.

Good, Drew Ellis is a waffler, a procrastinator.

"These look like bird poop." He picks up a tile and frowns at the coin-size brown splotches in the pattern. "Why are you smiling?" he asks, looking up at me.

Because you've got foibles. Now that I've got material for a good-riddance list, I may actually be able to date Drew Ellis.

20

"Wonderful, you're *dating*," Ruth says.

It's a hot Sunday afternoon in the first week of May. Ruth, Crystal, and I lounge on the porch at Colonel Cranson's, watching cars jerk and roll through the car wash.

"I guess you could call it that." Suddenly I want to slide my wedding ring back on. A wedding ring is something you can *hide* behind. It hangs from a gold chain around my neck now, resting against my sternum. Whenever I'm reading, I can't stop touching it, rubbing my thumb over the bumpy diamond, lifting the ring and holding it between my lips.

I remember thinking with tremendous relief on the morning I got married that I'd never be single again. Never have to worry whether a steamy soiree warranted a blood test. Never have to hide in the bathroom at midnight on New Year's Eve from the looming sweaty dateless guy at the party.

The leaves on the trees are so green that they look painted on, and the air smells sweet, like soap and wax. Cool spray drifts across the street from the car wash, tickling our skin.

"This should be a spa treatment," Ruth says, holding up her arms and closing her eyes. She looks beautiful in her long yellow sundress, which matches her hair. I'm proud of her; she came over to announce that she's not going to let her ex-husband, Mark, move back in.

"Ask me about mica!" Crystal kicks the wicker table and our

glasses of iced tea slosh over. A textbook lies open in her lap, a chunk of jagged black rock resting on the pages.

"What do you like about Drew?" Ruth asks me.

"He takes the grocery cart all the way back to the front of the store." For some reason this is the first thing that comes to mind: Drew's inherent conscientiousness.

"What's he look like?" Ruth asks.

"*Ask* me about *mica*," Crystal repeats. She squeezes the rock, its surface glittering in the sunlight. She's dying to impress her teacher with her earth science presentation. He's around her dad's age, and I think she's got a huge crush on him.

"I'll help you in a minute," I tell her. "You're interrupting."

"But this is *our* day." Crystal glances sideways at Ruth. "Why does *she* have to be here?"

"Feel free to address me directly anytime," Ruth says coolly.

Now I feel as though I've got two teenage daughters.

The sleeves of Crystal's football jersey hang in bell shapes over her wrists. She sucks some of the fabric into her mouth and chews.

Ruth's wicker chair creaks as she shifts her weight toward Crystal. "I'm sorry." She peers up from under the brim of her straw hat. "Tell us about mica."

"You don't have to apologize," I tell Ruth.

"Mica is any group of chemically and physically related mineral silicates . . ." Crystal shifts her eyes downward, peering at an index card on the table that's filled with her big loopy handwriting in blue ballpoint pen. "Um . . . common in igneous and metamorphic rocks, each containing, um . . ." She picks up the card and reads slowly, "Hydroxyl, *alk* . . . alkali, and aluminum silicate groups, characteristically splitting into flexible sheets used in insul, insul— *shit!*" She gives up, flipping the card like a Frisbee into the grass. "I'm so *stupid!*" She bangs her bare heel on the porch and slides down in her chair until her chin rests on her chest.

"No, you're not," I tell her, retrieving the card.

"What*ever.* I picked mica because it's, like, the prettiest, but I totally can't *say* all that stuff." She looks at the piece of inky rock accusingly.

"What's metamorphic rock?" Ruth asks, giggling. "Is that a genre of music?"

I laugh, spurting out a little tea.

"It's not *funny.*" Crystal snaps her textbook shut.

If Ethan were here, he'd have Crystal reciting eloquent paragraphs about mica in no time.

Last night, I dreamed Ethan and I were baking French bread on the big pine kitchen table at Colonel Cranson's. As he punched down the dough, there was color in his cheeks and his eyes were bright. Then I was awake, fumbling under the covers, expecting to feel his arm or leg or the river of his pulse running through his belly. I snapped on the light and recorded the dream in a notebook that Sandy said we should keep by our beds. I was relieved that Ethan wasn't ill in the dream. No tubes or bandages. It seemed possible that I might never dream of Ethan sick again, as though the cancer had gone away, as though he'd finally gotten better.

"Mr. Matthews is gonna think this *sucks,*" Crystal moans now. She picks at the mica's brittle top layer, which flakes off like nail polish.

"When's your project due?" Ruth asks.

The dryers in the car wash build to a high-pitched whir.

"Wednesday," Crystal says to me, ignoring Ruth.

"Don't worry," I urge, trying to adopt Ethan's optimism. "We'll do some research and present it in layman's terms that are easy to understand." I pace across the porch, brainstorming mica.

"What's *that* mean?" Crystal says.

"That means for people like you and me who aren't so good at math and science."

"But you're, like, good at *everything,*" Crystal says, annoyed.

I stop pacing, floored by Crystal's faith in me. She knows I can't sew or do algebra. The peeling paint on the porch tickles my bare feet. "Oh, no," I tell her. "*Ruth's* good at everything."

"Yeah, *right*," Ruth says, chewing her ice. In college, whenever she and I teamed up on something—a duet in choir or a doubles tennis match—she joked that we were like Lucy and Ethel. But I always thought we were like Lucy and Grace Kelly.

"I don't want to stand in front of the class and, like, *talk* in front of everyone." Crystal tosses the mica in the grass and chews her fingernails.

I pull her hand from her mouth.

"Amber and Tiffanie did their projects together on sand," she continues. "They, like, wore *bathing* suits and shorts, and they were such *dorks*. But Mr. Matthews laughed and gave them an A."

Crystal tosses her science book at the mica. It lands with a thud on the lawn. "I'm going to stay home sick next week," she says. "Why can't Mr. Matthews teach something easier? He's *totally* nice."

I remember admiring a teacher this much. In fourth grade I fell in love with Miss Brown. Everything about her was brown—long brown hair that swept across her back and a brown wool beret. She even drove a little brown Celica. During science class Miss Brown took us for walks in the woods to pick up litter, which she said was terrible for the environment. She was beautiful, unlike the third-grade teacher, Miss Dillon, who had a bulbous mole on her chin and a disposition that flashed like lightning, threatening to shut down recess at any moment. "Can Miss Brown live with us?" I begged my mother. I felt Miss Brown would make a perfect addition to our too-small family.

"No, sweetie, she has her own house."

"I'm *slow*," Crystal says now, snapping her lighter on to light a cigarette. "That's what my mom said."

"Well, I'm sure she meant slow as in it takes you a while to find your coat slow," I tell Crystal. "She didn't mean stupid slow."

"You can't *say* that to kids," Ruth says incredulously, frowning at Crystal's cigarette.

"What*ever*," Crystal snaps at her. "I'm, like, *flunking* pre-algebra."

"You are not flunking," I tell her. "You retook that test and got a C. That's a big improvement."

Crystal looks away and slides a hand up the sleeve of her jersey. I know she's picking at the scabs on her arms. She hasn't cut herself for almost two weeks. She's made a pact with her psychiatrist, promising to call her if she feels like cutting. Meanwhile, she's taken to compulsively drawing Xs in her notebooks, the pen slicing through the paper as she presses down.

"You're smart," I tell her. "You don't need Mr. Matthews or your mom or Tiffanie and Amber to tell you that. It's just true."

The praise makes her flinch. I feel like a dumb self-help cassette tape, but I know if I complimented Crystal ten times a day, she still wouldn't feel good about herself. She's the only person I know whose self-esteem is lower than mine right now.

"Maybe you just need a little help with math and science," Ruth offers.

"That's what the tutor's for," I agree.

Crystal shrugs. "My mom says I can't keep the tutor because it's expensive."

"I'll pay for it," I tell her. "It's not that much."

"What*ever*."

"No, not 'whatever.' We're going to get your grades up."

"Even if you don't get into vet school, there are lots of other jobs working with animals," Ruth says.

"Like what?" Crystal grumbles.

"Like working at a pet grooming place, for example," Ruth stammers, uncertain.

"Great, cutting dogs' *toenails*."

"No, and training dogs," Ruth adds. "Maybe training Seeing Eye dogs, and—"

"Or working with horses," I offer. "You know, brushing them."

"Horses are expensive," Crystal says. I can see her mother's logic at work here, telling Crystal that anything other than going to school and watching TV is too expensive.

"People pay you to take care of them," Ruth says.

Crystal carves her thumbnail into the paint on the wicker tabletop.

"How much time have you put into this project so far?" I ask her, nodding at the mica. "Honestly? About fifteen minutes copying that card out of the encyclopedia?"

"Yeah."

"Well, we just need to spend more time on it." I say this firmly but kindly, just like the mom in the salad dressing ad who insists that her daughter gently tear the lettuce.

When Chef calls me into his office Wednesday afternoon, I wonder if I'm getting fired or demoted again.

"Sophie, may I see you?" He pokes his big bearded head out of his office, juts out his plum of a lower lip.

"Just a minute." I set down the sifter, leaving a white spray of cake flour like a giant snowflake across the counter, and jot down how many cups I've measured so far.

If he fires me, maybe I'll start my own little bakery selling the savory cheesecakes I've been refining. The recipes are mine, after all. I've surfed the Web for tips on creating a business plan. My heart thrummed in my chest as I considered gambling my nest egg on my own little shop in town.

Chef pushes his door shut. His jeans and flannel shirt hang neatly from a hanger on a hook on the back of the door, and his toque sits at attention on the corner of his desk.

"Have a seat," he says, shuffling papers. My pink slip? News that you have to sit down for is never any good. I lean back in the Windsor chair, the spindles jabbing my spine.

"You've been doing a great job," he mumbles.

I'm waiting for the "but." I notice a lopsided clay bunny on Chef's desk that was obviously made by a child. Its head and ears are way too big for its body. I wonder if Chef has a kid or if he's an uncle, if he's got a soft spot somewhere.

"George loves the savory cheesecake," he continues. George is the persnickety owner of the restaurant who makes surprise reconnaissance visits. The first employee to spot George on the premises is supposed to yell, "Red light." The first person to notice him leave is supposed to say, "Green light." Then everyone goes back to sitting on the counters or swiping rolls out of the bread warmer.

"And the hazelnut torte is delicious." Chef closes his eyes and purses his thick lips as though tasting the torte. While he's one of the last people I'd relish praise from, I'm flattered.

"Thanks." *Get to the point!*

"I'm going to promote you to head baker."

"Really?" A *promotion*! A kooky swell of self-confidence warms my chest, like when you practice your Oscar acceptance speech in the shower despite the fact that you've never even acted. But it's only a job as a baker, for God's sake. It's not as though I'm secretary of state. Who *wouldn't* get promoted from this rinky-dink, college-student job? "But I'm the *only* baker," I remind Chef.

"True, but you'll get a raise and have expanded duties. You'll continue developing new recipes, order your own supplies, and manage the dishwasher. I may hire you a part-time helper so you won't have as much prep work." As he wheels his chair toward me, I catch his musky cologne and beef broth smell. "You're a hard worker and you've got great potential. You'll get your raise in your next paycheck." Chef extends a doughy hand. I'm afraid a neck rub's on the way, so I thank him and scoot out the door, bumping into the dishwasher, who's on his way in to work.

"Sorry, man," he says. He always calls me man.

Head baker. I turn back to my station, the late afternoon sun making the butcher block on the counter glow golden. Who knows, maybe one day I will open my own café. I picture customers sitting at sidewalk tables and tearing open sugary brioches, the sweet steam inside offering a bit of solace.

Early one Sunday morning the phone rings; it's Marion. She makes small talk for a few minutes, managing to be pleasant and insulting at the same time. She asks if I've had a chance to explore Oregon's beautiful hiking trails and maybe drop a few pounds in the process. Then she asks me to put Ethan on the line. At first I think she's joking.

"Yeah, right, there are a few things I'd love to ask him," I tell her. "Like where he put my passport!" To this day I haven't found it. "Oh, and I'd love to be able to tell him that I got a promotion at work."

"That's nice, dear. Are you trying cases now?"

I realize she's completely off her nut.

"I'm a baker," I tell her.

"Ohhhh. A *baker.*" She always went overboard in tone when trying to feign interest in my life. "Is Ethan out mowing the lawn?" she adds impatiently.

The *lawn*? Ethan? My breath catches in my chest.

"No. He's *dead*. Remember?"

The buzzer goes off in Marion's kitchen and she says she's got to run and take cookies out of the oven for the church bazaar. She asks me to have Ethan call her when he gets back in, then hangs up.

All week I think about calling Marion back, but I'm not sure what to say. It's as though grief has finally found her and she's denying everything, even denial.

The college parking lot sparkles optimistically on the first morning of classes. But I don't want to get out of the car. Students bustle toward the administration building with determination. They all look so *young*. Yesterday I couldn't wait to join the culinary arts program, to conquer Pastry Workshop: Pies, Cobblers, and Fruit Crisps. I even signed up for a class in how to start your own small business and called Kit to ask him to keep a lookout for commercial rental spaces. "My dream is to start my own bakery," I told him, caffeine and optimism sparking through my veins. But now my confidence has dwindled and my brain *feels* like a fruit crisp, bubbling over with anxiety, clear thoughts going soggy. Starting a new career means planning for the future. Without Ethan.

The car heats up in the sun, and my notebook feels slippery in my perspiring hands. The thought of starting over always gives me either a rush of excitement or a crush of dread. Nothing in between.

What if I fail at this career, too? After all, public relations seemed like a wise choice. The Advanced Cutlery Techniques class description said we'll learn to julienne vegetables and bone and ballottine a chicken, whatever that means. Maybe I should spare the chicken and drive home now.

I start the car and look over my shoulder to back up. A new lime green Volkswagen Bug is perched for my parking space, a twenty-something driver peering eagerly over her steering wheel. Suddenly my parking space defenses go up. This space is mine. *I'm late for class!* I shut off the car and wave the Volkswagen driver on. She guns her engine and shoots to the other end of the parking lot.

Honey, this is easy-peasy, I imagine my mother saying. She and her Delta Gamma sorority sisters always said "easy-peasy." *It's not like it's cordon bleu,* Ethan would point out.

I certainly can't tell Ruth I quit on my first day. Besides, who'd screw up a pastry class? Okay, *me,* quite possibly. But so what if I do? I at least want to learn to bake the pear pie with cheddar cheese crust. Ask the teacher for pointers on my savory cheesecake recipes. Does the smoked fontina overpower the mushrooms? More important, am I going to work at Le Petit Bistro until I'm sixty-five? I yank the keys out of the ignition, shove them in my bag, squeeze the notebook to my chest, and climb out of the car.

21

"It's a myth that people experience grief for a certain amount of time and then they're over it," Sandy says, clutching his clipboard to his chest and turning to scan the grief group circle. His baggy green fatigue pants and tan V-neck sweater make him look like a cross between Mr. Rogers and a private in the army fighting the war against grief. "Our culture assumes grief should be over in a year, so people may think they're going crazy if they can't 'wrap it up' by then."

Sandy begins every meeting with a sort of pep talk sermon, then invites discussion. I wish he'd open with a talk about intimacy, about what it's like to sleep with someone other than your husband or Ben & Jerry for the first time in six years.

Drew and I are soon to go on our fourth date, and I worry that it's going to be horizontal. Nine of the fifteen pounds I want to lose cling to me like an overprotective mother who doesn't want me to take my pants off until I'm married again.

"My women friends are a little impatient with me," says Gloria, who's sitting next to me. She's always draped in layers of woolen capes and smells cinnamony, like autumn. She lowers her voice and twists the tassels on her cape between her fingers. "They think I should be getting *on* with my life."

A man whose wife died of ovarian cancer nods.

Roger says, "*Fuck* them." Roger's son was accidentally killed by a neighbor kid who was playing with a gun, and Roger's the maddest person in the group.

"It's normal to feel angry," Sandy says. "But we have to work on that anger."

Roger digs his fist into his thigh and says, "Okay."

"Sophie," Sandy says, turning toward me, "we haven't heard from you. Are you up to sharing your feelings today?"

I don't want to tell the group that I've felt better in the past month. That seems like a betrayal.

"I still think of my husband every day," I tell them. "But now I smile when I think of him. Sometimes I cry, but I don't want to lie on the floor at the grocery store or inhale a whole box of Girl Scout cookies." The group chuckles and nods encouragingly, all those faces like a gentle wave moving toward me.

"How's your dream journal going?" Sandy asks. We're all supposed to keep a dream journal, and mine is the first-prize winner for cancer nightmares.

I explain to Sandy and the group that I haven't dreamed about Ethan being sick for several weeks now. No more hospital nightmares.

"It's such a relief," I tell them, embarrassed because now I'm crying. Gloria drapes a woolen wing around me and I burrow toward her, breathing her *chai* smell.

"After we've watched a loved one succumb to a terminal illness, it's very helpful to be able to remember them *before* they got sick," Sandy tells the group.

The guy whose wife died of ovarian cancer nods, wiping his cheeks with the heels of his palms. He has a large Grecian nose and black hair that curls around his forehead. He looks so young for a widower.

I'm still crying, and the guy whose wife died of cancer is crying, and Gloria's crying, black capes shaking. Then everyone around the room is crying, except Roger, who is pounding his thigh with his fist. Sandy tells us it's okay to feel terrible, and we feel terrible. It's like Simon Says. The boxes of Kleenex make the rounds.

"You've made remarkable progress, Sophie," Sandy says.

I shake my head and wave a hand at him dismissively, embarrassed by my grief gold star. Good girl. Good grief.

"We've all made remarkable progress," Sandy adds.

Roger is pounding his fist on the side of his chair now, unable to cry. I remember feeling like him back at the grief group in San Jose—being the only dry-eyed one in the room, your crying machine out of order.

Gloria stands, her silver bracelets jangling, crosses the circle to Roger, and crouches beside his chair. She takes his fist in her hands and brings it toward her chest, gently unfurling his knotted fingers one by one. Roger bristles, then relaxes and leans toward her. Gloria murmurs to him, her voice as husky as her woolen capes. Roger leans closer to hear what she's saying—the tops of their heads almost touching. His shoulders begin to shake and he nods yes to something. She takes his other hand and squeezes it, too, then sets them both in his lap and crosses the circle back to her seat. Roger glances down at his hands, which are finally still, then closes his eyes.

My next date with Drew is in two days, and I can't lose nine pounds or acquire a firm butt or suntan by then. "You look great," Ruth insists. "Shop for sexy lingerie if you're really worried."

I drive to Medford and hole up in the JCPenney's dressing room with an armload of slippery camisole tops. I finger the lace along a faux leopard number. Something like this under a sweater with jeans would be casual but sexy. The saleswoman, whose spiky orange hair looks like shag carpet, wants to know if I need help.

"Do they offer liposuction at the salon upstairs?" I ask her.

She giggles. "No, but you can get a bikini wax," she whispers loudly through the slats in the door.

"Can they wax away fat?"

"Aw, honey, don't worry. You're petite. You can keep the lights down low if you're shy. That's more romantic."

The leopard camisole is silky and scratchy at the same time, and the spaghetti straps keep falling down, as though the top is rejecting me instead of vice versa.

I spin in a half turn, dodging the pins on the dressing room floor, and have a three-way look at my figure. The fluorescent lights make my skin look blotchy and uneven, like old linoleum, and I'm certain these are someone else's thighs. Perhaps Margaret Thatcher's. *Attention, shoppers. If anyone is missing a pair of grand-piano-leg thighs, they have been found in the lingerie dressing area.*

I'm going to bring my savory blue-cheese-and-walnut cheesecake to try out on Drew, and a dark chocolate torte that I learned to make in class. I also want to show him the business plan for my bakery. He's going to open a bottle of port he's been saving for five years. The special occasionness of the port makes me nervous. It's clearly been held for a historical event, such as the first time you sleep with someone. Everything about the date makes me nervous: the intoxicating port, the aphrodisiac chocolate dessert, and the amorous hour of our meeting—ten-thirty in the evening, after his show and my shift.

The last person I slept with was my husband, and that was ten months and a hundred cartons of peanut-butter-cup ice cream ago. During my last life. The one that was supposed to be my *only* life. Ethan, my *only* love.

Despite my layers of fleshy padding, my stomach growls forlornly. *Do you think maybe there's a little something for us at the department store café?* it wants to know. *Maybe a croissant?* No! Nothing but tomato juice until after my potentially horizontal date with Drew.

I lift my chin, arch my back, suck in my belly. I remember holing up back in San Jose on the air mattress in my barren living room and working my way around the crust of an entire pizza, tearing off one comforting chunk of warm dough after another. I dread the thought of Drew running a hand over my round belly and comparing it to the washboard abs of certain breathy actresses with phony British accents and pompous heirloom jewelry. But wouldn't he tire of her bony shoulders and small breasts, which look as flat as drink coasters under those cashmere sweaters? Wouldn't he crave a bit of voluptuousness?

I switch to a lacy black camisole, but it's as scratchy as wool against my skin.

Certainly Ethan wouldn't mind my new full figure. He always thought I looked great, even when I was in sweatpants with hurricane hair.

I feel guilty for longing to sleep with anyone other than my husband. The last time Ethan and I made love should be my last time forever. It was right before he went into the hospital for good. I had called the doctor and explained that the Darvon shot wasn't helping with Ethan's pain this time. The doctor said to give Ethan another shot and bring him to the hospital, that he was terminal now and we wanted him to be comfortable. He said this slowly and gently, and I remember wanting to hang up on him.

I gave Ethan another shot and he lay back on the pillows and licked his lips, his eyelids fluttering. I rubbed his feet, then his legs, then his shoulders, and scratched his scalp vigorously. He said all those tingling nerve endings eased the pain. His once lustrous hair was thin now and came away in wispy clumps in my hands.

Ethan laughed, loopy from the shot, and pulled me close to him. His cleanly shaven face was smooth against my cheek. Even on days when he felt awful, he showered, shaved, and dressed in jeans and a T-shirt, the jeans hanging from his waist. That chore sapped all his energy, though, and he usually lay down again. Then I'd bring him some breakfast, which he pretended to enjoy.

His breath was sweet, like mint toothpaste. He tugged at my T-shirt, trying to pull it off. I swept it over my head and lay beside him in my bra, his skin hot and smooth against my stomach. He pointed at my jeans, and I peeled them off. He pointed at his jeans and then his shirt, and I helped him pull them off, too. Together we lay under the cotton summer sheet, which was as light as breath over our skin. Ethan's body seemed as thin and brittle as an old man's, his shoulder blades two sharp wings under the sheet. His breath was weak and rattled faintly in his chest. We lay on our sides and pressed our faces together, and I felt a surge of remaining strength in Ethan's arms as he wrapped them around me. Heat emanated from his chest, then the two of us were one and I hid my face in the pillow so he wouldn't see me weep.

Afterward, I helped him into the tub for a hot soak, which always eased the ache in his hips. I sat beside him on a wooden stool and read his book of Blake poems aloud. He dipped his head back against the edge of the tub and closed his eyes. His lashes were as long and thick and dark as they'd always been, and I remember thinking, *There is this one last healthy thing.* Looking back, I wish he would have died right then, comfortably.

Now, I choose a conservative apricot-colored camisole with a bow so tiny that it's almost invisible, and I begin to dress.

The warmth of Drew's raisiny port burns through my chest and into my arms and legs. Suddenly we're tumbling onto his bed, a feathery down cloud. We don't have far to go, since we started our late night dinner picnic on the floor in front of the fireplace in his room. Now the reflections of the flames samba across the ceiling, making the whole room seem on fire.

Drew's eyes are droopy—window shades drawn halfway. Drew-py.

He lifts up the down comforter, forming a cave to crawl into, and we nestle between the flannel sheets. He rubs the back of my neck and then my feet—massaging away my date anxiety. After he tugs off my jeans and sweater, I'm down to only my underwear and the peach camisole—a slippery wisp of fabric dividing my bare skin from his. Despite the warm, rubbery port sensation in my body, I dread losing my last protective layer. Would it be possible to keep on my undergarments and conduct our romance through a hole in the sheets, like the Shakers?

I lie still, not wanting anything to jiggle. Then again, I don't want to seem like an uptight, afraid-to-get-naked sort of girl. I hold my breath, suck in my stomach, and roll gingerly toward Drew, as though there's broken glass in the bed between us.

"Cold?" he whispers.

"Freezing," I lie. Maybe this means I'll get my sweater back.

But clearly there isn't going to be any sweater or jeans or underwear or camisole or anxiety. Only fire. On the walls, on the ceiling, between my jelly legs. I remember this: Being touched. Passion. Joy. A cut healing over.

In the morning I stand in Drew's bathroom, the plywood subfloor splintery beneath my bare feet, dreamily brushing my teeth with my finger and a gob of Drew's Crest. Turning my head in the mirror, I check out my crazy, just-had-sex-on-the-beach hairdo, which Drew said he loves. I poke my fingers into the curls, then give up trying to fix them and splash cold water on my face.

We slept only about four hours, and now my brain, soaked with port and sex and chocolate, feels numb and giddy.

"You okay in there?" Drew says through the door. He wants to give me a fresh towel and a clean warm sweatshirt with that alluring dryer smell of his. He wants to take me out for blueberry pancakes at his favorite diner on I-5, where you can sink into comfy Naugahyde booths and read the paper all morning.

But I don't feel up to breakfast and daylight. I'm dizzy and sleep deprived, my cheeks lacking last night's luster. Everything went so well on our date, I'm afraid somehow it'll get wrecked over break-fast. Maybe I'll find out Drew's secretly in a cult. Besides, I'm sup-posed to meet Kit in a few hours to check out commercial rental spaces in town. I thank Drew for the invite but tell him I've got to get going.

At home, while waiting for water to boil for tea, I do not want to make eye contact with the wedding picture on the kitchen counter of Ethan and me. I keep it by the sugar bowl, so that I'll see it first thing every morning when I'm groping for coffee fixings. It wasn't that I *had* sex with another man. It's that I *enjoyed* sex with another man. Clothes-strewn-everywhere date sex. Not carefully-timed-trying-to-have-a-baby sex. And last night, before heading off to Drew's, I took off the gold chain with my wedding ring. I laid the ring and chain in my jewelry box, beside the little note from Ethan saying that he'd just gone to Home Depot. The giddy delirium from my late night gives way to a leaden feeling in my chest. *I'm sorry,* I want to tell Ethan.

I shower, dress, and sit on the front porch waiting for Kit, staring at my feet in my sandals. Feet look strange if you stare at them long enough. Like flat, rectangular hands with tiny fingers.

Anything begins to look strange if you stare at it long enough. A hole in the plank on the porch looks like a gaping little mouth. *Oh,* it says. *Uh-oh.*

A word begins to sound odd if you turn it over in your mind enough times, like a stone from a river that's black, then blue, and then gray as it dries. Boyfriend. Boy. Friend. Boyfriendboyfriend. Do I have a boyfriend? A woodpecker hammers greedily at a tree beside the garage, the relentless rapping echoing through the yard. I cover my ears with my palms, which makes a new strange word beat louder in my head: *Lover, lover, lover.*

— 22 —

The old wooden door of what used to be the Fudge Shoppe on East Main is swollen shut, and Kit has to heave his weight into it. Finally it gives and he tumbles into the store, the bell on the door clanging cheerfully.

"Here we are." His voice echoes into the empty shop. There are two rooms: a sales area up front and a kitchen in the back, beyond a row of glass bakery cases.

This is the first of a number of commercial rental spaces Kit wants to show me, but I don't think I need to see the others. A few blocks from the theaters, this location is perfect. I picture tourists from San Francisco and Portland pouring down the street in the summer, the smell of baking pies luring them in.

The store has been closed for almost two months, since the Fudge Shoppe owners retired, and the air inside is warm and stale. A fly buzzes lazily against the glass in one of the dingy bakery cases. I notice that the racks are rusted. Still, I imagine the shelves sparkling and filled with cheesecakes.

I'd like to get Drew's opinion of the shop, but that might make me seem needy. Hot waves of date memory wash over me: port and flannel and skin against skin, slick with perspiration. The mattress moaning under our weight, the comforter tumbling off the bed.

"What do you think?" Kit asks.

Blushing, I shudder and turn to survey the shop. A long oak counter with bun feet runs perpendicular to the glass cases. The rest of the room is empty except for a wooden bench scabby with peeling paint. I picture a table by each window, where people can look out onto the street. "Perfect," I tell Kit.

"It's a bit grungy," he admits. "But nothing a little elbow grease can't fix."

I follow him into the kitchen, where a row of black ovens towers to the ceiling. I plan to use money from the sale of my house and stock from Ethan's company to start the bakery. I'll also need a bank loan.

"You may need some fireproofing work," Kit says, peering into one of the ovens. "But I'm sure it's nothing major. And look at this ceiling!" As we tip back our heads to admire the embossed tin ceiling overhead, I'm dizzy from my late night.

Maybe Kit's unflinching optimism is what lured me into getting a crush on him before. He made starting over seem easy, even fun. But thankfully I'm not fantasizing about going to the Ramada Inn with my realtor now that I have a . . . lover? Pending significant other? Drew needs a job title.

"I'll bet there's a great wood floor underneath here," Kit says, tapping his foot on the old black linoleum, which is flecked with gold sparkles.

We sit at a rickety table in the kitchen and go over the lease. It's for two years, with a five-year renewal and an option to sublet, which Kit says is optimal. That way, if things go well, I won't have to move anytime soon. "Then you've locked in five more years at a good rate," he explains.

The words *locked in* send a pain through my head. "Five years?"

"With the option to sublet, you have a backup plan in case you change your mind."

"Or the place flops!" I picture tourists sucking in their stomachs and hustling past the bakery toward the chain coffee shop down the street for a nonfat latte. Who needs all those sweets before a long play? Who wants to add to the calorie count after that heavy French onion soup and buttery escargots at Le Petit Bistro?

Kit smiles and squeezes my hand. "Sophie, you worry too much."

"Let's see what the bank thinks," I tell him.

Ruth helps me put the finishing touches on my business plan, which I take to the bank in town to apply for a loan. The loan officer, a thin woman with a pinched nose, is as brisk and humorless as a school nurse. The more she frowns at my loan application, the more I jabber on nervously about the savory cheesecakes. ("They *sound* strange, but really they make a wonderful hors d'oeuvre or first course.") Finally she says, "Everything looks satisfactory, Ms. Stanton. We'll be in touch. Good day." I sit in the chair beside her desk for a moment, trying to think of a compelling detail to add.

"Toppings will be sold separately for the sweet cheesecakes," I explain. "Cranberry at Thanksgiving."

She smiles stiffly. "I guess that's good. I'm diabetic."

After the bank, I stay up several nights poring over cookbooks and choosing recipes.

One or two nights a week I sleep at Drew's house, and a couple of nights a week he stays at my place. He leaves his deodorant, razor, and toothbrush in my bathroom. Meanwhile, I carry a toothbrush in my purse, not quite ready for bathroom cohabitation. Still, I'm grateful when Drew dotes over me with the concern a spouse would harbor. He doesn't think I should walk home alone from work every night.

"Can cars see you?" he asks. "In the dark?"

"I'm on the sidewalk."

"Well, there aren't very many streetlights. You should have air bags."

"I'm walking!"

"I know." He giggles. "Personal air bags. In your coat."

One morning a social worker from Big Brothers/Big Sisters calls. At first the graveness in her voice makes me worry that I've done something wrong. Did she find out about the time I let Crystal drive my car? It was in an empty parking lot. We wore our seat belts and only circled around a few times. Crystal was very good at shifting gears.

But the social worker's calling to tell me that Crystal's been expelled from school for blowing up M-80s in the girls' room. She explains that the whole student body had to evacuate and gather on the front lawn for over an hour. The band missed its recital. I clench my teeth angrily as I listen, sickened by Crystal's selfishness. The woman says that Crystal got the M-80s from her friend Melvin; she coerced him into stealing them from his older brother. Melvin has been suspended for two weeks, and his parents won't allow Crystal to see him anymore.

No more sleepovers with Pop-Tarts and Pringles, I think. Well, it's Crystal's own *fault.* Trying to blow up the school! Everything had been going so well for her lately. She was passing pre-algebra, and her science project on mica was chosen to be exhibited in the state science fair. I just took her to get a cute haircut. But it's as though Crystal doesn't want to allow herself to do better, as though she doesn't know *how* to be anything other than in trouble.

"Crystal hates gym class," I explain to the social worker. "The other girls are very mean to her." I know this is a weak defense, but I'm not sure anyone realizes how hard school is for her.

Crystal said that one day Amber asked if the two bony knobs on top of Crystal's shoulders were Crystal's breasts. "No, but they're larger than your brain," Crystal reputedly told Amber. I felt proud of her for at least having a comeback. But now I'd like to shake Crystal and yell at her.

"Since she's been expelled, she may want to spend all of her time with you," the social worker warns. "So be firm about your boundaries and don't feel bad about limiting her visits to once a week."

"Okay."

"Just remember, you're not her only resource. You're making a positive impact just by spending time with her. It's not your job to save her."

"I *like* spending time with her." That is, when she's not trying to burn down my house. Or steal lipstick at the drugstore. Or hang from the windmill at the mini-golf course until the motor whines and the manager yells at us.

"Crystal really seems to connect with you. I think it's because you're empathetic. Often, family and friends are disdainful of cutters. That just lowers the child's self-esteem, and the cutting gets worse."

I tell the social worker that I've seen my share of gore, that my husband died of cancer.

"I'm sorry."

"Thank you." I want to tell her that I think I'm feeling better now. Finally. And I've actually met someone else. *Slept* with someone else. Is this okay? But we're not talking about me.

I can't imagine what Crystal's going to do home alone all day in her pink house other than chain-smoke, burn things, and start cutting her arms again.

"What if I put Crystal to work?" I ask the social worker.

"Doing what?"

"I'm starting a business, a bakery." This is the first person I've told about the bakery other than Dad, Ruth, Drew, Kit, and the loan officer. I feel a rush of excitement as I describe this new stage in my life. My loan hasn't gone through yet, and I haven't signed the lease or received a business license from City Hall. But I've got what seems like the most difficult component: the confidence that I can do this. Maybe I'm crazy. But I'd rather be crazy with optimism than crazy with pessimism—crazy in my pajamas and unable to leave the house.

"That sounds good," the social worker says tentatively. "A job can help build a child's self-esteem."

As I head up the front walk to Crystal's house the next morning after class, I try to prepare a tough-love speech in my head. All that comes to mind is: *What were you thinking?* The metal storm door bangs open and shut in the wind, and the wind chimes clatter an eerie dissonant tune. Several stubbed-out cigarette butts line the porch steps. I'm surprised to find that the door is unlocked. I push it open and enter the hallway, which is dark and cold. Something crunches under my feet. I look down to see a broken Coke bottle, shards of glass strewn across the wood floor.

"Crystal?" Nothing. Sleeping in, probably. Hopefully. Like a normal teenager.

I crouch to sweep up the glass, using mail from the table by the door as broom and dustpan.

Maybe I should have agreed to let Crystal sleep over last night when she called and pleaded. It was around midnight, when Drew and I were just settling into bed. She said that her mother and a new boyfriend had gone up to Crater Lake and she didn't want to spend the night by herself. I paused, considering, worrying about Crystal being alone, then remembered what the counselor at Big Sisters had warned against. I told Crystal no to a sleepover but promised we'd get together today.

"How come?" Crystal had asked, sucking noisily on a cigarette. "Is actor boy there?" Drew's bare leg was hot and bristly against mine. I shuddered at the thought of him and Crystal sleeping over on the same night. But what difference would it have made, really?

This is the first time I've been all the way inside Crystal's house. Aside from the broken glass, it's remarkably tidy. Crystal's mother's favorite colors are obviously red and pink. The pink curtains are splashed with red hibiscus flowers, and the couch is lined with matching red chenille pillows. Two logs are stacked neatly in the fireplace, and the mantel is crowded with photos of her mother posing with various friends and boyfriends. There's only one picture of Crystal—a school portrait in which she's wearing a little too much blue eye shadow and smiling a little too fiercely at the camera, as if to say *Look at me, I don't hate junior high.*

The kitchen has a sharp acrid smell, like burned hair and rotten eggs.

"Crystal?" I call out, panicking. *"Crystal?"*

Nothing. There's a pot of congealed bright orange macaroni and cheese on the stove. I run water into the pan, then open the window over the sink to let in some air.

I head down the hall, looking for her room. "Crystal?"

Last night I told her I'd take her out to lunch today for veggie burgers. "Whatever," she said listlessly. I could tell something wasn't right. Still, I hung up and went back to Drew.

Now, I find a closed bedroom door and push it open.

The room is dark and the air smells of cigarettes. Crystal lies curled on her side in bed, facing the wall. She's so light that she hardly makes an indent in the mattress—a narrow boomerang lump that takes up only a tiny slice of space. A blue-and-yellow-checked down comforter is pulled all the way over her head. Just a few spikes of her blond hair stick out across her pillow.

"Crystal?"

"Unh," she says, not moving.

"Time to get up. Just because you're not going to school doesn't mean you can sleep all day."

"Un-unh," she groans, tugging the quilt higher.

I open one curtain, letting in a stream of sharp light. Sitting on the edge of her bed, I think of how this is like my dad trying to get me out of bed back in San Jose.

"Come on. I'll treat you to lunch."

Crystal rolls over on her back, the quilt falling away from her face. She stares at the ceiling, her cheeks flushed and creased from the covers, her eyes glassy, as though she has a fever. Her lips are swollen and chapped, with bits of peeling white skin.

"Honey, are you sick?" I splay the back of my hand across her forehead, which is sticky and warm.

"Un-unh." She slowly turns her head toward the wall and blinks, trying to focus.

I slide one of her arms out from under the covers and run my fingers lightly up and down her skin. I used to beg my mother to tickle my arms like this before bed. Crystal's scars are fading. They could just be lingering poison ivy now. Maybe a mild case of eczema.

"Your arms look better," I tell her. "I'll take you shopping today. Get you some new short-sleeved tops." I feel myself being too cheerful, overcompensating for the guilt from a lusty night with Drew.

Crystal doesn't say anything. She licks her lips and closes her eyes.

"Come on. Get up and take a shower and I'll make your bed." I slide my arm under her shoulders, trying to lift her. She curls toward me. I shove two pillows behind her to help hold her up.

Then I peel back the covers and see what's wrong.

At first I think there's something stuck on her leg: a purplish black leathery circle the size of a plate draped over her thigh. But then I realize it's her *skin*, which has been burned all the way through to a white, sinewy layer of flesh underneath. The top layer of skin hangs in white wrinkly blisters that weep yellow, staining the sheet.

Watery saliva rises in my throat. I'm afraid I'm going to vomit. I look away, at the floor.

"Crystal," I say slowly, "what happened?"

She stares at her leg vaguely, as if she knows it from somewhere.

"I burned myself," she finally says through shallow breaths.

"With what?"

"Teakettle." She winces as she tries to move her leg. Her pink tank top is hiked up, exposing her flat belly. She seems thinner than ever now.

"On purpose?" But I know the answer. I look back at the burn. The two dark red rings around the outside must be from the bottom of the kettle. "Does it hurt?" Dumb question.

Crystal nods. Tears stream down her cheeks, but her face remains still, trancelike.

"Okay." I take a deep breath and look around the room, unsure what to do. I head for the bathroom to look for bandages, wondering if I should call 911 or take Crystal to the emergency room myself. I decide to take her, since the hospital's only five minutes away, and I'm not sure if Crystal's medical insurance would cover an ambulance.

Rummaging through the medicine chest and cupboards under the sink, I find gauze and antibiotic cream. But nothing in the room will hold still. The air is starry and my head feels split open above my eyebrows, as though my skull is floating away. I grab the edge of the sink, fall back against the wall, then slide down until I'm sitting on a green fuzzy rug on the floor. With my forehead resting on my knees, I count slowly to ten.

"You're going to be okay," I call out to Crystal, hoping she can't tell that I've collapsed. "But your leg will probably hurt more later." My voice sounds far away and high-pitched. "The nerve endings go dead at first. That's your body's way of protecting you." Why am I telling her this? I don't even know if this is exactly how it works. It can't be comforting information. "Which is why we have to get you to the hospital right away." I try to say this more calmly.

Wrapping my fingers over the edge of the sink, I hoist myself up, grab the gauze and antibiotic ointment, and return to the bedroom.

"Why are you shouting?" Crystal asks.

She's sitting up now. Together we swing her legs around so her feet touch the floor. She winces again, shaking her head at the burn. "My dad?" she says.

"What about him?"

She points to a fan of greeting cards spread on the floor by the foot of the bed. I lean over to see that each of the different-colored envelopes has her father's name and address in Alaska printed in Crystal's loopy handwriting. They've all been marked UNDELIVER-ABLE. There's a faint purple stamp, a cartoon finger pointing to the words RETURN TO SENDER.

"All the cards I sent him, like, came *back*."

"Oh, honey, I'm sorry." I try to hug her, but I don't want to hurt her leg. "It's okay."

I push the covers aside, then help her stand and walk to the bathroom. Waiting outside the door as she pees, I worry she might faint.

In her drawer I find a pair of soft cotton shorts. She steps into them and I pull them up over her legs, careful not to let the fabric touch her skin. Tears run down her cheeks, but she doesn't make a sound. I decide against the ointment and gauze, figuring they might just add to her pain. I pull a sweatshirt over her head and slide clogs on her feet. Slowly we make our way out to my car. "Ow," she yelps when her leg bends as she's climbing into the front seat.

"I know," I tell her. "I know."

. . .

On the way home from the hospital, I try to comfort Crystal, telling her that the cards coming back is better than if her father had received them and not bothered to reply.

"Yeah." Crystal looks out the passenger window at a boy playing by himself in his yard. "Except now I don't even know where he lives. Or if he's even, like, *alive*. He could have died on a fishing boat. He could have fallen over."

The same emergency room doctor who saw me for my anxiety attack treated Crystal. Gentle and reassuring, he gave her a pair of scrubs to wear home over her bandage since we didn't have any pants for her. He gave her antibiotics and a pain pill and showed us both how to change the dressing. Crystal seems more comfortable now.

"I know, honey. It's a terrible thing."

"How do *you* know?"

"Well, I can't imagine what it's like not knowing where your dad is. But did you know that my mother died when I was your age?"

"Really? How?"

"Car accident."

Crystal considers this. "Were you in the car?"

"No. I was home with my dad."

"Did you ever *wish* you were in the car?"

Once I did wish that. Not that I was in the car, necessarily, but that I was with my mother, wherever she had gone. It was just before the first anniversary of her death, and my father was trying to help me hem my bell-bottoms. The stubborn denim fabric wadded up in the sewing machine, and he shouted frantically over the groan of the motor, "Is this the right needle?" Then he broke down and cried. Fathers weren't supposed to *cry*. I wanted my mother there so badly that I slammed my fingers in a kitchen drawer. I wasn't sure why, I just had to do something. Something had to be done.

"No, honey," I tell Crystal now. "I never wished that."

I remember waking up once in the middle of the night back in San Jose with a burning hole in my stomach from missing Ethan. I was certain something had ruptured inside of me. A tiny organ, maybe a spleen, was floating up into the back of my throat.

I wanted to call Dr. Rupert, but I realized there was nothing he could do. I wanted to call Dad, but I realized there was nothing he could do. I wanted to call Ruth, but I realized there was nothing she could do. No matter how much medication I took, or how many times a week I visited my shrink, or how many yoga poses I twisted myself into, or how many grief groups I wept through, or how many cartons of pralines and cream I polished off, it seemed there was no solace in the world.

I look over at Crystal. Today it seems there's solace in offering solace to others. Groggy from the pain pill, Crystal dozes off.

23

When the loan officer calls from the bank to tell me that my loan's been approved, I fight the unprofessional impulse to shout into the phone: *My own business!* I picture the woman perched behind her big desk, as thin and dignified as an egret. Suppressing my elation, I coolly go over the details of the loan with her, as though several other banks in town want to throw money my way, too.

After I hang up, I call Kit to tell him that I want to sign the lease to rent the old Fudge Shoppe. Then I head straight to Le Petit Bistro to give Chef Alan two weeks' notice.

"How can you *do* this to me?" he bellows, his breath smelling of sherry.

The dishwasher peers around the corner from his station, a mop of brown hair hanging in his eyes. When he sees Chef shaking a ham-hock fist at me, he quickly ducks behind the wall.

"I'm sure you'll find someone else good," I tell Chef. "I'll work two more weeks and help train the new person."

"No!" Chef snaps, turning his head toward the wall defiantly. "That won't be necessary. You are dismissed immediately." His coarse, wavy black hair sticks out in crazy directions, and I think he's had a bad night or maybe just a bad life.

The fact is, I *need* a paycheck while I'm fixing up the bakery and testing recipes. "I can stay three weeks if that helps—"

"I don't want anyone working in this kitchen who does not *wish* to work in this kitchen," Chef growls, still facing the wall. "Who does not appreciate the *privilege* of working here. Who thinks they are *too good* for this establishment—"

"I don't think I'm too good for anything. I *like* working here. Aren't you a little happy for me, though, that I'm striking out on my own?"

Chef marches toward his office. "It is very difficult to run your own establishment. You haven't *any* idea. You are naive and inexperienced and doomed to fail."

"Fine. Thanks for the pep talk." I wonder if maybe Chef opened his own place at one time and it went under. "I'll just finish up here and punch out."

"Punch out *immediately!*" he barks, then regains his composure. "Please turn in your uniform on your way out."

He disappears into his office, slamming the door.

"Open these and put them in the mixing bowl, please." I hand Crystal a package of cream cheese and wedge of Brie. I'm nervous about perfecting my recipes for prime time at the bakery and want to debut the porcini-and-Brie cheesecake at the party on the last day of my pastry class.

"I don't *feel* like baking." Crystal tosses the cheese on the counter. She licks her forefinger, dunks it into the open canister of sugar, then sucks noisily on it.

"Crystal!" I grab her hands and push them under the faucet. "First thing, wash your hands. Here's the deal: If you want to spend more time with me, you've got to help. I'm not forcing you; I'm giving you the option. Either we limit our visits to Sundays or we work together during the week. I'm going to pay you."

"How much?"

"Eight dollars an hour."

Crystal's eyebrows shoot up. "That's pretty good." She takes another pump of liquid soap and rubs her hands together vigorously, rinses, then dries.

"Put this on." I hand her an apron. She pulls it over her head, wrapping the ties twice around her straight, narrow waist. Then she opens the Brie and drops it into the KitchenAid bowl. As she flips the mixer to the highest setting, a glob of cheese flies across the room, sticking to a cupboard door. She doubles over, gulping with laughter.

"Come on now." I reach around her to turn down the mixer.

She points to the stack of cookbooks on the counter and raises her voice over the mixer. "Hey! Who's Fannie Farmer?"

"A famous East Coast cook." I hand her a container of porcini mushrooms. "Rinse these, put them in a small bowl, and pour hot water over them. Very hot, from the tap."

"These things smell like feet." She sticks out her tongue.

"They're pungent." I turn off the mixer. "This is going to be my signature item: savory porcini-and-Brie cheesecake."

"What*ever*, Fannie!" She rolls up her sleeves, and I see stripes of fresh, white skin where once there were cuts on her arms. I'm relieved to see this cycle of healing, and make a note to buy her vitamin E cream later. For now, I put her to work chopping onions.

"That dorky actor guy?" Crystal says, peeling away the papery skin of an onion, then cutting into it. "Is he, like, your real boyfriend now?"

I shrug and get to work crumbling sesame crackers into a bowl for the cheesecake crust.

"Do you think Ethan would want you to have a boyfriend?" Her eyes tear up from the onion. She wipes them with the backs of her hands, then pauses, considering her own question. "I think he would want you to."

.   .   .

"I saw Drew in town," Ruth says slowly, deliberately. She eases a miniature cheesecake out of its mold, being careful not to let it crack. She's helping me test the classic New York recipe, which I want to offer in a single-serving size.

"Did you say hi?"

"No. I was on the other side of the street. He didn't see me." She licks some crust off her finger. "He wasn't alone."

I turn off the mixer. The cheesecake batter emits one bubble of air, as if sighing.

"He was with that actress," Ruth continues. "The red-haired one."

"Oh, her. I hate her." I nod, slightly relieved. "But they're just friends. She has a boyfriend in New York. He's a big, rich soap opera star."

Ruth raises one arched brow doubtfully.

"They're *engaged*," I tell her.

"Well, Drew looked very smitten by her. They were arm in arm. Sort of leaning into each other."

"They've known each other for years. Went to Juilliard together." I turn the mixer back on.

"Un-hunh."

"*Maybe* they slept together," I ponder, raising my voice over the whir of the beaters. "Back in school?"

"I don't know. The point is they seem involved now. They had that nothing-else-in-the-world-matters-because-we're-in-lust aura."

I turn off the mixer. "What are you telling me?"

Ruth rearranges the cheesecakes on a platter unnecessarily. "That you should be careful. Don't get too attached."

"I'm *not* getting too attached." I bite into one of the cheesecakes that fell apart. It's warm and smooth and sweet, and I would like to plow through the rest.

"Oh, yes, you are. I know you." Ruth shakes a spatula at me.

"Fine. But so what? I told you, they've known each other for years and she's engaged."

"To a guy three thousand miles away." Ruth scrubs the cheese-cake molds in the sink. "I just want to be sure that Drew's actually available before you fall in love with him."

"He pursued *me*, remember?"

"I just can't bear to see you get your heart broken again."

Ruth's so jaded. Jaded and bitter and just plain wrong. *Isn't it time you got going?* I want to ask her. *Don't you have to be someplace?*

"What*ever*!" I tell her.

Drew and I are good together.

In the evenings after work we stroll through Lithia Park arm in arm, the sky a starlit navy bowl over our heads, tiny frogs singing to us. In the mornings we linger in bed, drinking lattes and working the crossword puzzle. We go out salsa dancing, and I teach him to program his VCR and make French toast, and he turns me on to Dixieland jazz and adds me to his speed dial, and I write his name down in case of emergency on my yoga sign-up sheet. I imagine collapsing during my extended wheel and Drew driving me to the chiropractor, holding my hand the whole way.

"I met someone," I tell Dad over the phone.

"Oh, *sweetie*." I picture him all the way across the country, sitting at his kitchen table in his khakis and chamois shirt. "When do I get to meet him?"

"Soon. He's an actor. You and Jill could fly out to see the plays. Drew can get you *great* seats."

But then late one Monday afternoon after a picnic in the park—I brought champagne and a cold frittata and fresh sliced tomatoes with basil and a wedge of chocolate rum cake—Drew says he doesn't feel well and would like to make it an early night.

I'm disappointed, because Monday is the only night when we're not working and can get together at a normal hour for a date.

I tell him sure, he probably just has a tension headache, and I've got aspirin and antacids back at my place. I'll set him up in front of the TV with the heating pad behind his neck.

"I'm an excellent nurse," I tell him.

"I don't think so. I have to get up early tomorrow."

"Since when do *you* get up early?"

Drew leads an actor's life, rolling out of bed around ten, going out for coffee at eleven, and hitting rehearsals at one. When I sleep over we stay up as late as two in the morning, making love and giggling and drinking wine and eating cold pizza in bed.

"I have a meeting." He winces, turning his head stiffly from side to side.

I rub the back of his neck, and his shoulders drop, relaxing.

"I'll walk you home," he says.

We walk in silence; he's studying the sidewalk as though it might crack open suddenly, while I'm too afraid to ask what's going on. A meeting? With whom? His wife? His drug dealer? His Mafia boss? What is the big secret?

When we get to my front porch he kisses my cheek: an airy sibling peck.

"Maybe we can get together for coffee later this week," he says.

"Coffee?" I try not to sound alarmed.

He nods.

How'd I get demoted to coffee? I'm the *girlfriend,* aren't I? I've been sleeping with this man for five weeks! I've borrowed his deodorant and seen his appendix scar. Didn't I recently move up the ranks from date to girlfriend? Just like getting promoted from salad girl to head baker? Wasn't I on the verge of meeting family?

Coffee?

Now I know how St. Christopher must have felt when they decided he wasn't a saint anymore, that maybe he hadn't really performed those three miracles. Now I know how Pluto must have felt when astronomers started saying maybe it wasn't a planet, maybe it was just a big dirty ice ball.

Maybe I'm not Drew's girlfriend. Maybe I'm just a fling, a *friend*. Someone you'd have coffee with. If you weren't busy with your glamorous actress friend with the Isadora Duncan scarves, Emma Peele eyeliner, Marilyn Monroe giggle, and Lauren Bacall waistline. This woman is a hybrid freak. A conglomeration of every glamorous star in history. I doubt she wears plain Jane Jockey For Her underwear. She probably doesn't wear *any* underwear.

"Um . . ." I clear my throat, mustering a fake cough. "Is anything wrong?" I'm trying to remain calm. I'm trying not to scream.

"I'm sorry." He looks at his perfectly white Nikes and closes his eyes as if this were causing *him* pain. "I'm just confused."

Confused! You're frigging confused?

"I see," I say softly. I find the key in my purse and clutch it in my thumb and forefinger, a reflection of sunlight bouncing off of it. No date should end this early, when the sun's still above the trees.

"Confused about what?" I ask. But I know I shouldn't ask. I'm not sure I want to know. Did he *sleep* with her while he was sleeping with me? The old key won't turn over in the lock, and I want to jam my fist through the glass on the front door.

"About us." He looks at the porch. "About someone else."

"Your actress friend?"

Drew nods. "Yes. Ginger."

Ruth was right. Waist-size-smaller-than-my-shoe-size Ginger. Cascading-red-hair-down-to-her-ass Ginger.

"Have I met her?" I ask, pretending I don't remember her from the restaurant.

Ginger is a seasoning, I want to tell him. *A knobby little root!*

I turn the key in the lock, and before Drew can answer I'm closing the door on the image of his face—slate-blue-gray eyes looking up sheepishly through brown schoolboy bangs, mouth parted slightly, one foot lifted as if to step forward.

I snap the lock shut and hurry down the hall to the kitchen. I close the kitchen door, pull down the shades, then crawl into the pantry, because that is one room farther away from Drew Ellis. As far inside my house as I can burrow. I yank the long cord to the bare bulb overhead, pull the door shut, and sit on the floor under the dim yellow light.

Although we just ate dinner, I'm hungry. There's nothing to eat in the pantry except for raw ingredients, though: flour, sugar, shortening, yeast, and polenta. I twist open a canister of rye flour and dig my hand into it. It's dry and silty and tickles as it runs between my fingers. I scoop some into my mouth and try chewing. But you cannot chew flour. I cough and choke, then swallow, saliva turning the flour to a sort of doughy glob that sticks in the back of my throat.

She's more beautiful, for one thing. And Drew mentioned that she's a Seattle SuperSonics fan. I tried to share Drew's enthusiasm for his stupid Seattle team. "They have a deep bench," I'd gush, watching the game with him, pretending not to prefer the Lakers, whom Ethan and I love. *Loved.* What*ever*! Drew says the Lakers are too Hollywood, though, and I pretended to agree. That's the dumb thing about dating—feigning similar interests.

I wish Ethan were here to kick Drew's skinny ass.

It doesn't matter, though, because I am never going to see Drew Ellis again. I'm not even going to stay in Ashland, where I might run into him.

No. I am going to move to the Southwest, to Phoenix or Santa Fe. I visited there once, and the air was so dry that my hair was almost straight. It hung in subdued elegant waves.

I could probably afford to buy a small stucco house in Santa Fe with a pool out back. Spend Saturday mornings lounging under a palm tree in the yard, nothing but the hum of the pool pump, a lizard skittering across the stone patio. Bright blue sky every day instead of this relentless Oregon rain.

I will marry again. I'll marry my Santa Fe neighbor, a beautiful man with skin the color of strong tea and coarse black hair. He will not get sick or break my heart. He will not leave me for a red-haired actress. In fact, he will have only one leg. I'll keep his artificial leg on my side of the bed while we sleep at night, so that he will have to *get past me* if he wants to leave.

I set the flour back on the shelf, reach up to pull off the light, and just sit there in the dark.

I picture Ginger in a string bikini sprawled seductively across Drew's bed, feeding him gingersnaps and ginger ale.

I don't know how long I've been crouching on the floor in the pantry when the doorbell rings. My throat is so dry, it makes me gag. I swallow, trying to generate saliva.

The doorbell rings again. It's old and funky and has a sharp, overzealous mechanical ring, like the doorbell on the set of a play.

I rest my forehead on my knees and study the sliver of yellow light under the door. Hopefully, whoever it is—Drew or Ruth—will give up and leave. If it's Ruth, I don't want to hear her say "I told you so." She wouldn't come out and say it, but it would be in her tone of voice, in the stiffness of her neck. If it's Drew, I don't want him to see how crushed I am. I don't want him to think I ever liked him that much in the first place. Maybe he's going to apologize, say he's not sure what came over him, explain how his sudden change of heart was probably an adverse reaction to the prescription medication that he didn't want to tell me he's taking.

There's a rattling knock on the glass window of the back door. I hold my breath.

"Hey, Fannie Farmer, are ya home?" Crystal shouts. "How come your car's here and the lights are, like, on?" She jiggles the doorknob, then shoves the door open. I didn't realize it was unlocked.

"Trick-or-treat!" she calls out. Then she mutters, "*Great.* Probably banging that stupid dork boyfriend."

She opens the refrigerator, then closes it, pulls a glass from the cupboard, and gets herself water from the tap.

I push open the door of the pantry with my heel and peer out at her, the kitchen light making me blink and squint.

"Hey, whatcha doin' in *there*?" She sets her glass on the counter and opens the pantry door all the way, then extends a small chapped hand to help me up. My legs are stiff and achy, and it's hard to stand.

"Hiding," I tell her.

"From me?"

"No."

"From who?"

"The world." I don't want to cry, but I can't help it. "Drew." I try to say, *He dumped me,* but it comes out: "Dummy."

"You've got flour on you." Crystal reaches out a hand to brush off my cheek. I look down and see that flour's sprayed across my lap and sprinkled in my hair.

I stop myself from crying, quickly wiping my eyes on the sleeve of my shirt. I spent way too much on this stupid transparent salmon-colored silk top with matching camisole. I thought it was simple but sexy and mysterious, my skin glowing pink underneath. I hoped it was alluring in a 1970s Stevie Nicks kind of way, but Drew didn't even seem to notice.

I slide into a kitchen chair and Crystal pours me a glass of orange juice from the refrigerator, pushing it slowly across the table as though I'm a wounded animal she's afraid she'll startle.

I drink half the glass in one gulp.

"That Drew guy?" Crystal says. "He's a *loser*. You could, like, totally land a cuter guy. You should forget about him."

"You hardly even met him."

"I could just tell."

"How's your leg?" I ask her, trying to change the subject.

"Kinda better." She lifts her foot off the floor to show her mobility.

"I need to make my good-riddance list," I mumble.

"Your what?"

"Good-riddance list. It's a list of all the stuff you don't like about a guy. You're supposed to make it when you break up with someone."

"Killer!" She digs into the drawer by the telephone, pulling out paper and pen. The pen won't work. She scratches in furious circles until a faint blue line finally emerges.

Stupid hair! she writes at the top of the list in her big block handwriting. The dots over her i's are little round circles. *Whistles fruity songs.* I watch Crystal read over the list so far. It's funny how you don't have to be related to someone to love them like family.

The good-riddance list is as long and detailed as any cheesecake recipe, but it does not prevent me from driving by Drew's house at three in the morning.

Three in the morning is a horrible hour. It's too late to be up and too early to get up. It's a limbo, a hell, when the sheets are damp and cold with nightmare perspiration and the blood in the veins moves too quickly, thumping up my neck into my temples like a crazy clock counting the millions of minutes until morning: *why, why, why?*

Was it because I said I don't like musicals? That I prefer plays? Because I was shy around his boisterous actor friends? Because I used a frigging pen to fill in the crossword puzzle? Or maybe the remaining extra pounds were coming off a little too slowly.

I get out of bed and march like a sleepwalker through the house, fixing a cup of tea, showering, dressing, then climbing into my car.

No one is on the streets of Ashland at three in the morning. I drive slowly toward Drew's house.

Don't do this, I tell myself, tell the steering wheel. *Let's drive to Ruth's house instead.*

Ruth is sleeping, the car hums. *Turn right here and just coast past Drew's place to see if her car is there.*

There aren't any cars parked in front of Drew's house or in his driveway, except for his old BMW. I had imagined there'd be something like an adorable powder blue vintage Volkswagen pulled self-confidently up to his garage. I turn off the Honda one house before Drew's. The engine ticks and sighs. Maybe he's at her place. He wouldn't have left his car behind, though. A dim light glows in Drew's kitchen. I try to focus on my good-riddance list. *Stupid seventies disco hair. No-good nose-whistling anal neat freak!* None of these faults wipe away the fantasy I have of Drew and Ginger having sex on his kitchen floor, Drew's face red and wrinkled with ecstasy.

BAKING

24

"Let's talk about tough days," Sandy says, opening up our Tuesday night grief group meeting. I brought banana cupcakes for the group, but Gloria is allergic to cheese so she has to scrape off the cream cheese icing, and Roger can't have walnuts, which I chopped finely and added to the batter, and Will, the man whose wife died of Alzheimer's, is a diabetic, it turns out. Comfort food is harder to pull off than you'd think.

"As if there are any *un*-tough days," Roger says sullenly. He always keeps his coat on and sits at the edge of his chair, as though he's on the verge of leaving. Apparently his son was a talented softball player. Now Roger seems to find the playoff season unbearable. No one to root for. From the way he talks, all the mistakes Roger ever made in his life were redeemed by his son, a strong student and talented ball player. Until that show-off neighbor kid came along. Now Roger's redemption, his reason for living, is gone.

"True, true," Sandy agrees, stroking his goatee, which has a bit of frosting in it. "But some days are even harder than others."

Will nods tentatively. I think he feels a little guilty for being relieved that his wife is finally gone. During her last year on earth, she didn't recognize him and was cruel. He said that whenever he went to visit her at the rest home, the first thing she said was, "What is that *smell?*" Now, he seems to have befriended a widowed lady in town. Sometimes I see them sharing an order of onion rings at the A&W.

"The holidays, of course," Sandy says. "Also birthdays, wedding anniversaries, and milestone events such as graduations."

Any day that you have to walk through town and potentially bump into the actor who dumped you, arm in arm with Ginger Gingivitis, I want to tell the group.

"The anniversary of their death," Gloria says, sighing heavily.

"Exactly," Sandy says. "That can be the most difficult day, and the first year is usually the worst. When the first anniversary hits, we realize that the person is really gone forever."

Great. I've got my wedding anniversary looming this week and the first anniversary of Ethan's death coming next month. Just when I'm beginning to feel human again, am I going to parade down East Main Street in my bathrobe?

"These are trigger days," Sandy continues, squeezing his clipboard. Sometimes it looks as though he's trying to wring all the grief and sadness in the world out of that clipboard. "Grief is literally triggered in the body, leaving you vulnerable and prone to setbacks. This doesn't mean you're not making overall progress. In fact, a trigger day can be part of your progress."

People shift in their chairs uncomfortably. It's no fun when Sandy goes on about how grief is such hard work.

I want to tell the group about my recent setback—how I've started sleeping with Ethan's ski sweater again since Drew broke up with me, bunching it into a ball and spooning the musty wool. But this seems like an embarrassing tangent.

"The good news is we're going to come up with a system for helping each other through these tough spots."

"It better involve Scotch," Roger says, rolling his eyes toward the ceiling.

"It sort of does," Sandy says, his voice rising with enthusiasm. "If you hit a tough day or a trigger and you feel terrible—like spending the day in bed or drinking to excess—you're going to call your grief partner."

Sandy divvies the group into sets of partners who are supposed to swap home and work phone numbers so we can call each other when we're feeling miserable.

Sandy points to me and Gloria, meaning she's my partner, and I feel lucky and guilty at the same time. Roger's the one who really needs her. Maybe we should swap. But Roger gets Emily, a woman in her twenties who recently joined the group after her boyfriend was killed in a motorcycle accident. She seems to have a sweet healing way about her, too. He leans toward her to copy down her information.

Sophie Stanton. My hands tremble as I sign the two-year bakery lease in Kit's office. I write in today's date—June 14—which is my wedding anniversary.

"Congratulations!" Kit hands over three keys on a no-frills silver ring.

Ethan and I would have been married four years today. If he had stayed in remission, maybe I could have talked him into quitting his job and we could have moved up to Ashland and started the bakery together.

"Call me if you need anything." Kit gives me a photocopy of the lease and smiles. "You know I want to be your *first* customer."

Sandy encouraged us to set aside quiet time on our tough days, to think about our lost loved one. When I get home on the night of my wedding anniversary, I dig my wedding album out of a box in the garage, open a bottle of wine, and sit in the living room.

The album's thick cardboard pages feel indestructible between my fingers. When we hired our photographer, the price for even the smallest package seemed outlandish. But not when you consider that photo paper, cardboard, leather, and gold trim outlive most people. The photos are as lustrous as the day we first got them from the photographer. Ethan has a precancer glow spiked by champagne and the heat of a June afternoon in San Jose. Now, when I look at pictures of Ethan I can tell whether they were taken before or after his diagnosis. Kodachrome has a way of capturing low hemoglobin—revealing the bluish gray tint of someone en route to another world. Here Ethan's cheeks are rosy, his green eyes bright with expectation. Despite his satin tuxedo lapels and stiff white cummerbund, he still looks like a boy ready for a game of Frisbee. I close my eyes and brush my hand across his face. The photo paper is tacky beneath my fingertips. The anniversary of Ethan's death is exactly five weeks away. All year the day has been behind me. Now it's before me, something to make my way through again.

I open my eyes, turn the album page. I laugh when I see Marion by the cake smiling stiffly. She looks pained, as though her corsage is pricking her.

Toward the back of the album there are candid shots of the reception. I forgot that Ethan's fraternity brothers charmed the bartender into getting drunk. In one picture, she's dancing in the middle of our family. Shortly after that, she left with one of the single guys and Dad had to mix drinks until the hotel sent a replacement bartender. At the end of the night, Dad paid the band to play for an extra hour, and people staying at the hotel called down to complain. I trace a finger along the gold trim. A great party. That's what a wedding should be.

I close the album, pour another glass of wine, and wander into the kitchen. Among the cookbooks I find an old etiquette book. I look up the gift for four-year wedding anniversaries. The traditional present is fruit or flowers. Two things as perishable as a husband with cancer. The contemporary gift is appliances. That seems more appropriate. Ethan shouldn't mind, then, if I buy myself a new industrial-grade mixer.

The next night I stay up until after midnight cleaning the bakery—scrubbing and scrubbing to get the dirt off the walls and counters, a primal layer of grease and gunk that roots itself under my finger-nails and turns the water in the bucket gray.

Screw Drew Ellis! Prince Too-Good-to-Be-True with his spooky good looks and knack for always saying just the right thing. *You're so smart and funny. Such a great mentor.* Brown-noser. He should run for office. Senator Scumbag.

I move on to the baseboards, crawling along the floor on my hands and knees, sponging away black sludge. Who cares that I awoke after sleeping with him feeling happy and rested for the first time in a year?

Ruth helped me flesh out my good-riddance list, adding that Drew was a procrastinating commitment-phobe who didn't appre-ciate me. She didn't say "I told you so." She said I was right—there was no reason to be overly suspicious and paranoid like her. Drew had said Ginger was engaged.

After cleaning the front of the store, I move to the kitchen, where the previous tenants left behind an old pockmarked copper kettle encrusted with chocolate. While I'll probably never use it, I scrub the kettle until my fingers are raw and a shiny layer of cop-per finally emerges.

In the middle of the kitchen there's a small table with a marble slab top for cutting fudge. I try pushing it against the wall, but it's heavy and obstinate, as if to say *Who are you to think people will want to buy cheesecake instead of fudge?*

I wish I had a helper: Dad or Ethan or . . . *not* Drew. Add this to the list: Who the hell keeps *books* in his dishwasher? And who wants to eat with someone whose teeth clack as if they're wooden when he chews? At first it didn't bother me, but somewhere around our fifth meal together I wanted to squeeze Drew's jaw shut to make the noise stop.

Tomorrow I'll enlist Crystal's help with the cleanup, get her to heave her scrawny hundred pounds into a mop.

I tug open the drawer under the marble tabletop. It's full of cracked wooden spoons, fudge knives, and a wooden paddle for stirring chocolate. Nothing very useful for cheesecakes. A few mouse droppings fleck the back of the drawer. Suddenly this place seems too dirty and funky for a bakery. I'm overwhelmed by everything that needs to be done before I can open: cleaning, inspections, permits, a new exhaust system, paint, varnish, curtains, tables, a sign and a logo, and printed menus. Sampling and advertising. What if Chef Alan's right and I'm making a terrible mistake? What if I don't even turn a profit in the first year? I'll sap my nest egg and wind up living in a rented room over the bus station with a bunch of cats.

I pull a stool up to the marble slab and sit down to take a break, squeezing my eyes shut and trying to will optimism into my bloodstream.

It's completely dark outside the bakery now, the empty street shining with rain, the only light a dim glow in the bookstore window across the way. I try to remind myself that life often seems unmanageable at night. Then somehow, as sunlight finally streaks the sky in the morning, everything seems possible again.

I grab a pad and pen out of my bag and start a list. *Paint. How much? Color?*

I flip through the paint samples in my folder and consider Pineapple Crème, a yellow that's as satiny as cake batter. Even when it's raining for days, the bakery will look sunny and Ashlanders will be tempted to wander in for a slice of pear pie and a cup of tea.

My mind wanders back to Drew, but I force myself to focus on the shopping list: *drop cloths, ladder, masking tape, brushes, rollers, nose hairs.* Despite Drew's good looks, weren't there nose hairs? I fight to recall long, black, homely nose hairs. Not just slow dances and flannel sheets, deep dimples and his sweet knack for making kids laugh.

When life gives you lemons, you make lemonade. When guys break your heart, you conjure nose hairs. Good riddance.

25

Crystal climbs to the top step on the ladder and yanks down the brown paper covering the bakery windows; it crackles and cascades over her head like a giant ribbon. The grand opening party is one week from today, but we're technically open for business this morning. I want to get a little experience before the mayor, newspaper food critic, Chamber of Commerce president, and the rest of the town show up for the opening.

"Careful!" I shout, dizzy as I look up at Crystal.

She clambers down the ladder and runs through the bakery, still favoring the leg she burned. "I'm a mummy!" she shrieks, wrapping herself in the paper.

While I wash the windows with Windex and paper towels, Crystal makes a sign with colored markers.

Grand opening party this weekend, she writes, the tip of her tongue pointing out of the corner of her mouth as she concentrates. Underneath: *Come in for a free sample now!* She runs out of room on the paper and has to scrunch several letters into one corner. I wish we had a more professional-looking sign, but I don't want to hurt her feelings.

"Great." I hand her the tape. "Hang it in the window."

I flip over the OPEN sign, and Crystal and I stand behind the register, waiting for our first customer.

During the weeks I was preparing to open—haggling with the health department, meeting with the graphic designer, perfecting the pie dough recipe—it seemed this day would never come. Now, the sidewalk outside is empty. A car slowly splashes by in the street. Sometimes the Oregon weather makes the whole day look like four in the afternoon. Inside the bakery seems sunny, though, and the place looks edible to me: buttery yellow walls and crown molding as glossy white as marshmallow icing. The refinished wood floors shine like honey, punctuated with chocolaty knots.

Over the register I've hung a framed picture of me as a kid standing with my mother beside a new Suzie Homemaker oven on Christmas morning. Mother's wearing a white apron over a red-and-green-print dress, her beautiful mouth outlined in red lipstick. You'd never guess that she was a terrible cook or that a week after I got the oven, an evil neighbor boy named Jeremy bullied me into letting him bake a frog in it. The house filled with a putrid stench, and Dad tossed the oven out onto the curb.

Crystal helps me load a tray with free samples to put by the register: miniature cherry cheesecakes, walnut brownies, slices of lemon butter pound cake, and wedges of ollallieberry muffin.

Finally, our first official customer shows up—a mother with twins who wrestles a gigantic stroller through the door. I bolt across the room to help her, then adjust my speed en route, not wanting to seem desperate for business. The woman's eyes widen as she surveys the cookies and muffins.

Crystal stands at attention on the other side of the case, holding a sheet of waxed paper in one hand and an empty white bag in the other. I convinced her to swap her jeans and giant sweatshirt for pressed khakis, a pink T-shirt, and a white apron. She looks much more approachable now. The twins tip their chins back to look up at her, fluttering their fingers over their heads as though playing castanets. Their mother chooses two maple moons, two sugar cookies, and a blondie.

"Will that be all?" Crystal asks with Miss America poise I never knew she had. "The angel food meringues are very light and non-fat." She's a great low-pressure salesman. Rows of pink and blue barrettes line either side of the zigzag part in her hair. You'd never imagine that she would have the capacity to give herself a second-degree burn with a teakettle.

Our customer plucks a miniature cherry cheesecake from the sample tray and takes a tentative nibble.

"Oh," she moans. "Mmmmm." She licks crumbs of crust from her lip.

Crystal points to the full-size cheesecakes in the case, and suddenly the woman is committing to a New York style that serves ten, and blackberry topping.

"You have a nice day," Crystal trills as the woman heaves the big stroller through the door.

"You sold our first cheesecake!" I give Crystal a high five, and she takes a bow.

Last week I called Crystal's school guidance counselor to tell him how helpful she's been to me in opening the bakery. I wanted him to know that Crystal's time off from school has been productive. She's even better than I am at maneuvering the high-strung cash register. I felt like a bragging parent as I explained this.

"Dude! My first paycheck *ever*," Crystal said when I handed over a check from my business account. She closed her eyes and kissed the check. I worried that she would blow her earnings on junk food, CDs, and firecrackers. But she bought only one thing: a mail-order taxidermy kit.

"Are you sure you want that?" I asked, looking over her shoulder at the kit in the catalog, shuddering at the description of the glass eyes included.

"Sometimes animals, like, die by accident and you want to fix them so you can look at them later," she explained, filling in the mail-order form in her loopy handwriting.

Weird kid, I thought. "Okay, sounds good," I said.

Around lunchtime two giggling teenage girls crash through the bakery door. Even though it's barely sixty degrees outside, they wear halter tops that expose wide stripes of bare white belly over their tight, low-rider jeans. Tiny silver hoop earrings shimmer in their belly buttons.

"Oh, Crystal," one of them says sarcastically when she spots her behind the counter. "I didn't know you, like, had a *job.*" Neon green and orange rubber bands flash in the braces on the girl's teeth.

"It's my aunt's bakery," Crystal says, her back straightening as she rearranges a row of carrot-raisin muffins. "She *owns* it."

I duck behind the kitchen wall so the girls can't see me, afraid I might embarrass Crystal.

"Cool," the other girl sniffs indifferently.

They choose peanut-butter chocolate-chip brownies and cans of Coke from the cooler, and Crystal rings them up. As she hands them their change, one of the girls looks over the counter at Crystal's feet and giggles.

"*What?*" Crystal says.

"Nothing," the two chime in unison, bumping against each other as they pop open their Cokes.

"You look like a *nurse,*" one girl teases. She wrinkles her nose and points at Crystal's squishy white shoes. Now I regret forcing the shoes on Crystal.

"Later," the other one says.

"See you at school," the first one says. "Oh yeah, you can't *go* to school." They both giggle, their cheeks bulging with brownie, and clomp back through the door onto the street, doubling over with laughter.

"Whatever," Crystal says quietly to herself, apparently out of her cutting comebacks.

I poke my head around the corner. "Don't tell me. Amber and Tiffanie?"

She nods and wipes the already clean counter with a rag. I want to run outside and throttle those two snotty girls. As I watch them turn up the street, I can't believe what I'm seeing: black thong underwear riding above the ridiculously low-slung waist of one of the girls' jeans.

"They don't seem particularly pretty or smart or nice," I tell Crystal, wishing I could come up with a more clever jab. Teenage plumber's crack!

Crystal shrugs. "Everyone likes them."

Later in the afternoon, Crystal leaves for the first of the horseback-riding lessons that I gave her as a birthday gift. I start a new batch of cheesecakes. It's as warm as summer in the kitchen, and I peel off my sweater and work in my T-shirt. Closing my eyes for a moment, I breathe in the scents of butter, sugar, and vanilla. The bakery smells like a safer time to me, a time before Ethan died and Johnny Carson went off the air, and there was that hole in the ozone. It smells like a time when you'd come home from school and your mom would be baking cookies. Actually, *my* mom wouldn't be baking cookies, since she didn't bake. There were always warm slices of cinnamon toast, though, and a cup of cocoa. While I ate she sat with me at the table, reading her big *Art Through the Ages* book, fantasizing about a trip to the Parthenon the way some people might fantasize about meeting their favorite celebrity.

"How'd you learn to cook like this?" Drew asked one night at my house, tasting a spoonful of spaghetti sauce from the pot with admiration. *Good question,* I thought, *since I barely passed home ec, got kicked out of Girl Scouts, and my mother couldn't cook.* Maybe it was just the love of eating and the search for comfort since the time of her death.

"Self-taught," I told him.

Now, I grate lemon rind and measure sugar.

After Drew dumped me, I had to buy new sheets so I could lie in my bed again. I'd owned the former sheets for years, and they reminded me of sleeping with Ethan and sleeping alone and sleeping with Drew. The new sheets are splashed with bunches of blue hydrangea with bright yellow centers—happy, single-girl bedding.

"Madame?" a voice calls out from the front room.

I switch off the mixer and step through the kitchen door to discover Chef Alan standing stiffly in front of the bakery cases. He's wearing jeans and a T-shirt, and his thick hair is wet and slicked back.

"Chef." I figured I'd run into him in town at some point, but certainly not in my bakery.

He makes his signature little bow.

"George would like to keep your cheesecakes on the menu." He avoids eye contact, cracking his knuckles as he peers into the bakery case. "And I agree. They are . . . *adequate.*" Before, Chef praised my savory cheesecakes. "Perhaps I will be your first commercial customer."

I figure this is as close to an apology as I'm going to get. "Thank you," I say. Maybe I can persuade other restaurants to carry the cheesecakes.

"I want to offer the Brie-and-porcini as a first course and the New York style for dessert." He furrows his brow at the case. With Chef, ordering food is serious business. He prides himself in choosing just the right amount of everything, allowing little to go to waste.

Finally, he peers over the top of the case and makes eye contact with me. His eyes are nearly black, without pupils, and he seems tired and hungry for something beyond food. "I am ready to place my order."

"Sophie?" Drew's voice echoes through my answering machine one morning as I'm heading out to the bakery. I freeze, clutching the front door handle.

Drew pauses. "I'm sorry," he continues.

Squeezing a stack of cookbooks to my chest, I creep back down the hall to the kitchen, holding my breath as if he might hear me through the answering machine.

This better be good.

"I'd like to talk to you. Are you there? Will you pick up?"

Why? So we can go have coffee?

"Some things happened before you moved up here that I'd like to explain."

Things? By any chance sex-related *things?* I tiptoe closer to the machine.

He clears his throat. For an actor with perfect diction and delivery, suddenly he's fumbling. "It's all over now." He pauses. "With Ginger."

I lean toward the answering machine as if to sniff it. Clean laundry smell, broad shoulders, narrow waist, callused warm hands. None of my good-riddance list items come to mind.

"I'd like to see you." His voice lowers. "*Soon.* Please call me."

Fat chance, Mr. Coffee.

He sighs, hangs up.

I set my cookbooks and purse on the counter, open the refrigerator, and stare inside. This is me not calling Drew Ellis back. The air is cool against my face and arms. A bottle of Drew's Bloody Mary mix stares at me. I pour it down the drain and torpedo the bottle into the recycling bin. It pops and shatters.

I drink a little milk from the carton, then close the refrigerator door and calmly cross the room to the phone. I've forgotten how dating bestows your answering machine with such power. How you yearn to drive an ax through the thing just because the little red light isn't flashing. Once you're married, you could care less about the light. If it's blinking, it's probably some other married couple calling to ask you to a barbecue.

As I stand over my answering machine, I imagine my handsome fantasy husband with the prosthetic leg in Santa Fe. He will serve me tall glasses of iced tea by the pool with fresh mint and sugar cubes. I will put *his* name down in case of emergency.

Crystal hovers over the long wooden table in the kitchen at the bakery, pounding her fist into her science book.

"Shit!"

"Watch the language." I slide a tray of oatmeal cookies out of the oven, closing my eyes. I'm overwhelmed by the amount of work left to do for the opening. My feet and back hurt today, and I'm actually tired of the thick, sweet smell of the bakery. The loan, the lease, the insurance payments. It all feels like too much.

"I *hate* summer school!" Tears fill Crystal's eyes.

The social worker at Big Sisters warned that Crystal might become more agitated after the cutting stopped. "However inappropriate it was, her self-medication has been taken away," she explained. "But the rage is still there."

"I know it's not fun," I tell Crystal. She has to complete three courses before she can join the ninth grade next year, and the condensed summer school classes seem even harder for her.

"I don't want to go back to school anyway." She scratches at the last scab on her arms. It breaks open and bleeds a streak of bright red.

"Don't." I take her hand, squeeze it, close the textbook. "Forget about it now. The tutor's coming tomorrow."

She nibbles the edge of a cookie. "I don't give a *shit* about the

Earth's core anyway. I don't like minerals. I like animals. How come there's no class about animals?"

I try to steer the conversation in a more positive direction. "What's your favorite animal?"

"Marmoset. I *want* one. They're so small and they're, like, totally—"

Crystal's interrupted by a loud knock at the front door of the bakery, which is locked, since we're closed for the day. I peer out of the kitchen and see Drew cupping his hands around his face, peeking through the glass. He smiles and waves when he sees me. I duck back behind the wall, sucking in my breath.

"Crystal," I say mechanically. "Unlock the door."

She heads to the front of the bakery, spinning back toward me when she sees Drew. Her mouth drops open and she stops in protest.

I glare at her. "Go."

She backs toward the entrance, eyes on me the whole way. She snaps the lock open but lets Drew struggle with the sticky door. The bell rings cheerfully.

"Hi," he says, extending a hand to Crystal. "Drew Ellis."

"I *know*." She folds her arms over her chest. "Whatcha want?"

"Here to see Sophie."

"About what?" She forms a blockade in the doorway to the kitchen, her feet spread wide.

Drew looks over her shoulder at me. Turning away, I dunk the cookie sheets into the sink.

"I want to tell her I'm sorry and ask her if she'll have dinner with me."

"I don't *think* so, jackass," Crystal snaps.

"Hi," I hear him say, stepping past Crystal into the kitchen, exuding his same old Drew exuberance, as if he hadn't dumped me for a red-haired harpy. I turn from the sink. He looks sexy in black jeans and a white T-shirt. "Too Dudley Do-Right," Ruth said of his square, cleft chin. But I like it. I shudder, turn back to the sink, grip the faucet.

"We're closed," Crystal says, following behind him.

He kneads his New York Mets cap with both hands and looks at the floor.

"Crystal . . ." I untie my apron, wad it up, and toss it on the table. "Why don't you go home and I'll see you in the morning?"

"Uh!" She stomps her foot on the floor.

"*Now.*"

She turns on her heels, grabs her jacket and science book, and hurries out the back door, slamming it behind her.

"She doesn't like me," Drew says.

I shrug, moving the cookie sheets to a rack to dry.

"I don't blame her," he says, gesturing toward one of the chairs at the table. "May I?"

"Sure. Whatever." I've learned the value of this word during my time with Crystal. How it can provide a shell of indifference that prevents your feelings from getting hurt.

"Listen, I want to apologize." Drew rubs his face with his hands. "I know it sounds stupid. But I've been through a very difficult time these past two weeks."

"And now you want to go out for coffee?" I wipe down the ovens.

He looks at me quizzically; I don't think he realizes this is the last thing he said to me.

"I was confused."

"I remember. About Ginger."

He nods. "I fell for her two years ago. Before you even moved here."

"That's supposed to make me feel better?"

Drew holds up a hand to stop me. "She had a fiancé in New York, as I told you. Still, she and I spent a lot of time together as friends. I always hoped it would be more. Until I met you."

"Great, so I was the booby prize?"

"No! As soon as I met you, I wasn't attracted to Ginger in the same way anymore. We still spent time together, but I didn't pine for her. And she *missed* that. She missed the buzz she got from me wanting her. I realize now that's what fueled our friendship. She got high on my attraction to her. Actors can be *very* narcissistic."

Drew's face is pale, eyes sunken. I want to sit at the table with him. Instead, I grab my jacket and purse off the hook by the back door.

"As soon as I told her how much I liked you, how happy I was, she wanted me. She couldn't stand to see me happy with someone else. Suddenly I was confused and had a choice to make."

Maybe I don't need to hear this story. I don't feel up to the details of Ginger's seduction tactics.

I turn off the lights in the front room and switch the fan off over the oven.

"So I thought I'd better not see you for a while." Drew looks up, his face pleading. "But it was terrible not seeing you."

I back up against the double sink, rooting in my purse for my car keys.

He sighs and drops his hands at his sides. "I won't be seeing her anymore, not even as a friend. She's meddlesome and controlling, and I don't want you to worry about her. It's over. It never even started." He adds quietly, "I didn't sleep with her."

I find my keys and jab them in the air at Drew. "You *work* with her," I say, as though this is worse than sex. In a way, it is. Seeing a woman every day whom he *wants* to sleep with might be worse than actually sleeping with her and getting the fantasy over with. Finding the bumps and lumps of her imperfections, rather than leaving everything to his imagination. Assuming Ginger *has* any bumps and lumps. I hate to even theorize.

"I do. I work with her. She's joining another company next season, though. So it's only six more months."

"Six months is a long time."

"It is. But please, give me another chance."

"We'll see," I say. *Dangerous rebound guy,* Ruth insisted months ago.

"We'll have to take it slowly," I finally tell him.

Drew gets up from the table and steps toward me, reaching out a hand. "I understand."

I'm afraid he's going to touch me or hug me or dump me again. I shuffle backward, bumping against the sink.

"Very slowly." I flip off the kitchen lights.

Drew drops his hand, bows his head. "I'm sorry," he says softly. "I—"

I unlock the back door and hold it open for him, nodding at the parking lot. "So slowly that you have to leave now."

26

The next morning Marion's sister, Jolene, who's ten years younger than Marion and lives in Sacramento, calls.

After commenting on what a nice young man Ethan was and expressing shock over the fact that her neighbor's cat recently snuck into her house and fell asleep in a basket of freshly laundered towels, Jolene finally cuts to the chase.

"It's Marion," she says, sighing wearily.

"Is she all right?"

"Yes and no. She's been diagnosed with Alzheimer's disease."

I can't imagine this. Marion never forgets anything. She always remembers where she parked her car, never misses anyone's birthday, and commits casserole recipes to memory: one can of mushroom soup, one can of tuna, a half teaspoon of cayenne, a cup of potato sticks. She knows all the words to the old songs she and Charlie used to dance to, singing along to *Big Sal's Swing Show* on the car radio.

"Really? I'm so sorry."

"She wants to come and see you."

"*Me?*" I consider the controlled disdain Marion always had for me, as though I were a failing houseplant she kept watering and fertilizing but it just wouldn't bloom.

"Okay," I answer tentatively. "When?" I try to sound brighter, hospitable.

"This week."

My stomach cramps with panic. I recall the brusque efficiency with which Marion whisked Ethan's belongings into my garage in San Jose. Now I've moved his boxes from storage into Colonel Cranson's garage, to save on the storage fees. Will Marion repossess them?

"She won't be able to travel alone much longer," Jolene explains. "This will be her last trip."

"Is it that bad?"

"She has some good days."

When Marion shows up, it's apparent she's not having one of her good days. I can't believe Jolene let her travel alone.

In the car on the way to my house from the airport in Medford, she wraps her arms tightly around her hard, toaster-size cosmetics case as though someone might steal it. Worry wrinkles her powdery brow as she tries to tell me about how Jolene is forcing her to move to a new place. (A very lovely assisted living facility, Jolene insisted on the phone.) But nouns confound Marion. She'll struggle to think of a word, rapping her forehead with her knuckles in frustration. The word will always be a simple noun, such as house or sky.

I think of how busy Marion has always been—an activity for every day of the week. Church and bowling and bridge and her hospital auxiliary group.

We head toward the grocery store to buy Marion a new romance novel, since she finished hers on the plane. I remember how she devours the books intently, snapping through the pages while clucking her tongue with disapproval. She favors the raciest titles with oil paintings on the covers of men with coppery skin and glistening biceps embracing women with sweaty cleavage, heads thrown back with abandon.

Seeing me obviously makes Marion's brain hurt as she struggles for context. She wants to know where Ethan and his father, Charlie are, assuming they must be in Oregon, too. She's suspicious, as though I'm hiding them from her.

"They died," I remind her.

It's ironic that Marion has shown up six days before the first anniversary of Ethan's death, apparently unaware of the fact that he's no longer with us. Equally ironic is the fact that I've scheduled the grand opening for the bakery to take place a day before the anniversary. I've managed to surround this grief sinkhole with a to-do list that would make a speed freak blanch. And Ethan's death looms larger now than it did when he was terminally ill, which certainly isn't helping me finish the party preparations. "Is there any way to postpone it?" Sandy asked when I confessed to my odd scheduling. Not unless I want to call the two hundred people I've invited—from local bed-and-breakfast owners to festival employees to city officials. So I'm soldiering on with the preparations, stacks of plastic champagne glasses towering on my kitchen counters.

When Ethan died, Marion shot straight to the acceptance stage of grief. Now she's regressed into a haven't-heard-the-news-yet fog that I kind of envy. Meanwhile, I'm in a manic, perfect-the-lemon-cream-frosting phase. But this is all I can conceive of doing. When I consider July 19—the day of Ethan's death—I can imagine screaming, sobbing, and clawing the carpet or filling two hundred little paper cups with cashews. I cannot imagine sitting calmly with my grief journal and photo albums.

"Ethan and Charlie are gone," I tell her, reaching across the seat and patting the slippery knee of her polyester slacks. "You're stuck with me."

"I never wanted a daughter," Marion replies primly. "I wanted three sons." She hugs the powder blue case tighter and looks out the window. Her eyes dart back and forth at the passing scenery, and her head trembles slightly, like a cat watching a bird.

"You want your money back?" I ask her.

She nods, purses her lips.

"If you find out where to submit a claim, let me know," I tell her. "I'd like a refund, too."

The next morning I awaken to a loud clatter coming from the kitchen: ba-*bang*, ba-*bang*! I hurry downstairs to find that the racket's coming from the laundry room. Inside the dryer I find a frying pan.

"Better get our chores done, dear!" Marion chirps from behind me, scrubbing the kitchen counters with an SOS pad. "Can't sleep all day!" Blue foam bubbles up between her fingers.

It's only six-thirty, barely light outside. She's already dressed in bright green slacks and a lemon yellow cotton sweater. She always wears bold, country club colors and thick-soled white shoes that make a squishing sound when she walks. Despite her child-of-the-Depression frugality, she buys a new pair of the shoes every six months so they're always spotless, never a scuff or scrape.

I decide to harness Marion's energy. If she wants to work, she can help me get ready for the bakery opening, which is only four days away.

When Crystal shows up at the bakery midmorning to help, she's quickly irritated by Marion's confusion.

"Quit it!" Crystal whines, slapping at Marion's hands as Marion tries to load blackberry muffins into the dishwasher.

"Be patient," I tell Crystal. I figured the more helpers I had, the faster the preparations would go, but now I wonder if I'd be better off without these two.

I steer Marion away from the dishwasher, pulling out the muffins and arranging them on a plate. "The guests are going to sample these," I tell Marion. "Don't they look good?" The muffins are golden brown and sprinkled with clumps of white sugar.

"Who *is* this young lady?" Marion asks haughtily, glaring at Crystal and biting into a muffin.

"Hand it over, grandma," Crystal says, reaching for the muffin. "Those are for the party."

Marion holds the muffin behind her back, narrowing her topaz blue eyes.

"Let her have one," I tell Crystal.

"Why? You make me eat the broken ones."

"Ethan won't care for this behavior," Marion tells Crystal, wagging a crooked finger at her. "Where *is* he?"

Crystal rolls her eyes and shoves a clump of frosting into her mouth. "He died," she says through the mouthful of frosting. "Of cancer. Hello! Like, almost a *year* ago."

Marion sets down her muffin. She looks at Crystal, looks at me. Then her gnarled little hand flies up and she slaps Crystal sharply on the face.

Crystal rears backward, her tongue exploring the inside of her cheek. "You're a fruitcake!" she shrieks, looking to me for help.

"Marion doesn't feel good," I tell Crystal.

I pour Marion some milk. She wraps her knobby fingers around the glass and stares vacantly at the wall, as though she's already forgotten what just happened.

"She *hit* me," Crystal says with disbelief, still running her fingers over her cheek.

"She didn't mean it," I tell her. "You're okay."

"What*ever*," Crystal says. "Who does she think she is?"

"She's confused," I try to explain.

"I'm confused," Marion says. She begins to weep. "I am." Jolene said that Marion knows she has Alzheimer's, but she's too embarrassed to talk about it. Her shoulders shake as she emits little ladylike sobs. Crying and succumbing to confusion is probably her worst fear. Marion has always loathed weakness, dreaded the thought of becoming a sloppy, wallowing widow like me. This is the first time I've seen her cry since Ethan's memorial service. That day, tears streaked her cheeks as she stood on the beach. But they dried quickly in the wind, and we were back at her house in no time, arranging daffodils in vases and setting out trays of deviled eggs.

"I don't want to live in a home," she moans.

"Then you can't *hit* people," Crystal says.

"It's not a home," I tell Marion. "It's assisted living. Jolene says there's a yard with a garden and a nice communal dining room. I'll help you pack and move. I'll sleep over with you for the first few nights."

I'm not sure how I'll manage to go down to San Jose to participate in the move and keep the bakery open. But I want to help. Marion's even more alone in the world than I am. At least I have Dad and Jill, Ruth and Crystal. I wish Ethan were here to console her. "Try not to worry so much, Mom," he used to say, squeezing her small pink hand until she stopped fretting.

Marion looks up at me. She wipes her eyes with her sleeve, sips the milk. "That would be nice, dear," she says.

As I wash a stack of dirty bowls, my party anxiety builds. What if no one shows? Maybe no one cares about a bakery opening. Or worse, what if *everyone* comes and there's not enough food?

"We're falling behind here," Crystal says, clapping her hands. "Let's frost these." She sets a plate of banana cupcakes and a bowl of icing in front of Marion.

"Hellooooo!" a voice calls out from the front of the store. Drew. Great. All I need right now is His Coffeeness messing with my mind.

"Hi," I call out tentatively.

Loser! Crystal mouths.

"Who is it?" Marion whispers.

"It's her *boyfriend*," Crystal says, licking icing off the edge of her palm.

Marion draws in a sharp breath. "But she's *married*." She says this with the same disdain she uses to describe the lascivious women in her romance novels.

Drew stands in the doorway to the kitchen. Deep dimples, smoky blue-gray eyes. My hand wanders up to my curls, patting them into place. This is the first time I've seen him since his apology. After that day he sent a big bouquet of lobbying-for-a-second-chance roses, but I didn't call him.

"Hi," he says brightly. Marion melts, splaying a hand across her chest. Her mouth forms a little coral-colored O, and her eyebrows arch with delight.

"This is my mother-in-law, Marion Stanton," I tell Drew.

"My pleasure," Drew says, tipping his head and taking her hand in his. "How do you like Oregon so far?"

"It's *lovely*," Marion purrs. Just yesterday she said it looked like a dreary watercolor.

"Have you been to the theater yet?"

Marion looks at me forlornly, as though I've cheated her.

"We've been working on the party," I tell him.

"Well, you must come. I'll get you front row center seats."

Marion tips her head and looks at him demurely through lowered lashes.

"We're, like, *working* here," Crystal snaps.

"And you're doing a great job," Drew tells her.

She huffs a sigh, pretending not to be flattered, and keeps frosting. "Were you ever in, like, a *real* movie or TV show?" she asks suspiciously.

"I was on a soap opera," Drew says, shuddering at the memory. "I was Anthony, the brother from Albany who had a tumor."

I find myself grateful for Crystal's innate ability to tap into Drew's worst fear—being a B-grade actor. Somehow I want to hurt Drew back, even if in a small way.

"What kinda tumor?" Crystal asks.

"Brain. I had amnesia and couldn't remember Rachel."

"My goodness," Marion says. "Is your tumor *growing?*"

"On TV, stupid," Crystal tells her.

"I am not stupid," Marion says, pride burning in her eyes.

"Who was Rachel?" Crystal asks Drew.

"Old girlfriend."

"Did you have sex on TV?" Crystal asks eagerly.

The thought of Drew lip-locked with a soap opera starlet wearing gobs of greasy lip gloss makes me bristle. I'm irritated by my jealousy, by Drew's ability to distract me.

"Nah." He turns to me. "I've got something for you," he says.

I look at his empty hands, peer behind his back.

"It's outside."

I don't have time for a second-chance sales pitch right now.

I've got something for you, Crystal mouths, standing behind Drew, mocking him. He's working hard to win Crystal over and win me back, but we're both tough nuts.

"Come on." He leads me by the elbow through the back door. In the parking lot, something large and rectangular is hidden under a green tarp.

"Close your eyes," he says.

I close my eyes and cup a hand over my face, listening to the snap of the tarp as he yanks it off.

"Ta-da!"

I open my eyes, squinting. It's an oven. Not just any oven, but a circa 1937 Westinghouse automatic painted cherry red with chrome trim and four gas burners with white oversize knobs. It's the oven that Drew and I found in an antique shop in Jackson when we first started dating. I spent half an hour running my hands over the smooth paint on its swollen belly of a door and opening the bun warmer underneath and wishing the oven were mine.

"This would look so great in my bakery," I told Drew.

"What bakery?" he asked.

"The bakery I'm going to open one day."

The store owner said that the old woman who sold it to him claimed that when her brother was born prematurely he was put in a shoebox and kept alive in the bun warmer. I know for a fact that the oven cost around $2,300. I know for a fact that Drew doesn't make a lot of money, that this probably put a hefty dent in his savings. I know for a fact that this is a perfectly thought-out gift.

"It's beautiful." I admire its squat legs and padded feet. I'm afraid to look at Drew, to let him see how pleased I am.

"It would look great in the corner in the front room," he says.

I hug my arms around my chest, shivering a little now that I'm outside of the warm bakery. "Thank you." *But this doesn't mean we're back together!* I want to add. Still, I feel a little shift of forgiveness in my heart, like tectonic plates creaking under the Earth's crust.

"I've got to get to work," Drew says. "The movers will be back in an hour to put the oven wherever you want." He kisses me lightly on the cheek. "This is going to be a great party," he adds, heading toward his truck. And that is *just* like him, damn it. To say the *one* thing I've needed to hear all morning.

27

There's obviously little to do in Ashland on a Monday afternoon in July. At least a hundred people show up at the grand opening. Guests jostle elbow to elbow in the front room, shouting over the cacophony of chatter, laughter, and big band songs Drew's cued up on Crystal's CD player. The crowd even spills out the door onto the sidewalk.

"These people aren't nibblers, they're gobblers," I tell Ruth, loading trays with cookies, tartlets, brownies, and miniature cupcakes.

"Slow *down*." Ruth squeezes my arm. "Everyone's having a great time."

I smooth my fingers over the scalloped white apron tied around the waist of my powder blue 1950s-style waitress uniform. I rented the outfits for Ruth, Marion, Crystal, and me to wear, and so far we've been showered with compliments.

Crystal takes a platter and winds her way into the crowd, her uniform hanging a bit on her boyish figure. This morning she prepared for the party as though primping for the prom—her chapped hands fumbling to apply blue eye shadow and pink lip gloss. She used a Magic Marker–like tube of dye from the drugstore to paint magenta stripes in her hair. I thought this made her look a little like a laundry disaster but didn't say anything, striving to embrace this teen fad. Now, she offers the Chamber of Commerce president a macaroon.

"Don't you look pretty," the woman coos, taking a step backward to admire Crystal. Crystal ducks her head shyly, loving and hating compliments at the same time.

As soon as the mayor gets here, she'll cut the red ribbon—which Ruth draped across the bakery cases in two big swags with bows in the middle. Then Drew will pour the champagne.

In a short time, Drew has managed to make himself indispensable in preparing for the opening—blowing up balloons, buying flower arrangements, setting up the bar, helping Crystal braid and hang streamers. Still, I've kept a safe distance from him, letting my work absorb my attention. Because Redemption Drew makes me nervous. I worry that Real Drew might come back. The Drew who bristles when I do the crossword puzzle in pen and lusts after certain red-haired actresses. The Drew who might downgrade me to coffee again.

"Work the room," Ruth insists, shoving a tray into my hands and pushing me through the kitchen door.

As I scan the clusters of guests, I spot the visitors bureau ladies, the downtown business association president, my pastry class teacher, and a slew of new faces. A spark of party anxiety makes my pulse race. When Ethan and I entertained, he usually greeted the guests—taking coats and pouring drinks—while I finished up in the kitchen. I often felt a burst of shyness when the doorbell rang. It soothed my nerves to dress the salad and slice the bread while Ethan navigated the group through the first few awkward minutes that every party seems to have.

"Remind me why I threw a party for the entire *town,*" I ask Ruth, wishing I could slide back into the kitchen.

"Don't worry. They *love* you. They're so relieved this isn't another potpourri-and-scented-soap tchotchke shack."

Just then Chef Alan sidles up between me and Ruth. I introduce the two.

"Sophie has a special talent," Chef says, leaning flirtatiously toward Ruth. His belly swells under an aloha shirt that hangs over his khaki shorts. Bits of sugar cookie crumbs dot his black beard. Oh sure. *Now* I have a special talent. Ruth has a way of bringing out the Eddie Haskell unctuousness in men.

"I've always known that," Ruth says, taking a step away from him. She looks like a 1950s movie star in her uniform, her hair pulled up into a golden twist. Chef crowds her against the bakery case, grilling her on her vocation, his eyes drifting to her sternum. Ruth shoots a pleading look over Chef's shoulder as I leave them. When I'd complained before to Ruth about Chef, she'd insisted that he couldn't be *that* much of a nuisance. *Feel my pain,* I mouth now as I turn into the crowd.

I move through the room passing out the miniature cheese-cakes, guests swarming around me. My ears ring with their com-pliments: *scrumptious, to die for, congratulations!* I hand an empty tray to Crystal and turn from side to side to accept the whirl of warm handshakes and soft perfumed cheeks of women giving kisses. I meet the Arnolds, who own the Hummingbird Bed and Breakfast, and the Wisemans, who own the Traveling Bard. Both couples insist they'll order at least one chocolate torte a week for their dessert and sherry hour.

I spot Crystal's mother, who's talking to an actress from the fes-tival while keeping a captious eye on Chef and Ruth. Roxanne's dressed like the girls at Crystal's school—low-rider jeans and a shim-mering red halter top. I encouraged Crystal to invite her mother, but now the boozy way Roxanne sways on her feet makes me nervous. I duck to avoid her gaze, snaking through the group. I find my grief partner, Gloria, talking with my realtor, Kit, and his wife. They laugh as Kit's twin daughters lick the chocolate icing from their cupcakes, their lips turning into big brown clown mouths.

"We're going to have to bring these two here every day, I'm afraid," Kit's wife tells me.

I'm about to compliment her on the girls' flowered dresses when I spot Marjorie Bison, the newspaper's restaurant critic, hovering in the corner by the old Westinghouse oven. A photographer hangs at her side as dutifully as a shadow. A white-haired woman with thin white eyebrows creased into a permanent frown, Marjorie is stingy with the stars. She actually *looks* like a bison, with broad, boxy shoulders and a tiny rear end. I hide behind Gloria's flowing caftan and watch as Marjorie takes tentative bites out of cookies and tarts without finishing any of them. She balances her plateful of half-eaten treats in one hand as she scribbles in her notebook and whispers to the photographer.

Marion breezes up to them with a platter of something. Marjorie leans toward the tray, as if to sniff it. Then she scoops up a clump of what appears to be raw sugar-cookie dough. As she brings the glob to her mouth, I dive out from behind Gloria and cross the room to snatch it from her, but I'm too late. The gluey dough forms a ball in Marjorie's cheek. Her tongue protrudes from between her lips as though she'd like to spit, but she's not sure where. I introduce myself. She gags a little and looks at me, a tear forming in the corner of one eye.

"What *was* that?" she asks thickly.

Ruth appears at our sides. She hands Marjorie Bison a few napkins and a Brie-and-porcini cheesecake, then grabs the platter of dough from Marion. "Let's get these in the oven!" she says, leading Marion into the kitchen.

"I'm so sorry," I tell Marjorie. "My mother-in-law's not well. She has Alzheimer's."

Marjorie works the dough down her throat, like a gull trying to swallow a too-big piece of garbage.

"Please, try the savory cheesecake," I say. "It's meant to be served as an hors d'oeuvre."

"Was there by chance raw egg in what I just ate?" Marjorie runs her tongue over her teeth as though she'd kill for a toothbrush.

"Yes, I'm so sorry. It was an accident." I look around the room desperately, wondering if I should get her a drink of water. "My mother-in-law is only helping with the party. She won't be working at the bakery."

"I understand." Marjorie pinches the cheesecake between her fingers and jots something in her notebook.

What's she writing? *Salmonella dough?*

"How many employees do you have?" she asks.

"One." I look at Crystal, who is coughing without covering her mouth, the magenta stripes in her hair looking as if they could be food related. "So far."

On the other side of the room, I notice that Roxanne's clutching a glass of wine in each hand now. She's pitched forward, as though leaning into the wind. I must be cracking under the stress; suddenly I want to shove the cheesecake between Marjorie's thin lips.

"I plan to sell cheesecakes by mail order, too," I tell her. "Ship them frozen so they're ready to eat upon arrival."

She nods at the ice buckets of champagne on the counter by the cash register where Drew is stationed as bartender, pouring wine for the adults and milk for the kids. "Do you have a liquor license?"

"No." I shake my head, feeling as though I'm in the principal's office.

"Sophie, over here!" Drew calls out, waving me toward the bar. The photographer points her camera at him, slicing through film as he uncorks another illicit bottle of Sauvignon Blanc.

"Excuse me," I tell Marjorie, figuring there's nothing more I can do to earn her praise.

Drew's actor friends swarm around the bar, laughing and tossing back little plastic cups of wine. Drew's the only guy I've ever known who owns his own tuxedo, and he's wearing it for the party, the little black bow tie and white collar framing his square chin.

Like Ethan, he has a flair for making guests feel funny, interesting, and welcome. I wonder if I could have pulled off the opening without him.

"Wow," Ruth whispers, stopping me a few feet from the bar, "Prince Charming's in full form."

Crystal glides up beside Ruth with a tray of glazed apricot tarts. "Drew looks totally fruity in that suit," she says.

While I'm grateful that they're both protective of me—unwilling to let Drew off the hook just yet—I can tell Crystal likes having him around. He laughs at all her jokes and shares her algebra loathing and even bought her Doors and Janis Joplin CDs last week, pointing out which songs to listen to first. "Yeah, thanks, whatever," Crystal said, sliding the CDs into the back of her case with disinterest. As soon as Drew left the house she ripped open the wrappers, jammed her headphones over her ears, and bounced around my living room, kicking her stocking feet.

The three of us make our way up to the bar now. Drew pours Ruth and me glasses of wine and makes Crystal an Italian soda with fizzy water and cherry syrup.

"Cheers!" he says. Suddenly I'm surrounded by a protective circle of glasses, obstructing my view of Marjorie Bison and her little notebook.

Everyone seems to be having a good enough time without me, so I sneak back into the kitchen to put the lemon soufflés in the oven.

As I whip egg whites into foamy peaks, I'm grateful for a reprieve from the party. The approaching anniversary of Ethan's death has cast a pall on my ability to make small talk. *These are called Mexican wedding cakes. . . . Oh, and my husband died a year ago, and now I'm baking our life savings.*

"Create a grief sanctuary," Sandy had advised at our last meeting. "Spend time alone with photos and letters, light a candle." Instead, I've created a sturdy wall of busywork around the anniversary. Yesterday I prepared for the party, today I'll throw the party, tomorrow I'll clean up after the party. It's funny how you can be dumb in an organized fashion. Plan a party for the day before the anniversary of your husband's death. Let the guy who dumped you pitch in!

After folding the egg whites into the already prepared batter, I drizzle the mixture into ramekins. As I open the oven, I'm blasted by a wall of heat. Did I even remember to butter the cups? Perspiration trickles down my chest, and my head feels light. I realize that I haven't eaten all day. My stomach feels as though it's actually returned to its former flatter self.

I haven't told Drew about the anniversary. Ruth knows, and I told Crystal this morning. I yelled at her when she accidentally tipped over my cup of tea on the bathroom counter, then quickly apologized, explaining about tomorrow.

"Oh," she said, standing in her stocking feet, her sheer white tights stretching all the way up to her pink bra. "Do you want to, like, do something?"

I shrugged, unsure. Albums, letters, candles. It all seems hopelessly corny and insufficient.

I close the oven door on the soufflés.

When I return to the party, I find Marion passing a tray of empty cupcake liners. Gloria graciously takes a pink liner from the tray and holds it in the air with admiration, as though it's a fancy pastry. She smiles and winks at me. I steer Marion by the shoulders into the kitchen. She frowns, peering back over her shoulder at Gloria's flowing leopard-print caftan.

"Oh, *my*," Marion whispers loudly. "What an outfit! Is she going on safari?"

I'm afraid Gloria might have heard her. For the first time since Marion's arrival I'm mad at her, sick of her supercilious wardrobe criteria, which has probably hurt my new friend's feelings.

"That's enough passing for now." I push on her shoulders firmly until she takes a seat at the table. She looks dejected, like a child who's being punished.

"I'm so sorry!" I hear a voice call out. The mayor appears in the kitchen doorway, out of breath. "We got a flat tire."

I pour her a glass of water and assure her that it's no problem. But I'm relieved that she's finally here and we can move toward wrapping up the party. She blots her forehead with a napkin, re-applies her lipstick. Then I hand her the scissors and we head out to the crowd. Marion follows. I nod at Drew to get the champagne ready. He quickly arranges glasses on the table and passes bottles around for his friends to open.

"Everyone!" the mayor calls out. The crowd keeps chattering.

Crystal jams two fingers between her teeth and lets out a pierc-ing whistle, blushing when people turn and look at her.

"Hello and welcome!" The mayor positions herself beside the red ribbon. "We're happy to welcome this wonderful new business to Ashland," she says. "It's been two months since the Fudge Shoppe closed, and this community's gone far too long without chocolate."

"Here, here!" cries an actress who's wearing a tank top deco-rated with safety pins.

"We wish Sophie the best of luck," the mayor adds. "And we beg her to bake her chocolate rum cake every day!"

With a snip of the scissors, the ribbon cascades to the floor. The crowd applauds, champagne corks pop, and a balloon bursts over-head with a startling bang. Marion yelps and covers her ears. The actors cheer and glasses foam over. I lean back against the corner of the bakery case, relieved. Everything feels official now, and people do seem to love the place. I raise a plastic glass to my mouth, champagne bubbles tickling my lips.

"Congratu-*fucking*-lations," a husky voice slurs from behind me.

I turn to find Crystal's mother lunging toward me, red wine slosh-ing out of her glass. I don't mind that Roxanne's never thanked me for Crystal's tutor or the horseback-riding lessons, but I mind that she's hammered at my opening. I snatch her glass and toss it into a nearby garbage can.

"I never thought I'd need a bouncer for a bakery party," I tell her quietly, trying to steer her into the kitchen before anyone sees her. "Let me show you to the back door."

There's a sharp burn across my forearm as Roxanne digs her nails into my skin, leaving four red crescents. I pull away and she teeters backward, as though the floor's icy.

"Suzie Fucking Homemaker," she growls. Her hair falls around her face. "I'll bet you think you're quite the *role* model."

"Just the opposite, I guarantee you."

I spot Marjorie Bison watching us through the crowd, her notebook poised.

"*Ma,*" Crystal whines, cutting in between Roxanne and me. "Quit it!" Mortified, Crystal turns toward the wall and hooks her hand into her mouth, chewing her nails. I want to tell her not to worry, no one knows Roxanne's her mother, but that's certainly not an encouraging observation.

"Someone's been hitting the sauce too hard," the receptionist from the downtown business association whispers loudly.

Just then Drew crosses the room quickly but smoothly, like one of the officers on *Cops* sneaking up on a suspect. He curls an arm around Roxanne's waist and leads her toward the kitchen.

"You don't know how *hard* it is," she slurs, crying now.

For a moment I am sorry for her, knowing just *how* hard it is to make it in this world. But she should see Crystal as a blessing, not a burden.

Roxanne squirms and kicks the Westinghouse oven. "What's this old piece of shit?"

People look away, pretending not to be interested.

"Get your *own* daughter," Roxanne mumbles as Drew wrestles her into the kitchen. "Don't touch me," she adds, slapping at his arms and chest.

"Let's get you some coffee," he says.

I'm grateful for Drew's ability to avert disaster. It occurs to me that he was actually like this before he became Redemption Drew. Helpful and well-intentioned. Maybe Redemption Drew and Real Drew are the same guy. Confused, flawed, but honest, with a good heart. Maybe he deserves a second chance.

As Drew and Roxanne disappear, the guests continue chattering and laughing. Ruth slides a new CD into the player. Two actors break into a swing dance, spinning into a tray of maple moons and sending them toppling over and skittering across the floor. Marjorie Bison takes a step backward to clear the impromptu dance floor, and the heel of her shoe pierces a cookie.

Crystal fumbles through her backpack and lights a cigarette.

Outside, I mouth to her. The last thing I need is Marjorie spying the underage help smoking.

I finish my champagne, grab a tray of banana cupcakes from Ruth, and head toward Marjorie, determined to win her over. The banana cupcakes are my favorite, with thick cream cheese frosting sprinkled with chopped walnuts and toasted coconut. She must try one.

I stop halfway across the room. There, leaning in the front doorway of the bakery, is Ginger. Five feet eight willowy inches of come-hither sexpot sleaze. She's lit from behind by the afternoon sun—fiery red hair and bare long legs outlined in a transparent blue organza dress. The dress is a tight, wraparound number with a V-neck plunging into a creamy crease of cleavage. Guys' heads snap around like compass needles swinging due north. Suddenly their expressions say: *No bra . . . nipple alert!*

Ginger's eyes scan past me. She spots Drew as he emerges from the kitchen and saunters toward him, hips swaying.

"What are *you* doing here?" Drew squawks as she approaches. She's like a test that he has to pass, perhaps as difficult for him as algebra is for Crystal.

Dear Miss Manners: What should you do if a red-haired praying mantis crashes your party?

I forget about Marjorie and veer toward Drew and Ginger. Let's get this over with for good.

"I don't recall sending you an invitation," I tell Ginger. The tray of cupcakes wobbles in my hands.

Ginger wrinkles her nose at the cupcakes. *"Carbs,"* she says, as though there's a cockroach on the tray. She tosses back her wavy hair, slick red lips shimmering like cinnamon candies. "They *ruin* your waistline." She scans my figure, smirking at my uniform.

This is the closest I've ever been to her, and I notice a tiny spray of endearing freckles across her button nose.

"I know," I tell her, shifting the tray to my hip. "Some people are too vain to enjoy food."

"Darling," she coos at Drew, ignoring me, breathy fake English accent heating up. She slides the plastic champagne glass from his hand and finishes it in one swallow. "Let's go get a *real* drink." She tips her heart-shaped face up at him, her thin eyebrows arched across her smooth, high forehead, emerald eyes twinkling.

I watch Drew struggle against her undertow. He slowly shakes his head and looks to me, helpless.

Get a spine! I want to shout.

Ginger turns to me, waves a hand at my head. "Shouldn't you wear a hair net?" She shudders dramatically. "I'd hate to think of all that hair getting in my cupcakes."

"I'd hate to think of cupcakes getting in your *hair,*" hisses a voice from behind me. In the next moment a flying cupcake smacks Ginger in the side of the head, glops of cream cheese icing and chunks of cake tumbling through her red locks and landing in her cleavage. Her glossy mouth drops open. Crystal bumps up against me, pulling another cupcake off the platter.

"Nobody invited you, Cruella!" she says, hitting Ginger smack in the forehead with icing.

"Who the hell are *you?*" Ginger asks, lunging toward me and snatching a cupcake. She winds up and chucks it at Crystal, who runs toward the kitchen. The cupcake sails past Crystal and hits the Chamber of Commerce president square in the middle of her stiff white hairdo. The hair is resilient, and the cupcake bounces to the floor.

Suddenly the crowd is quiet, the guests gathering in a circle around the fracas, clutching their plates and champagne glasses. I see strained smiles, raised eyebrows, mouths ajar. They look at Ginger, look at Drew, look at me. I can tell they won't be ordering their wedding cakes or party platters from *this* unreliable trouble magnet anytime soon.

"Food fight!" the safety pin actress cries with glee, lobbing a miniature cherry cheesecake at her date. He retaliates by tossing his champagne across her chest.

Food fight? But this is the part where I'm supposed to start living happily ever after. Just like the opening of *The Mary Tyler Moore Show,* where Mary spins and throws her beret in the air, the theme song cheering "You're gonna make it after all!" Food fight! Where did these people get their manners?

"Oh, my, what a *zoo,*" the Chamber of Commerce president tells her assistant as they bustle toward the door.

"Wait!" I call after them. I want to apologize for the ruckus and explain how I intend to contribute to the community: tours for elementary school kids and cookie day for the senior center. They vanish through the door and up the street.

Marion sidles into the middle of the dwindling crowd. "No one treats my daughter this way." She pivots on one heel, scanning the group with a menacing gaze. "*No* one." She narrows her eyes at Marjorie Bison. "Sophie has worked very hard to become a lawyer. You people must learn to appreciate her. My *son* appreciates her."

Again I'm flattered that she thinks I'm a lawyer. At least her dementia classifies me as a capable person, someone who could take depositions and fire off legal briefs. Maybe the lawyer daughter-in-law is the daughter-in-law Marion always dreamed of.

"A baker lawyer?" Ginger seethes, wiping icing out of her hair with a paper napkin.

Drew circles an arm around my waist. "Are you all right?" he asks. I unhook myself from his grip and brush off my uniform. "Fine."

Ginger turns toward Drew to say something, but then Ruth's standing between them, hands on her hips. "How can I help expedite your departure?" she asks Ginger.

"Did someone clone Betty Crocker?" Ginger asks, looking at Ruth's uniform.

"Bette Davis's botox injections are making her cranky!" the safety pin actress says, giggling.

"I thought we agreed you'd dump Little Miss Muffet," Ginger tells Drew, nodding at me. I see now that I was dumped not just by Drew, but by a coalition.

"We didn't *agree* on anything," Drew tells her. "Except that you'd leave me alone."

"Alone?" she purrs, tickling the underside of his chin with her red fingernails. "You don't want to be *alone*, do you?"

"No," Drew says, stepping aside to dodge her touch and brushing up beside me. "I want to be with Sophie. I *am* with Sophie." He looks at me, looks around the room. "I love Sophie," he announces.

"Yeah!" the safety pin actress cheers.

The small crowd breaks into applause and whistles.

I back away from the group, feeling my face flush. Drew never said the L-word when we were dating. A few times I thought he would: once after sex as he stared dreamily at the ceiling; the time we stayed up until three in the morning talking about our childhoods.

Now he's decided to profess his love, publicly, further humiliating me in the middle of my party flop. Making a big speech as though we're all in a Shakespeare festival drama. *This isn't a play!*

I want to shout at him and Ginger, irritated by their histrionics. *This is life. My life!*

"Sophie's *married*," Marion tells them.

"See, she's already married," Ginger tells Drew.

"She *was* married," Crystal tells Ginger, stabbing a stubby finger at her. "She's a widow now. Which is why you should butt out of her life and let Actor Boy decide for himself."

I back away, toward the kitchen. If Drew hadn't dumped me in the first place, we wouldn't be in this mess.

"I *have* decided," Drew says. He takes a shaky step in my direction, then swoops down on one knee and reaches for my hand. "Sophie . . ." He hesitates, wipes his brow with his free arm. I notice that his hand shakes around mine. "M-marry me." His fingers are warm and callused. Even in a tuxedo he has that clean laundry smell. I pull my hand away, wondering how this day could possibly get any weirder.

Crystal bounces on her toes, clapping her hands. "Killer! Can I be the flower girl?"

"No," I tell her.

"Why not?" she whines. "Who's gonna be flower girl? Not *Simone*. Hey, can I be bridesmaid?"

Ginger grabs her bag and clicks across the floor in her high-heeled sandals, her skinny organza ass swishing through the door.

"There's not going to *be* any wedding." I turn from Crystal to Drew.

Drew's face sinks with disappointment, his dimples disappearing.

"We'll see," I tell him.

"You're *already* married," Marion sniffs.

"I said, we'll *see*," I tell her.

Crystal turns pleading eyes on me. "But—"

"We'll see!" I shout into the small crowd, clutching my throbbing head.

Suddenly the piercing wail of the smoke alarm slices through the room. People grimace and cup their ears with their hands.

"The soufflés!" Ruth gasps, running to the back of the bakery as smoke roils through the kitchen doors.

"What happened to the timer?" Drew asks.

I forgot to set it.

The smoke smells sour and chemical, like burned lemons or something you'd use to clean the floor. Ruth manages to silence the alarm. Everyone sighs with relief. But then there's a snapping noise overhead, followed by a low hiss. The sprinklers explode, a sharp spray shooting over the group.

The safety pin actress tips her head back with her mouth wide open.

"The floors!" I hear myself shout. The newly restored maple, which cost about $5,000 to have refinished, isn't supposed to get wet. I grab napkins from the top of the bakery case and fall to my knees, trying frantically to wipe up the mess.

The remaining guests swarm toward the door, everyone trying to squeeze through at the same time.

"*My silk!*" someone yelps.

In the distance a siren wails.

"I called the fire department," Crystal says proudly.

Great. The Ashland Fire Department has already been to my house and now they're coming to my business. What a way to establish yourself when you're new in town.

I feel water drench my back as I blot at the maple. In a matter of moments two firemen charge through the door, their yellow coats flapping around them.

"No fire," Drew says. "Just smoke. It's under control."

The firemen hold their hose and ax poised, ready to spray and chop their way through my nest egg. Instead they head for the back of the building to turn off the sprinklers. Finally the water stops.

"Oh my," Ruth says, looking at the drenched floor. She quickly tries to adopt a positive spin. "Well, this is one way to wash up."

Everyone is gone now except for Drew, Marion, Ruth, Crystal, and me.

"It was a lovely party," Marion coos, hugging me.

"Are you crazy?" I ask her.

Yes, Crystal mouths.

"Don't worry," Drew says, looking over the smashed cupcakes and cookies, cups and champagne glasses on the tables and floor, everything drenched in water. "I'll help you clean this up."

Working in silence, the five of us mop the floor, using the big string mops and all the dish towels and paper towels we can find. When we're finished I leave the mops and towels in the sink and the rest of the mess for the morning.

"It wasn't as bad as you think," Ruth insists. "Everyone had a ball. Usually these things are boring."

"I could have used boring," I tell her.

I lock the front door and flip the sign over in the window: SORRY, WE'RE CLOSED. It makes me sad to think how many days the sign might have to hang there.

Part Three

ACCEPTANCE

28

I awaken from a starchy dreamless sleep, dim brown light seeping through the window shade and lace curtains. The numbers on the clock radio click forward to ten-thirty. The air in the room is thick and sour and presses down on me, making it impossible to lift my head. Another hot day.

A year without Ethan.

I am matter, and the pain of missing him is antimatter, and when you put the two together, *kaboom,* there's nothing left of me to get out of bed and go clean up the bakery.

I'll never miss Ethan any less than I did on the day that he died. I know this, because I don't miss my mother any less than the day she drove off the road twenty-three years ago. My grief is diminished, but it feels permanent, like a small scar. I have brown hair, brown eyes, wear size seven shoes. I miss my husband, miss my mother. Two chips out of my heart like birthmarks. Today I'm exhausted from carrying on as though this is all right. *I'm starting over! I'm moving! I'm sleeping with someone else! I'm going back to school! I'm opening a business!* Screw it. I'm lying down.

I tug the hydrangea coverlet over my head.

I'll clean the bakery tomorrow. Stay in bed today. Create a sanctuary of sheets and pillows.

But how pathetic to call in sick to your own business. No matter how ill Ethan felt, no matter how loosely his pants hung from his winnowing waist, he rarely missed a day of work, unless he was in the hospital. Every morning he waved and blew me a kiss from the driveway, then climbed into his car and drove off, fueled by optimism I envied. I waved back from the dining room window, drumming up the nerve to go to my own new job.

I smell coffee and hear the tinkering of dishes in the kitchen, where Marion is probably reading over Miss Manners and eating her two slices of rye with marmalade. Peering over the side of the bed, I spot my waitress uniform balled in a clump on the floor. Nest egg overboard. My bladder feels on the verge of bursting, and my throat's parched from the champagne. Colonel Cranson stares down at me angrily. *Get up and check on Marion,* he demands. *Take a shower, get back to work!* But a magnet pulls me into the center of the bed.

Sandy's right. It's easy to believe for several months that someone who died is just out of town. But the one-year mark brings certainty.

A year ago today I was at the hospital with Ethan. The last day was the worst, because he had such trouble breathing. His lungs sounded as though they were trying to percolate coffee. His chart said he didn't want CPR or tube feeding, only a morphine drip. The oncologist said we would keep him comfortable. Everything had been as calmly and carefully planned as a trip out of town. Still, I felt hysteria boil under my skin. It made me fidget and itch and want to holler at the people coming off the elevators. *Somebody do something!*

"This is called the agonal phase," the doctor explained, touching my elbow. "Many family members prefer not to stay for this." He assured me that while it sounded as though Ethan were in pain, he was not. I remember straining to concentrate on noises other than Ethan's breathing: the tap-tap of Marion's knitting needles and the squish-squish of sneakers and the click-click of high heels passing in the hall. The *bing!* of the elevator bell and the rush of TV sitcom laughter fading in and out like surf.

I close my eyes now and try to think of something else. All I can see is the panicked look on Marjorie Bison's face as she choked down a clump of raw cookie dough. My whole body shudders with remorse. Sometimes you want to turn back the clock so far that it seems you'd have to go all the way back to second grade to fix everything.

The phone rings. I hear Marion tiptoe up the creaky stairs and hover outside my room. "She's sleeping, Drew," she whispers loudly. "I'll tell her—"

I hold my breath as she shuffles back down the stairs, wishing that it were my grief partner, Gloria, who had called.

Gloria says that if you're going to have a bad day, you should have a *good* bad day. Go all out on a pity party with whatever you want. Sandy looked a little uncomfortable as she recommended this, worried that we'd drink too much or overmedicate. Now I want to call Gloria and ask her how to have a good bad day instead of just a *bad* bad day.

I pull my purse off the night table, dig her number out of my wallet, and dial her house on the old black rotary phone by the bed.

"Rachel?" a gruff voice answers. "Don't hang up this time." I figure it must be Teddy, Gloria's teenage son.

"Is Gloria there?"

"She's not home." The boy sounds disappointed, irritated.

"Teddy?" I remember how when Crystal blew up M-80s at school, Gloria said that was nothing compared to Teddy's deeds: He was caught skinny-dipping at the town pool and even hot-wired and "borrowed" the neighbor's car.

"It's Sophie Stanton. Your mom's friend? Would you please tell her I called?"

"Okay," he mumbles. I can tell he's not going to write down the message. He takes a deep breath.

"You okay?" I ask him.

"Yeah." But he sounds despondent.

"Rachel your girlfriend?"

"She broke up with me." His voice quavers. "Last night."

"That hurts. I know."

"It *sucks*," he says accusingly.

"My husband died," I tell him. I have the urge to eat something hearty. A steak.

"I'm sorry." He blows his nose loudly.

"It's okay," I say, a little embarrassed. "It was a year ago." The wind picks up outside. "A year ago today."

"My sister died."

"I know." I wonder what it's like to be the child who lived. How much pressure that must be. "Do you miss her?"

"Yeah," he says tentatively. "Of course." *But why all the fuss?* his tone seems to say. *Why not just love the living now?*

"Dead people never do anything wrong," I tell him.

"What are you *talking* about?"

"What do you do that drives your mother crazy?"

"Everything. Leave, like, *one* dirty dish in the living room. She's so anal."

"Your sister never did stuff like that, right?"

"She got straight As," he says, annoyed.

"My new boyfriend has faults." I lie back against the pillows. The word *boyfriend* still sounds dippy to me, as though I'm a teenager who should be gabbing on a Princess phone. "But my dead husband is perfect. That's how it works."

"Yeah," Teddy says, perking up a little.

I notice that the wallpaper's curling away from the wall in one corner of the room. There's a pause. Inertia prevents me from saying good-bye and hanging up.

"I'm not sure this guy's really my boyfriend," I tell Teddy, considering Drew's public marriage proposal at the party. Down on one knee in his tuxedo, already looking like a groom.

"Oh." I hear Teddy losing interest, his fingers clacking on a keyboard.

"What do you like about Rachel?" I ask, trying to win back his attention.

"I don't know." Teddy stops typing and sniffles. "She makes me feel good." There's a pause and he coughs. "Her hair and stuff."

"You'll meet someone else," I tell him. "Someone pretty who will love you back."

"What are you, like, the psychic hotline?"

I laugh.

"I don't want anyone else," he grumbles.

"I know."

As I hang up the phone the wind gusts suddenly, sucking the window shade against the screen. Maybe this is a sign from Ethan. But it feels more like the grief and depression scratching to get back in.

What I really want is some sort of "It's okay, I'm here" sign from Ethan. The worst part about grief is that it's so one-sided, so unrequited. Lost loved ones don't reciprocate, when you get right down to it. You try to convince yourself that they do. But Ethan hurts me every day with his indifference, his aloofness. I pray, I journal, I speak to him. Not a peep. He's like the popular kids in high school, breezing by in a flash with no eye contact or acknowledgment of my existence.

I flop back against the pillows, irritated. The nerve of these dead people! Not a single word from Mother or Ethan. What do they have to do that's so important? Sure, you're dead. But there's such a thing as *manners*. The lengths I've gone to: the flowers tossed into the sea, the candles burned, the photo albums. The shrink visits, the grief groups, the antidepressants. Nothing from them.

I miss Ethan, but I *blame* him, too. Blame him for this pain, for his illness and death, even. Working himself to the point of exhaustion! Returning to that poisonous cubicle as soon as his cancer was in remission. Roasting his privates with that stinking laptop. Maybe *that's* why we couldn't have a baby.

Before, I blamed medical technology. (You call this advanced? We'll burn it out or poison you or cut it out? *Hello!*) I blamed bum luck. I searched for meaning, read books: *When Bad Things Happen to Good People. The Problem with Pain.*

I sit up and grab the framed picture of Ethan and me that I keep on the night table. We're at a party, arm in arm, laughing. While I'm looking at the photographer, Ethan's distracted by something, gazing off to the side at someone who's probably told a joke. *Look at me when I'm talking to you!* Hot tears make my cheeks itch. I set down the picture and pick up the little china mouse that sits on the lace doily beside it. I've tried not to move too much of the bed-and-breakfast bric-a-brac at Colonel Cranson's house, since I don't really live here. I don't really live *anywhere.* I hurl the mouse against the wall and it pops and shatters, making room for something else on the night table. Clearing one or two cobwebs from my heart.

Somehow the broken mouse makes me feel a little better, as an aspirin might. I wipe my eyes with a corner of the sheet. The house is eerily quiet. I wonder what Marion's up to, whether she's broiling mail in the oven. I picture black smoke snaking up the stairs, flames eating through the calico wallpaper. Slowly, I slide my legs out of bed. Somehow I will make it through this day. The first day of the second year without my husband.

In the kitchen, I find Marion at the ironing board with the radio tuned to the oldies station, singing along while she presses rags.

"'Sweet Caroline . . .'!" she belts out merrily, jumping when I appear beside her. "You're up? I made you soup."

A pot of chicken and rice soup simmers vigorously on the stove. Marion ladles some into a bowl and sets it on the table with crackers and a spoon. *It's too hot for soup,* I want to tell her. *And no one eats soup for breakfast. Okay, maybe in Korea they do. Or on your planet, where they iron rags.* I sit down and take a sip of the soup. It feels good against the back of my throat. A salve.

"Can I take you somewhere?" I ask Marion. "Shopping?" I don't think she remembers this is the anniversary of Ethan's death. "Out to lunch?" I decide not to mention Ethan. If I didn't remember that he died on this day, I probably wouldn't want someone to remind me. Lucidity can be a drag.

"We better stay home," Marion says, frowning. "So you can get well and go back to school tomorrow."

"Work," I tell her.

"Pardon?"

"Back to work."

"Right. At the bakery." She raises a crooked finger in the air, proud of this recollection.

I take a handful of crackers and leave her with the rags, heading out the back door across the porch and into the garden.

It's a bright July morning that promises something. Green trees, blue sky, pink roses. It all seems like false advertising.

"Ethan?" I say.

Nothing.

I toss the crackers into the grass and sit cross-legged on the brick path. It's warm from the sun.

I feel a twang of guilt as I recall how sometimes I had to get away from Ethan when he was sick, get away from his illness. I'd make up an errand—a trip to the store or post office—so I could escape the house. I'd take my time, then drive home slowly, crying in the car, not wanting to cry too much in front of Ethan.

One afternoon, a cop pulled me over. There was no siren, just the blue swirl of his lights in my rearview mirror, slow, like a dream. I pulled off the road. I was way over to the side anyway, hugging the edge in case anyone wanted to get by. The cop probably figured I was drunk.

"You all right?" he asked, peering past me into the backseat.

I nodded, handed him my license. He looked at it and handed it back.

"You should wear your seat belt." He pointed to my chest. Seat belts seemed unnecessary by then. Seat belts, sunblock, life vests. Why bother? I pulled on the seat belt and tried to smile.

"Mind if I ask you to get out of the car?" He was apologetic, gently patting the side of my door.

I killed the engine, unhooked the belt, and crawled out. The policeman asked me to put my feet together, close my eyes, and count to thirty. I obeyed, hoping I wasn't swaying like a palm tree in the wind. The whole time I wanted to explain that I wasn't drunk, just afraid.

Now, I lean against the edge of the porch. An ant crawls along a crack in the brick that must be like the Grand Canyon to him. He carries a speck of something white.

One year.

The wind picks up suddenly and a swirl of dust forms in a funnel, leaves and a bit of trash spiraling toward the top. Grit flies around me. I close my eyes, clenching them shut. The world inside my eyelids is a burnt red color. Then I feel something. A breath, a sigh, a chuckle. A tiny hug. It's not external, as I had expected. It isn't in the sky or in the trees. It's somewhere quiet and safe within me.

I hear the crunching of footsteps on the path and realize I'm lying on my back beside the porch, the sun warming my face. Shielding my eyes with one hand, I peer up through my fingers at stripes of blue sky. Then Crystal's face appears, followed by a swatch of pink tank top.

"Dude," she says. The sky turns yellow as she holds a bouquet of yellow roses over me. "Here."

I sit up, clamber onto the edge of the porch. Yesterday morning when we were getting ready for the party, I told her that Ethan always got me yellow roses on my birthday and our anniversary. I take the flowers from her, surprised by their weight. I dip my face into the blossoms, breathe in their sweet smell.

"Don't cry," she says.

"I'm not," I insist, wiping my eyes.

"Okay, you can," she says.

I laugh.

Crystal sits beside me on the porch. She's wearing loose linen pants to cover the scar on her leg and dirty white sneakers without socks. I clumsily wrap an arm around her, kneading her bony shoulder blade.

"I tried to pick ones Ethan would have picked."

It's good to have someone else acknowledge this day. To say: *Yes, this did happen.*

"Thank you." The roses have faint peach-colored stripes along the top of each petal. I am grateful for their uniqueness.

A voice floats through the garden—Drew's voice. "'After years of mediocre sweet shops and stale-bagel cafés, Ashland finally has a first-rate bakery!'" he booms theatrically. His shadowy figure appears through the gate by the garage. Then he steps onto the path, waving a sheet of newspaper in the air. "Look, bakery review!"

My stomach tightens. Critics, reporters. *Gentlemen, start your hair dryers.*

Marion shuffles out onto the porch.

Drew kisses me on the forehead and Marion on the cheek. Marion giggles and smiles demurely. He gives Crystal a high five. Crystal accepts it but rolls her eyes.

"'While the opening party was a bit of a boisterous mess,'" Drew reads, "'this establishment is bound to flourish. The cheesecakes are the highlight, with a sublime consistency that isn't too dry or gummy, and there are a number of clever savory choices, such as the delicious Brie-and-porcini. These are sure to be a hit, so place your party orders early.'"

I climb up into a chair, cradling the roses in my lap. But I thought Marjorie *hated* the place. We fed her raw cookie dough! "How many stars?" I ask Drew, immediately afraid of finding out.

"Four."

"Out of how many?"

"Four! You can only *get* four. Did you want a fifth star? I'll give you one." He stands behind my chair, kisses my neck.

Marion giggles. I grab the section of newspaper from Drew and continue reading the review.

Frosted when warm, the maple moon cookies hark back to a day when soft cookies and lemonade were a mainstay in the South, where I grew up. The cupcakes are airy and light, with generous dollops of frosting. There are even a few low-fat and sugar-free options. In short, a treat for everyone.

"'NEW BAKERY BOUND TO BOOM,'" I read the headline aloud, savoring the alliteration. "Assuming the baker can drag her butt to work," I add, standing up. "I've got to get a move on."

"Sublime," Marion coos.

"Bound to boom," Drew says, stepping off the porch and swinging an imaginary golf club Johnny Carson style. He's wearing a black T-shirt and khaki shorts. I don't think I've ever noticed how nice his legs are. Thick, curvy calves. Strong, square knees with halos of golden hair that beg to be touched. We haven't slept together since he dumped me. I've been cautious, like someone who's afraid to get back in a car after being in a wreck. Meanwhile, Ethan's ski sweater has been a scratchy, passionless lover. Suddenly I long to break my take-it-slow vow and have sweaty sex with Drew right now, upstairs, defiling the froofy hydrangea bedding.

"Hey, howdja get my mother home yesterday, anyway?" Crystal asks him.

"I asked Chef Alan to drive her."

I consider the image of Roxanne and Chef packed into Chef's little Miata convertible, Roxanne's long hair like a bride's veil in the wind.

Marion and Crystal head into the kitchen for iced tea. Drew seems relieved once they're gone.

"Listen . . ." He clears his throat, lowers his voice. "I'm sorry about proposing at the party. I think I embarrassed you."

"At least Ginger got the message."

"The offer's still good, but I know you want to take it slow."

"Slowly," I say, correcting his grammar. The prospect of needing Drew scares me; I don't think I need him the way you need a vitamin or a good night's sleep. I'm afraid I need him the way you need a cigarette or a drink. Besides, I don't want to be engaged right now. I don't even want to be single or widowed. I just want to be a sane person.

"Slowly," Drew repeats, giving me a quick PG-13 kiss on the mouth. "I've got a two o'clock curtain and my call's at one. Can you go for a picnic tomorrow?"

"We'll see," I tell him, turning to the roses. "I have a lot of work to do. I'll call you."

The porch steps groan as he turns to go. He whistles a tune as he makes his way through the garden. I'm a little annoyed by his cheerfulness on this day. And equally relieved to be free of those legs.

Marion and Crystal clamber back out onto the porch to settle an argument over whether you can drink iced tea out of a cereal bowl.

"Well, you *could*," I tell Marion, never wanting to make her feel ridiculous. "But a glass is easier."

"See!" Crystal says. She is always a little too vindicated when Marion is wrong.

Marion succumbs to the iced tea glass and they head back into the house for lemon. I realize there's no way Marion can fly home alone next week. I'll have to travel with her. I should go inside and call to make a reservation on her flight right now. But first I've got to clean up the bakery—assess the water damage to the floors, return the rented uniforms and punch bowls, and check the answering machine in case there are any orders.

I'm grateful for the bakery's demand for attention. For the longest time after Ethan died, it seemed no one needed me. Is there anyone less essential in the world than an unemployed widow without children? But now Marion needs me to help her get home. Crystal needs me to help her get through summer school. The bank needs me to stay in business so I can pay off my loan. Ruth needs me to baby-sit—*tonight,* so she can go to her book club! As I remember this, I stand up and clutch the roses to my chest. The porch is reassuringly firm and certain beneath my bare toes.

I close my eyes and imagine the baby shampoo smell of Simone's hair and the pale green vein pumping in her temple as she concentrates on staying within the lines in her coloring book.

Suddenly I relish the thought of a shower. Sweet warm water trickling into my mouth and a cloud of shampoo foaming up between my fingers. On some mornings back in San Jose, it would take me hours to work up the courage to take a shower, the busy scallop-shell motif on the shower curtain terrifying me. Now I quickly head inside to find a vase for the roses.

GOODWILL

29

"After we straighten up the bakery, I want to clean out my garage," I tell Crystal as we pull away from the senior center, where I've dropped Marion off for a bird-watching expedition.

"That doesn't sound fun."

"I know. But I want to go through Ethan's stuff." I'm determined to sort through Ethan's boxes, to salvage the things I really care about and move them into the house. Pack up the rest and deliver it to Goodwill. Shut down the Ethan museum. I squeeze the steering wheel, bracing myself for this onerous chore.

I wait for Crystal's signature response to something she doesn't want to do: What*ever*! Sometimes she's like a song you know all the words to. I look at her flat bare feet on the dashboard, her toenails painted pink with sparkly daisy decals on every other one.

"Okay," she says. "I'll help you."

I'm surprised by her willingness. I don't think Crystal really minds the fact that her mother doesn't pay the electric bill or sign her up for horseback-riding lessons. I think what really bothers her is that Roxanne doesn't include Crystal in her life. While Crystal can be a difficult person, in some ways she's easy; all she really wants is to be included.

"You and I will go through the stuff," I tell her, "then I'll get Ruth to help me with her truck."

Crystal nods seriously, as though she can hear all the little cracks in my airy, no-problem tone.

. . .

The garage smells like cedar and motor oil. The roof creaks over-head, as though buckling in the heat. Crystal and I sit on the chalky floor, sorting through Ethan's cardboard boxes and creating four piles: *Goodwill, Trash, Keep, Maybe Keep.* I'll review the *Maybe* pile before loading the car.

Crystal's pulled her hair into two spiky pigtails on top of her head. The magenta streaks make them look like flares. She sorts carefully through Ethan's socks, matching them and tossing the ones with holes. She blows her bangs off her forehead as she concentrates. I'm surprised by her patience. When I first met her, she lacked the ability to concentrate on anything but video games, spending entire Sun-day afternoons pumping my dollar bills into the token machine at the arcade while I looked on, pretending to have fun.

I scan the stacks of boxes. The only things of Ethan's I threw away after he died were his medical paraphernalia: prescriptions, Ensure, X-rays, the sharps container that held the syringes from his pain shots. I edited the illness out of his life story and saved everything else, even his doodles on the phone pad and his nameplate from his cubicle at work.

Lifting one of Ethan's flannel shirts to my face, I close my eyes, hoping to discover his smell. But the clothes have absorbed a neu-tral, cardboard aroma. I dig into the box marked *Bathroom.* A sharp pain burns my finger. Razor blade. A bright drop of blood bubbles up from the cut. I suck gently on it. The blood tastes salty. Ethan's hairbrush peers out from the *Bathroom* box. I lift it and tug my fin-gers through the bristles, soft brown hair coming free with a rip-ping noise. It's smooth and tickly, with the still-sweet, eggy smell of Ethan's Flex shampoo. I want to lie down.

"You could, like, put that in a locket," Crystal says, nodding at the hair.

I set the tuft at the edge of the *Maybe* pile. Wind creaks through the garage and the hair blows under a wheelbarrow, settling in among cobwebs, dead leaves, and the remnants of a moth. Organic matter. I shove the *Bathroom* box into the throwaway pile and head into the house for a Band-Aid.

After bandaging my finger, I stop in my room. I scoop Ethan's ski sweater out from under my pillow and knead a pinch of the coarse wool between my thumb and forefinger. Just as children have to surrender their pacifiers, and smokers have to toss their cigarettes when they kick the habit, I should probably give up the sweater.

I carry it to the garage.

"I think I have to give this away." I hold the sweater toward Crystal, hoping she'll take it from me.

"Okay." She shrugs and digs into a box of books. "It's not like you ever go skiing."

"But I want to keep it." I hug the sweater to my chest, inhaling its smoky wool smell.

"So keep it." She flips through the pages of Ethan's yearbook. "Wow." Her lips move as she reads the inscriptions. "Some people *like* high school."

"Ethan was a great student." I crunch the sweater against my belly and sit on the stool beside her. "He was president of his class."

"He was, like, totally smart," Crystal says as if she knew him, too.

"He could have helped you with your math. He would have made it fun."

"There's no *way* math is fun."

"I know. Which is what was so incredible about him."

I set the sweater in the *Maybe* pile and move on. My whole life seems to be in the maybe pile right now. Maybe I can run a successful business on my own, maybe I'll stay with Drew.

"Did you ever think you didn't want to live?" Crystal asks. "Since Ethan wasn't living?" She closes the yearbook and places it gently in the *Keep* pile. She asked me this same question when I told her about my mother dying. It worries me that she can muster these dark thoughts so easily.

"Yes," I admit, remembering lying alone in the dark on an air mattress in my living room in San Jose, the eerie blue light of the TV glowing on the ceiling. Too tired to turn it off, too tired to watch, too tired to sleep. "But I'm better now."

Crystal looks at the ski sweater. "'Cause you met me?"

I look at her, thinking.

She laughs. "I'm *joking.*"

"Kind of. Your family doesn't necessarily have to be your husband or blood relatives."

"Cool." She burrows into a box and pulls out Ethan's softball trophy.

"That's to keep." I lurch toward the trophy.

"Don't worry." She cradles the trophy to her chest, smoothing her palm over the brass head of the baseball player. "I never won anything," she says quietly, then sets the trophy in the *Keep* pile.

We continue working in silence. Sandy and Gloria will be proud of me for launching this cleanup project on the anniversary of Ethan's death. Another grief gold star.

"Hey." Crystal fingers the cleats on the golf shoes Ethan never wore and looks down at the floor. "My mom says she'll buy me a horse if I don't hang out with you anymore."

"Oh, really?" I throw an old computer mouse in the *Goodwill* pile a little too hard and it cracks. I move it to the *Trash* pile. "I thought horses were too expensive." Roxanne's like Ginger; even though she's not especially *nice* to the people she's close to, she wants to hoard them for herself. God forbid anyone else should love them.

Crystal shrugs. "She says she can get a loan."

Maybe a horse is to Crystal what Ginger is to Drew. A sexy upgrade.

Crystal holds up the dusty golf shoes and raises her eyebrows.

"Goodwill," I tell her.

"Anyways, I told her to shove her horse up her ass." She sets the golf shoes in the *Goodwill* pile. "Besides, she'd probably screw up the loan somehow."

"You really shouldn't talk to your mother that way." I look away, hoping Crystal hasn't seen me smile.

By the time Ruth and I reach the Goodwill in her truck later that day, it's closed. I cup my hands around my face and peer through the glass door at the rounders of clothes. They're sorted by colors ranging from turquoise to orange to black. I imagine Ethan's olive rugby shirt sidling up to a stranger's lime green aloha shirt. But his ski sweater is equally red, yellow, and navy. Will there be a home for it in this strict, color-coded system?

"Closed?" Ruth asks, digging her hands into the pockets of her jeans.

I turn toward the truck, which is so jammed with boxes that all Ruth could see out the back when we were driving was cardboard. I know exactly which box holds Ethan's ski sweater.

"There's a donation bin." Ruth points to a yellow Dumpster-like container at the rear of the parking lot. She climbs into the truck and backs it up to the bin, leaning out the door to see. Then she hops out and swings a box onto the ground. I follow her toward the bin, noticing that it's completely full. The mailbox-style door bulges open, choked with the hood of a down jacket. The coat looks as if it's trying to climb out.

"We'll just put them here." Ruth stacks the box beside the container.

"Uh, okay." The sour smell of unwashed fabric sticks in my throat.

No! Ethan says. *Don't leave my worldly possessions in a filthy parking lot.*

Discarded belongings litter the asphalt around the donation

bin: a curled-up huarache sandal, a snarl of bent hangers, a silk scarf streaked with black tire marks. The greasy smell of French fries wafts over from the fast-food place next door. Across the parking lot, a faded futon leans against the back wall of the Goodwill building. Beside it, plastic tubs overflow with shoes, toys, and small appliances. There's simply too much junk in the world. Each person should be allowed a small quota, the way you're allowed only two bags when you fly.

Ruth drops a box of books with a loud smack on the pavement, making me jump.

"Careful," I tell her.

"It's heavy. You need to give me a hand!"

"Okay." But I can't move. Suddenly I feel as though I've orchestrated a crime I can't bring myself to go through with.

"Help," Ruth yelps. As she wrestles the big suitcase of Ethan's coats out of the truck, her slender back bows under the weight. Together we drag the bag across the parking lot and lean it against the bin.

As we're returning to the truck, I notice a sign screwed to the chain-link fence behind the donation box: WARNING: DONATIONS LEFT WHEN GOODWILL IS CLOSED IS CONSIDERED DUMPING. VIOLATORS WILL BE PROSECUTED.

"We can't leave this stuff here," I tell Ruth, pointing to the sign.

Her lips move as she reads. "Oh, for God's sake. You can go to jail for cutting off your mattress tag, too, you know."

"Right." I laugh weakly, noticing another sign on the side of the container: THANK YOU FOR HELPING PEOPLE WITH DISABILITIES LEAD PRODUCTIVE LIVES. I think of Ethan's fancy Bose clock radio, which I've decided to give away so I won't always imagine him lying in bed listening to the news in the morning. They can probably get at least fifty bucks for it. I continue unloading. Surely someone will be here first thing tomorrow to unpack the stuff and move it indoors.

As we finally drive out of the Goodwill parking lot, I focus on Ethan's boxes in the rearview mirror the way you might locate the North Star in the sky at night.

I get up at four the next morning and head straight to the bakery to start the cheesecakes, pies, and muffins. *This is me, throwing myself into my work,* I think as I lean my weight into the pie dough, the rolling pin smacking the counter. Back in San Jose, work threw itself at me, deadlines wrapping their tentacles around my legs and pulling me down. Crystal shows up shortly after dawn, her eyes puffy with sleep. She lifts the cheesecakes out of their molds, picks the final bits of streamers and tape off the walls. I'm relieved when we're finally able to flip the sign in the window over to the OPEN side at ten. By then a small cluster of customers waits on the sidewalk, and they all seem to have read Marjorie's review. Drew's already framed the review and hung it over the cash register. The article has a big color picture of Crystal and me standing behind a row of cheesecakes. By some miracle I'm having a good hair day in the photo: soft ringlets instead of wiry frizz. Crystal looks serious, leaning toward the cakes as though they might tell her something.

A young actress from the festival wants to order her wedding cake. I'm nervous as she spreads pages torn from magazines across the kitchen table with pictures of cakes decorated as intricately as Fabergé eggs.

In the afternoon, customers fill the bakery, struggling to see into the glass cases, which are emptying fast. People want cupcakes for birthday parties, cookies for softball games, carrot cakes and cheesecakes for dessert. I work the counter while Crystal mans the register, fretting as she hurries to count change.

I try to talk to everyone, ask if they live in Ashland or if they're just visiting, suggest wines to serve with the savory cheesecakes, remind them to order their birthday cakes earlier next time. As I grab sheet after sheet of waxed paper to fill the orders, I feel a year's worth of isolation and shyness evaporate in the heat of the bakery.

"That should be a five," a woman buying a peach pie tells Crystal sweetly. Crystal reddens and pops open the drawer to recount the bills.

"Don't worry," I tell Crystal when there's finally a lull. "Take your time."

We do $752.86 worth of business over the course of the afternoon, selling out of cheesecakes, savory and sweet. While I figured I wouldn't need to hire employees for at least the first month of business, obviously I need more helpers right away. As the dinner hour approaches and the bakery finally empties, I sit in the kitchen to draft a help wanted ad: *Sales clerk, weekday afternoons.* Then it hits me: the image of Ethan's ski sweater suffocating under a mountain of dead people's musty sweatshirts and jerseys.

"It's cathartic to let go of their belongings," Gloria said when I told her that I finally cleaned out the garage. She told me that she left jeans and a T-shirt laid out on her daughter's bed for six months after the girl died. Finally she gave away the clothes, and turned the room into a study.

I force myself to forget Ethan's sweater for now, to forget the image of his tuft of hair under the wheelbarrow in the garage, and turn back to the ad. *Busy downtown bakery . . .*

By the time I make it home that evening, I can't wait to lie on the couch and put my feet up. But as soon as I'm through the door the phone rings. Marion answers it.

"Uh," she stammers, "he's not here right now." She thrusts the receiver at me.

"Hello?" I cradle the phone between my shoulder and ear as I open the mail.

"I'm trying to locate a Mr. Ethan Stanton?" a man says. Telemarketers. Rude slime.

"He died." I drop the envelopes. "A *year* ago. Who's calling, please?"

There's a scratchy silence at the other end.

"I'm sorry," the man says tentatively.

"He died," I repeat, pressing guilt.

"Are you sure?" the man shouts over wind that rumbles into the receiver, and I realize he must be outdoors.

"Of course I'm sure. I'm his widow. Who *is* this, please?"

"*Who* died?" Marion asks.

"I've found some of his belongings." The man's hoarse voice struggles through the crackly connection. "Coats? On I-5 at a rest stop. I pulled off to use the rest room and when I got back to the parking lot a suitcase was dumped beside my car. I thought someone might have stolen Mr. Stanton's belongings, or that something might have happened to him. A tag in one of the coats had his name on it. I got your number from information. There was another Stanton, but they weren't home."

The Marlboro Man coat. I tried to cut out the tag with Ethan's name, but Marion had sewn it deep into the silk lining years ago when we were at her house for dinner.

"You don't want someone stealing this beautiful coat," she fretted, dragging her needle and thread through the slick lining. I was annoyed with Ethan for letting his mother be so meddlesome, treating him as though he were a kid headed for camp. But her bossy behavior never fazed him.

"There are several boxes, too," the man shouts. "They've been opened and clothes are everywhere. I'm sorry, I have to get going to make it to Spokane to see my son."

Someone must have stolen the boxes, decided they weren't worth anything, and dumped the contents. Suddenly I'm offended by these low-life thieves. Why did they dump the coats? What were they expecting from the Goodwill parking lot? That was a $300 suede coat!

"You go on," I tell the man. "I'll be there soon. Thank you," I add. I can't imagine that very many people would have bothered to call.

"Exit forty-seven," he says before I hear the ghostly hum of the dial tone.

I drop Marion off at Ruth's house for dinner, borrow her truck again, and pick up Crystal en route to the rest stop. As Crystal braces an arm against the dashboard, I realize I'm driving eighty-five on the freeway.

"Sorry." But if I drive fast enough, maybe I can undo the terrible mistake of abandoning Ethan's possessions. DUMPING, the Goodwill sign said. ILLEGAL.

There are a few hours of daylight left, but a storm is brewing, grayish green mashed-potato clouds roiling along the horizon.

"There." Crystal points to the sign for the exit, which I'm about to pass.

I don't think we can make it, but I swerve off the road anyway. We jerk across two double white lines, lurch over the curb onto a median strip, and squeal through the grass, gravel and mud shooting up behind the truck.

"Shit!" Crystal shouts. "They're only clothes!"

A rock pops loudly under the truck, as though it's ruptured something. *Don't worry, I'll fix it,* I'll tell Ruth. *I'll fix everything.* We bump over the curb onto the other side of the median strip and speed into the rest stop parking lot. Clothes, *Ethan's* clothes, are strewn everywhere—the only streaks of color in an otherwise gray landscape. I stomp on the brake. Crystal lurches forward. The engine stalls and stutters.

A sudden gust of wind makes the trees twist and strain toward the heavens. Ethan's Christmas necktie spirals in the air like a red streamer. The arm of his navy windbreaker flaps over the top of a box, waving at us.

Across the lawn there's a low, sand-colored building as bleak as a prison with a row of vending machines out front. I shove open the truck door, but the wind is stubborn, slamming the door shut against my calf. Pain sears my leg.

We finally push our way out of the truck, bending our heads into the wind. Something bangs loudly inside the rest stop building. Crystal jumps and grabs my arm.

"This place is creepy," she says.

It's odd how many things don't frighten her—blowing up M-80s, starting fires, cutting herself—while other scenarios freak her out.

"We'll be out of here soon," I tell her. "Let's just gather the clothes."

Children's screams from a nearby field curl through the wind.

"I don't think we *can* get rid of these clothes." Crystal shudders and shoves her hands inside her sleeves, hopping up and down to keep warm. She bends over, plucks a soggy sock out of a puddle, shakes it, and drops it into a box.

A pair of Ethan's khakis are strewn in the grass beside a metal garbage can that's chained to a pole. Wind tunnels through the legs of the pants, making them dance a little jig. Maybe a person never really leaves this world. You can pack up their belongings, deliver their clothes to Goodwill, put their letters away in shoeboxes. But they will always inhabit the landscape in some way. If not in a rest stop parking lot, then in the first smell of cut grass in the spring.

I try to refold Ethan's T-shirts. This proves futile as the wind yanks everything apart. I give up, balling and stuffing the clothes into the boxes. As I turn over the suitcase, I find that it's been sliced open with a knife. A black nylon wound flaps open, a slash all the way through the soft suede arm of the Marlboro Man coat. I collapse, sitting cross-legged beside the suitcase, and begin to sob, choking on the wind.

Crystal looks up from a box, her face flushed. "What're ya doing? Let's get out of here!"

"Buh!" My eyes and nose and mouth gush as though I've sprung a leak. A strand of drool hangs from my mouth, but I don't care. I double over my legs and pound the pavement with my fists, tiny rocks piercing the skin.

"Hey, it's all right." Crystal's thin arms circle my middle, the goose bumps on her skin as rough as a cat's tongue. She crouches and grunts, trying to lift me. "We're almost done." Her breath is warm in my ear.

"Everything's ruined!"

"Nah, *look*." She points to Ethan's ski sweater, which lies folded neatly at the top of a nearby box. She manages to get us both standing, bending her knees into the backs of mine to right me. My arms flop at my sides, and my hair whips and stings my cheeks.

"Okay," I tell her, tell myself. I concentrate on taking deep breaths, wiping away hair and tears and drool with the sleeve of my corduroy jacket. "Okay." I want to be strong for Crystal. Strong for Marion and Ruth and Dad. For Ethan. Strong for people I haven't even met yet, for prospective customers, future grandchildren. Strong for me. Person to contact in case of emergency? Put my name down: Sophie Stanton.

I brush dirt off my jeans. After I open the bakery tomorrow morning, I'll leave Crystal in charge and deliver the boxes to the Goodwill when they're actually open.

As Crystal and I wedge the suitcase between the last of the boxes, the rain blows in sheets, soaking our clothes and drumming the car roof.

Soon we're back on the freeway, windshield wipers squeaking, the cab of the truck smelling like mealy wet cardboard, the whole Oregon sky turning inside out.

30

It's still dark as I trudge up East Main Street to work, orange light tingeing the sky, the asphalt glistening black like the still surface of a lake. I'm groggy from lack of sleep. Last night Drew and I slept together for the first time since our breakup. After dinner and a bottle of Chianti at an Italian restaurant, followed by a furtive make-out session in the car outside Colonel Cranson's, Drew tried to persuade me to stay at his house. I didn't want to leave Marion home alone, though. "May I come in, then?" he asked, rubbing his arms to keep warm.

"Come in. Meaning sleep *over*," I said, not as a question, but as a statement.

He looked down, searching for the right words. As he opened his mouth to speak, I leaned across the seat and bit into the soft flesh of his lower lip and tried to tell myself not to worry so much.

Now I anticipate drinking my first cup of coffee at the bakery kitchen table, eager to inhale the rich, roasted steam as the ovens preheat and the sweet-roll dough rises. I walk faster, working out the day in my head: bake sweet rolls, muffins, and scones; serve morning rush of coffee-and-muffin customers; unpack supplies. Fill birthday cake orders, bake cookies, prepare and chill pie dough, balance books, schedule employee interviews.

As I reach the gallery beside my shop, I glance down to step over a puddle. When I look up, a car accident jolt of adrenaline shoots through my body because I think I see *Ethan* standing in front of the bakery. His back is toward me as he bends over the trash can on the corner. The three thick stripes of red, yellow, and navy on his ski sweater stand out like a flag.

My bowels rumble and my legs wobble. I almost kneel on the sidewalk involuntarily.

Ethan plucks a Coke can out of the trash and turns, looking at me. I realize it's not Ethan, but an elderly gentleman I've often seen in town sitting on a bench in front of the post office, smoking hand-rolled cigarettes. He's short and stout, with a long Santa Claus beard that hangs in a V shape over his chest. His belly swells under the sweater, round and hard like a basketball.

When I finally left the sweater at the Goodwill, handed it over to the woman behind the counter as though it were the Holy Grail, she pointed out that winter items aren't big sellers in August. Yet this gentleman certainly snatched it up in a hurry.

"Good morning," I say, trying to smile. The man wears too-big khakis slung low around his hips, fastened with a woman's shiny faux crocodile belt. He shuffles his feet a little on the sidewalk. His sneakers have one white and one yellow shoelace. Ethan's ski sweater looks rumpled, slept in, one sleeve caked with something brown. The man looks like Colonel Sanders's black sheep brother. Clearly not a skier. He smiles and cocks his head. I'm surprised at how straight and glossy his teeth are. Dentures, maybe.

"Ma'am." He brings his hand to his forehead, as though tipping a hat, then pops the soda can into a bulging garbage bag resting at his feet.

I wonder what Ethan would have looked like as an old man. Even when he was sick he never developed wrinkles or a single gray hair. He just lost his vibrancy, as though cancer had rendered him in black and white while the rest of the world remained in color.

"Would you like to come in for coffee?" I pull my keys out of my purse and nod toward the bakery door.

The man cocks his head the other way.

"I own the bakery," I tell him. Once I get him inside, I'll ask for the sweater. I'll offer to pay three times what he paid for it at Goodwill or ask if I can buy him another. Maybe he'd like a coat. A tuxedo. Whatever. I'll explain there's been a mistake.

"Don't mind if I do." The man claps his hands clean. As he shuffles in behind me, he sets his bag of cans in the doorway, looking back to make sure he can keep an eye on it. I seat him at one of the tables in the front window, start the coffee, and turn on the ovens. Then I slice open a blackberry muffin from yesterday, toast it in the oven, spread it with butter, and pour him a cup of coffee.

While he eats, I pull on a chef's jacket and apron. I slide the sweet-roll dough out of the refrigerator, throw a moist dish towel over the bowl, and leave it beside the ovens to rise. Sitting next to the man, I cradle a cup of coffee in my hands.

He takes big bites of the muffin, looking up at me shyly. I notice he has the same sour fabric smell as the Goodwill. He's not as old as I originally thought, maybe only in his early sixties. More weathered than elderly. Deep grooves line his forehead, and red leathery skin hangs from his chin.

"Where do you live?" I ask, and immediately regret the question. Maybe he doesn't have a home.

"At a boardinghouse," he says through a mouthful. His nose is purplish and vein riddled, like a plum. "They serve dinner, but not breakfast." He holds up the muffin. "Delicious."

"Would you like another?"

"No, thank you. I have to be going." But he sits back in his chair, relaxing.

I think that's my sweater, I could explain. *I donated it to the Goodwill, but it has great sentimental value and I'd like to have it back. May I buy it from you?* Instead of saying anything, I drum my fingers on the table and gulp my coffee, skipping the slow, pleasure-filled sips.

The man rests his bearded chin on his chest, peering down over his belly. He runs a thick finger along the line between the red and yellow stripes. My fingertips flutter as I imagine the sensation of the bristly wool. It always felt good to bunch the sweater in a ball against my stomach as I slept. For some reason, I like to have something against my belly when I sleep. It used to be the curve of Ethan's spine, his lungs expanding and contracting. After he died, I tried several different pillows. Somehow the lumped-up sweater fit just right.

"You won't need that in an hour," I tell the man, nodding at the sweater. "It's going to be a scorcher."

The man thrusts back his shoulders and puffs up his chest, modeling. "I rather like the stripes, though, don't you?"

"Yes." The red is as lustrous as a fire engine, the yellow as bright as lemons, the navy as rich as midnight. I know it's a ten-year-old sweater with a tea stain, but I envisioned someone more . . . *appealing* inheriting it from Ethan. Maybe Brad Pitt or Mel Gibson. Why can't *they* shop at the Goodwill in Ashland?

The man squeezes his chin in one hand and looks up at the ceiling. Ethan always did this when he was thinking. As if there were answers on the ceiling. This is an *Ethan* gesture. I remember a TV news story about a heart transplant patient who insisted that her new heart made her more artistic. Suddenly she could paint watercolors and throw pots. Could Ethan's sweater carry similar powers? Will the man start writing software code?

Of course not. But if you can donate a heart or kidney, why not a ski sweater? How lame to renege on this small gift of charity. I tighten my grip around my coffee mug, even though it's empty now.

"My wife was a good baker." The man picks crumbs from the muffin wrapper. "She made the best pie crust." He pauses and gazes up at the ceiling again, thinking. "With lard."

"Did you lose your wife?" At least I'll see the sweater on occasion, when I run into the man in town.

"Divorced me." He glances out across the street as the owner of the bookstore unlocks her shop.

"I'm sorry." The buzzer in the kitchen goes off. I get up to punch down the dough, then return to the table.

"It was my fault."

I'm not sure what to say. "I'm sorry," I repeat.

We sit and listen to the ovens tick.

"By the way, my name's Sophie Stanton," I finally tell him.

He smiles, tips his head toward me. "Jasper Jenkins."

"Let me pack you something to go, Jasper." I get up and fold one of the pink boxes into a square, then line it with waxed paper. I choose a miniature jalapeño cheesecake, ham-and-chive croissant, and two egg brioches. Savory items that seem filling and meal-like. I want to pack the box until it's bursting, but I worry the food will go stale and that sometimes charity can be overbearing, even condescending.

"You ski?" I ask Jasper, hovering near the sweater as I hand him the box of goodies.

"Never learned how." He uses his napkin to wipe the crumbs from the table into his cupped palm, then shakes them into his empty coffee cup. "My wife knew how to ski." Jasper cradles the bakery box in his lap.

"Maybe you could get back together," I offer. "There's always hope, as long as someone's alive."

"It's too late. She married someone else."

"Oh, I'm sorry." I feel as though I've ruined the guy's day, interviewing him like a nosy talk show host. "You mustn't worry too much about the past," I tell him, knowing this is impossible.

"You ski?," Jasper asks.

"Not anymore. Want to, though." Maybe next winter Crystal and I will go skiing. Ruth and Simone could join us. But I'll wear my own ski sweater.

THANKSGIVING

31

Two days before Thanksgiving, Crystal, Marion, and I sit in the living room at Colonel Cranson's. Crystal paints Marion's fingernails while I snap green beans.

"Hold *still*, please," Crystal commands as she anchors Marion's fidgety hand and dabs her nails with Misty Mauve polish. Crystal's adopted a chiding but protective attitude toward Marion, as an older sibling might. Marion fidgets, her foot tapping the TV tray. Her fingernails are yellow, hard, and ridged—sort of the way she is. "This color matches your Thanksgiving outfit perfectly," Crystal tells her. Although she usually favors black nail polish, she spent a long time choosing this pinkish shade for Marion.

"That's going to look pretty," I agree, trying to encourage Marion to relax and focus on her hands.

Both Marion and Crystal have moved in with me. They're sort of like my two kids now. I knew Ethan would be sad to see his mother spend her final years alone in a facility in San Jose, and at the end of her three-week summer visit I invited Marion to live with me. We rented her house back home. I flew down with her and helped her pack. She wanted to bring everything to Ashland, even the food in her refrigerator. This time *I* was the bossy packing coordinator putting my foot down.

"We *have* melon in Oregon," I told her, wrestling a five-pound bag of frozen cantaloupe balls from the Price Club out of her gnarled hands, the icy wrapper nipping at my fingers.

After Labor Day, Crystal's mother announced she was moving to Texas with her new boyfriend, an electrician with broad shoulders and blond hair pulled into a rock star ponytail who bought Roxanne a ring with an almond-size ruby. Crystal lobbied to move in with me so she wouldn't have to switch schools. I reminded her that she tried to *blow up* her school. Still, she insisted she didn't want to leave Ashland and talked her mother into letting her stay. Apparently Roxanne likes her new boyfriend more than she loathes me.

Some nights, I lie awake worrying about Marion. Will she wander through the car wash or tumble down the stairs? Other nights, I toss and turn fretting about Crystal. Will she revert to cutting herself or get kicked out of school again? Then there's the bakery to lose sleep over. How far will my sales dip in the slow months of January and February? At least I'm not plagued by the fears I had back in San Jose, where I couldn't even muster enough courage for the produce section.

Now, Marion gazes up at her burgundy dress, which hangs from the back of the living room door. "I went dancing one time with Anthony in an outfit like that," she says.

"Who's Anthony?" Crystal asks.

"Old boyfriend." A web of thin blue veins pulses along Marion's temple as she struggles to remember. "In junior high. We won a dance contest." Her left hand is finished. She blows on her nails, reflecting.

"We're going to have a great Thanksgiving," I tell Marion, trying to bring her back to the present. This seems remarkable, given that I've always *hated* Thanksgiving. When I was a kid, no relatives lived close enough to come to our house. I longed for bustling gatherings with brothers, sisters, and cousins overflowing onto card tables. Grandparents belting out Broadway tunes around a grand piano. Glamorous aunts whipping cream in the kitchen. After Mother died, it was always just Dad and me, moping over Stove Top stuffing. Ethan never really appreciated the holiday; he always insisted on working.

I still won't have to put leaves in the dining room table this year, but at least we'll have a group of nine, including Crystal, Marion, Dad, Jill, Ruth, Simone, me, and Drew. Even without Ethan, this finally seems like the Thanksgiving I've always longed for.

The pies are finished, the turkey is soaking in brine, the silver is polished, the tablecloths are pressed, and the house is filled with red roses from Drew. Dad and Jill are flying into Medford tonight. Our ninth guest will be Jasper Jenkins, the inheritor of Ethan's ski sweater. I've treated Jasper to a cup of coffee and blackberry muffin once a week or so since the first morning he and I met. While I work, he sits at the table in the window at the bakery, looking out at the street and harboring conspiracy theories: The moon landing was all plaster of Paris and string; the CIA offed Jim Morrison; drug companies want to clone Elvis with nail clippings. These ideas seem to help Jasper stop thinking about his wife.

Last week I stopped by the post office, where Jasper smokes on the front steps, and asked if he had Thanksgiving plans. He said the boardinghouse was serving dinner, but it was "usually crap." He picked bits of tobacco from his lips, considering my invitation.

"What are you having?" he finally asked.

When I told him turkey, the usual, he decided that would be acceptable.

Now, Crystal finishes Marion's last nail, using a wisp of cotton to dab at the polish pooling around her cuticles.

"Just sit for a few minutes," Crystal tells her.

"But we need to make the yam puff before everyone gets here." Panic creases Marion's brow. "Where's Ethan?" she adds. Marion is convinced Ethan's coming for Thanksgiving dinner, that he's somewhere in the house and she just hasn't run into him yet. She looks wistfully through the living room door toward the stairs. "Is he sleeping in?"

32

"Sophie!" a man's voice booms, full of fear.

What? Oh! Fire, earthquake, Crystal, emergency room. I fly out of bed, only to discover that I'm still in bed, sitting up, a corner of the sheet clenched between my teeth. A tangle of arms, Drew's arms, circles my waist. We're in bed. Together. It's Thanksgiving morning.

"You're still *here*," Drew says. He pulls me down, burrows his head into my chest.

"Yes," I tell him, heaving a sigh of relief. "I don't leave the house in my pajamas anymore." The warm sheets feel almost damp against my bare skin. "Or naked."

There's a faint knock on the door. "Everything all right?" Jill whispers.

"Fine," I assure her, embarrassed that Drew's in my room. I didn't want him sleeping over during Dad and Jill's visit. But last night he joined us for pizza, and after dinner, as he played the piano and sang Jill's favorite Broadway song with her—"If I Were a Rich Man"—his voice grew croaky. He was obviously coming down with a cold.

"You mustn't go out in this weather," Jill insisted, heading to the kitchen to fix him a cup of Sleepytime tea. She's as smitten with Drew as Marion is. "You better stay here and let us take care of you."

Dad nodded, but I was self-conscious, wondering if everyone knew that this meant Drew would stay in *my* room. I felt as if I were in an ad for the Charming New Boyfriend™. *The Charming New Boyfriend™ loves your parents! He plays the piano and sings!*

Now, I hear Jill continue down the hall.

"Just a bad dream," Drew whispers. He tightens his arms around my waist. His breath is hot against my cheek. "I dreamed that you were *gone*. That I lost you."

"How? That's silly." But I know this anxiety dream by heart. In it the person sleeping beside you suddenly vanishes. I had this nightmare for months. Only when I woke up, it wasn't just a dream—Ethan was really gone.

"You left," Drew says.

"I'm not going anywhere." I hold his face in my hands. His whiskers are rough against my palms. "For starters, I've got a year's supply of cake flour." The *upper hand* with my boyfriend. Is it all right to be grateful for this on Thanksgiving?

Drew drifts back to sleep, his cold making him snore slightly. His pink lips are parted and squashed against the pillow, his unshaven cheeks bluish with beard. My good-riddance list for him has dwindled to nil. He's great at keeping Marion company. The two of them sit for hours on the porch, Drew practicing his monologues, while Marion comments on the car wash as though it's a sporting event. ("A coat hanger! Why can't they get a real antenna?") For my birthday, in August, he gave me a pair of antique teardrop diamond earrings. Last week, he bought Crystal the potbellied pig she's been pining after. "Great! Where is *he* going to live?" I asked. Drew hadn't thought through the details. But he quickly offered to keep the pig in his yard, which is twice as big as mine, and he even rushed the thing to the vet when it choked on a crab apple.

While Drew had originally planned on going out to New York for the six weeks the festival is closed, he's decided to stay in Ashland to be with me. According to Ruth, who heard it from a friend who works at the festival, Ginger's left town for the winter break on a Caribbean cruise with the phantom fiancé. When I heard this news I had a vivid fantasy in which Ginger contracted food poisoning from a sketchy shrimp curry at the cruise buffet, leaned over the edge of the boat to retch, her skinny ass perched in the air, and fell overboard, strands of long red hair floating in the sea like kelp, the body never to be found.

I watch Drew sleep. While today I have the upper hand, it seems it would be easy for him to derail my recently acquired happily-ever-after status. All he would have to do is downgrade me to coffee again or announce that he's gay or moving to Seattle. He could get hit by a bus or diagnosed with cancer. A pea-size tumor somewhere in his body would be the size of a walnut by the time I let myself fall completely in love with him. It would be the size of a baseball by the time we got married. He'd be a walking tumor by the time we had kids.

I smell toast burning downstairs. At least I hope it's toast. Last week Marion stuffed a glove in the toaster. I gently lift Drew's arm from around my waist, slide out from under the covers and into my robe, and head for the kitchen.

Marion sits at the table, wrapped in her pink chenille robe, hugging herself and shaking her head as she reads Miss Manners. "Freeloaders," she squawks. "They should pay their share!"

I'm always relieved to find that Marion's in the house when I get up in the morning. Once I awoke to discover that she and the car had vanished. I called the senior center, then the coffee shop downtown, then the police. An hour later, an officer called back to report that Marion had been on her way to the senior center—not wanting to bother me by asking for a ride—got muddled, went to the park instead, drove over the grass, got stuck in the mud, and backed into a fountain. Marion and I had a talk about how she shouldn't drive anymore. She agreed and gave me a little hug. Since then, I hide the car keys in an empty flour canister.

The doctor in Medford suggested putting Marion in a home. Instead, I've convinced Marion to let me use some of her savings to hire a caregiver to come to the house while I'm at work.

"Good morning." I kiss Marion on the forehead, then turn on the oven.

I hoist the turkey out of its brine bath in the refrigerator and pat it dry with paper towels. It took forever to finish the stuffing yesterday because Marion wanted sausage and Crystal wanted plain white bread without any meat. Drew wanted chestnuts, which Crystal said were for squirrels. I ended up fixing three batches, and now I'm not sure which to stuff the bird with. It never occurred to me that my Thanksgiving fantasy dinner would be complicated by so many culinary demands. I choose Marion's stuffing to fill the bird, honoring her seniority before realizing that she probably won't remember that she *likes* sausage. After I shove the roasting pan into the oven, I pour a glass of cranberry juice for Drew.

Back in my room, I push aside the lace curtains and snap open the window shades. In the distance, snow dusts the Siskiyous.

Drew lifts his head from the pillow and blinks at the daylight. "Brrrr," he says as I push open a window, anxious to rid the room of its sour sick odor. The earthy smells of wood fires and damp leaves outside are a relief.

I turn toward the bed. Drew's shoulders and chest are smooth and muscular, and I want to touch his skin. I hand him the juice, which he swallows in two gulps.

"Ow!" He clutches his throat. "Feel my forehead." He reclines on the pillows, rolling his eyes toward the ceiling dramatically. I sit on the edge of the bed and lay a hand across his brow. It's damp but cool.

"I think you're fine." I keep one foot firmly on the floor, resisting the temptation to dive under the covers with him. "Why don't you get up and take a shower? Split some wood and build a fire?"

"C'mere, Nurse Naughty." He tugs my arm and I fall onto him, feeling his chest purr. He tightens his hands around my wrists, pinning them behind me. As he burrows his face under my sweater, his whiskers are rough against my belly. "Will you shower with me?" We toss and tumble and giggle, his skin hot and smooth against mine. He tries to pull my sweater over my head, but I tug it back down and free myself, worrying that Dad and Jill might hear us.

Drew sits up and moans. "My throaaaaat! Would you look in there?" He opens his mouth wide and sticks out his tongue. "Ahhhh," he honks.

His throat is rimmed scarlet, with a few raised white spots in the back. He probably needs a throat culture and antibiotics. I should want to coddle him, but I'm irritated by his illness. I don't want anyone in my life to ever get sick again. Not even a sniffle or hangnail.

In the bathroom I refill Drew's glass with water and grab a few Tylenol from the medicine chest.

"I think you're fine, Falstaff," I repeat, handing him the pills. I bend over to retie my sneaker.

"I love you," Drew says.

Panic sears my heart. I retie my other shoe. Now they're both too tight. "I, uh . . ." I don't want to stand up. Drew told me he loved me at the bakery party. But he hasn't said it since. Neither have I. I've been resisting loving him the way you'd resist a box of chocolate truffles or a pair of expensive shoes. You can't get in a train wreck if you don't board the train. But how can I live happily ever after without loving someone again? How can I love someone again without granting him the power to crush me?

Suddenly I want to see my entire future. I'd like to be able to drop a quarter into one of those viewing machines at a scenic lookout and gaze all the way past the horizon to the rest home and see whose picture is on my bedside table and how many husbands there were and whether there were children.

I figured that if Drew and I ever exchanged the L-word again, it would be in front of a roaring fire or after sex. Not while I'm tying my sneaker. And not until a few months from now. After the holidays, maybe.

"Thanks," I finally stutter.

A head rush makes the room tilt sideways as I stand up. Drew's smiling. His face is flushed and his eyes are glassy. He doesn't seem to mind that I haven't reciprocated. I sit beside him on the bed, rubbing his neck and shoulders, then pulling the quilt up to his chin.

"Let's go to New York," he says. "Next week. I'll treat you. It's the best time of year in the city. Let me take you to the Waldorf."

"I can't leave work," I remind him. While it's the slowest time of year for Ashland, I've barely been able to keep up with holiday orders at the bakery. "Maybe in February." I'm glad I'm unable to bend to Drew's schedule. When we first started dating, I always seemed to be available.

"I want to help with dinner," he says huskily, coughing and then blowing his nose.

"Forget it. You're quarantined. I'm not letting you touch the food."

"Okay." He grabs at me again.

I'd like to strip off my clothes and slide back under the covers, to risk ruining the dinner and catching the white spots in Drew's throat. Instead, I tip my head toward the door. "The turkey," I tell him.

I'm heading down the hall to the kitchen when I hear Crystal calling me.

"Fannie? Are you there?" At first her voice is quiet, almost a whisper, but then it fills with anxiety.

I freeze, worried that maybe Crystal's cut herself, overwhelmed by the holidays. I hurry down the hall and peer into her room. Jimi

Hendrix and Janis Joplin peer back at me from posters covering the lilac wallpaper. Red scarves drape the lampshades, giving the room a bordello glow. Instead of stuffed teddy bears, Crystal owns real taxidermist-stuffed animals she bought from a musty antiques store in town—a raccoon rearing on its haunches beside her desk and an opossum crouched on top of her dresser. Crystal's not in her room. The opossum's beady eyes make him look guilty, as though he's stolen something out of her top drawer.

"Sophie? Can you *help* me?" Crystal's voice, from the bathroom across the hall. I knock, then push the door open a crack and find her sitting doubled over on the toilet, her bare knees pressed together, her pajama bottoms tossed in the corner.

"I got my period." Her underwear is wadded in her fist.

I assumed Crystal already *had* her period. She turned fourteen last month and she's so worldly and tough—with the smoking, eyeliner, and cutting. Fourteen going on forty. She never brought it up. She just bemoaned her tiny breasts and boyish waistline, which I tried to make her feel better about, telling her that people do crazy stuff to be thin.

"Oh, okay." I slide in through the door and close it behind me.

Are you there, God? It's me, Sophie! What do I tell a teenage girl who just got her period? I'm not sure, because my mother had already died by the time I got mine, so I never got a proper birds-and-bees, coming-of-age lecture. My father just went to the store and returned with two grocery bags brimming with packages of pads and tampons—probably every variety they sold, unsure of which one I might need. I curled up on the couch with cramps and he fixed me a cup of tea with a tablespoon of whiskey, fetched me the heating pad, and sat with my feet in his lap. He kept opening his mouth as though he were going to say something, but then he'd close it again. Finally we watched *The Gong Show* on TV.

I leave Crystal to fetch her some clean underwear, a tampon, and a sanitary pad. When I return to the bathroom, I close the door and hand her the things, wondering if maybe I should have stayed in the hall. "You just—"

"I *know* how to use them," she says, irritated. "I just don't have any." She chooses the pad and steps into the underwear I brought her. I pretend to be busy refolding the towels as she flushes the toilet and washes her hands. "I'm, like, the last girl in my class, you know." She rinses out her underwear in the sink.

"Oh, honey, that must have been hard. But now you don't have to worry about it anymore." The radiator in the bathroom rattles and clanks. I'd like to make an eloquent "You're a woman now!" speech. "Want to call your mom?" I finally ask Crystal.

"What *for?*" She loops her underwear over the towel rack to dry, then leans over the sink to look in the mirror. Her cheeks are red and still creased with wrinkles from the sheets. She rubs at a smudge of black eyeliner under her eye.

"Right." A new wave of worry for Crystal washes over me. Now she can get pregnant! I think of the long list of gynecological troubles outlined in *Our Bodies, Ourselves,* which we all kept tucked under our beds in college. (Not that we were ashamed of the book, but when guys came to your room for a beer, you wanted them to see your Fitzgerald and Hemingway.)

I reach out to hug Crystal, but she dips her head into the sink to wash her face. When she's finished I hand her a towel. She turns and pulls on her pajama bottoms, then takes a step toward the door.

"Gah! This is like having a roll of paper towels in your pants!"

"They have all kinds of maxi-mini skinny-thinny better ones at the store," I tell her. "Wait until you see the choices."

"I *know.*"

"Okay."

Somehow, Crystal's grateful and aggravated with me at the same time. I think I know how the mother of a teenage daughter must feel. Like an indispensable annoyance.

"Would you like a little glass of wine with dinner?" I ask her.

"Yes, please."

Back in the kitchen, Dad and Jill are up and dressed, peeling potatoes at the table. They look like twins in their matching chamois
shirts and khakis, laughing in unison as they work. I hope that by
some miracle they die at the same time.

"How many should we peel?" Jill asks me, holding up a potato.
Her white hair is cut into a pageboy that curls around her ears.

Ruth has arrived and she wants to know about the stuffing.
"Should I cover it?" She seems irritated by the stuffing, holding it
away from her as though it smells bad. She looks beautiful in her
long brown velvet dress, her yellow hair fanning across her narrow
waist. Simone clings to her legs, peering out shyly at Dad and Jill,
who are trying to coax her across the room with a gingersnap. I'm
about to tell Ruth not to worry about the stuffing when Crystal
spins into the kitchen in her stocking feet.

"Hey, does this go?" she asks me, holding a necklace up to the
collar of her dress. The dress has a black velvet bodice and long
lacy sleeves that are pretty in a Gothic sort of way. As she does a
pirouette to model the ensemble, she loses her balance and
stumbles.

"Sophie?" Drew calls out raspily from the bedroom. "Hot tea?"

I turn from Dad to Jill to Ruth to Crystal toward my bedroom.
Everyone is asking me what to do here. Wears-her-bathrobe-to-
work *me*. I'm in charge.

"Peel all of the potatoes, please," I tell Jill.

"Just throw some foil over it," I tell Ruth. "Then sit down and
relax."

I put the kettle on for Drew's tea.

"That looks pretty, honey," I tell Crystal, clasping her necklace.

The doorbell rings; I answer it to find Jasper Jenkins standing on the porch in a Goodwill ensemble that suggests he might be color blind. His signature khakis are fastened with a woman's belt, and he's replaced Ethan's ski sweater with a kelly green button-down shirt and a purple tie speckled with yellow diamonds. I feel silly for missing the sweater. Jasper's outfit is finished off with a professorial tweed jacket, the too-short sleeves exposing tufts of curly white hair around his wrists. One arm is bent behind his back. He brings it forward to present a bouquet of gold mums tied with a red ribbon.

"Happy Thanksgiving," he says.

Stepping off the porch, I take the flowers and give him a hug. His scratchy blazer smells of cherry pipe tobacco. He smiles broadly, exposing a flash of glossy white dentures.

In the kitchen, I introduce Jasper. He's more nervous and for-mal than usual, kneading his hands and bowing ceremoniously. Jill makes a fuss over the flowers, putting them in a vase on the hutch in the dining room.

"Would you like a glass of wine?" Ruth asks Jasper.

"I'm off the sauce," he tells her.

There's a silence, the kitchen timer ticking. Pots of water for the potatoes and peas boil away on the stove, steam filling the room. Jasper dabs perspiration from his forehead with a tweed sleeve as Ruth pours him a ginger ale. Finally he sheds the jacket. The out-line of his belly button looks like an eye peering through the thin knit fabric of his shirt.

Simone claps and points a finger at his white beard, which he seems to have trimmed for the occasion. "Santa!"

Soon the whole house smells like Thanksgiving—like sage, cinna-mon, and pie filling that's dribbled over onto the bottom of the oven and burned. The sky clears and sun filters through the dining room windows, making the crystal and china on the table twinkle.

I've set out my grandmother's silver, which I've rarely had occasion to use before today. There are a few odd pieces I'm unsure of.

"What's this?" I ask Ruth, holding up a wide, flat, forklike spatula.

She pours ice water into the goblets. "Cucumber and tomato server," she says. She points to another piece that I always assumed was for picking up ice cubes. "Asparagus tongs."

"How did you *know* that?" Jill asks.

"She knows everything," I tell her. "It's annoying."

Ruth sets the water pitcher on the buffet. "That thing would be handy to clean out the cat's box," she says bitterly, pointing to the tomato server. I notice that her hands tremble and her eyes are glassy with tears.

"You okay?" I ask Ruth after Jill leaves the room.

"Today is the first day of the rest of my nervous breakdown," she says, running a finger through the condensation on the water pitcher.

"I know the holidays are hard."

"Yeah. Mark called last night. He and Missy are back together for good."

"I'm sorry." Only a few weeks ago, Ruth and Mark had talked again about patching things up.

"Missy's pregnant."

"Oh, Ruth." I give her a hug, closing my eyes, wishing there were something more I could do.

"Apparently my husband's midlife crisis is a whole-life crisis."

I'd like to assure her that she's not going to be alone forever, but I'm not sure this is true for either of us.

"Who's going to say grace?" Marion asks as we finally sit down to eat. Her face clouds with worry. She smoothes the napkin in her lap over and over, as if the cloth won't hold still. "Charlie?"

There's a moment of silence in which pained glances are exchanged across the table.

Dad bows his head. "Whoever you are up there, thank you for this wonderful meal and for bringing us together—"

"Amen!" Jasper says.

I don't think Dad was finished, but he looks relieved. We begin passing the platters and bowls and tureens of food.

"Look at *this*," Jill says of Marion's yam puff, which is cobbled with a coating of golden brown marshmallows.

"That's Drew's stuffing with chestnuts," I explain, "and that's Crystal's with white bread, and Marion's with sausage."

"Wow! Thank you," Drew says with a nasally twang, cradling a cup of hot tea in his hands.

"Where's my customized stuffing?" Ruth asks loudly. "You know how I like mine with oysters and prawns." Missy and Mark have clearly ruined the day for her.

Crystal giggles. She looks up to Ruth when Ruth's in smart-ass mode.

Jill fusses over Simone, buttering her roll and cutting her turkey into teeny pieces.

"Now what do *you* do?" Marion asks, turning to Jasper, who's seated beside her. She sets her fork on her plate, brings two polished fingertips demurely to her lips, and bats her eyelashes. I wish I could have told her ten months ago that she'd be flirting with a guy who collects cans for a living.

"Sell real estate," Jasper tells her. "Mostly commercial." His gray hair is parted neatly in the middle and greased down a bit in two flat sheets.

"Oh," Marion coos. "*Real* estate."

I look at Ruth, who knows from what I've told her that Jasper used to sell life insurance but hasn't worked for years.

"Big stuff," Jasper continues. "Stores, office buildings, supermarkets." He takes a bite of turkey.

"*My*," Marion says, splaying a hand across his sleeve. As far as I know, she's never dated anyone since Charlie died. There was a man who played the cello in the San Jose Symphony, but they seemed to be just friends, meeting for coffee on Sunday afternoons.

"Don't you usually lease commercial real estate?" Dad asks. "Rather than selling it?"

"*Exactly,*" Jasper says, leaning over the table and pointing at Dad as though he'd just solved a great puzzle.

"Sophie has a commercial lease," Crystal says proudly.

"Before that I was an inventor," Jasper says, herding peas to the edge of his plate.

"What did you invent?" Drew asks him.

"Nondairy creamer."

"Gross!" Crystal says.

"Well, I *like* it," Jill says. "You know, in a pinch."

"I must have gone through a case in college," Ruth tells Jasper. She isn't really touching her food, focusing instead on her wine.

All eyes are on Jasper. He basks in the attention, tipping back his head and gazing at the ceiling. "Convenience," he says. "Every good invention addresses convenience."

"Necessity is the mother of invention, and convenience is the father," Dad says.

"You said it," Jill agrees.

"I'd like to toast the chef," Drew says raspily, raising his glass and winking at me. His hair is damp from the shower, and I can imagine his clean laundry smell. I think of how we made love as quietly as possible last night, how I bit into my lip until it stung as Drew tightened his hands around my shoulders. I look away, embarrassed. "To Sophie, the best cook I know. She's what I'm most thankful for this year."

"To the cook," Dad agrees.

"We all cooked," I say, raising my glass.

"To my beautiful bride, Jill," Dad says. He always calls her his bride, even though they've been married a few years. "My KP duty partner."

Jill giggles and squeezes Dad's hand.

Poor Ruth! If there's any more happy-loving coupleness at this table, she might stab herself with the asparagus tongs.

Jill raises her glass. "I've decided it's important to love the life you get and somehow learn to let go of the life you dreamed of."

I'm about to agree wholeheartedly when Ruth says, "Really? Do you have to love *all* of it? Even bad drapes and cheating husbands?"

Jill chokes a little on her stuffing. Dad pats her on the back, encourages her to sip water. I know it's a bad day for Ruth, but she's wrecking my fantasy Thanksgiving.

"You can switch bad drapes," Crystal says.

"If you can *afford* to," Ruth says dryly.

"I'm thankful for Argentina," Jasper says.

"Me too," Marion agrees. "Why?" she whispers to him.

Simone shrieks and bangs her spoon on her Dora the Explorer plate.

I want to say something to reroute the conversation, but mashed potatoes and disappointment clog my throat.

"I'm sorry, Jill," Ruth says. "I'm the Grinch who stole Thanksgiving."

"You're too pretty to be the Grinch," Crystal tells Ruth. I think this is the first compliment she's ever paid Ruth, and I'm grateful for her timing. Crystal takes a big bite of mashed potatoes. "My dad?" she says through a mouthful. "He's, like, *totally* handsome. If he ever moves back to town, you could marry him." She flips her fork over and gives the tines a long lick. "Except he's kind of a loser."

"Where does your dad live?" Jill asks.

"On a fishing boat," Crystal says tentatively. "I think. In, like, Alaska?"

"That's neat," Jill says, trying to muster enthusiasm for this bit of information.

I excuse myself to check on the pies.

. . .

As I pull the apple pie out of the oven, the smells of cinnamon and cloves embrace me like a tonic. I leave in the pecan pie to get a little browner, which is how Ethan always liked it—almost burned.

Suddenly Ruth's beside me, clutching the gravy boat.

Crystal follows her, carrying an empty bread basket. "Dude, Marion and Jasper are *totally* hooking up," she says.

"Really?" Ruth giggles, ladling more gravy into the boat.

"They're holding *hands* under the table," Crystal tells her.

"Oh, great," I say.

"Why do you care?" Ruth asks, irritated.

"Because Marion's enough to handle. Now I've got to deal with her tall-tale boyfriend, too?"

"You'd rather have Marion be lonely?" Ruth says.

Crystal hums nervously, refilling the bread basket.

"Of course not," I tell Ruth. She doesn't seem to understand that I've got a lot going on in the next few months: making it through the holiday season at the bakery, making sure Crystal passes Algebra I, making sure Marion doesn't find the car keys and drive through the park's duck pond. Right now I just want to make it through pie and coffee.

"Just because Jasper's down on his luck," Ruth continues. "You're a snob—"

"No, I'm *not*," I tell her. "You need a time-out. I'm going to lock you in the living room with a *Barney* video."

Ruth's regal posture stiffens. Then she slumps, laughing for the first time all day. "I'm sorry." She covers her face with her delicate hands.

"Actually, it's kind of a relief to see you misbehave for once," I admit. "Usually you're so perfect."

Ruth snorts.

"Yeah," Crystal agrees. "It's annoying."

"I know there's nothing worse than the holidays when you're single," I say.

"How come?" Crystal asks.

Before I can answer, Jill bumps through the swinging door from the dining room, pinching the sleeve of her turtleneck, which is splashed with red wine.

"Sophie, have you got any soda water?" she asks, panicked.

Ruth lurches toward the refrigerator to check, obviously hoping to make it up to Jill. Dad swings through the door, wanting to help. Marion follows behind them, wondering if we should rewarm the yam puff.

Next, Jasper and Drew stride into the kitchen. Drew holds Simone, balancing her on his hip, his wineglass in the other hand. "Party moved in here?" he asks.

No one wants to sit at the dining room table anymore. The problem with Thanksgiving is that the pressure for the meal and the conversation to be perfect is daunting. Somehow it's easier to hang back in the kitchen, picking turkey off the carcass, gossiping about the guests, and confessing your holiday dread.

The fan over the stove rattles and clanks. Drew turns it off and everyone sighs, enjoying the silence.

Ruth holds the gravy boat, Crystal holds the bread basket, Drew holds a new bottle of Cabernet, and Dad holds Jill's hand.

"Shall we?" I ask the group. We all turn and file back into the dining room.

"Hey," Ruth tells Crystal as she sits down, "I'm glad that you and my friend Sophie are such good cooks."

Crystal raises her eyebrows, her cheeks bulging with bread. "Sophie taught me."

"Best rhubarb pie west of Minneapolis," Jasper says, winking at Marion.

"Can we have *baked* potatoes next year?" Crystal asks me, digging a trench through her uneaten mashed potatoes.

"Baked potatoes?" I ask skeptically. But it's not the potatoes I'm hesitating over. It's the plausibility that there will *be* a next year. That Crystal may be a part of it.

"Hey, the wishbone!" Crystal jumps up, accidentally tugging a corner of the tablecloth and sending the wineglasses teetering. We grab our glasses as she bounds into the kitchen. She returns, squeezing the wishbone between her fingers.

"Wanna split it?" she asks me, sinking back into her chair. She leans across the table, centering her elbow as though bracing for an arm-wrestling match.

"Okay." I pinch the other side of the bone. A sharp bit of turkey pokes my thumb.

Crystal frowns at the wishbone with the seriousness of a chess player. She sucks in her lower lip.

"Make a secret wish!" Drew whispers loudly.

"Okay," I tell him.

"Duh," Crystal says, and I wonder what she's wishing for. Maybe for a horse or for her dad to come back.

I lean closer to Crystal, inhaling the smell of my own Joy perfume, which she seems to have borrowed. I pretend to hang on tight to the wishbone. But really I grasp it loosely, considering its brittle frailness between my fingers. My secret wish is for Crystal to break off the bigger half.

"Do you think Ethan will make it in time for *dessert*?" Marion frets, peeling back the sleeve of her dress to check her watch.

A hush falls over the table, forks of food frozen in the air. Dad looks at me. Crystal rolls her eyes.

I lay my free hand across Marion's bowed back, which is hard and hollow like a gourd.

"Ethan died," I remind her.

"How?" she asks, incredulous.

While nothing about Marion reminds me of Ethan, he is our common denominator. "Cancer, remember? You and I are both widows." I squeeze her arm, feeling the slender bone beneath a handful of papery loose skin.

"Oh." There's a stricken look on her face as she forgets and then remembers in the same split second. "That's right." She smacks her head lightly, as though she's trying to tune in the reception. "I'm sorry. I do remember."

"It's okay," I tell her. And in a way I'm glad she makes me say this almost every day now. "It's okay."

Acknowledgments

First, thanks to Frank Baldwin, the most generous reader a writer could hope for.

Thanks to my agent, Laurie Fox, my all-time stroke of good luck. For her enthusiasm and smarts, thanks to my editor Amy Einhorn.

I couldn't have finished this book without the help of my San Francisco writer's group: Rich Register, Susan Edmiston, Cheyenne Richards, Karen Roy, Laurence Howard, Gordon Jack, Julie Knight, Greta Wu, Joan Minninger. Wonderful writers, readers, friends.

Thanks to those who gave the manuscript thoughtful reads from start to finish: Aimee Prall, Nicolle Henneusse, Eileen Bordy. And especially Sona Vogel, copy editor extraordinaire.

Thanks to my earliest supporter and oldest friend, Quee Nelson.

For their unyielding encouragement from day one, thanks to my South Bay writer's group: April Flowers, Judy Cowell, Deb Gale, Nancy Shearer, Marilyn Rosenberg, Nancy Sully, and Cristina Spencer. And thanks to my brainstorming buddies: Bobbi Fagone and Charles King.

Thanks to teachers Bud Roper, Tom Parker, and Ellen Sussman, for offering worldly wisdom along the way, and to Tom Anfuso, for his editing savvy.

For helping me keep the facts factual, thanks to Bob Aimone, Karen Eberle, and my beloved friend Ede Sabo.

Finally, thanks to my writing partners and fellow graduates of The Los Gatos Café School of Journalism: Vicky Mlyniec and Kim Ratcliff.

And of course thanks to my loyal office assistant, Popoki, for manning the fax machine and keeping all moths at bay.